"I reckon the whole thing started in Nevada, in a little place called Flat Rock. . . ."

The U.S. needed men. Men who were ready for adventure, ready to fight . . . and ready to die.

In 1917, you could still find those kind of men riding from one Western town to the next, defying the law and daring authorities to catch them. But one day, the authorities *did* catch up with the Tacker Gang. And sent them off to Europe to prove that the spirit of the Wild West was still alive and kicking. . . .

UNDER OUTLAW FLAGS

From the Frontier to the Front:
An American Story

UNDER OUTLAW FLAGS

From the Frontier to the Front:
An American Story

James Reasoner

BERKLEY BOOKS, NEW YORK

UNDER OUTLAW FLAGS

A Berkley Book / published by arrangement with the author

PRINTING HISTORY
Berkley edition / May 1998

The Penguin Putnam Inc. World Wide Web site address is
http://www.penguinputnam.com

ISBN: 0-425-16305-9

BERKLEY®
Berkley Books are published by The Berkley Publishing Group,
a member of Penguin Putnam Inc.,
200 Madison Avenue, New York, New York 10016.
BERKLEY and the "B" design
are trademarks belonging to Berkley Publishing Corporation.

PRINTED IN THE UNITED STATES OF AMERICA

10 9 8 7 6 5 4 3 2 1

Special thanks are due to the following people for helping to make this novel possible: Kimberly Waltemyer, John Talbot, and Gary Goldstein. I would like to thank as well my cousin Richard Finley, the first person I knew who wrote something and actually got it published. He inspired me to think that maybe someday I could do the same.

This book is for Livia, Shayna, and Joanna.

UNDER OUTLAW FLAGS

PROLOGUE

1965

It was a mom-and-pop grocery store, too small to be air-conditioned, but the shade was still a welcome relief from the blazing heat of the Texas summer afternoon outside. The man stopped just inside the screen doors, pushed back his hat, and pulled a handkerchief from his pocket to mop away the sweat from his forehead. His tie hung loose around his throat, his coat was slung over one arm, and the sleeves of his white shirt were rolled up. He looked around.

A square formed by waist-high wooden counters filled the center of the big room. The cash register, an old-fashioned model with a pull handle on the side, stood behind the counter facing the doors. In front of that same counter was a red metal box shaped like a coffin, with *COCA-COLA* written on it in white letters. A metal spinner rack stood at the right end of the soda pop box, and a sign on top of it read *HEY KIDS! COMICS!* Two little boys were turning the rack slowly, studying intently the array of colorful comic books displayed on it. The fat one wore glasses that constantly slipped down on his nose and had to be pushed back up.

Shelves full of canned goods, bread, bags of flour and sugar, cans of motor oil and dog food, and bags of potato chips ran to the right and left, forming precise aisles. Shovels and fishing poles hung on hooks on the right half of the store's rear wall. To the left, with room to walk behind it, sat a refrigerated, glass-fronted butcher case full of hamburger meat, steaks, ribs, and chickens. The door that led to storage rooms was in the center of the rear wall. Somewhere back there, a swamp cooler banged and rattled.

"Howdy," said the man who sat on a stool behind the cash register. "Come on in out of the heat, mister. What can I do for you?"

The stranger moved deeper into the almost cavernlike interior of the store. He was slender, dark, intense, a vivid contrast to the burly, genial man behind the counter. The storekeeper's hair had been brown once, but nearly all of that hue had faded away with the years, leaving the thinning strands silver. The stranger figured the storekeeper was at least seventy.

"Mighty hot outside," the stranger said.

"Got popsicles in the box back here," the storekeeper said, turning on the stool to gesture at another metal box next to the rear counter. "They'll cool you right off. Got Cokes in the front box if you'd rather have that."

"Thanks." The stranger hung his coat on the back of a wicker chair at the left end of the Coke box and dropped his hat on the seat. He lifted the lid of the box, reached in, pulled a six-ounce bottle from the bed of crushed ice. An opener was attached to the front of the box. He used it to pry the cap off, then lifted the bottle quickly to his mouth as the drink inside began to well out of the neck. The stranger sucked greedily on it, then sighed in appreciation as he lowered the bottle a moment later. "Half-frozen. Can't beat that."

"Not even with a stick," the storekeeper agreed. He grinned, then glanced over at the spinner rack. "You boys figured out which o' them funny books you want yet?"

"Just about, Mr. Matthews," the fat kid replied.

The stranger took another swig of the melting Coke and said to the storekeeper, "You must be Drew Matthews."

"That's right. We haven't met, have we?"

"No, sir."

"But I know who you are. You're one o' them newspaper fellas, ain't you?"

The stranger smiled. "Does that bother you?"

"Nope. One o' you boys shows up about every ten years or so, when they figure everybody's forgotten again about the Tacker Gang."

"Are you willing to talk about it?" asked the reporter. "Especially the part about the war? I understand it's quite a story."

Short, silvery bristles stood out on Drew Matthews's jaw and chin. He lifted his hand and rubbed it over the stubble, making a faint rasping sound. "I suppose I could reminisce a little," he said. "If you're really interested, that is."

The reporter nodded. "I am. And I think my readers will be too."

"Well, since business ain't very brisk this afternoon— and ain't likely to be until after it starts to cool off a little— why don't you pull up that chair and sit down while we talk?"

The reporter picked up the wicker chair and carried it over by the side counter. As he did so, the two little boys brought a stack of comic books to the counter on the other side. "Can we get these and a couple of root beer popsicles, Mr. Matthews?" one of them asked.

"How many funny books you got there? One, two, three, four, five of 'em, at twelve cents apiece, that's sixty cents, and them popsicles are twenty-five cents each. . . ."

"I got a dollar," the fat kid said.

Matthews nodded. "Close enough for gover'ment work. Get your popsicles and go on out on the sidewalk while you eat 'em, so you won't be drippin' on the floor in here."

The boys got their popsicles from the freezer and hurried out, arguing over which one of them would get to read the new issue of *Spider-Man* first.

When the screen doors had slammed behind the boys, Matthews leaned back a little on his stool and said, "Thought it might be a good idea if them little fellas left before I started tellin' you about what happened back in the old days. Some of it wasn't very pretty, you know."

"Whatever you want to tell me," the reporter said, "I want to hear it."

"You understand, I wasn't there for everything that happened. Most of it, but not everything. Course, I heard all about it later from the other fellas. I'll just tell it the best way I know how. I reckon the whole thing started in Nevada, in a little place called Flat Rock. . . ."

ONE

We were double-crossed, plain and simple. If not for what Murph Skinner did, might not any of it would have happened the way it did. But it did, and before we knew it, it was way too late to change things. That's always the way, seems like.

But I'm getting ahead of myself. It was a while after we all got together in '17 that the real trouble started. The first few months the Tacker Gang rode, things went just fine. We walked into that bank in Flat Rock as bold as brass and smooth as silk, and nobody inside dared move a muscle when we drew our guns and Roy said in a loud voice, "This is a holdup. Everybody just stay still, and nobody gets hurt."

Seven of us went into that bank. Roy Tacker, he was our leader, and the oldest one of the bunch, around forty-five years old. Tall and a little on the skinny side, with as much gray in his hair and mustache as black, but I'd as soon tackle a wolf with my bare hands than get in a fight with Roy. Then there was his little brother, Jace. Half brother, really, since Roy's mother had died a long time before and Roy's daddy up and married him a younger woman when he was getting on in years, and they had Jace.

But that never affected the way Roy felt about Jace. They were as close as any full-blood brothers you ever saw.

Aaron Gault was from California—Bakersfield, I think. He'd drifted east after some trouble out there, just like I'd drifted west from Texas, and we both wound up in Nevada and fell in with Roy. Aaron was a good-looking fella with blond hair, and the gals all loved him as soon as they saw him. That never gave him a big head, though. He was down-to-earth, and a good man to ride with.

Big Boy was with us too, of course. Wherever Roy was, Big Boy wasn't far off. His real name was Alfred Guinness, but he never cared for it—the Alfred part, I mean. And Big Boy suited him just fine, since he was so tall and wide we used to rib him by saying it'd take a man on horseback a day just to ride around him. He'd been riding with Roy the longest, even longer than Jace.

The last two who went into the bank were the Gunderson brothers, a couple of Swedes who had just joined up with us. This was their first job. Outside, seeing to the horses, was Murph Skinner. Roy never gave that chore to a new man. It was too important. Being able to keep a cool head while you were inside a bank robbing it was pretty important too, but you sure as hell wanted your horses to be there waiting for you when you came out. And Murph was cool-headed, right enough. A treacherous son of a buck, but not prone to panic.

So we all had our guns out, but there were more of us than there were other people in the bank. A manager, a couple of tellers, and an old man standing at one of the tellers' windows were the only folks there, and they were all gawping at us like they'd never seen a gang of outlaws in dusters and Stetsons, with bandannas tied over their faces, before.

And maybe they hadn't, since it was 1917, after all, and most people thought the Wild West was dead and buried. Some of the streets were paved now, even in a little burg like Flat Rock, and there were gaslights on every block. Flivvers were parked along the boardwalks, instead of buckboards.

But there were still hitching posts along the street too, because this was ranching country and a lot of cowboys still rode their horses into town on payday—which was, of course, the very next day, and that was why the bank was full of money today.

"Nobody gets hurt," Roy said again. "All we want is the cash."

The bank manager was a dried-up little prune of a man, and he puffed up like a toad and said, "Well, you can't have it, you hooligan."

Roy pointed his gun at the man's face and said, "You best think about that for a minute, mister, but no longer, 'cause we ain't got the time."

The bank manager swallowed hard as he stared down the barrel of that Colt. Then he looked over at the tellers. "Give 'em what they want."

"Figured you'd see the light of reason," Roy said.

Big Boy and the Gunderson brothers holstered their guns and took canvas bags from under their dusters. They went behind the counter and started emptying the cash drawers in the tellers' cages. While they were doing that, Roy said to the manager, "You'd best open the vault now."

"I . . . I can't. The key's not here—"

"Sure it is. I never saw a banker yet who couldn't get into the vault whenever he wanted. I'll bet you like to go in there and just look at all those greenbacks. Makes you feel all nice and tingly inside, don't it?"

The bank manager heaved a disgusted sigh. Roy had him pegged, all right. "The key's in my pocket," he said. "I'll get it out."

"You do that."

The fella reached into his coat and brought out a gun instead of the key to the vault. I don't know what he thought he was going to do with one piddling little pocket pistol against four Colts, but he never got a chance to do much of anything. As always, Roy had told us that there wouldn't be any shooting unless it was to save our lives, so he jumped at that bank manager and cracked the barrel of his gun across the gent's scrawny little wrist. The

manager yelped and dropped his pistol before he could even
come close to getting a shot off. Roy whacked the little gun
with the side of his boot and sent it sliding across the floor,
well out of reach.

"That was a damned stupid thing to do," he told the
bank manager, who was bent over holding his broken wrist
and whimpering. Roy reached into the man's coat, found
the vault key, tossed it to Jace. Jace opened the vault door,
and Big Boy went in there with his sack, leaving the Gundersons to finish cleaning out the tellers' cash.

Big Boy came out a few minutes later and held the sack
up to let us know he was finished. Nobody ever talked
while we were pulling a job except Roy. That was the rule,
and we followed it as closely as possible.

That day, though, Aaron had to break it, because he had
backed off to keep an eye out through the bank's front
window, and he said sharp-like, "Men coming."

Roy stepped back so he could look out the window too.
"They're still a block away. Let's go."

Those of us still holding guns holstered them, and Aaron
opened the door. Roy looked at the bank manager and the
other three men in the room and said, "Just remember, we
could have killed all of you." Then he turned and went out
onto the boardwalk, not hurrying. The rest of us followed
him.

There was a time, I suppose, when the sight of a bunch
of masked men in dusters coming out of a bank would have
instantly alerted the folks in a town to what was going on.
But like I said, nobody expected such a thing to happen in
this modern day and age, so the men down the street just
stopped and stared at us in confusion for a few seconds as
we mounted up. Then one of them yelled, "Hey! What the
hell!"

The bank manager popped his head out the door and
squalled, "Stop them! They robbed the bank!"

Roy palmed his Colt out slick as you please and put a
bullet in the doorjamb about a foot above the manager's
head. The fella screamed like he'd been shot and vanished
back inside the building. More yelling came from down the

street, but we didn't pay any attention to it. We just put the spurs to our horses and rode like blazes out of there.

Most of the side streets weren't paved. Roy swung into the first one he came to, and almost before you knew it, we were out of town. The street we were on petered out into a broad, open flat covered with short-grown sage. On the far side of the flat was a line of green trees that marked the course of a creek, and beyond the creek the terrain started to slope up toward the Prophet Mountains, which rose gray and purple against a blue sky. As I rode along with the others, I pulled down my bandanna so that the wind could blow in my face.

God, what a beautiful day!

Where we went, there weren't any roads. Sooner or later the people back in Flat Rock probably came up with the idea of getting together a posse on horseback, but by then it was too late, of course. They were used to turning to the law for help whenever there was trouble, instead of handling things themselves. Flat Rock had a deputy sheriff stationed there, but he was the sort who didn't like to go anywhere that he couldn't get to by automobile. Roy had checked into that before we decided to hit the bank. The deputy likely ran around for a while like a chicken with its head cut off, trying to figure out how he could use his car to chase us into the mountains, and by the time he realized he couldn't, we were long gone. We never saw any sign of pursuit at all.

We took a little over sixteen thousand dollars out of that bank. Two thousand a man, share and share alike. Everybody was happy.

Well, nearly everybody.

We made camp that night way up in the high lonesome of the Prophets, not lighting a fire just in case somebody was looking for us, and as we sat around gnawing on jerky and biscuits and washing it down with whiskey, Roy said to Big Boy, "How much did you leave in the vault this time?"

"Don't know for sure," Big Boy said. "Four or five thousand, I reckon."

Roy nodded. "Good. That ought to be enough to tide folks over."

Murph spoke up, saying, "I still don't see why the hell we have to leave *anything*. We were robbing the damn bank, f' Christ's sake. You ought to've just cleaned it out."

"If we had, then every cowhand around Flat Rock would've had to do without a whole month's pay," Roy said. "How much credit you think the bartenders and the whores would extend to them under those circumstances? This way, when we leave a little cash behind, at least they still get a couple of bucks to jingle in their pockets. It ain't much, but it's better'n nothin'."

Murph shook his head. "Still seems mighty wasteful to me. What do I care whether or not some cow nurse can buy a drink or a whore?"

"You were never a cowboy," Roy said. "I was. I know what it's like."

And he did. Roy had ridden for several spreads in Colorado and Wyoming before heading out to Nevada to become a badman. He and Big Boy had punched cows together on one of those ranches, which was how they met. Roy didn't talk about himself much, but I'd heard some yarns about those days from Big Boy. It seemed that Roy had found himself with an almighty powerful crush on the daughter of one of the men he'd worked for, and she felt the same way about him, but that rancher hadn't been about to let his little girl get hitched to some no-account line rider. So Roy took off, and Big Boy, being Big Boy, went with him.

Roy had always had a bit of a reckless streak, and if he'd been able to do anything in the world that he wanted to, he'd have ridden with the Wild Bunch. But by that time, Butch Cassidy and Harry Longbaugh, the one they called the Sundance Kid, had already sailed off to South America with Etta Place, and the Wild Bunch was no more. Roy and Big Boy rustled a few cattle and robbed a store now and then, but they did some honest work too, prospecting and the like. I figure that in the back of his mind, Roy always thought that he'd hit it big somehow and then go back to Wyoming for that girl, but the years went by and he never did. His folks died back in Kansas, taken by a fever, and Roy and Big Boy went to see about Jace, who rode back to Nevada with them, not much more'n a kid, but with the same wild streak that Roy had. They must have gotten it from their old man.

I don't know who first came up with the idea to rob a bank. I've got a feeling it was Jace, after he'd been listening to Roy talk about Butch and Sundance and the old days, the days that Roy had been born just a little too late for. Big Boy told me that Roy pondered over the idea for a long time before they finally did it, and it was during that time that Roy came up with the rules he had for bank robbing, such as how nobody talked but him (so that if there was ever any question about it, the law couldn't prove that any of the rest of us had even been there), and how there'd be no shooting unless we just had to, and how we'd always leave a little money instead of cleaning out the vault entirely. Some might call him good-hearted for thinking up those rules, despite his being a bank robber, but that wasn't really why he came up with them. He just didn't think it was fair to do things any other way.

Aaron and I met up with Roy and Jace and Big Boy about a week apart, as it happened. Each of us had pulled a few small jobs on our way to Nevada, but we weren't what you'd call hardened criminals. We were just young fellas down on our luck, and to tell you the truth, neither of us saw much wrong with lifting a few bucks from a store owner now and then. We were crooks, right enough, and I know now we were in the wrong, but it didn't seem that way at the time. Everybody carries their past around with them, and there's not a blasted thing anybody can do to change it.

Other gents came and went, riding with Roy and the rest of us for a while and then going their own way. Murph Skinner had been with us for a few months when we robbed the bank in Flat Rock, and like I said, the Gunderson brothers were new. The Swedes never said much, but Murph complained all the time, and I was already getting tired of it. So was Roy.

"That's enough," he said when Murph started in again a few minutes later about leaving some of the cash behind in the vault. "You know the way we do things, Murph. If you don't like 'em, you're free to leave. I never forced a man to ride with me, and I don't intend to start now."

"Never said I wanted to leave," Murph groused. "I just don't see any point in losin' out on an extra five hundred bucks a man."

Big Boy shoved a bottle in Murph's hand. "Here. Have a drink and quit your bitchin', why don't you? I don't know about you, but I feel downright rich."

So did I. I couldn't remember ever having two thousand dollars in my pocket before. It seemed like just about all the money in the world.

Wanting to keep peace in the gang, Roy came up with an idea that I figured was aimed mainly at making Murph happy. He leaned forward, and I saw him grin in the moonlight. "Why don't we pay a visit to Harrigan's place?" he suggested.

That brought a grunt from Murph, but when he spoke he sounded happily surprised. "That's a damned good idea," he said.

One of the Gundersons asked, "Vat is this Harrigan's?"

Big Boy laughed and gave him a friendly little slap on the shoulder, which nearly knocked the big Swede off the log where he was sitting. "You'll see," Big Boy said, "and you'll be mighty pleased when you do."

TWO

We had a regular hideout in the mountains, an old stone house that had probably been built by some rancher fifty or sixty years earlier. Something had happened to make him abandon it, though, and it had been deserted for a long time. The roof had fallen in, but the walls were still standing.

And thick walls they were too, which was what had attracted Roy to the place. The old house was the closest thing to a fort you could find in the mountains, and if ever a posse tracked us there, they'd have a tough time trying to root us out as long as our food and water and cartridges lasted.

Not a one of us thought much about dying in those days, unless it was Roy and Big Boy, because they were older. Jace and Aaron and me, we were young bucks and likely thought we would live forever, if we thought about it at all. But there was always a chance our luck would run out and we'd wind up on the wrong end of a bullet. It was just part of the game.

A couple of days after robbing the bank in Flat Rock, we reached the hideout, riding single file through the twisting, sheer-walled slash in the rock that was the only way in and out of the high mountain valley where the old stone house was located. This was *our* Hole in the Wall, and while it was never as famous as the one the Wild Bunch used, we were all proud of it.

We didn't stay long, though. Everybody was anxious to get to Harrigan's. We hadn't kept the Gundersons in suspense; it would have been downright cruel not to tell those Swedish boys about all the good things they had to look forward to.

Harrigan was a failed rancher too, but unlike the fella who had built our hideout, he had done something to salvage the situation. He'd turned his place into a whorehouse.

We left the hideout after stashing a little of the loot there, and spent a day riding down out of the mountains into a greener, more gentle land. Harrigan's ranch house sat on top of a small hill surrounded by pines. It was a sprawling, two-story place built of logs. To one side was a big, open-fronted barn where visitors could leave their mounts if they came in on horseback. Sometimes Model A's were parked there too, because there was a road leading south from Harrigan's that connected up with the highway between Elko and Reno, and Harrigan regularly got folks coming up there from the cities too. His whores were young and pretty and his whiskey wasn't watered-down and his poker games were honest, and what more could you ask for in those days?

I'd only been there once, but that had been enough to make me look forward to another visit. I'd gone upstairs with a redhead named Becky, and she'd managed to seem totally innocent while showing me some of the dangedest tricks you ever did see. I wanted to spend some more time with her. I sure hoped she was still working there.

A few cars were parked in the open area in front of the barn when we rode up. A Mex who worked for Harrigan came out of the barn and took our horses, promising to look after them special-like. Being from Texas, I spoke a little of his lingo, and I said, *"Muchas gracias,"* and flipped him a silver dollar.

Murph leaned his head toward the cars as we walked past them and said to Roy, "You reckon any of the folks who came up here in those are lookin' for us?"

"Not very likely. It's been almost a week since we were in Flat Rock," Roy said. "Besides, Harrigan's got a deal with the law. They don't come up here."

That was another good thing about the place. Harrigan greased enough palms so that the authorities left him alone. Of course, he could afford to, because he knew his customers weren't the sort to balk at the high prices he charged for everything he had to offer.

He met us at the door, a big man bald as a cue ball. I never saw him when he didn't have a suit and tie on, and he didn't look anything like a rancher. I doubt if the way he looked had anything to do with the fact that he had been a piss-poor cattleman, but maybe it had. All I knew was that he was damned good at running a whorehouse.

"Hello, boys," he said as he pumped Roy's hand. He shook with each of us as we trooped into the big, high-ceilinged main room. It was furnished mighty fancy, with soft rugs on the floor and heavy furniture scattered around. Some old rifles were hung on the walls, along with a couple of moose heads, and a huge stone fireplace took up nearly one whole wall. A long mahogany bar sat on the other side of the room. In between were tables for the games of chance and the drinking. Stairs in the back of the room led up to the second floor, where the girls who were circulating through the room did their real work.

Not counting us, I could see twelve men in the room: Harrigan, the bartender working behind the bar, and ten men sitting at the tables. Of those ten customers, six of them were drinking and laughing and talking with some of Harrigan's girls. The other four were all sitting together at one table, playing cards. Three of them were wearing range clothes, like us, and the fourth cardplayer sported a pin-striped suit and a derby hat.

Some of the whores were wearing silk dressing gowns, while the others had lacy getups that left them more bare than not. My eyes went right away to one of them with plenty of reddish-orange hair and fair skin dotted with freckles. I could see a lot of that skin because she wasn't

wearing anything except some frilly black step-ins and a
band of black silk around her breasts. She saw me too, and
let out a squeal as she jumped off the lap of the man who
had been cuddling her and ran over to me. I just had time
to see that the gent who'd been deserted didn't look too
happy about the state of affairs, and then Becky was grabbing onto me and practically jumping up into my arms like
a puppy. She damned near knocked me over, but I caught
myself as she wrapped her legs around my hips and just
sort of hung there as she kissed me.

Well, with my arms full of a pretty, nearly naked, red-
headed whore, I didn't think much about anything else for
a few seconds, but then I heard Roy say, "I'd just let it go
if I was you, mister." The sound of his voice told me plain
as day that there might be trouble.

I'd closed my eyes while I was kissing Becky, but I
opened them now and turned a little so that I could see.
The man she'd been with was standing up and glaring at
me and her. His hands were balled into fists, and his shoulders were set for a fight. Roy stood a few feet away from
him, his left hand raised slightly. The gent looked like he
couldn't decide if he wanted to take a swing at Roy or come
after me and Becky first.

Then, before anybody could do anything, the cardplayer
wearing the town suit spoke up and said, "If you boys are
going to fight over that young lady, why don't you do it
outside? We're playing poker here, and the ladies in my
hand are demanding even more attention than the one in
that young cowboy's arms."

Now, I don't believe for a minute he was actually holding any queens in his hand. I think he just said that to throw
off the other fellas in the game. Or maybe he did, I don't
know. But it sort of broke the tension anyway. The man
Becky had deserted so sudden-like said, "Hell, a whore's
a whore. There's always another of 'em."

That wasn't really fair to Becky, and I wouldn't have
blamed her a bit if she'd taken offense at it, but she just
giggled and rubbed herself against me some more, and I
sort of lost interest in everything else again. Aaron told me

later that Harrigan gave the gent a couple of free drinks and steered one of the other girls over to him, and that satisfied him just fine.

Roy and the rest of the gang went over to a big table in the corner, but I was already heading for the stairs, carrying Becky with me. Jace looked back over his shoulder at us and called, "Drew, are you comin' or not?" and that made everybody else hoot with laughter. I didn't bother answering.

I just took Becky upstairs to see if she'd learned any more tricks since the last time I'd been there.

Turned out she had, but I've always prided myself on at least trying to be a gentleman, so I won't go into that. I'll just say that I was a tired son of a buck when I came back downstairs a couple of hours later. Becky had told me she was going to take a little nap, but she made me promise before I left that I'd be back later.

Night had fallen while I was upstairs, and the big room was lit by the glow of several kerosene lamps. The air was smoky from the lamps and the cheroots clamped between the teeth of several of the customers, as well as Harrigan himself. Big Boy, Jace, and Aaron were sitting at the same table where they had been earlier. Big Boy had a blond whore sitting on his lap. She was small to start with, and cuddled up next to such a big fella like that, she looked even tinier. Aaron had two girls with him—no surprise there—one on each side. One was a redhead, but her curls were a darker shade than Becky's hair. The other was a Chinese girl, with long straight hair black as midnight flowing down her back. A girl was sitting next to Jace too, on a chair pulled up next to his, and she was a brunette with just a little paint on her face, which was unusual for a girl like that. Even Becky, who was young enough and pretty enough not to really need it, painted herself up. It was just the way of things.

The table was littered with glasses and empty whiskey bottles. As I came up, Big Boy waved a hand in greeting and said, "Pull up a chair, Drew."

I looked around. "Where's Roy?"

Big Boy nodded toward one of the other tables. "Over there."

I looked and saw that Roy had joined the same poker game that had been going on earlier. One of the players had dropped out, but the dude and the other two were still there. Roy had his hat shoved to the back of his head. A glass of whiskey sat at his elbow, but it didn't look like he had touched it. Roy wasn't much of one for drinking when he was playing cards. He liked to be clearheaded whenever he was doing anything important.

"What about Murph and the Gundersons?"

"Upstairs," Aaron said. "Those Swedes' eyes got so big when a couple of Wing's cousins got hold of them, I thought they were goin' to pop." He patted the bare thigh of the Chinese girl, who had to be Wing.

"Where's Becky?" asked the brunette sitting with Jace.

"Still upstairs," I told her. "She said she was going to take a nap."

That brought a laugh from the others. The little blonde on Big Boy's lap said, "Wore her out, did you, Drew?"

I grinned and said, "She's an enthusiastic girl."

Aaron reached for a bottle with a few inches of whiskey still in it and poured some of the hooch into a glass. He slid it over to me. "Here. Get your strength back."

I felt like I needed more than whiskey, but I knocked it back anyway, then said, "What about something to eat?"

"Harrigan had his cook fry us up some steaks earlier," Big Boy said. "Not all of us were so danged impatient that we didn't stop to eat first."

"Well, I'm about ready to go upstairs, Big Boy," said the blonde. "From what I hear from the other girls, you live up to your name."

Damned if he didn't blush a little when she said that.

Big Boy and Aaron scraped their chairs back and stood up, and Aaron solved the problem of deciding which girl to take with him by taking both of them. I just shook my head in wonderment as they all headed up the stairs.

Jace and the brunette were still sitting there at the table, though, and I realized then that Jace hadn't said a word since I'd come downstairs. His jaw was set tight, in fact. The brunette looked at him, then looked at me, then said, "My name is Cecilia, by the way." She stuck her hand out.

I shook it and said polite-like, "Pleased to make your acquaintance, ma'am. I'm Drew Matthews."

"I know who you are," Cecilia said. "You and your friends are the famous Tacker Gang."

I shrugged. I didn't know how famous we were, but I suppose a few people had heard of us. The newspapers had gotten hold of Roy's name somehow and tagged it on the whole bunch, since they didn't know our names.

"I've read about you," Cecilia went on.

"That's one thing about the newspapers," I told her. "You can't believe but about half of what you read in them. If those reporter fellas don't know what they're writin' about, they just make something up."

Now, I know that was maybe overstating things a mite, but I was young and I was talking to a whore, so I didn't really mean anything by it.

She talked to me for a few minutes more, mostly about nothing, but I wasn't really paying attention. I looked over at Jace and when Cecilia gave me a chance, I asked him, "Are you all right?"

"Sure," he said tightly. "I'm fine. Why wouldn't I be?"

"Well, you haven't said nothin' since I came down, and you're still sittin' here—"

He didn't let me go any further. He reached over and grabbed Cecilia's hand and said, "Let's go."

"There's no hurry," she said to him. "Just whenever you're ready—"

He interrupted her too, pushing back his chair and standing up as he said, "I'm ready now."

Cecilia glanced at me, and this time it was her turn to shrug, and then she let Jace lead her over to the stairs and up to the second floor.

I caught Harrigan's eye and asked him if I could get a steak.

"With all the trimmin's?" he asked.

"Damn right."

We were rich, after all.

I ate the steak, along with a mess of potatoes and biscuits and gravy, washing it all down with beer instead of whiskey. Then I went over and watched the poker game for a while so that my food could set a spell before I went back upstairs to Becky. While I was doing that, Murph Skinner and the Gunderson boys came downstairs with their whores to fortify themselves with some more liquor before going back up for another bout.

Some cardplayers don't like it when anybody watches them, but others don't seem to mind. This appeared to be an easygoing bunch. The fella in the pin-striped suit was called Ford, and he was from Los Angeles, over in California. The other two men were ranchers, which was what I had pegged them for from the first. It didn't take me long to figure out that Roy and Ford were the best poker players in the game. They won the biggest pots, about half going to Roy and half to Ford. The ranchers settled for raking in some of the little ones.

I'm not much of a cardplayer myself. Give me some dominoes and a good game of Forty-Two. So it didn't take me long to get a little bored watching Roy and the others play. By that time, I was feeling a mite stronger, and I figured Becky had gotten enough sleep to last her a while. So I drank the last of the beer in my mug and headed upstairs again.

Becky was awake and waiting for me, and she said she had dreamed about us. She started showing me some of the things she'd been dreaming about. I allowed that those must have been pretty nice dreams, and she was showing me just how nice when the door of the room suddenly burst open and a stark naked, sobbing woman ran into the room.

I surely do hate it when that happens.

THREE

As she ran across the room and threw herself down on the bed next to Becky and me, I recognized her as Cecilia, the pretty brunette who had come upstairs with Jace. Like most fellas, I reckon, I'd wondered sometimes what I'd do if I ever found myself in bed with two naked women at the same time. Well, here it was happening, but somehow it wasn't anything at all like what I'd imagined. In fact, it was downright embarrassing.

So I rolled out of bed, grabbed for my pants, and said, "What the hell!"

Cecilia was lying facedown, her back heaving as she cried. Becky put a hand on her shoulder and asked, "What is it, honey? What's wrong?"

Cecilia's voice came back muffled by the bedding and distorted by her sobs. "It . . . it's that Jace!"

Becky threw an angry glance my way. I don't know why she was mad at me, unless maybe it was because Jace and me were both men. She asked Cecilia, "Did he hurt you?"

"N-no. He . . . he didn't do *anything* to me."

"Oh." There was a world of understanding packed into that word as Becky said it.

I didn't catch on right away, though. I had pulled my pants on by this time, so I felt a little braver. "If he didn't do anything," I said to Cecilia, "then why in blazes did you run in here cryin' like that?"

The question just brought more boo-hoos from Cecilia, and got me a glare that would curl your toes from Becky. She sat next to Cecilia and sort of hovered over her like a mama hen, and said to me, "Why don't you go talk to that friend of yours? You're not doing any good in here."

I looked at her for a second, with her sitting there naked like that, and felt a pang of pure regret. But even though I was never the smartest fella in the world, I was smart enough to see that there wasn't going to be any more loving for me as long as Cecilia was so upset. So I sighed and asked, "Which one is her room?"

"Three doors down on the left," Becky told me. "Now get out of here. I'll take care of Cecilia."

I put my shirt on but didn't button it. Then I settled my hat on my head and picked up my boots and duster, carrying them with me as I left Becky's room and went down the hall. The door of Cecilia's room was open a few inches, so I put my foot against it and shoved. It swung open the rest of the way.

Jace was sitting on the bed, his back to me, smoke curling up from the quirly he had in his mouth. Around it, he said tight-lipped, "Look, I told you I'll be out of your hair in just a minute."

"You ain't in my hair, hoss."

He jumped up and turned around in a hurry. "Damn it, Drew," he said, "don't go sneakin' up on a fella like that! That's a good way to get yourself shot. I thought you were Cecilia."

I closed the door behind me with my heel and said, "In the first place, you couldn't beat me to the draw on your best day, and in the second place, you're not even packin' iron. So I don't think there was much chance of me gettin' shot."

As a matter of fact, he wasn't wearing anything except the bottoms from a pair of long underwear, never mind a gun. He scowled at me, took a drag on the smoke, and said, "What are you doin' here? I figured you had business of your own with that Becky girl."

"I did," I said, trying not to sigh again as I thought about red hair and fair skin. "And things were goin' just fine until that gal of yours came runnin' in, bawlin' about you."

His face stiffened even more than it already was. "I didn't touch her. I don't care what she says, I didn't hurt her."

"I believe you."

He frowned. "You do?"

"Yep. First thing I thought was that you'd gotten riled for some reason and took a swing at her, but I ought to've known you better than that, Jace. I *do* know you better'n that. Cecilia said you didn't touch her. Said you didn't touch her at all." By now I was starting to understand what she'd meant by that.

The end of the cigarette glowed bright red in the dimness of the room as he smoked it down with one long pull. Then he said, "What I do or don't do with a whore is none of your business, Drew."

"Normally I'd agree with you, but seein' as how I'd be back in that other room with Becky right now if you hadn't got Cecilia so upset, I figure I got a right to know what happened."

For about half a minute, he didn't say anything. Then: "I just didn't feel like doin' it, okay?"

I shrugged. "Don't matter to me either way. You must've said something to Cecilia to get her that upset, though. What'd you do, tell her it was her fault you couldn't get it up?"

"That's not what I said!" he practically yelped. "I could've done it! I . . . I just didn't want to."

I knew we'd been to Harrigan's once before since I'd started riding with the gang, and I didn't have any idea how many times Jace and Roy and Big Boy might've been there before Aaron and me showed up. I figured Jace had done his share of dallying, though, so I said, "Hell, I wouldn't worry about it. All the other times went fine, so I reckon it will again later on."

He stared at me, his eyes all narrow-like, then gave a sharp shake of his head. "There weren't any other times," he said.

"What?"

"I said there weren't any other times!" He pulled in a deep breath. "Don't you say anything about this to any of the other fellas, Drew. If you do, I'll have to try to gun you, and one of us'll get killed. But I sort of . . . haven't ever done it yet."

Now, I don't mind telling you, that came as a surprise to me. "But you've been here to Harrigan's before," I said. "I saw you take a whore upstairs, saw it with my own two eyes."

"Yeah, but we didn't do anything. I just . . . talked to her for a while. And I paid her extra to lie about me to the other girls, if they ever asked."

"Well, I'll swan. I never heard of such a thing."

"You have now," he snapped. "I don't want you blabbin' it all over the place either."

My right hand was free, since I was holding my boots in my left hand and had my duster draped over that arm. I held up the right, palm out, and said, "Don't worry. Like I told you, what you do or don't do with a whore ain't none of my business. I won't say anything."

He grunted. "Thanks. I guess."

"But there's still a little matter of a sobbin' gal to deal with."

Jace looked pained. "I didn't mean to hurt her feelin's. I was just so . . . so upset with myself that I reckon I said some things I shouldn't have." He scrubbed a hand over his face, then said, "Can you send her back in here? I ought to apologize to her."

"That sounds like a good idea. You just hang on a minute."

In my bare feet, I went back down the hall and tapped on the door of Becky's room. "Who is it?" she called, not sounding any too happy.

"It's me," I said. "I got to talk to Cecilia."

"She doesn't want to talk to you."

I leaned closer to the door. "Well, it ain't really me who's got something to say to her. It's Jace."

I heard the two of them talking quiet-like for a minute. Then somebody padded over to the door and opened it. Becky looked out at me. "Where is he?"

"Waiting in Cecilia's room." The door was only open a couple of inches, but I tried to get a look at Becky anyway so that I could see if she was still naked. She wasn't. She was wearing a dark green silk robe.

"I don't think Cecilia ought to have anything to do with him," she said after a few seconds. "He was rude to her. You men ought to be at least a little bit polite to us, even if we are whores."

I nodded. "Yes, ma'am, I couldn't agree more. I've always tried to be nice to you, haven't I?"

The door opened a couple more inches, and the mad look on her face softened a little. "Yeah," she said, "you have." She looked back over her shoulder for a second, then said to me, "All right, it's against my better judgment, but if Cecilia wants to talk to him, I suppose it's her decision."

Cecilia must have come up behind Becky, because she was there at the door all of a sudden, and she said, "I'll talk to Jace."

"Good," I said. "He'll be glad to hear that."

Becky stepped aside so that Cecilia could come out of the room. She had borrowed one of Becky's robes and had the belt tied tight around her waist. She started down the hall toward her room, and Becky followed her. I wasn't expecting that, but a couple of long strides let me catch up to them.

"I imagine Jace wants to talk to her alone," I said in a half whisper to Becky.

"I don't care. If he gets her upset again, I'm going to be there to give him a piece of my mind. I might even ask Mr. Harrigan not to let you boys come back here again."

The thought of that made me gulp. I didn't argue with Becky. I didn't want to rile her more than she was already riled.

Cecilia went into her room. Through the open door I could see that Jace had pulled his pants on but still wasn't wearing his shirt. As Becky and I watched from the hallway, Cecilia faced him and used the back of her hand to wipe away the streaks that tears had made on her cheeks. "What do you want?" she said to Jace.

"I just want to say that . . . I'm sorry. It wasn't your fault, Cecilia. None of it was your fault."

"I know that. I just wasn't sure you did."

"Well, I didn't mean what I said," he told her earnestly. "You're just about the prettiest . . . the nicest girl I ever saw."

Cecilia looked down at the faded, threadbare rug on the floor. "No, I'm not," she said. "I'm a whore. That's all I am and all I'll ever be."

What she said was likely true enough, even though it wasn't something that any of us who came up to the second floor of Harrigan's liked to dwell on. The whole point of it was not to think about the money that changed hands, or the other gents who spent some time in those beds with those girls. I reckon what we really wanted was just a few minutes of softness, a few minutes when we didn't have to worry about heat and dust and danger. I wouldn't pretend to know what the girls thought about or what they wanted; females have always been pretty much a mystery to me, be they whores or ladies.

Somehow, though, Jace picked that moment to say and do the right thing. He stepped up to Cecilia and put his arms around her and pulled her tight against him. "You're more than that to me," he said. "You always will be."

Out in the hall, Becky sighed and turned her head to look at me, then balled up her fist and punched me in the arm. I said, "Ow! What the hell was that for?"

"Oh, shut up and come on," she said as she reached down and caught hold of my hand. With her other hand, she pulled the door of Cecilia's room shut. She started tugging me down the hall.

I looked back over my shoulder. "Seems to me that havin' those two shut up in the same room was what started the trouble in the first place. How do you know Cecilia won't come bustin' out of there cryin' again in five minutes?"

"She won't," Becky said confidently. "Take my word for it."

She was right, of course. When I walked by Cecilia's room on my way to the stairs an hour or so later, the bed-springs were still singing their song inside.

It was the middle of the night by now, and the big room downstairs was mostly empty. Harrigan sat at one of the tables, counting money, while the bartender made tired swipes over the mahogany with a rag. Several thousand dollars were spread out on the table in front of Harrigan, and the thought occurred to me that if a gang was to stick up this place, they could carry off a lot of loot.

But nobody was going to try to rob Harrigan's. Anybody fool enough to do that would be hunted down by half the men in Nevada, and likely some from California and Utah and Oregon too. The money wouldn't be worth what would happen to a fella if he ever got caught.

The poker game was still going on. Roy, Ford, and the other two men had been at it for hours now. I wasn't sure how they kept playing for such a long time. The lure of those pasteboards had to be mighty strong, whether or not I understood it myself.

Roy saw me come down the stairs and amble toward the bar. His eyes flicked over to me for an instant, then went back to the cards in his hand. Curious, I looked closer at the table and saw that the pile of money and chips in front of Roy was considerably smaller than it had been earlier in the evening. On the other hand, Ford's pile was a whole heap bigger. It didn't take a college professor to figure out what had happened. Roy's luck had changed. His run was over.

I heard him cuss, something he didn't do overmuch, as he threw in his cards a minute later. Ford raked in the pot.

I leaned on the hardwood, and the bartender came over to ask, "Beer or whiskey?"

"Coffee." A pot was sitting on the stove at the end of the bar, and I could smell the strong black brew inside it.

The bartender filled a cup and brought it to me. I held it under my nose for a second, took a deep breath, and felt a little stronger and more clearheaded just from the smell. Harrigan's liquor was prime stuff, but I'd had my fill of it for now. The same was true of his whores. I was fuzzy-headed and worn out, and I just wanted to drink some coffee and clean some of the musty staleness out of my insides. I took a sip.

The coffee was blistering hot and strong enough to peel paint. It was damned near the best I'd ever had.

Roy pushed back his chair and stood up. I figured he was quitting before he got cleaned out, but I heard him say to the other players, "I'll be back in a minute." Then he started over toward me.

That was when I started to have a bad feeling.

"I need some more money, Drew," Roy said in a low voice when he came up to me. No *howdy* or *how ya doin'*.

I put the coffee cup on the bar and rubbed my chin. I hated to say no to Roy about anything, but I didn't much like the looks of this. "I don't know, Roy," I said slowly. "Don't look like the cards are runnin' your way no more."

"That's just it," he said. "My luck's bound to change any hand now. Ford's had it too good for too damned long."

"Maybe so, but one of those other fellas might start rakin' in the pots."

Roy shook his head. "Nope. Not the way they play cards. They're afraid to take chances."

Nobody could ever say that about Roy Tacker. Most of the time, he was about the calmest fella I ever knew, and he played most things close to the vest, especially robbing banks. But sometimes when he got to playing cards, something happened to Roy. His eyes lit up, and all you had to do was look at him to tell that he was being pulled along by something bigger than him.

This was one of those times.

"Come on, Drew," he said. "The other boys kicked in already with some of their shares."

Well, now, that just about floored me. I hadn't realized that I was the last one left who Roy hadn't put the touch on. Jace and Aaron and Big Boy and the others were all upstairs right then, but I figured they must have come down from time to time during the evening like I had just done, and when they did, Roy had asked them to bankroll him.

I looked at the piddling pile of chips in front of Roy's chair and knew that he hadn't just lost most of his own money. He had gambled away most of the gang's too.

Knowing that put me in an even worse spot. Roy was our leader; how could I tell him no? But obviously, his luck had turned really bad, and if I gave him my money, he'd be likely to lose it too.

"It's a sure thing, Drew," he said. "I've got Ford right where I want him. He's overconfident now."

Ford had reason to be confident, I thought, but I kept that reaction to myself. Instead I sighed and did the only thing it seemed like I could do. I reached in my pocket and brought out the roll of bills I had left. As I slapped the greenbacks into Roy's outstretched palm, I summoned up a grin and managed to say, "Go get 'em, Roy."

"Thanks, Drew. You'll get this back in spades. All you boys will."

I hoped he was right. Jace and Big Boy might be able to shrug it off if Roy wound up losing all our money in a poker game, but I didn't know about Aaron or Murph or the Gundersons. Hell, I didn't know how *I* would take it. I sure wouldn't be happy, though. I knew that.

Roy took my money back to the table. I could follow the game pretty well from where I was, so I stayed at the bar and kept drinking coffee.

The first hand went Roy's way for a change, and he pulled in a nice little pot. Then he lost a couple of small ones before winning again. That started a run of three winning hands in a row, and the pot in each one of them was a little bigger than the one before. I could see Roy's excitement growing. In the early stages of a game, he had a pretty fair poker face, but not when things had gone this far. If even I knew that he was about to start plunging again, I was certain a slick-haired gent like Ford knew it, too.

The clump of footsteps on the stairs made me turn my head and look in that direction.

The evening had been a fairly busy one, what with tumbling Becky and settling that misunderstanding between Jace and Cecilia. I hadn't kept track of anybody else's comings and goings. I wasn't surprised that the three men coming down the stairs were strangers to me. A dozen men could have arrived at Harrigan's and gone upstairs during the time I'd been otherwise occupied.

These three weren't cowboys. They all wore town suits, like Ford, and had fedoras on their heads instead of Stetsons. Hard-faced hombres, every man-jack of them, and the uneasy feeling I'd had earlier when I realized Roy was going to try to borrow money from me had just gotten worse. These men looked like the sort who might be friends with the gambler called Ford, and as they reached the bottom of the stairs, I saw the slight bulges under their suit coats that told me they were carrying guns.

Which meant it was just about the worse possible time Roy could have picked to slam his hand down on the poker table and yell, "Damn it, Ford, you're nothin' but a no-good, cheatin' bastard!"

FOUR

The place went so quiet it was like nobody was even breathing in there. I know for a fact I wasn't. All I could do was stand there next to the bar and watch what was about to happen.

After a few seconds that seemed more like an hour had gone by, Ford tipped his head back and looked lazylike up at Roy, who was standing on the other side of the table, his left palm still resting on the felt where he had slapped it.

"For the sake of the game, I'm going to pretend I didn't hear that, friend," Ford said.

"Then I'll say it again," snapped Roy. "You're a lyin', cheatin' bastard."

Actually, he'd said *no-good, cheating bastard* the first time around, but I didn't figure it was the right time or place to go correcting him.

Roy pointed with his right hand toward the cards lying facedown on the table in front of Ford. "I saw you come off the bottom of the deck with one of those," he said. "Is that how you've been winnin' all night, by bottom-dealin'? Or have you been markin' the cards too? I figure a sharper like you's got to know how."

Ford sighed. "I truly do enjoy the game of poker, the interplay of minds as each of the players tries to figure out what the others are thinking. It's a challenge unlike any in the world. Why would I ruin the most enjoyable aspect of the game by doing anything so crude and crass as cheating?"

"Because you want to win, and that's the only way you can when I'm sittin' at the table."

I saw Ford's face go hard, and I realized he was more bothered by the fact that Roy thought he couldn't win fair and square than he was by the accusation of cheating. But he still said, "Sit down and let's get on with the game. I've got no quarrel with you, Tacker."

"No, sir," Roy said stubbornly. "I ain't playin' with a cheat."

I decided it might be a good idea to glance around the room. The bartender was standing motionless behind the bar, but I could tell from the wide-eyed look on his face that he was ready to head for the floor as soon as trouble broke out. Harrigan was still sitting at the table where he had been counting money, but instead of continuing to count, he was putting the bills into little stacks and stuffing them in pockets inside his coat. He didn't want those greenbacks getting scattered in a fracas. Harrigan was known for not taking sides whenever there was a dispute amongst his customers; staying out of fights was the only way for him to stay in business. I knew Roy couldn't expect any help from him. The other two players at the poker table were a lot like the bartender—ready to dive for cover at a second's notice.

That left just me to side with Roy in any sort of showdown. I had a hunch the three city boys standing stiffly at the bottom of the stairs would back up Ford, and that suspicion was confirmed when one of them said, "You need some help with this cowboy, Chuck?"

Ford shook his head. "No, I don't think so." He placed his hands flat on the table and pushed himself to his feet so that he could look straight across at Roy. He gestured at the pile of chips in front of him and said, "Maybe you're right. Maybe we ought to just call it quits. Take your stake back out of there, Tacker. I don't want your money.''

Well, that threw Roy for a loop. He hadn't expected Ford to offer to give any of the money back. His eyes narrowed into a squint, and he hesitated before doing anything.

I've thought about it some since then, and I can't decide if Ford meant what he said or not. Maybe if Roy had just picked up the money, that would have been the end of it. Or maybe Ford was just suckering him, waiting until Roy leaned forward over the table to whip out a blackjack and clout him over the head with it. I don't even know if Ford was really dealing off the bottom of the deck, although some things that happened later on made me feel pretty strongly that he was cheating like Roy said.

But whatever Ford had in mind, I'll never know, because Roy just looked at him, said, ''The hell with that,'' and threw a punch at his head.

At least Roy didn't go for his gun. There was that much to be thankful for.

As it was, though, Ford's friends still reached under their coats and yanked out pistols, even as Roy's fist was smacking into the middle of Ford's face and knocking him back away from the table. Ford staggered, overturning the chair where he had been sitting, and crashed to the floor. By that time, the other gents had their guns drawn and were turning them toward Roy.

My Colt was upstairs where it wasn't going to do me a damned bit of good, and I cussed myself for that bit of carelessness. But at the same time I was already reaching for a half-empty whiskey bottle that was sitting on the bar a couple of feet away. I turned toward the men at the foot of the stairs as I snatched up the bottle and let fly with it. The whiskey in it gave it enough weight to make it fly straight and true, and it caught one of the men in the jaw with an ugly thud. The bottle didn't break, but it sure jerked that fella's head back. He fell back against the stairs.

I threw the only other thing that was handy, which happened to be my coffee cup. It was still half full of coffee, and the coffee was still pretty hot. Hot enough, anyway, to make one of the other men yelp in pain as it splashed across his face. About that time, I tackled the third man, diving under his gun, grabbing him around the middle, and driving with my feet so that we crashed back on the stairs and on top of the fella I had downed with the whiskey bottle.

Roy was doing all right, I figured, from the sound of the fracas going on behind me. I sure didn't have time to turn around and look to be certain, though. My hands were full right then. The hombre I'd tackled was trying to dent my skull with his pistol barrel, so I latched onto the wrist of his gun hand and hung on for dear life. That left me one hand free to pound him in the face as he squirmed under me and the gent on the bottom struggled to get both of us off him.

One of the city boys was still on the loose and able to cause trouble, the one who'd taken the hot coffee in the face. I couldn't deal with him, so I yelled as loud as I could, "Big Boy! Jace! Aaron!"

I hoped at least one of them would show up to lend a hand, but for all I knew, they were all so busy with their whores that they wouldn't even hear me.

Luck was with me. A door slammed open upstairs, and feet ran along the hallway. I heard Aaron yell, "What the hell!" Then somebody jumped over me as I lay there on the stairs wrestling with the two fellas I'd knocked down. Somebody else crashed to the floor behind us, and I figured Aaron had tackled the third man. More yelling and running sounds came from upstairs.

Then the fella who was trying to clout me over the noggin slipped his hand loose just long enough to bang the barrel of his gun off my skull. Everything turned black for a second, and he shoved me away hard. The staircase banister hit me in the back, but I barely noticed the pain because of the fireworks that had started going off in my head.

Somebody was going to shoot me. I was sure of it. I braced myself for the impact of the bullet.

Somebody screeched instead. At first I thought the sound came from a panther, but then I realized there wouldn't be a panther inside Harrigan's. So I figured out then that it was coming from a woman, and as my sight cleared, I saw Becky clawing at the eyes of one of the gunmen from the city. She was naked as a jaybird, but that didn't stop her, didn't even slow her down. She must have heard the commotion and come a-runnin', then thrown herself into the fight when she saw that I was in danger of getting my head blown off.

Whores tend to run like the dickens whenever there's trouble. In their line of work, they can't afford to take sides, just like Harrigan. So the fact that Becky hadn't hesitated to jump to my defense would have made me feel pretty darned good if I'd had the time to think about it. But right then, I was struggling back to my feet. As soon as I was upright, I set myself and threw a punch into the belly of the nearest gunman. Everything was so confused I couldn't tell any of them apart anymore. All I knew was that anybody in a pin-striped suit was the enemy.

Finally, I caught a glimpse of Roy again. He and Ford were on the sawdust-sprinkled floor, hands locked around each other's neck, rolling over and over. Likely they would have wound up killing each other if they'd kept that up, but Roy managed to bang Ford's head against the leg of a table as they rolled past it. Those tables in Harrigan's place were built sturdy. Ford went limp, and his fingers fell away from Roy's throat.

I ducked as one of the other gents tried again to pistol-whip me. His swing missed and threw him off balance, which left me in position to bring up an uppercut to his jaw. I felt the impact all the way to my shoulder as the punch landed. I swear, the fella's feet lifted a couple of inches off the floor, and he sailed backward to land on an empty table. It didn't collapse under him, so he just lay there on it with his arms and legs spraddled, out cold.

I twisted around, trying to see what was going on. There were fellas throwing punches everywhere I looked. Some of them were just wearing their underwear, so I knew they'd come running down from the second floor to get in on the brawl. I saw Jace and Aaron and Big Boy trading punches with some gents I didn't recognize. They weren't part of the original scrap, but they seemed to be after us. The Tacker Gang against the whole world, as usual. Everything was out of control now, and there was only one thing left to do.

Roy had had the same idea. He popped up sudden-like beside me and gripped my arm, squeezing it hard. "We better get out of here!" he shouted at me over all the yelling and thudding of fists against flesh and bone.

A huge crash made us both look around. The poker table had gotten knocked over, and money and chips went flying everywhere. Roy let out a groan. He had probably figured on grabbing at least some of that pile as we left, to try to recoup his losses. But now that would be impossible, because the money was scattered across the floor under the feet of the struggling men.

Somebody came at Roy swinging a broken bottle. Roy blocked the attempt to rip his face open and laid the gent out with a short, straight-arm punch. At the same time, somebody grabbed me from behind, looping an arm around my neck and cutting off my air. I stomped back, glad I had put my boots on, and felt my heel grind down on a bare foot. As the fella howled in my ear, I brought an elbow back into his belly and broke his hold on my neck. I lifted the elbow and cracked him under the chin with it, and he fell away.

Roy grabbed me again and tugged me across the room through the melee, both of us fending off attacks as we went. Along the way, we gathered up Jace, Aaron, Big Boy, and Murph Skinner, who was in the thick of things too. Roy looked around, his eyes wide and a little wild, and yelled, "Where the hell are the Swedes?"

I didn't see the Gunderson brothers anywhere. Maybe they had stayed upstairs instead of rushing down to join the fight. If that was the case, then they had more sense than everybody else in the place, I remember thinking.

But then both of those big Swedish boys stood up from behind the bar, and they had the bartender with them. One of the Gundersons had hold of his legs while the other one had his arms. The bartender was yelling like crazy as the Gundersons lifted him. With grunts of effort that I could hear clear across the room, they swung him up over their heads and then flung him across the bar. He crashed into some of the fighters and mowed them down like a scythe going through wheat.

"Come on, boys!" Roy shouted at the Gundersons.

Those Swedes vaulted the bar and started across the room through the path they had cleared with the flying bartender, stomping on sprawled bodies as they came. Just as they reached us, somebody yelled, "Look out!" and I heard the most god-awful sound I'd ever experienced.

It was like the roar of thunder and the crackle of lightning all in one, and it filled the room. A line of splinters flew up from the floor, and a chair that was sitting about five feet to my left practically exploded into kindling. Roy grabbed the collar of my shirt and slung me to the right, away from the hail of bullets that were now chewing up the wall near the door. He palmed out his Colt and triggered a couple of shots, and as I fell I caught a glimpse of what he was shooting at.

Ford had climbed a few steps up the staircase across the room, and he had some sort of contraption clutched in his hands. I found out later it was a machine gun, but right then I didn't know what to make of it. All I knew was that it was making a horrible racket and spitting out bullets faster than you could say Jack Robinson. Everybody in the place had given up fighting and gone diving for the floor instead when Ford opened up with the hellacious thing. It fell silent as the slugs from Roy's Colt whipped past Ford and smacked into the stairs beside him. The nearness of the shots made him stumble back.

I reckon Ford must not have been real familiar with that machine gun, else he would have been able to control it better and would have likely shot us all to doll rags. As it was, Roy's shots distracted him enough to give us a chance to scramble out the front door of Harrigan's. "Get the horses!" Roy yelled, and we headed for the barn.

Ford ran out after us and started shooting that machine gun again. But it was dark outside, being the middle of the night and all, and the thing had such a powerful recoil that the barrel kept riding up on him. I could tell that much when I threw a glance over my shoulder and saw him silhouetted there in the doorway with the light behind him. After a minute or so, Ford gave up and yelled to his pards, "Get 'em! Don't let 'em get away!"

But if there was one thing we'd had some experience with, it was getaways. It didn't take us long at all to run into that barn, find our horses, and slap blankets and saddles on them. We busted out of that barn and rode right through the boys who came running out of Harrigan's to try to stop us. They scattered like a flock of ducks to keep from getting trampled.

Ford let off another couple of bursts from the machine gun, but they didn't come anywhere near us. We hit the trail, galloping off into the night.

FIVE

Not that we were real happy with the way things had turned out, mind you. We were alive, and that was a hell of a lot better than getting our behinds shot off, but other than that, we were in piss-poor shape.

Roy and I were the only ones fully dressed, and I didn't have my gun. Roy's Colt was the only weapon we had. Everybody else in the gang was missing at least one article of clothing, and Aaron was in nothing but his long underwear. He was shivering from the chill in the night air, so I took off my duster and handed it to him when we finally slowed our horses to a walk after putting several miles between us and Harrigan's place. He shrugged into it with a grateful nod. He was barefooted too, but there was nothing I could do about that. I wasn't going to give up my boots.

The trail we were on was too rugged for cars to follow us, so we weren't worried about those flivvers that had been parked at Harrigan's. We didn't figure Ford and his cronies were very likely to come after us on horseback either. Not city boys like them. So we'd gotten out of the mess with our hides intact, but that was about all.

Except for the hoofbeats of our mounts, the night was quiet. It was a mighty tight silence too, and Big Boy finally broke it by asking, "What in blazes was that all about?"

"That fella Ford was cheatin'," Roy said. "I caught him dealin' off the bottom of the deck."

Big Boy sighed. "So I reckon you just had to call him on it."

"What else was I supposed to do? Let him get away with it? He'd taken most of our money with his cheatin' ways!"

"And now *all* our money's gone," Murph said bitterly. "Along with our guns and most of our clothes."

Even in the faint starlight, I saw Roy's shoulders twitch a little. He wasn't used to being talked to like that. "Harrigan will keep our guns for us," Roy said, "and we can pick 'em up next time we're there. Anyway, there are plenty of guns back at the camp."

That was true. We all had spare revolvers at the old abandoned ranch house, and there were a couple of rifles there too. We wouldn't be outgunned for long. But there was still the principle of the thing—and the money.

One of the Gundersons said, "We cannot get our loot back, yah?"

"I reckon that'd be a little too much to hope for," Roy told him. "Any of it that Harrigan gets his hands on, he's goin' to keep to help pay for the damages. The rest of it likely got snatched up by the other fellas who were left back there."

"So that job we pulled in Flat Rock was all for nothing." That was Murph again, still sounding mad and bitter.

Roy tried to laugh, but it came out flat and hollow. "There are plenty of other banks in Nevada. We'll be rollin' in cash again before you know it."

"Sure we will," Murph said, but he didn't sound like he believed it for a second.

Jace turned on him hotly. "If Roy says it, that's the way it's goin' to be!" he said to Murph. Sticking up for his big brother came natural to him.

"Back off, kid," Murph told him. "If there's goin' to be trouble, it's between Roy and me, not you."

"There's not goin' to be any trouble," Big Boy said heavily. "We ran into some bad luck. It's over, and that's the way it is. Let it go, Murph."

Sometimes I thought Big Boy was really the smartest one of all of us, even though he took a back seat to Roy when it came to planning. But he knew when to cut his losses and move on, and that was something none of the rest of us ever quite seemed to grasp.

"You stay out of this too," Murph began, but Big Boy reached over and rested a hand on his shoulder.

"No good's goin' to come of pokin' at it, Murph," he said. "No good at all."

Murph grumbled something I couldn't understand, but then he shut up. One of the Gundersons prodded his horse up next to Roy's and said, "You better come up with a mighty good job for us next time, Roy, to make up for this."

"Don't you worry," Roy said. "I'll see to it that we're all as rich as kings."

It was a long, miserable ride back into the mountains, and by the time we got to the hideout, we were all out of sorts with each other. It wasn't a matter of just a few of us resenting what Roy had done anymore. For two cents, the gang might've busted up then and there.

But nobody offered us two cents, so we stayed together, and Roy started planning again.

Looking back on it now, I can see that what happened at Harrigan's had a mighty big effect on Roy. He knew he shouldn't have lost his temper with Ford, and he knew he had let us down. He was smarting under that knowledge, just like a proud kid who's been forced to take a whipping. That was why, when he set his sights on our next job, he made sure it was a good one.

Too good, maybe.

There were spare clothes at the hideout too, along with the extra guns, so we were all outfitted just fine again when Roy gathered us around him a couple of weeks later. The abandoned ranch house was laid out sort of like a Mexican hacienda, with a courtyard inside the outer wall, and in the middle of the courtyard was an old well with a low stone wall around it. That was where we sat as Roy explained the plan.

"We're going to hit the First Cattleman's Bank in Reno," he said simply.

I reckon we all just stared at him for several seconds. Murph had been drinking from a little silver flask that he carried with him most of the time, and he paused with it halfway to his mouth. He was the first one to respond to what Roy had told us. He said, "Damn it, Tacker! Have you gone crazy?"

"Reno's a big town, Roy," Big Boy said quietly. "It's not like the other places we've hit."

"Yah," one of the Gundersons agreed. "Too many people. We get caught for sure, you bet."

Jace said, "Why don't you all just shut up and listen to what Roy has to say? He's bound to know what he's talkin' about."

Roy smiled and said sort of dry-like, "Thanks for the vote of confidence, Jace."

Jace flushed. "I meant what I said. If you think we can pull it off, Roy, then that's all I need to know."

"I wouldn't mind hearin' some of the details," Aaron said.

Roy nodded. "The Cattleman's Bank is the biggest one in Reno. Even though they call it the Cattleman's, it handles the payrolls for several of the mines in the area too. If we hit it when the vault's full, I figure we can take at least a hundred thousand out of there, maybe more."

Aaron let out a whistle of admiration and said, "That's a lot of money."

"Damn right it is. More money than fellas like us have ever seen before."

"How we gonna get in there and back out again?" asked Murph. "There's too damned many people all over the place. Reno's got its own police force too, not just a constable or a deputy sheriff like most of the jerkwater towns where we've been robbin' the banks."

"We can do it," Roy said stubbornly. "I've been thinkin' on it."

"Thinkin' about how the citizens are goin' to react when they see a bunch of desperadoes on horseback ride up to the bank?" Murph demanded.

Roy had taken about all the lip he was going to take from Murph. "Shut up and listen," he growled. "We're not goin' to ride up on horseback, and we're not goin' to be dressed like desperadoes. The only thing the folks in Reno will see is a bunch of businessmen in automobiles."

Now *that* scared me. I took a deep breath and said, "I don't much like them things, Roy."

"It'll be all right, Drew," he assured me. "I know how to drive just fine."

"Back in Minnesota, I drive a farm truck," one of the Gundersons put in.

Murph said, "I can drive a little too," and the way he sounded made me think that maybe he was coming around a little—grudgingly—to Roy's way of thinking.

"So you see," Roy said to me, "we won't have any trouble finding somebody to handle the cars. All you have to do is ride, Drew."

Knowing that didn't make me feel much better. The only time in my life I'd ever been in a car was when the sheriff of Parker County, Texas, had put me in one and taken me to Weatherford to see a judge about some cattle that had wound up on the wrong side of a fence. That would have been enough by itself to cause some bad memories, but I also remembered the way that contraption had sputtered and spat and rumbled, and how nervous I'd been when it started tearing down the road faster than I had ever gone before.

"And we won't be in the automobiles very long," Roy went on. "We'll ride our horses most of the way, then swipe a car or two when we get close to town. After we've pulled the job, we'll hightail it back to where we left the horses and head for the high country."

I was glad to hear that our getaway didn't depend entirely on mechanical things. They break down too easy. A good horse, now, you can depend on him until the crack of doomsday.

"You know the layout of that bank, Roy?" asked Big Boy. As always, he knew what the sensible questions were.

"I've been there, but I want to refresh my memory. That's why we're goin' into town and scoutin' around for a while before we pull the job."

That brought another frown to my face. I didn't like the idea of going into Reno and showing our faces around town just before we planned to rob the bank. Like Roy had said, though, the folks there wouldn't be seeing hard-faced outlaws in range clothes. We were going to be like kids playing dress-up, pretending to be something we weren't.

"You best lay out all the details," Big Boy urged. "Sounds a mite complicated to me."

So for the next few minutes, that's what Roy did. He told us how we'd ride into Reno on our best behavior and find a boardinghouse where we could spend the night. He figured we'd tell anybody who asked that we were on our way to California to take riding jobs on a ranch there. Roy knew of a ranch there in northern California, not far over the border from Nevada, called the Diamond F, and knew that they were hiring right now. He'd found out that much from the talk that went on over cards between the two ranchers back there at Harrigan's place. So maybe our visit there wouldn't turn out to be a total disaster after all. While we were in Reno, a couple of us would take a *pasear* down to the First Cattleman's Bank so we could look it over. Then we'd move on, heading west for California.

At least, that was what it would look like. What we would really do was circle back around to the east, find someplace we could steal a car or two and some clothes, and start the ball rolling. It was simple enough, despite what Big Boy had said, and it even sounded like it could work if everything went right. Seemed to me that the only problem might be finding those automobiles. The whole plan would fall apart if we couldn't lay our hands on a couple of the damned things, because I didn't think we could get out of town on horseback. Reno was too big, too modern, and too populated. A lot of folks who lived there might be old enough to remember when the West was wild, but these days eight men galloping down Virginia Street would attract way too much attention.

When Roy was finished, none of us said anything at first. Finally, Aaron spoke up. "Sounds like it might work, Roy . . . but it's risky."

"Yeah," Roy said, "it is. But think about the payoff, boys. We could come out of that bank with enough money so that we wouldn't have to worry about anything for a long time."

There was no denying that. If there was a hundred thousand dollars in the bank, that meant more than twelve thousand bucks for each of us. I'd known men who worked honest jobs all their lives and never made that much money. And Roy seemed to think that was about the least we could expect to find in the bank.

Murph took a healthy swig from his flask and said, "I say we do it."

"I reckon I'm in too," Aaron said with a slow nod.

"You know I'm with you, Roy." That came from Jace.

"Me too," rumbled Big Boy.

Both of the Swedes nodded, and one of them said, "Yah, we ride with you, Roy."

Roy looked at me. "What about it, Drew?"

He knew what I was going to say. Just like back at Harrigan's place when he'd asked me to stake him in the poker game. He knew I wasn't going to say no to him.

"Somebody fetch a bottle," I said. "Let's drink to the First Cattleman's Bank of Reno, Nevada . . . soon to be a whole lot poorer."

SIX

If there had never been a Comstock Lode, there might not have ever been a Reno. But a loudmouthed fella named Henry P. Comstock came along in 1859 and started claiming he'd discovered silver in the Washoe country of northwestern Nevada—when all along it was some other gents who had really made the strikes—and the boom was off and running. By 1868 Reno had grown up on the banks of the Truckee River, and I don't reckon I've ever seen a prettier place for a town. The Truckee Meadows, as the valley along the river was called, was surrounded by desert and mountains, but the valley itself was green and the weather was mild most of the time. Reno got its start because that was where the railroad crossed the Truckee, and when the silver boom was over, some folks thought the settlement was likely to dry up and blow away. But it didn't. It grew to the point that Reno started calling itself the Biggest Little City in the World.

I can't vouch for the truth of that claim. All I can say is that when we rode down into the Truckee Meadows and got our first good look at the place, I was impressed.

On the outskirts of town were nice neighborhoods of big houses and quiet, tree-lined streets. The folks who lived there had money, and you could tell it. Things got rowdier the closer we came to the downtown area, though. The buildings were made of brick, and some of them were three or four stories tall. I tried not to stare at them like I was some sort of barefoot country boy. We passed the Majestic Theater, the city hall, and a fancy four-story building with *Reno Evening Gazette* painted in big letters on the outside wall. Hell, I thought, even the newspaper office is bigger than anything I ever saw.

Roy leaned his head toward a big white building with a dome on top and columns out front and said, "That's the Washoe County Courthouse. Lots of folks get divorced there."

I'd heard about how it was easier to get a divorce in Reno, Nevada, than just about anywhere else in the country. I had to frown a little in disapproval as we rode past the courthouse. It may sound strange for a bank robber to be talking about what's right and what's wrong, but I never held much with divorce. Seemed to me that if a fella cared enough about a gal to say, "Until death do us part," he damned well ought to mean it.

"Where's the bank?" Murph asked.

"Keep your shirt on," Roy told him. "We're gettin' there." A couple of minutes later, he said, "It's up ahead on the left. Now, don't start gawkin' at it. How would that look?"

The First Cattleman's Bank was a square, red brick building like a lot of others in Reno. Just looking at it gave a fella a feeling of downright respectability. Men in sober dark suits were going in and out of the place, and several cars were parked in front of it. I thought about all the money in there, and I had to grit my teeth and force myself to look away. We rode on by without slowing down, and as far as I could tell, all the glances we threw toward the bank were casual ones.

Reno had a lot more automobiles in it than horses, but I saw a few horse-drawn wagons and carriages as we rode along, the hooves of our mounts clopping loudly on the paved street. Most of the men wore town clothes, rather than Stetsons and range garb, but we weren't the only cowboys in town either. Nobody paid much attention to us, and that was good.

Roy turned off Virginia Street onto one of the cross streets, and we all followed. Within a couple of blocks, we were back in one of the residential neighborhoods, though this one wasn't as fancy as the area on the other side of town. The streets were lined with trees, but the houses were smaller. They were plenty respectable anyway, with neatly kept lawns and flower beds along the front porches. Roy stopped at a house with a sign in the front yard that read ROOMS AND MEALS—LADIES AND GENTLEMEN ONLY.

I wasn't sure we fell into the category of gentlemen, but we could always pretend we were, I supposed. Roy turned to us and said in a quiet voice, "Just like robbin' a bank, boys. Let me do the talkin'."

We swung down from our horses and tied the reins to a fence of black wrought iron that ran along the sidewalk. Roy opened a gate in the fence and walked up to the house. We trailed along behind him, and when we reached the porch, he took his hat off and motioned for us to do likewise. He rubbed his other hand over his hair, smoothing it, and me and the other boys did that too. It was almost like we had come a-courtin'.

Roy knocked on the front door.

It was the middle of the afternoon, well past dinner, but I could still smell some mighty appealing aromas floating in the air as the door was opened. Pot roast, I guessed, with potatoes and onions cooked in with the gravy, and mixed in with that . . . apple pie, that was what it was. Deep-dish, with cinnamon sprinkled on the top.

The woman who opened the door was probably forty years old and not much more than five feet tall. She had to tilt her head back to look up at Roy. "Yes?" she said. "What can I do for you?"

Roy smiled, and even though he was grizzled and sort of craggy, the smile made him look a whole lot less dangerous than he really was. "Afternoon, ma'am," he said. "Would you be the owner of this place?"

"I am. I'm Mrs. Whaley." She looked along the porch at the rest of us, who were holding our hats in our hands and smiling too. "If you and your friends are looking for rooms to rent, I'm afraid I only have two vacancies at the moment."

"That'd be just fine, ma'am," Roy told her without hesitating. "We're used to bunkin' in together, and we'll only be stayin' the night."

Mrs. Whaley's face hardened a little, and she said, "Transients, eh?"

"We're on our way to California, ma'am," Roy said. "Got good ridin' jobs lined up there on a spread called the Diamond F."

"I see." Mrs. Whaley tapped her foot softly as she considered for a minute or so. I was about to decide she was going to turn us away when she said, "I don't normally rent my rooms by the night, but I suppose in the case of you gentlemen, I could make an exception. The price, however, will be a bit higher per night than my regular boarders pay."

Roy nodded. "That's just fine, ma'am, as long as it's reasonable."

"Two dollars for each room," Mrs. Whaley said.

I thought that was a mite steep, but Roy just nodded and said, "That's agreeable, ma'am."

"In advance."

"Of course." Roy reached in the pocket of his jeans and dug out four silver dollars, which left us pretty low on funds—for the time being anyway. I hoped we'd be a lot richer soon. He handed over the coins and said to Mrs. Whaley, "I reckon that includes meals?"

"Supper tonight and breakfast in the morning," she said.

Roy nodded. "That's all right. We'll be on our way west by noontime."

Mrs. Whaley looked past us at our horses. "There's a stable in the back," she told us. "Tend to your own animals, then bring your things in. I'll have the rooms ready. They're on the second floor, rear."

"Nice and quiet," Roy said, still smiling. "That'll suit us to a T."

We started to turn away, but Mrs. Whaley stopped us by saying, "There are plenty of hotels downtown. I'm surprised you didn't rent rooms in one of them."

"No, ma'am, we always find a boardin'house if we can," Roy said. "Can't get the kind of home cookin' I just know you'll dish up when you stay in a hotel."

That flattered her. Looked like she was proud of the table she set. She smiled up at Roy.

To tell the truth, I'm not sure why he really picked that place. It was quiet and out of the way, yet still close to downtown. But I saw the way Roy was looking at Mrs. Whaley too, and even though she was a little long in the tooth for me, I had to admit she was still a handsome woman. Her fluffy brown hair didn't have too many strands of gray in it, and she was a fine figure of a woman with the sort of ample bosom that some men like to wallow in. Thinking about such things reminded me of Becky, and I really missed her right then.

We put away our horses and carried our war bags inside through the back door, where Mrs. Whaley was waiting for us. As she led us upstairs, Roy said, "You and Mr. Whaley run this place by yourselves, do you?"

"Mr. Whaley passed away five years ago," she said. "I run the boardinghouse by myself."

"Sorry to hear about your loss, ma'am," Roy told her, and I'd've sworn he meant it. I wasn't surprised to hear that Mr. Whaley was dead; a lot of boardinghouses were run by widow women. They owned their houses anyway, and it was something respectable they could do to make ends meet.

At that hour of the afternoon, we were the only ones in the house except for Mrs. Whaley and a colored lady who worked as the cook and maid. Her name was Inez, and Mrs. Whaley spoke of her several times as she was showing us the rooms. The rest of her boarders were at their jobs. She told us about them too—a couple of old bachelors who owned a hardware store, a clerk in the local assay office, a schoolteacher, and some traveling men. They were all quiet, morally upstanding folks, to hear Mrs. Whaley tell it, and I had no doubt it was true. The best thing, though, was that none of them sounded like the sort to give us any trouble if anything went wrong.

"Now, then, is there anything else I can do for you?" Mrs. Whaley asked when we'd dumped our war bags in the rooms.

"Yes, ma'am," Roy said. "Could you tell me where I might find a bank?"

"Why, certainly. There are several banking institutions right downtown. The Farmers and Merchants Bank, the Reno National Bank, the Cattleman's Bank . . ."

Roy tugged on the brim of his hat. "Much obliged, ma'am."

You could tell by looking at Mrs. Whaley that she was curious about why a hardscrabble lot such as the eight of us would have need of a bank, and after a few seconds she indulged that curiosity by asking, "Do you have some banking to do, Mr. . . . . ?"

"Royce, ma'am," he told her, using the phony name he usually pulled out when he didn't want folks to know he was really the infamous Roy Tacker. "John Royce. And I have to send a draft back to my family in Kansas."

"Your . . . wife and children?"

Roy chuckled. "No, ma'am, I never got hitched. The money's goin' to my old mama and my little brother." Roy lowered his voice and said in a half whisper, "He's touched in the head, you know."

Behind Mrs. Whaley's back, Jace just glared at Roy.

"Oh, dear, I'm sorry to hear that," Mrs. Whaley said. "But you're certainly to be commended for looking out for them."

"A fella does what he can," Roy said modestly. He glanced over at me and went on. "Why don't you walk down to the bank with me, Dave?"

"Be glad to," I said. Dave was my alias when I had to have one.

We left the boys at the boardinghouse to settle in, and strolled back along the tree-shaded sidewalks to Virginia Street. As we walked, I said, "That Mrs. Whaley is a nice-lookin' woman."

"Yep," Roy agreed.

"You figure on humpin' her tonight?"

He looked over at me, frowning and narrow-eyed. "What the hell kind of a question is that?"

I shrugged and said, "Well, she's a widow woman and all. If her man's been dead for five years, likely she's got a mighty strong itch by now. And the way she was lookin' at you, I don't think she'd mind if you was the one to scratch it."

Roy just shook his head. "You youngsters think too much with what's below your belt. Mrs. Whaley's a nice, respectable woman, and she runs a clean place and sets a good table. Right now, that's all I care about." He paused, then added, "Besides, after we hit the bank, she's liable to figure out who we really are, and I wouldn't want her to have to live with knowin' she took an outlaw to her bed."

"Well, all right. But she's liable to be disappointed."

"Better that than for her to have to feel bad about herself later on."

It was none of my business who Roy did or didn't bed, so I let the matter drop. Besides, we were nearly at the bank, and I felt my nerves getting all tight and drawn up, like a new barbed-wire fence.

Our gunbelts were rolled up and stashed inside our war bags back at Mrs. Whaley's place. None of us had ridden into town with iron on our hips. Nor were we wearing our dusters. But Roy and I both had on shorter coats that hung down over the butts of the six-guns we had tucked into our belts at the small of our backs. We didn't want anybody knowing that we were armed as we walked casually into the Cattleman's Bank.

Roy walked straight up to one of the tellers' cages and asked the fella behind the wicket if Mr. Kirman was in, using a name he'd read off the front window of one of the other banks as we walked past it.

"You mean Mr. Richard Kirman?" the teller asked with a frown.

"That's right," Roy said. "I'm supposed to see him about a financial matter. A loan, in fact."

The teller laughed. "I'm afraid you're in the wrong place, cowboy. Richard Kirman is the president over at the Farmers and Merchants Bank. This is the Cattleman's Bank."

"It is?" Roy asked with a surprised frown. "I'd've sworn this was the Farmers and Merchants."

The teller was rapidly getting bored with what he considered to be just another dumb cowboy. "Go back down this street three blocks, and it'll be on your right," he said.

Roy nodded and said, "Much obliged, mister," then turned to me and said, "Come on, Dave."

I followed him out of the bank without a word.

All the time we'd been in there, I had been looking around without being too obvious about it. I knew Roy had been doing the same thing, only with an even keener eye. He would have taken in all the details of how the bank was set up. I had seen quite a few of them myself.

The lobby was spacious, with a row of six tellers' cages to the right. To the left had been an area of desks set off by a wooden railing with a couple of gates in it. In the middle of the lobby's rear wall were two doors, and I figured one of them opened into the bank president's office while the other led to the vault. Most importantly, I had seen only one guard, a middle-aged gent in a blue uniform with a Smith & Wesson double-action .38 on his hip. He'd probably been a lawman at one time or another, and looked salty enough to handle one or two men—but not eight.

"What do you think?" Roy asked me in a low voice as we walked along. "We park the cars right in front, go in and do our business, and get out of there before anybody knows what's happenin'."

"Sounds good to me," I told him. "We're really goin' to do this, aren't we?" Even then, a part of me didn't want to believe it.

"Damn right we are," Roy said.

SEVEN

The food at Mrs. Whaley's was every bit as good as I expected it to be. Inez fried up a mess of chicken for supper, and served it with mashed potatoes and green beans and biscuits that were almost fluffy enough to float right up off the plate. In those days, I was pretty skinny, but I could still put away the food. Wasn't until I got older that it started catching up with me.

Anyway, we ate supper there with the other boarders, and they were a pleasant bunch. Not that I could've spent much time around storekeepers and clerks and schoolteachers without going a little crazy. I was too reckless and fiddlefooted back then. But their company made for a nice change from that of outlaws and gamblers and whores.

Not everybody saw it that way. When we went back upstairs after supper, we all gathered in one of the rooms we'd rented, and first thing, Murph started complaining.

"I need a drink, Roy," he said. "Let's go find us a saloon."

Roy shook his head. "No, we're stayin' close here tonight. We don't need any trouble."

"I'm not lookin' for trouble," Murph said, "just a drink."

"Well, haul out your flask and take one," Big Boy said. "I've never knowed you to be without a pint of who-hit-John in your pocket, Murph."

"It ain't the same thing," Murph snapped. "I've spent the past couple of weeks with you boys, and I'm tired of your ugly faces. I need to see some pretty women and listen to a piano player while I'm havin' my drink."

"What you want's a whore," Aaron said.

"Well, what of it?" Murph challenged. "Ain't no crime for a fella to be feelin' a little randy, is it?"

"This ain't the time, Murph," Roy said. "Too much is ridin' on what's goin' to happen in the next few days to risk it all for a whore."

"Yah, Roy is right," one of the Gundersons told Murph. "Is better to wait."

"Soon you can buy all the women you want," the other Gunderson said.

Murph didn't like it, but he could see that we were all opposed to the idea, so he shut up. Jace, Aaron, Big Boy, the Gundersons, and me all played cards for a while. Like I said before, I'm not much on poker, but I can stand a friendly game every now and then. Roy read a newspaper he'd brought upstairs from Mrs. Whaley's parlor, while Murph nipped on his flask and turned the pages in an old dime novel some other boarder had left behind in one of the dresser drawers.

Along about ten o'clock, we turned in. Big Boy bunked with Murph and the Gundersons, since they were the newest members of the gang and Roy wanted somebody reliable in with them. He and Jace took the bed in the other room, while Aaron and me spread our bedrolls on the floor on either side of the bed. The space was narrow, but I reckon we were comfortable enough. Roy blew out the lamp and we went to sleep.

Sometime later, I heard voices, and after a few minutes I realized I wasn't dreaming. Somebody was in the room talking, and a second later I distinctly heard Roy say, "Damn!"

"I'm sorry, Roy." That was Big Boy's rumble. He was trying to keep his voice down, but with Big Boy, that was hard. "I reckon I was tireder than I thought I was. I slept right through it when he snuck out. Wouldn't know about it yet if I hadn't had to get up and take a leak."

I sat up and whispered, "What's goin' on?"

Roy was sitting on the foot of the bed, with Big Boy standing beside him. Roy turned his head and hissed at me, "Go back to sleep, Drew."

"No, something's wrong," I said. "What is it?"

"Murph's gone."

My thinking had still been a little fuzzy until Roy said that, but his words cleared all the cobwebs out of my head right fast. Murph knew what we were planning to do here in Reno, and despite the fact that he'd never given us any reason to think he was less than trustworthy, not having him around where we could keep an eye on him was downright scary.

I pushed myself to my feet and went to the foot of the bed. "Reckon we better roust the others and go look for him?" I asked Roy.

Before he could answer, Jace lifted his head from the pillow and asked, "What's all the jabberin' about? Can't you let a fella sleep?"

"Murph's gone," Roy said again, and Jace reacted pretty much like I had. He sat up straight in bed and cussed.

That woke Aaron up, and within a minute or so, all four of us were standing around the foot of the bed where Roy was sitting. He asked Big Boy, "What about the Gundersons?"

Big Boy snorted. "Them Swedes are sawin' logs like they're tryin' to clear a whole forest by mornin'. I don't know if they'd wake up even if the Angel Gabriel started blowin' his horn."

"All right," Roy said with a nod. "Jace, you go next door and keep an eye on 'em. The rest of us'll go look for Murph."

"Why do I have to stay here?" Jace asked. "I ought to go with you."

"Nope, I want somebody here in case the Gundersons wake up. I don't want them findin' everybody else gone. They might figure we were double-crossin' 'em, and that could ruin everything."

Jace grumbled a little more, but he wasn't going to refuse one of Roy's orders. The other four of us pulled our clothes on, except for our boots, and slipped out of the room in our sock feet.

We walked quiet as Apaches downstairs in the dark and let ourselves out the front door of the boardinghouse, which wasn't locked. Folks never locked their doors then; there wasn't any need. We put our boots on and started toward downtown. There on the side street, it was pretty shadowy under the trees, but I could see the glow of electric lights a couple of blocks away on Virginia Street. When we got closer, I pulled my watch out of my pocket, flipped open the turnip, and held it so that I could read the time. It was just after two o'clock in the morning.

We were still half a block away from Virginia Street when Roy held up his hand to stop us and said, "Look there."

A fella was just turning the corner up ahead. He came toward us in a stumbling gait. I could hear him talking to himself, and as he got closer, I realized he wasn't just talking, he was singing.

"Oh, the moon shines tonight on purty red wings . . . on purty red wings . . . on purty red wings . . ."

"That's Murph," Roy said, "and he's drunk as a skunk."

He sure was. I was a little surprised we couldn't smell the booze on him, even at that distance. We could sure smell it strong enough a minute later when he came stumbling up to us. Realizing that somebody was blocking his path, he stopped short, or at least tried to. He wavered and said, " 'Scuse me, gennelmen, but you seem to be in my way."

"Damn it, Murph, it's us," Roy said.

"Roy! You and the boys come to . . . to j-join me in celebratin'—"

"We're not celebratin' anything, you idiot," Roy told him savagely, "unless it's the fact you didn't get thrown in the hoosegow! Where've you been?"

"Downtown at a fine establishment known as Red Mike's." Murph let out a loud belch. "Fine establishment," he said again.

I could smell not only rotgut, but also cheap perfume on him, and I knew he'd found himself a whore to go along with his drinking. I hoped he hadn't said anything to her that he shouldn't have.

Roy was worried about that too. "Did you talk to anybody? Did you tell anybody what we're plannin'?"

Murph put his hand over his heart. "Roy! You wound me deeply, ol' son. Hell, I know not to run off at the mouth."

"You've been drinkin'," Big Boy said.

"Whiskey don't muddle my brain nor loosen my tongue." Murph glared at us, and he seemed a little more sober than he had been a moment earlier. "You boys shouldn't ought to think such things 'bout me."

Roy sighed. "All right. No harm done, I reckon. Come on, Murph. You need to sleep off this bender as best you can before morning."

"You're gonna have a hell of a hangover," Aaron told Murph. "My daddy had a good cure for that. Had to do with tabasco sauce and cayenne pepper and a dash o' black powder for seasonin'."

Murph groaned. He was already thinking about how he was going to feel in the morning, and I reckon he was dreading his punishment.

He got what was coming to him, I guess. But that came later.

I've seen fellas who had worse hangovers. Reckon I've had worse myself. But Murph was miserable enough the next morning. Roy warned him to keep it to himself, because he didn't want Mrs. Whaley knowing that any of us had sneaked out during the night. Murph didn't say anything during breakfast, but he couldn't stop himself from turning green around the gills when Mrs. Whaley's colored lady set a big plate full of hash browns and sausage swimming in grease in front of him. Murph stared at the food for a minute, then bolted from the table, drawing an exclamation of "My lands!" from Mrs. Whaley. She turned to Roy and asked, "What in the world is wrong with your friend, Mr. Royce?"

"He's got a delicate disposition," Roy said grimly. "He's prone to these spells."

"Oh. I see." Mrs. Whaley looked down at her coffee cup, and I would've sworn she was smiling a little. "Mr. Whaley's disposition could be a touch delicate at times too."

"We all have our crosses to bear," Roy said.

"Yes, indeed we do."

The rest of us kept eating, and I reckon I probably tied each of the Gunderson boys for the number of flapjacks we put away. That Inez could surely cook. If I'd been Roy, I might've been sorely tempted to give up the outlaw life and ask Mrs. Whaley if she needed any permanent, full-time help running the boardinghouse. What with Mrs. Whaley's bosom and Inez's cooking, a fella could have surely done worse.

But I knew Roy wouldn't have done it. None of us would. Once the open air and the high lonesome get in a man's blood, it takes a long time to get them out. Most fellas who rode the trails we did would die there and never settle down, and they knew it. That was the way they wanted it.

Murph stumbled back into the dining room before we were done, but he didn't eat any. He just slugged down two or three cups of coffee and then muttered, "I'm ready to ride."

"So are the rest of us," Roy said. He scraped his chair back and stood up, then nodded to Mrs. Whaley. "We're much obliged to you for your hospitality, ma'am. It's time for us to be ridin'."

"You're quite welcome, Mr. Royce," she told him. "If you and your friends ever come through Reno again, feel free to stop."

"We'll sure do that, ma'am," Roy lied. We'd be coming back to Reno, all right, and we'd be stopping too—but not at Mrs. Whaley's boardinghouse.

We gathered up our gear, saddled our horses, and rode off, and as we did so, I noticed that Mrs. Whaley had come out onto the porch to watch us leave. I thought for a second she was going to wave, but she didn't. I figure she was thinking about Roy, maybe wondering what it would have been like if he had stayed. It's easy to do that. You meet somebody and then they go out of your life, and you ask yourself what it would have been like if things were different.

But there's no way to answer that question, and if you ask it too much, you're liable to drive yourself plumb crazy.

We rode west out of Reno, just as Roy had worked it out, then swung back to the north when we were about ten miles out of town. That took us almost to the California line. As we rode north, Virginia Peak rose in the distance in front of us, its slopes covered with pine. We were still a good distance away from it when we turned back east.

While we were coming into Reno the first time, we had kept our eyes open for a likely place where we could get our hands on a couple of automobiles and some town clothes. I hadn't seen anything too promising, but I figured Roy would come up with something, and sure enough he did. We camped that night a good ways out of town, and as we sat around the fire he took a folded-up piece of newspaper from the pocket of his duster. "I tore this out of the paper I found at Mrs. Whaley's," he said as he unfolded it and handed it to Jace. "Pass it around and let all the boys take a look at it."

When the piece of newsprint came to me, I saw that on one side of it was an advertisement for some place called Moana Hot Springs. I glanced around at the other boys, and saw that they looked as confused as I felt. "What the hell is this?" I asked Roy.

"It's a health resort just a little ways out of Reno," he said. "The place is built on some natural hot springs, and the fella who owns it called it Moana because that's a Hawaiian name, and it reminded him of a resort he'd been to in Hawaii. Folks go there to take mineral baths. That's where we're headed first.''

''You think we need baths?'' Jace asked.

''We need clothes, town clothes. And what do people do before they take a bath?''

Aaron grinned. ''They take off their clothes.''

I had figured it out too at the same time as Aaron. He just spoke up quicker than I did. I said, ''I'll bet folks drive their cars out to this hot springs place too, don't they?''

''Bound to,'' Roy said.

''They're bound to have a telephone there too,'' Big Boy pointed out. ''What if they call ahead to Reno and tell the police somebody stole some clothes and automobiles? The law's liable to be waitin' for us when we get to town.''

''A telephone's got to have wires, and wires can be cut. That'll be a good job for you, Aaron. You can shinny up a pole about as fast as anybody I've ever seen.''

Aaron thought about it a little, then nodded. ''All right. I reckon I can do that.''

''We'll fix the other cars so they can't chase us in them,'' Roy went on, ''and we'll run off any horses they have out there. Then we'll stash our own mounts somewhere between the resort and Reno and get on into town as quick as we can. Once we've done the job and are back on our horses headin' for the high country, nobody's goin' to catch us. You boys know that.''

''Yeah,'' I said. ''We know it.''

None of us slept too good that night. The excitement of what the next day would bring was just too much to let us relax. I was rarin' to go when I got up the next morning, and the other boys seemed to feel the same way.

We skirted to the east around not only Reno, but also Sparks, the smaller town right next door where the Southern Pacific Railroad had its repair yards. Then we cut back to the west, and after a while reached a set of narrow-gauge railroad tracks that had wires strung above them on poles. Roy told us that the tracks belonged to the electric-powered

interurban trolley that ran between Reno and Moana Hot
Springs. A dirt road and another set of wires followed the
tracks. Roy pointed to the wires and said, ''That'd be the
telephone line.''

Aaron edged his horse over next to one of the poles.
''Ain't nobody comin','' he said. ''Want me to go ahead
and cut that wire, Roy?''

''Might as well,'' Roy decided.

Aaron stood up in his saddle while Big Boy held the
reins for him. He got hold of that pole and scrambled up
it like a monkey climbing a tree. When he got to the top,
he slipped his knife from its sheath on his belt and sawed
through the wires. The loose ends fell to the ground, coiling
like snakes. ''What about them others that run above the
trolley tracks?'' he called down to Roy. ''Want me to climb
one of those poles and cut them too?''

''You stay away from those wires,'' Roy told him
sternly. ''They carry electrical current, and they'll bite you
worse'n any sidewinder.''

Aaron climbed down the pole and got back on his horse.
''Nobody's goin' to be callin' for help over those telephone
wires for a while,'' he said proudly.

Roy waved us on toward the south. ''Let's go, before
somebody notices the telephone's out and starts gettin' suspicious.''

From where we had stopped to let Aaron cut the telephone wires, we could see both Reno in the distance to the
north and a clump of green to the south that turned out to
be Moana Hot Springs. The resort was a huge white building that was surrounded by trees. It had so many small
windows that it reminded me of a gigantic chicken house.
Part of it stuck out in the middle where the entrance was,
and the words MOANA BATHS were painted over the doors.
Almost two dozen cars were parked in front of the building,
along with a few horse-drawn buggies. As we rode up, Roy
said to the Gundersons, ''Cut those teams loose and haze
'em off.'' He turned to Murph. ''Pick us out a couple of
good cars, then you and Jace fix all the others so they won't
run.''

Murph nodded. "Got it." He had recovered from his hangover of the day before, but he still had a haggard, strained look about him. I didn't think anything of it, though, since he'd never been what you'd call an overly handsome cuss.

Jace looked like he wanted to come with the rest of us, but he didn't say anything, just went along with Murph like Roy had said. Roy, Big Boy, Aaron, and me swung down from our horses and walked inside like we owned the place. A fella in a white shirt and white pants came out of a little office to one side of the entrance and started to smile at us. He stopped when he saw how we were dressed. "What can I do for you?" he asked. He was being polite, but you could tell he didn't like our looks. We weren't the sort of people he usually saw in a fancy place like this.

Before Roy could say anything, the fella in white looked past us and saw Jace, Murph, and the Gundersons going about their work out front. "Hey!" he exclaimed as he started toward the door. "You can't—"

Roy palmed his Colt and said, "Don't go raisin' no ruckus. Just stand still and keep your mouth shut."

The fella stood still, all right, but he couldn't seem to shut his mouth. It hung open as he stared at us.

"Take us to the dressin' room, and nobody will get hurt," Roy told him.

"You . . . you're going to rob . . ."

Roy lifted the barrel of his gun a little. "I didn't say talk. I said take us to the dressin' room."

I could hear a lot of talking and laughing elsewhere in the big building; sounds had a hollow echo to them there. But there was nobody around out in the entrance area except that one fella. So far, so good, I thought as he led the four of us down a short hall and into a big room with a damp stone floor and a rank smell to it. The baths themselves were on the far side of the room, through some big double doors.

"This . . . this is the men's dressing room," the fella said. His face was as white as his shirt and pants. He had to be convinced these crazy cowboys were going to gun him down at any second.

Instead, Roy just said, "Much obliged," and tapped him on the head with the butt of his gun. The fella folded up and stretched out next to one of the benches that were in front of a whole wall full of open-fronted cubbyholes. About three-fourths of the spaces were empty, since it was fairly early in the day, but the others had clothes hanging in them. Aaron and I started grabbing clothes while Roy and Big Boy stood lookout.

It only took a couple of minutes for Aaron and me to each gather up an armful of clothes. We headed for the door of the dressing room, and we almost got out without any trouble. But then a couple of heavyset, elderly gents wearing nothing but towels around their waists sauntered out of the room where the baths were. They saw the four of us standing there, and the fella in the white outfit sprawled out on the floor, and they both started hollering as they backed up toward the doors as fast as they could.

Roy lifted his gun, and for a second I thought he was going to send a shot or two after them, just to hurry them on their way, you understand, but then he jammed the Colt back in its holster and said, "Let's go!"

We ran out of there and found that Jace, Murph, and the Gundersons had done their jobs. Murph had a couple of the cars already running, and the others all had one side of their hoods raised. "We yanked out all the wires we could find," Murph called to us as he motioned for us to hurry. He was sitting behind the wheel of one of the cars.

Jace and the Gunderson brothers were already mounted up again. Jace had the reins of Roy's mount, and one of the Gundersons was leading Murph's horse. Roy jumped into the second car while Aaron and I threw the clothes we'd stolen into the passenger seat. Then we swung up into our saddles, following Big Boy's lead. We tore out of there, Roy and Murph driving the cars, the rest of us on horseback.

I heard yelling behind us, and looked back to see several men spilling out of the big white building. They'd never be able to catch us, and dressed in towels like they were, I didn't figure they'd even try.

I couldn't help but let out a whoop. We were a long way from being finished, but the first step of Roy's plan had gone off without a hitch.

Now all we had to do was rob the First Cattleman's Bank, and we'd be rich men.

Rich as kings, Roy had said.

EIGHT

We were about as fancy a bunch as you ever saw when we drove into Reno a short while later. In lightweight town suits, boiled white shirts, bow ties, and bowler hats, we were downright dandies.

We had stopped a couple of miles from Moana Hot Springs and hidden our horses in a little draw that was partially concealed by brush. While we were there, we'd gone through the clothes we'd stolen from the dressing room, and each of us had found a suit that fit fairly well, except for Big Boy. The suit he was wearing was too small, but we hoped it wouldn't be too noticeable.

The disguises wouldn't have to pass muster for very long. Just long enough for us to get into the bank and back out again.

I kept one hand on my head so that my hat wouldn't blow off as Roy drove the flivver that carried him, me, Jace, and Big Boy. Aaron was behind us in the other car with Murph and the Gundersons.

We drove down the main drag, Roy's car in the lead, Murph following closely behind us. It was the middle of the morning, and the street was fairly busy. I didn't see anybody on horseback today, just folks in cars and on bicycles. None of them paid much attention to us, and neither did the people on the sidewalks. Roy had been right: Dressed like this, driving up to the bank in automobiles, we blended right in and nobody gave us a second thought.

Word hadn't reached town yet of the robbery at the bathhouse. It would take at least another fifteen minutes before anybody from out there could hoof it into Reno. And by the time a quarter of an hour had passed, we planned to be on our way back out of town with all that money.

The Cattleman's Bank loomed up on our left. Roy angled the car toward the sidewalk, and I grabbed onto the door beside me. It still made me nervous when we changed direction like that. I halfway expected the car to tip over and dump us all in the street. Roy knew what he was doing, though, and he brought the thing to a smooth stop next to the sidewalk. Murph piloted his car in right behind us.

Roy had already decided we would leave the engines running while we went into the bank; it was too much trouble and took too long to crank them and get them started again. We stepped out onto the sidewalk. Nobody was wearing a gunbelt, but we each had our Colts tucked into our belts behind the tails of our coats. Moving briskly, like businessmen on an important errand, we crossed the sidewalk and stepped into the bank.

Stepped into Hell was more like it.

But we didn't know that at first. Everything looked normal when we glanced around the big room. As far as we could tell, nothing had changed since Roy and I had paid it a visit a couple of days earlier. I did notice that there weren't any women in the bank, but that didn't surprise me. To the best of my recollection, I hadn't seen any women in the place on our previous visit either.

Roy went in first, followed by Big Boy and Aaron, then Jace and me, the Gundersons, and Murph bringing up the rear. That put Murph closest to the door, which was right where he was supposed to be. When I glanced over my shoulder, I saw him hanging back some, but I didn't think anything of it. One of his jobs was to throw the latch on the doors so that no unsuspecting customers could barge in from the street in the middle of the robbery.

But Murph didn't throw the latch. Instead he just reached down and grabbed the door handle, like he was ready to twist it and yank the door open again. . . .

I knew right then and there that something was wrong, but I hadn't figured out just what. I opened my mouth, thinking that I ought to say something to Roy, even though it might make him mad if I broke the rules and spoke up. But it was too late, because he'd already slipped his hand behind his back and pulled his gun, and as he brought it out he said in a loud voice, "All right, this is a holdup! Everybody just stay still, and nobody will get hurt!"

Instead of the shocked silence that usually followed that order, a door slammed open, and Roy turned quickly toward the sound. I saw a man step through a door on one side of the bank lobby, and I never will forget what he looked like. I can still see him in my mind's eye to this day. He was a big fella, middle-aged, with long white mustaches that hung down on both sides of his mouth. He wore a brown suit and a cream-colored Stetson, and he had a lawman's badge pinned to his vest. In his hands he was holding a double-barreled shotgun, and it was pointing right at Roy. The fella bellowed, "Drop your guns! You're all under arrest!"

Murph. That bastard. He sold us out to the law!

Those thoughts flashed through my head even as I instinctively spun around and grabbed my gun. I was going to put a hole in that son of a bitch if it was the last thing I ever did, and I remember thinking that it likely would be. Because even as I turned toward the door, from the corner of my eye I saw more men popping up behind the tellers' cages, and they were armed with scatterguns too. Through the front windows of the bank I saw deputies running toward the doors, cutting off our escape. We were trapped good and proper.

A pistol cracked and a greener roared at the same time. More guns began to bang all around me. Glass exploded from the front windows. I didn't pay any mind to any of it. All I could think about was Murph, and how he must have gone to the law when he sneaked out of Mrs. Whaley's house. Instead of finding himself a whore, he had found the local sheriff and set up this trap. Then he had probably splashed whiskey over his clothes and pretended to be drunk when he came back to the boardinghouse. We'd already discovered he was gone, but the ruse had worked anyway.

I wondered how much money he had been promised for betraying the Tacker Gang. Whatever the amount, it was going to be the price of his life, because I was going to kill the no-good skunk.

But I didn't have to, because even as Murph tried desperately to yank the door open and escape from the bloodbath inside the bank, the glass in the upper half of the door blew in, shattered by both barrels of a shotgun blast. The buckshot and the shards of glass tore into Murph's face and chest and ripped the hell out of him. He gave a bubbly little half-scream as he flopped backward, his hands over the mess that had been his face. He landed hard on his back, kicked a couple of times, then relaxed as the blood started to pool under his head. One of the deputies outside the door had been too quick on the trigger, and it had cost Murph his life.

Good riddance, I thought as I triggered a couple of shots toward the door, firing over Murph's sprawled body in hopes of driving the deputies away from the entrance.

A powerful hand gripped my arm, and Big Boy yelled in my ear, "Go! Go!" We started toward the door, firing as we went. I couldn't tell where my bullets were going, and I didn't care. There was nothing in my mind but anger and the terrible certainty that I was going to die at any instant. So far, though, none of the bullets flying around the place had touched me.

The Gundersons hadn't been so lucky. I saw both of them lying on the floor not far from Murph. Shotgun blasts from the sidewalk, fired through the windows, had brought them down. I couldn't tell if they were alive or not, but as bloody as they were, I doubted it.

More shooting was still going on behind us. Roy, Jace, and Aaron were putting up a fight. I was convinced it didn't matter. None of us were going to make it out of that bank lobby alive. I was never more sure of anything in my life.

Then something slapped at my leg and I felt myself falling. Big Boy's hand tightened on my arm, and he would have been able to hold me upright and keep hauling me toward the door, but he was hit just then too. His fingers slipped off my sleeve as he grunted and stumbled forward. I thumped hard against the floor, knocking the wind out of me. I lay there gasping for breath, and to my considerable surprise, I noticed that my right leg didn't hurt. In fact, I couldn't even feel it, couldn't tell whether or not it was still there. I looked, just to be sure.

There was a bloodstain on the outside of my thigh, almost exactly halfway between my knee and my hip. Part of my brain knew that the wound wasn't a bad one, just a deep graze, but the other part didn't know anything except that I was bleeding, dark red blood soaking into the pants leg of that stolen town suit. I yelled in horror, and since I'd already dropped my pistol and my right hand was free, I clamped it over the bloody place and held on tight.

Big Boy was down too, curled up in a ball and clutching at himself, and I was afraid that he was gutshot. But then he rolled onto his back and I didn't see any blood, so I didn't know what had happened to him. Right then, I didn't particularly care. I was too busy holding on to my own leg and yelling to beat the band.

I wasn't the only one yelling. Deputies crashed in through the buckshot-shredded front doors of the bank and covered us with scatterguns as they shouted for us not to move. I realized nobody was shooting anymore. It took craning my neck and twisting my head around, but I saw that Roy, Jace, and Aaron were all still on their feet. Their hands were in the air and they weren't fighting back anymore. They had dropped their guns and were surrendering. Jace swayed, and Roy reached over to steady him. A few drops of blood oozed from a bullet burn on Roy's cheek; he had come *that* close to dying. More blood dripped from the fingers of Jace's left hand. As far as I could tell, Aaron was the only one of us who hadn't gotten a scratch in all the shooting. He always was lucky.

That was the last thought I had before my head suddenly fell back and thumped against the floor. Blackness loomed up all around me, and I didn't mind letting it take me away for a while.

I didn't know if I was alive or dead, but when I woke up smelling carbolic acid and bedpans instead of brimstone, I figured I was alive. Sure enough, when I was able to pry my eyes open and take a look around, I saw that I was in a hospital, lying in a bed covered by stiffly starched white sheets, a pillow with an equally stiff pillowcase under my head.

"So you're awake, are you?"

I didn't recognize the voice. It came from my right. I turned my head to look in that direction, and saw a lantern-jawed, jug-eared man about thirty years old. He was wearing a suit but no hat, and his dark hair was slicked down and parted in the middle. He was sitting in a straight-backed chair, and behind him, leaning in a corner of the room, was a shotgun. He was wearing a holstered revolver, too.

"You're . . . a lawman." My lips and tongue were dry as Death Valley, and the words came out in a croak.

"That's right. I'm Deputy Gilliam. And you're a prisoner, even if you are in the hospital, so don't get no funny ideas."

I gave a little shake of my head. I was too tired to have any ideas, let alone funny ones.

But I was curious too, so I asked, "What about . . . the others?"

"Got two of 'em locked up down at the county jail and two more here at the hospital. They ain't hurt bad, and neither are you. And then there's the three who're already at the undertaker's."

Three dead . . . that would be Murph and the Gunder-sons, I thought. None of the rest of us had looked to be hurt bad enough to need the services of an undertaker. At least, not yet.

The deputy must've had the same thought, because he got this ugly grin on his face and said, "The rest of you could wind up there too, depending on how your trial goes. It's a good thing you didn't kill nobody with all that lead you slung around, or else you'd hang for sure."

He was trying to get my goat, but what he'd done instead was give me a tiny little sliver of hope. Roy, Jace, Aaron, and Big Boy were still alive, and since nobody had died in the trap except three members of the gang, the law might just send us to prison instead of the gallows. Prison was pretty bad, but it was better than dancing on the end of a rope.

"Somebody better . . . see to our horses . . ."

"They've already been brought into town and put up at the livery barn. One of the others told us where to find 'em." Deputy Gilliam snorted contemptuously. "If you boys was half as worried about how you've been stealing money from poor honest folks as you are about them horses—"

I was so tired I couldn't help it. I went back to sleep while the deputy was still yammering at me.

I was only in the hospital for a couple of days before I was taken to jail. My right leg was sore and stiff and had a heavy bandage wrapped around the thigh, but I could hobble along without too much trouble. The deputies took Jace and Big Boy to jail the same time they took me. A piece of buckshot had plowed a furrow along Jace's left forearm, but it was bandaged up like my leg and seemed to be healing all right. Big Boy wasn't wounded at all except for a deep bruise and some scratches on his belly. He had stuck a spare pistol under his shirt before we went into the bank, and a bullet had hit it during the fracas. That was what had doubled him over and knocked him off his feet. He had been kept in the hospital for a while because the doctors said that a blow to the stomach like that could sometimes

cause "internal injuries," but they were satisfied by now
that his guts were all right.

We were the only prisoners at the time, so each of us
was locked in a different cell, but the cell block was fairly
small and we could talk to each other, which was a relief.
I was sorry when Roy told me that the Gunderson brothers
were sure enough dead. That was a real shame; I liked those
Swedes.

Murph, now, I didn't shed any tears for him. None of
us did. Everybody had figured out by now that he had
double-crossed us, and as far as we were concerned, he had
gotten what was coming to him. His death had been an
accident, sure, just something that happened in the heat of
battle, but some things have a way of working themselves
out. That was how I looked at it. It was sure a bad break,
though, that the Gundersons had had to die too.

After a couple more days, a young fella about the same
age as me and Aaron came to see us. He said his name was
Darnell and told us that he was our court-appointed attorney. Roy was stretched out on the bunk in his cell while
Darnell was talking, and he interrupted to ask, "Does that
mean you're goin' to get us off for the crimes we're
charged with?"

"Every man is entitled to a defense," Darnell said. "I'll
do my best for you, Mr. Tacker. That's all I can promise
you."

He had curly red hair and freckles all over his face, and
he looked like he would have been more at home clerking
behind a store counter than defending us in front of a judge
and jury. I didn't hold out any hope of being found not
guilty. Hell, under the circumstances, Clarence Darrow
himself couldn't have kept a jury from convicting us. All
I was hoping for was that we'd escape the hangman.

Well, that was how it turned out, of course. But not the
way I figured it would.

The trial began a week later—and ended the same day. The
sheriff, who was the big gent with the white mustaches who
had first challenged us in the bank, testified first and said

that he had received an anonymous tip that the Cattleman's Bank was going to be robbed. Anonymous, hell. He was talking about Murph Skinner and we all knew it. But the District Attorney didn't press him on that point. The sheriff told about how him and his deputies had set up an ambush and how we had walked into the trap. There wasn't any way of getting around the facts of the story. Everybody in town knew what had happened.

But then Darnell got up and asked, "Sheriff, how did Mr. Roy Tacker react when you called on him to throw down his weapon and surrender?"

The sheriff looked surprised. "How'd he react? He tried to shoot me!"

"Did he really, Sheriff? Are you sure of that? Couldn't he have simply been trying to wound you, or even to frighten you off, rather than killing you?"

"Looked to me like he was trying to blow a hole right through me," the sheriff said with a frown.

"*Were* you injured, Sheriff?"

"Nope. Nary a scratch." The lawman said it proudly.

"I see." Darnell sounded satisfied with that answer, and from where I was sitting at the defense table, I saw the District Attorney wince a little, like somebody had poked him. "And how far away from you was Mr. Tacker standing when he allegedly fired at you?" Darnell asked.

"Oh, twelve, fifteen feet, I suppose."

"Practically point-blank range."

"Well, I wouldn't say that. Say, are you trying to claim that outlaw missed me on purpose?"

"I'm asking the questions, Sheriff, not you," Darnell said. "And I have no more for this witness."

"Wait just a dad-blasted minute! I know good and well Tacker tried to shoot me. Hell, I let off a load of buckshot at him, and all of it except one piece missed!"

Darnell just looked at the judge and said, "Move to strike the witness's last comments as not responsive to a question. My cross-examination is over."

The judge nodded in agreement.

It wasn't much, but it was something to hang on to for the time being. We hadn't gone into that bank planning to kill anybody. Truth to tell—and I told it when my time on the witness stand came, after the prosecution had rested and all of us were called to testify—I hadn't aimed right at anybody when I squeezed off the shots I had fired during the fight. I was just throwing lead in the general direction of the door.

Now, I wouldn't even start to claim that we were *trying* not to shoot any of those lawmen. They had been on one side and we were on the other, and all of us had known the chances we were taking when we chose the trails we would follow in life. I won't claim we were in the right either, because we sure enough weren't. I've been a law-abiding citizen for a long time now, and I know that robbing banks and shooting at lawmen is wrong, whether you actually hit anything or not. But Darnell did a good job of making us seem to the jury to be not quite as bad as we really were, and when they came back with their verdict late that afternoon, they found us guilty of attempted bank robbery, but innocent of the attempted murder charges that had been filed against us. It was left up to the judge to sentence us, and I knew what that sentence would likely be.

Twenty years at hard labor in the state penitentiary.

Only the judge didn't sentence us right away. Instead the District Attorney and Darnell went into his chambers with him and jawed for a long time, leaving us sitting out in the courtroom at the defense table, wrists and ankles shackled, wondering what in blazes was going on. The five of us just looked at each other and frowned. Even Roy was starting to look worried. We couldn't be sentenced to hang for attempted bank robbery, but we were all convinced the judge and the two lawyers were cooking up something else for us.

Finally, everybody came out of the judge's chambers, and His Honor took his place behind the bench again. Darnell said quietly to us, "I did the best I could for you, boys. The rest is up to you."

He didn't have time to say anything else, because the judge smacked his gavel down a couple of times and said, "Court is back in session. The defendants will stand and face the bench."

We did, and he went on. "As you may be aware, war has been raging in Europe for the past three years."

Now, that sure wasn't what any of us expected to hear. We saw a newspaper every now and then, and they had stories about what was being called the World War, but all that fighting over in Europe didn't have anything to do with the United States, or with a ragtag bunch of bank robbers.

That showed how well we kept up with the news, because the judge said, "The United States declared war on the Central Powers several months ago, and American troops are already being sent to join the Allied forces in France. However, more men are needed for the American Expeditionary Force, and broad latitude has been granted to the judiciary in the matter of clemency for potential enlistees. Do you men understand what I'm saying to you?"

I didn't, not really, but Roy did, and he put it in words we could all understand. "You're sayin' that if we sign up to go fight in Europe, you won't throw us in prison."

The judge got a stern look on his face. "You have all been found guilty of serious charges, and I hereby sentence you to be incarcerated for the next twenty years in the state penitentiary."

I bit back a groan. Why had he given us that song and dance about the war in Europe if he was just going to send us to prison anyway?

But then he went on. "However, that sentence will be suspended in the event that you enlist in the American Expeditionary Forces. What will it be, gentlemen?" His voice got all loud and dramatic, because all judges are politicians at heart, I reckon. "Prison—or fighting to make the world safe for democracy against the hordes of Kaiser Bill?"

He even clenched a fist and thumped it on the bench in front of him when he got to that last part.

The five of us looked at each other, and Big Boy said, "I don't much hanker to go to prison, Roy."

"Neither do I," said Aaron. "I never figured I'd get any further east than Nevada, but I don't suppose goin' to Europe would be all that bad."

Jace said, "I'll do whatever you say, Roy."

As usual, I was the last one to make up his mind, but this wasn't a hard choice. I nodded and said, "I'm for it, Roy."

"I guess that's it, then," Roy said. He turned back to the judge. "Your Honor, we accept."

The sheriff was still sitting in the courtroom, and that was all he could stand. He jumped up on his feet and yelled, "Wait just a damned minute! Do you mean to tell me that you're letting these outlaws go?"

"There are other outlaws in the world, Sheriff," the judge said. "There are entire nations of outlaws, and we have to deal with them any way we can." He banged his gavel down. "I order that these men be taken to the nearest military installation and enrolled among the ranks of the American Expeditionary Forces." He looked at us and added out of habit, "And may God have mercy on your souls."

When I heard that, I thought about asking if it was too late for us to pick prison instead. But it wouldn't have done any good. By the next morning, we were already sworn in and on a train heading east with a couple of hundred other recruits, bound for the 36th Division that was training at Camp Bowie, in Fort Worth, Texas.

I was headed home.

NINE

It's easy to talk about those times now, but let me tell you, it wasn't so easy living through them. Many's the time I woke up sweating and shaking in the middle of the night, first in the hospital in Reno, then in the jail cell, and then on that train bound for Texas. I'd come closer to dying than I ever had before, and when you're lying there in the darkness thinking about that, you have to ask yourself some mighty hard questions.

And the hardest of them all is, how in the hell did I wind up in such a mess?

I won't bore you with a lot of details about my life, since nobody asked, but I will say that I was born on a farm in Parker County, Texas, just outside a wide place in the road called Peaster. I was delivered by a midwife, since there was no doctor closer than the county seat in Weatherford in those days, though a sawbones named Howard moved to Peaster in time to set my arm after I busted it falling out of a tree when I was twelve years old. I was already pretty wild by then, since my mama had died when I was just a toddler and I'd been raised by my dad and three older brothers who were all too busy working to pay much attention to a kid. Wasn't long after that broken arm healed up that I fell into bad company, as the old saying goes, and sure enough, it caught up to me a few years later when I got in trouble with the law and lit out for the tall and uncut. Over the next few years I saw some rough places and rougher men, went hungry and near froze to death plenty of times, and learned that the only person you can really trust is yourself.

That's a harsh way of looking at things, I know, and I've since found out that it's not always true. But that's the way I felt when I drifted into Nevada and hooked up with Roy and the other fellas. They were the ones who first started teaching me what it's like to have real friends.

We spent a lot of time on the train talking and playing cards. Everybody was excited about getting to go overseas and fight the Boche. Of course, I couldn't have told you *why* we were at war with the Germans, and I suspect most of those other recruits couldn't have either. European political alliances were a maze we didn't even try to find our way through. It was enough for us to know that the Germans were our enemy and Kaiser Bill was a dirty son of a bitch who was trying to run roughshod over everybody else. Now that America was in the war, we'd settle his hash for him soon enough, we all told ourselves.

The trip from Reno to Fort Worth took three days, and by the third day, word had got around about who we really were. Sheriff's deputies had delivered us under armed guard to the recruiting station in Carson City, where we were sworn in, and somebody must have seen that and told somebody else, who told somebody else, until finally, as the train was rolling across the high plains of the Texas Panhandle, a group of fellas came to the car where we were sitting around a makeshift table and playing poker. I knew by the looks on their faces that they were hunting for trouble.

Those troop trains were nothing but baggage cars with narrow bunks rigged inside them. The five of us were sitting cross-legged on the floor with a barrel lid propped up

on some boxes between us serving as a poker table. The
doors on the sides of the car were each open a couple of
feet to let some air through. We had to hold on tight to our
cards to keep the wind from blowing them away.

"You Tacker?" one of the gents said to Roy.

We all looked up at him. All of us on that train might
have been sworn members of the United States Army, but
we were still wearing our own clothes. We'd been told that
we would be issued uniforms when we got to Camp Bowie.
The fella who had asked the question was wearing corduroy
pants and a wool shirt, along with lace-up work shoes. His
face was burned by the sun and wind under a mess of thick
black hair, and his hands were knobby-knuckled and cal-
lused. He looked like somebody who had spent just about
his whole life working outside, and the men who were
standing just behind him were more of the same.

"I'm one of the Tackers," Roy said mild-like. He leaned
his head toward Jace, who was sitting next to him. "This
is another."

The man didn't look at Jace. He had all his attention on
Roy. "You don't know me, do you?" he said.

Roy considered for a couple of seconds, then shook his
head and said, "No, I reckon not."

"No reason for you to. I'm just somebody who had his
money in the bank in Auroraville."

That name brought back some memories. We'd held up
the bank in Auroraville about four months earlier. There
hadn't been much money in the vault, only four thousand
dollars.

"Two hundred and forty-three dollars," the man went
on. "Don't sound like much, but it was all the money I
had to my name. I worked for months stringin' electric line
for that money."

"I'm sorry to hear that," Roy said. "I really am."

The man stuck out his hand. "I want it back, right now.
Every penny of it."

Roy just shook his head and said, "If I had it, I'd give
it to you, hoss. But that money's long gone."

"You took it, you can give it back." The man jerked a thumb over his shoulder toward the other fellas with him. "These guys want their money back too. You made poor men out of all of us, Tacker."

Roy evened up the cards in his hand and put them face-down on the barrel lid, stacking some coins on them to hold them down in the wind. He looked back up at the man and shook his head again. "I told you, the money's gone. I'm sorry for any hardship we caused you gents, but there's nothing we can do about it now."

"The hell you say. Maybe we'll just take it out of your hide!"

We were expecting a ruckus, so it didn't come as any surprise when the fella lashed out with his foot and kicked over the barrel lid. Cards and coins went flying, and the barrel lid spun across the car. The fella tried to kick Roy in the same motion, but Roy was ready for him and grabbed his foot. Roy heaved, and the gent went over backward, spilling into the boys who had come with him.

There were maybe thirty men in that train car, and twenty of them started yelling, "Fight! Fight!" The rest of us were already on our feet and throwing punches.

I hadn't gotten back all the strength in the leg that had been bullet-creased, so I was a little slower getting up than the others. That gave one of the men time enough to swing a punch at my head. I was able to block it and keep him from breaking my jaw, but I hadn't quite got my balance and the impact against my forearm made me stumble back a few steps. The sound of the train's wheels click-clacking over the rails suddenly got louder, and I remembered that the door on the side of the troop car had been slid back. The opening was only a couple of feet, but that was wide enough for somebody to fall out if he wasn't careful— somebody like me.

Visions of tumbling under the train and being cut to pieces flashed through my mind, and bloody visions they were. I flung my arms out to the side and caught myself as my back hit the edge of the door. I was mad now. This had started out as just another brawl, but after what had happened back in Reno, life was more precious to me than it had ever been. That didn't stop me from risking it on occasion, but it sure made me fight back harder when somebody tried to kill me.

I dove into the melee, swinging my fists as hard and fast as I could. It didn't matter who I was hitting; anybody who got in front of me who wasn't one of my friends was fair game. The rest of the boys likely felt the same way, which meant the fight spread all through the car in a matter of minutes, involving even the fellas who hadn't been part of the original tussle.

Roy and the others seemed to be holding their own. I saw Jace trading punches with a baby-faced recruit who fought older than he looked. Aaron was ducking and bobbing around and jabbing his fists in the faces of anybody who got too close to him. Big Boy had two fellas by the nape of the neck, and from the corner of my eye, I saw him bang their heads together. I heard the crack even over the yelling that filled the car, and when Big Boy let go of those fellas, they fell straight down and didn't move again. I hoped like the dickens that he hadn't busted their skulls and killed them.

Roy was doing some stand-up, toe-to-toe slugging, and I wound up beside him. He glanced over at me and grinned just a little, and I knew he was enjoying this. It broke the monotony, sure as shooting. And there's nothing much more monotonous than riding on a slow-moving train through the Texas Panhandle, which is about as flat and empty as any place on Earth.

Somebody might've been hurt bad if the fight had gone on, but after about seven or eight minutes, somebody started blowing a whistle; then a man let out with about the bluest string of profanity I'd ever heard, and I'd heard plenty. When he got through cussing, he bellered, "Fall in! Fall in, you jackasses! Fall in, damn you!"

All of us recruits had been jawed at enough when we signed up and during the train ride to know that the order meant we were supposed to form up into orderly lines. We stopped throwing punches and shuffled around a little, but

I wouldn't call what we did falling in. The fella who was doing the yelling took care of that for us. He started grabbing folks and throwing them across the car, and as they bounced off the wall, they sort of naturally made a line. The rest of us gave in and formed up like we were supposed to before that gent could get his hands on us.

I hadn't seen him before. From the sound of his voice I expected him to be a big fella, but he was shorter than me by a couple of inches. He was broader than me too, but there wasn't any lard on him. It was all muscle. He was wearing an olive-green wool uniform with yellow stripes on the sleeves, and even somebody like me, who knew more about mules than military matters, could tell that he was a sergeant. Only sergeants could yell that loud and cuss so much. He was wearing a brown hat with the crown pinched in all around, and on his hip was a pistol in a holster with a snapped-down flap.

"What the hell do you boys think you're doing?" the sergeant shouted at us as he stalked along in front of us, his hands clasped together behind his back. "Are you so anxious to start fighting the Boche that you're practicing on each other? You make me want to puke!"

He had a real precise way of talking, even at the top of his lungs. His accent didn't sound like anybody else that I knew, so I figured he was from back East somewhere. A Yankee, more than likely.

"I'm Sergeant Cribbage," he yelled as he walked in front of me, and it was just my bad luck that he happened to be right there, because he stopped short and spun around and stuck his face right up in mine. His nose wasn't more than an inch or two away from mine as he said, "It's spelled just like the game, but don't any of you bastards get the idea that you can play me. You can't!"

I just sort of blinked a few times as he screamed in my face. I'd only vaguely heard of a game called cribbage, and nobody I knew played it, so what he was saying didn't mean a whole lot to me. Now, if he'd said something about dominoes or Forty-two or Moon, I would've known what he was talking about.

Anyway, he stomped on down the line and kept bellowing. He told us how he'd boarded the train when it stopped at Amarillo, and then said, "I'm going to be in charge of you ladies when we get to Camp Bowie, so you better get used to me now. I won't tolerate any insubordination or goldbricking. You will do *what* I say, *when* I say, *how* I say! Do you understand?"

A few of the braver souls sort of nodded their heads and muttered that they understood.

"What did you say?" Sergeant Cribbage hollered. "I asked, do you understand?"

Some of the boys got the idea then and piped up, "Yes, sir!"

"I don't *hear* you!"

"Yes, sir!" we yelled back at him.

"I *still* don't *hear* you!"

We all opened our mouths wide and shouted *"Yes, sir"* as loud as we could, and that seemed to satisfy the sergeant, at least a little bit. He gave a curt nod and swung around to pace back along in front of us.

"I don't give a damn what this fight was about! But I'll not stand for any brawling amongst my men. We'll be getting into Fort Worth tomorrow morning, and between now and then there'll be no more fighting! Understood?"

This time we knew what to do. "Yes, sir!"

"And while I'm training you sorry excuses for soldiers at Camp Bowie, there'll be no fighting! Understood?"

"Yes, sir!"

Sergeant Cribbage glowered down at the cards and money scattered on the floor of the troop car and snapped, "Get this damn mess cleaned up."

Then he walked to the front of the car and stomped out through the door, and a fella I hadn't noticed before followed him. This fella was taller and skinnier but wore the same sort of uniform as the sergeant. He only had one stripe on his sleeve, though, and I found out later he was a corporal. His name was Stiles, and he was Sergeant Cribbage's *segundo,* or right-hand man. Stiles and me were never what you would call friends later on, but he got to where he'd talk to me some, and he told me once about how Sergeant Cribbage was grinning to beat the band as soon as he got out of that troop car and we couldn't see him anymore. "About time those boys showed a little spirit," he said to Corporal Stiles.

But like I said, I didn't know that then. I thought the sergeant was really and truly mad at us, because he sure seemed like it.

Once he was gone, we all started milling around. Jace picked up the cards and counted them, then told us that nearly half of them were gone. They'd flown out the open doors of the troop car during the fight, we figured. That meant the poker game was over until we got a chance to buy another deck of cards, and who knew when that would be?

The big electric lineman who had started the ruckus came over to Roy and growled, "This ain't over, Tacker, no matter what that tight-ass sergeant says."

"You'd best let it go, mister," Roy told him. "Like the sergeant said, we're goin' to be fightin' Germans soon enough. We don't need to fight each other."

But the fella just glared at him and said again, "This ain't over."

Of course it wasn't. If there's one thing I've learned, it's that trouble is just about the stubbornest damned thing in the world.

TEN

Even though I'd been born and raised less than forty miles from Fort Worth, I'd only been there a few times as a boy. It used to be called Panther City, because some wag from Dallas had claimed that Fort Worth was such a quiet place that a panther had been spotted sleeping in the middle of Main Street. That was just a story, of course, told because of the rivalry between the two towns. Once the Swift and Armour meatpacking plants opened up on the north side of town, Fort Worth wasn't sleepy at all. In fact, it became sort of a boom town, only instead of oil or gold, cattle was its main industry. Gold on the hoof, I suppose you could say.

So even though I remembered it as a good-sized place, by the time the United States got mixed up in the war and Camp Bowie was built just west of town, there were at least a hundred thousand people living there. It was big, even bigger than Reno. As we filed off the train at the depot downtown, I had to stare at the tall buildings a couple of blocks away. One of them was at least eight stories high.

"Lordy, did you ever see such?" Big Boy asked beside me, and all I could do was shake my head and say, "Nope."

Sergeant Cribbage and the other sergeants in charge of the recruits got us all loaded on electric-powered streetcars, and pretty soon we were bumping along down the middle of Arlington Heights Boulevard, heading west from downtown toward the army camp. My eyes got even wider as I saw all the buildings stretching out to the north and south from the boulevard, filling up what had been open, rolling prairie the last time I had been there.

I found out later that most of the men assigned to Camp Bowie were from National Guard units in Texas and Oklahoma that had been called into active duty. But there were also some oddball recruits like us mixed in with them who came from other parts of the country. So many men had enlisted in the outburst of patriotism that came after the United States declared war on Germany, and there was such a push to get them trained and shipped overseas to join in the fighting, that folks were sent to whatever camp had the most room at the moment. So we became part of the 36th Division, under the command of Major General Edwin St. John Greble, and found ourselves members of the 142nd Infantry Regiment.

We'd rolled into Fort Worth about noon, and once we got to the camp, the rest of the day was spent standing in line. First we stood in line to get our hair cut off short, and the barber shaved off Roy's mustache too, which pained him considerable. Then we lined up in a big warehouse to get our uniforms, which were shoved into our arms by supply sergeants on the other side of a long counter. Several of them had to get together and palaver for a while when they saw Big Boy, but they finally dug up a uniform that was almost big enough for him. "Where the hell did they find you?" one of the sergeants grumbled.

"Nevada," Big Boy said.

Then we marched, sort of ragged-like, over to another warehouse, where they gave us our rifles. Only they weren't real rifles at all. They were wooden, just made to look like rifles. Aaron hefted his and asked the soldier who had given it to him, "What's this?"

The soldier laughed. "You don't think we'd trust you plowboys with the real thing right away, do you? Those Springfields ain't squirrel guns, you know."

Aaron and I just looked at each other and tried not to grin. I'd seen Aaron make a Winchester do just about everything except sing and dance, so I figured he could handle any kind of rifle the army might give him. But there was no point in telling that to that soldier.

When we were through at the warehouses, we marched back west and then north, to the infantry camp. Row after row after row of tents ran for just about as far as the eye could see. Seemed like we marched for a couple of miles before we got to the ones where we'd be staying. When we went inside, we found that there were eight cots in each tent, four on a side with a narrow aisle running down the middle. I reached over and prodded the thin mattress on one of the cots. I'd felt worse. So far, compared to some of the places I'd been, this was damned near the lap of luxury.

I suppose the army had some method of deciding which soldier would be assigned to which tent, but if they did, it never made any sense to me. All five of us were stuck in different tents, and I wasn't a bit happy about it when I found out one of the other fellas in my tent was the big black-haired lineman who'd kept his money in the Auroraville bank until the Tacker Gang took it out. He had already tossed his uniform and wooden rifle down on one of the bunks, so I picked one that was as far away from him as possible. Still, that wasn't very far, because those tents weren't very big. I told myself that I'd have to keep an eye out behind me and sleep with one eye open as long as the two of us were bunking together.

Sergeant Cribbage came around to the tents and told us to put our uniforms on and report with our rifles to the drill field. He didn't bother explaining where that was, but I figured I could find it. I'd just go where everybody else was going. It was late in the afternoon when we all wound up in this big open pasture between two groups of tents. I looked around for Roy and Jace and Aaron and Big Boy, and I was able to find them because Big Boy stood nearly a head taller than most of the other recruits. I hurried over to them, grinned, and said, "Howdy. Don't you boys look spiffy?"

I reckon we all did in those brown wool uniforms. The tight leggings below the blousy trousers had been a pain to get on, but they sure looked snappy. I had my hat cocked at a jaunty angle on my head, and I put that wooden rifle on my shoulder the way I'd seen some of the other recruits doing. I was a doughboy, just like the others.

A whole mess of sergeants showed up, Sergeant Cribbage among them, and they all started hollering at once. Somehow, though, they got us sorted out and lined up. We were broken down into eight-man squads, and naturally enough, the eight men from each tent formed a squad. That meant I wouldn't be with Roy and the others during training, which bothered me. There was nothing I could do about it, though, and I had to admit it was still a lot better than being in prison—or dead.

We drilled for about an hour that afternoon, and even though Sergeant Cribbage said we were the worst-looking excuses for soldiers he'd ever seen, I thought we did pretty good. By the time we were dismissed and told to go to chow at the mess hall, I figured we had improved so much that it wouldn't take more than a few days of drilling before we'd be ready to go to France and kick the bejabbers out of those godless Huns.

The mess halls were these huge wooden buildings with steps leading up to them. As we filed in, I could hear the clatter of silverware inside and smell the food, and it was mighty enticing. Plenty of folks complained about the army food, but to somebody like me who had lived on hardtack and jerky part of the time, it wasn't bad at all. Roy and me and the other boys sat together at one of the tables and dug in.

While we were eating, I told Roy, "That fella from the train who's got a grudge against us is in my tent."

I hadn't gotten used to the look of Roy without his mustache yet, and when he frowned he looked so odd I had to laugh. "There's nothing funny about it, Drew," he said, not understanding why I was laughing. "You best watch yourself, because that fella's liable to try to get even with you."

"I'll be careful, Roy," I promised.

I wondered if I looked as funny with most of my hair cut off as the rest of them did.

Well, I was wrong about how long it was going to take to train us, of course. Sergeant Cribbage said we were the slowest bunch of muleheads to ever join the army as we marched up and down that drill field. He took us down to the western part of the camp, where trenches like those in France had been dug, and for several days we practiced jumping in and out of those overgrown bar ditches. You wouldn't think that jumping into a ditch would be very hard to master, but evidently there was a right way and a wrong way to do it, and we were nearly always doing it wrong.

The boys and I weren't able to get together again until the next Sunday, which we all had free since the rotating schedule of kitchen and latrine duty hadn't gotten around to our squads yet. Roy wanted to know how things were going and if I'd had any trouble, and I told him that Private Gechter—that was the name of the lineman from Auroraville, Calvin Gechter—hadn't done anything but ignore me. He didn't even glare at me anymore. Roy warned me to be careful anyway.

He was right, of course, because it turned out Gechter was just biding his time.

After a week of drilling and jumping in and out of trenches with those wooden rifles, we were finally issued our real weapons, Springfield '03 bolt-action rifles, each with a five-shot clip. They were thirty-ought-sixes with twenty-four-inch barrels and a rear sight that you could flip up. I'd never been any great shakes with a long gun—or a pistol either, for that matter—but the first time I handled one of those Springfields, I knew I'd do pretty well with it. Sure enough, the first time on the firing range I outshot everybody else in my squad. Sergeant Cribbage came along and stood behind me while I was squeezing off my rounds, and when I was finished he said, "Not bad, Matthews. If the broad side of a barn ever attacks you, you should be able to hit it."

I turned my head around and looked at him with a grin and said, "Thank you, sir."

He just rolled his eyes and went on to holler at the next man.

By the time the afternoon was over, my ears were ringing and aching from all the gunshots I'd listened to, but as we were marching back to our tents, I heard the fella next to me say, "Boy, what I'd give to be back on a horse right now."

I looked over at him and saw that he was a tall, rawboned, skinny sort with the look of a gent who'd spent a lot of time outside. "You a cowboy?" I asked.

He looked a little surprised by the question. "Was," he admitted. "Gave it up and went to Hollywood."

"Hollywood? You mean that place where they make movin' pictures?"

He grinned. "Yep." He stuck out his paw at me. "Hank Ball's my handle."

I shook with him and told him my name. "Did quite a bit of ridin' myself, up Nevada way."

"What spreads did you work for?"

"Oh, just about all of 'em at one time or another," I said, not wanting to tell Hank that I'd been an outlaw. I'd already started thinking that maybe it wasn't something to be very proud of.

"I rode for the JA, the XIT, and the Four Sixes up in the Panhandle," Hank said. "Then I heard that this old codger I used to know had gone on out to Hollywood and got him a job in movin' pictures, so I decided to give it a try too."

"I saw one of them once, in a medicine show. They strung up a bedsheet for a screen and showed the picture on it." I shook my head at the memory. "Dangedest thing I ever saw. Maybe you were in it."

"Not likely. I only worked on a few pictures before a bunch of the boys and I decided to enlist. I figure I'll go back out in a few months after the war's over, though."

"How'd you get to be an actor?"

Hank shook his head. "I wasn't never what you'd call an actor. They called us ridin' extras. We'd just chase around pretendin' to shoot at each other and fall off our horses when the director told us to. He's the ramrod of the whole thing."

"You'd fall off on purpose?"

"Hell of a note, ain't it? You work like the dickens to learn how to stay in a saddle, and then some fella pays you to fall out of it instead."

I had to laugh at that. Sounded to me like those fellas in Hollywood sure had things bass-ackwards.

Hank promised to introduce me to some of his pards from Hollywood, then gave me a wave when we reached the tent where his squad was bunking. I marched on to my tent and got there just as Calvin Gechter did. We both started for the entrance at the same time, but he took a quick step and bumped me hard with his shoulder, pushing me to one side.

"Hey!" I said without thinking. "Watch where you're goin'."

He swung around right quick-like, and since he had his rifle on his shoulder, that meant I had to duck to keep from getting hit in the head with the barrel. "You got a problem, outlaw?" he snapped at me.

"Take it easy," I told him. "I just don't like folks runnin' into me."

He slipped that Springfield off his shoulder and let it drop into his hand. As he did, I saw his finger go inside the trigger guard, and I saw too that he hadn't pulled the bolt, like he was supposed to before leaving the firing range. That rifle might still be loaded, and if it was, it was also capable of being fired.

So naturally, I yelped, "Watch it!" and reached out and slapped the barrel down, away from me.

The Springfield roared and the bullet smacked into the ground about six inches away from my left foot, kicking up some dust and clods of dirt. I hollered and then dropped my own rifle as I jumped toward Gechter. I lowered my shoulder and tackled him, and we both went down.

There were quite a few recruits around, making their way back to their tents, and they cussed and hollered in surprise at the sound of the shot, then started running over to see what in blazes was going on. By that time I had Gechter flat on his back and was punching him in the face. I was mad as hell, because I knew he'd meant to shoot me and then claim it was an accident. He probably couldn't have gotten away with that, but Gechter was dumb as a rock to start with, and probably didn't look past wanting me dead.

Like I said, coming as close as I had to getting killed in that Reno bank had done something to my head. I didn't see things too straight when somebody tried to do me in. I just let the anger take over, and Gechter was on the wrong end of it. In less than a minute, I'd pounded him enough so that his face was all bloody and his nose was sort of flat. I don't know how long I'd have kept hitting him if Big Boy hadn't come along and grabbed me under the arms and lifted me up off Gechter like I was a baby.

"Son of a bitch, son of a bitch, son of a bitch!" I was yelling as I punched, and I kept it up even after Big Boy snatched me up. I kept flailing away with my fists too, until Roy got hold of my arms and said, "Stop it, Drew! Take it easy, son!"

I was used to listening to what Roy told me, so that got through to me. I stopped lashing out and took a couple of deep, ragged breaths as I hung there from Big Boy's mitts. After a minute, Roy said, "Put him down, Big Boy."

About the time I got back on my feet, Sergeant Cribbage pushed his way through the crowd of recruits around us and saw Gechter sprawled out on the ground, all bloody and limp. He saw me standing there breathing hard, with Gechter's blood all over my skinned-up knuckles, which were already starting to swell pretty good. The sergeant took it all in for a few seconds, then blew up.

He chewed my rear end up one way and down the other, then had some fellas drag Gechter off to the infirmary. Then he chewed on me some more. I took it, knowing I had it coming, but eventually I got a mite tired of it, and when Sergeant Cribbage slowed down to take a breath, I said, "He tried to shoot me."

That stopped him cold. He stared at me and said, "What?"

"Private Gechter tried to shoot me." I pointed at Gechter's Springfield, which was still lying on the ground nearby. "He didn't unload his rifle and pull the bolt before he left the firing range, like he was supposed to. When we got back here to the tent, he bumped into me on purpose and then slid that rifle off his shoulder like he was going to put it down and offer to fight me. Only it was pointed toward me, and he had his finger on the trigger. He was going to shoot me and claim it was an accident."

Sergeant Cribbage was still staring at me when I finished. "How in the name of George's old tomcat do you know *what* he intended to do?" the sergeant demanded.

I shrugged. "Saw it in his eyes, just before I knocked the barrel down and jumped him. Folks have tried to shoot me before."

That was true enough. There's a certain look in a man's eyes when he means to take a life. Roy and Big Boy and Jace and Aaron all nodded. They had seen the same thing enough times to know I was telling the truth.

Sergeant Cribbage glared at me and blew his breath out between his teeth, then said, "There's no proof that Private Gechter meant you any harm. You're going to spend two days in the stockade for this, Matthews. We can't have you killing your fellow doughboys before Kaiser Bill's troops get a chance to."

Roy started to say, "That ain't hardly fair, Sarge—"

Sergeant Cribbage turned on him and yelled, "This is the army, Private! Fair hasn't got a damned thing to do with it!"

"It's all right, Roy," I said. "I reckon I can do two days' time."

"And I'm putting you in a different squad," the sergeant told me. "I don't want any more 'accidents.'"

Neither did I, especially the kind that involved me nearly getting shot. I'd be glad to be in a different squad . . . once I'd done my time, that is.

ELEVEN

The stockade wasn't too bad. The little room where I was locked up had only one window, and it was small and set high up in the wall opposite the door. So it was gloomy and hot and stuffy, but that was all. I caught up on my sleep the two days I was in there.

Sergeant Cribbage was true to his word: He had me moved to another tent. I was surprised but pleased to find out that I was now in the same squad as Roy. I don't know if the sergeant did that on purpose or not.

One of the other recruits in that squad was a friend of Hank Ball's named Pike Carson. Pike had been in the moving pictures too, working as a riding extra along with Hank. He and Roy and I all got along just fine.

"I've been thinkin'," Pike said one evening as we sat around the tent, cleaning our rifles, "that once we get finished with this basic trainin', we ought to put in for the cavalry. Seems foolish to waste all this ridin' talent we got amongst us."

Roy nodded, all solemn-like. "That's a good idea, Pike."

Now me, I'd never even thought of such. Ever since we'd joined up in the AEF after that disaster in Reno, I'd been content to go where the army told me to go and do what the army told me to do. It never occurred to me that we might have any choice in the matter. And we didn't, not really, but our sergeants could recommend us for certain assignments if they thought we'd be suited for them.

There was nothing we'd be better suited for than the cavalry, because all of us—Roy, Jace, Aaron, Big Boy, Pike, Hank, and me—were just as much at home on the back of a horse as we were on our feet. Maybe more so. Of course, the army might not see it that way, but all we could do was try.

"I'll say something to Sergeant Cribbage," Pike decided, and Roy and I told him to mention us too. He said he would.

I didn't know it then, but something else had happened that sort of put a crimp in the plans we'd started making.

This is one of those parts I wasn't there for, but I heard all about it later, so I'm pretty sure I've got it right.

Jace and Aaron had wound up in squads that trained together most of the time, so they saw a lot of each other. Their squads were drilling in the trenches, not far from the western edge of camp, on this day I'm talking about. Just beyond the camp boundaries was a little lake called Lake Como. It was a man-made lake, and had been put in back in the 1880s by a rich man from Denver named H. B. Chamberlain. It was Chamberlain's idea that he was going to build a resort in this area, so he bought a bunch of land from a rancher named McCart, put in the lake, and built a big fancy hotel right next to it called the Arlington Inn. Chamberlain was the one who'd put in the streetcar line, so that folks could get from downtown Fort Worth out to his resort. Other land developers followed Chamberlain's lead and decided to build a residential community out there called Arlington Heights.

Well, the whole thing went bust. It was just too far out of town back then. But the lake was still there, and a few decades later the war had come along and Camp Bowie was built right next door. Somebody had put up a two-story

pavilion there on the lake shore, and it was a popular place
with the soldiers who were off duty. Dances were held
there, and there were rowboats that a fella could rent and
take his best girl for a ride in. There was even a roller
coaster.

But on this day, nobody was boating out on the lake,
and that was a good thing, because as they stood in one of
the trenches Jace and Aaron heard this loud *pop-pop-pop,*
and looked up to see an airplane go right over their heads,
not more than twenty feet in the air.

We called them aeroplanes then, mind you, but nobody
does anymore.

Anyway, Jace and Aaron and everybody else in the
trenches saw that airplane fly over, and they could tell it
was in trouble. They jumped up out of the trenches to see
what was going to happen, and watched as the plane
zoomed out over Lake Como, its engine sounding worse
and worse.

"That fella's goin' down," Aaron said, and Jace nodded.

None of us had ever seen an airplane until we got to
Camp Bowie, but we saw a lot of them there. They flew
over all the time, seemed like. There was a training field at
Benbrook, southwest of Camp Bowie, where British and
Canadian pilots from the Royal Flying Corps learned to fly.
Why they were sent all the way to Texas to learn such a
thing, I don't know, but they were there anyway. An American flying corps was being formed at Barron Field in Everman, south of Fort Worth, and there were even a few
would-be pilots out at Lake Worth, northwest of town.
Planes from all three fields went zipping over Camp Bowie
night and day, and after a while the fellas on the ground
got used to them and didn't even look up much when one
flew over.

But this plane was different, because it was getting lower
all the time, and as Jace and Aaron and the other recruits
watched, it slammed into the waters of Lake Como with a
huge splash.

The lake wasn't but a couple of hundred yards from where Jace and Aaron were standing, and they sort of looked at each other for a second before they took off running. They had seen two men in that airplane when it flew over, and if those pilots had survived the crash, it was a good bet they were in pretty bad shape. Jace and Aaron didn't pay any attention to the sergeants yelling behind them. They just headed for the lake.

Now, I never learned to swim myself, and I've regretted that. But Aaron was a good swimmer, and Jace handled himself in the water pretty good for a boy who'd grown up in a land-locked state like Kansas. They threw off their hats and their uniform jackets, then stopped on the shore of the lake long enough to yank off their boots. Then they dived in and started swimming toward that wrecked plane, which was still floating about a hundred yards offshore. The plane was busted up pretty bad, though, and it was breaking apart. The body of it was made of wood and canvas, but it didn't float well enough to keep the weight of the motor from dragging it down.

Jace and Aaron got there when the tail and one wing were still sticking up above the water. The places where the pilots sat were pretty much submerged already, but they were close enough to the surface for Jace and Aaron to see that the pilots were still sitting in them. Jace and Aaron each gulped down a deep breath and ducked under the water.

Those fliers were wearing safety belts, of course; they had to, the way they turned those planes upside down and every which way. But right then, those belts were holding them in their seats when they needed to be loose. Jace was able to unfasten the belt around the gent he went after, but Aaron had to use his knife to saw through the tough leather around his fella. The pilot Jace pulled out of the plane came back to his senses as Jace broke the water with him, and he started thrashing around. "Stop it!" Jace yelled at him, trying not to swallow too much water himself as he did it. "I've got you! You're all right!"

Aaron was having a harder time of it, and Jace looked
back over his shoulder worried-like as he started swimming
toward shore, dragging that first pilot with him. By that
time, there were more than a hundred soldiers standing on
the bank of the lake, yelling encouragement to Jace. He
paddled on with one arm and his legs, and hoped that Aaron
wouldn't drown down there trying to get that other flier
loose.

When Jace got to the shore, plenty of hands reached out
to grab him and the pilot and haul them up out of the lake.
Jace shook the water out of his eyes and looked toward the
center of the lake again, and he was mighty relieved to see
Aaron swimming toward shore, towing the second flier.

That fella hadn't been as lucky. When Aaron got him
on shore, it became obvious pretty quick that he was dead.
His neck was broke.

The other fella was all right, though, just shaken up a
mite, except for a gash over his right eye where he'd
banged his head when the plane hit the water. He was up
and on his feet, and when he saw that his partner was dead,
he started cussing about what he called the bloody bad luck
of the whole thing. He dropped onto his knees next to the
other pilot and tugged the fella's leather helmet off, and
that's when Jace and Aaron saw that the dead man couldn't
have been more than twenty years old. The other pilot
brushed the wet hair back out of his friend's face and said,
all choked up, "Clear skies on your journey, old chum,
clear skies."

That got to Jace and Aaron, because it was clear the two
pilots had been good friends, and each of them knew what
they'd feel like if one of us went down. Aaron stepped over
to the surviving pilot and clapped a hand on his shoulder.
"Sorry I couldn't save your pard, mister. I gave it a try,
but it was already too late when I got him out of that aeroplane."

The flier pushed himself to his feet with a sigh and then
turned to Aaron and Jace. "I know. The impact of the crash
killed poor Charles." He stuck his hand out. "I'm Leften-

ant Edmund Rattigan. Thank you, lads, for saving me and for trying to save Charles.''

Jace and Aaron shook with the Englishman, because that's what he was, a member of the Royal Flying Corps stationed at Benbrook. He took off his wet flying jacket to reveal a uniform that would have been mighty snappy if it hadn't been soaked.

The sergeant who was in charge of the training exercise in the trenches came boiling up and started in on Jace and Aaron. ''What in blue blazes did you two think you were doing?'' he demanded. ''I gave you a direct order to halt, you lame-brained, ignorant bast—''

''Excuse me, Sergeant,'' Lieutenant Rattigan said. ''These gentlemen you've chosen to lambaste undoubtedly saved my life at great risk of their own, and they attempted to save my copilot as well. I should think you'd be congratulating them, rather than dressing them down.''

Well, that didn't go over too well with that American sergeant, having an Englishman tell him what he should or shouldn't be doing. Jace said the sergeant got all red in the face and swelled up like a toad until he looked fit to bust. Before he could blow up, though, a major drove up in a staff car and wanted to know what was going on. Lieutenant Rattigan told him.

That got Jace and Aaron off the hook for disobeying the sergeant's commands. Our brass had orders to cooperate with the British and Canadian officers as much as possible. The major warned Jace and Aaron to pay more attention to their sergeant in the future, but promised there wouldn't be any repercussions from this tragic incident. He offered to take Lieutenant Rattigan in his car to the camp infirmary so the gash could be looked at, and then he would drive the lieutenant back to the airfield in Benbrook. The dead flier's body would be returned in an ambulance.

Rattigan agreed, but as he was about to climb into the major's car, he paused and looked at Jace and Aaron. ''I say, lads,'' he said, ''whenever you've some time off, I'd love for you to come out to the field and say hello. I'd like to show you around.''

They both nodded, and Aaron said, "Sure, Leftenant. We'd be glad to."

The two officers drove off, and Jace asked Aaron, "What's the difference between a leftenant and a rightenant?"

"Damned if I know," Aaron said.

That was when the training sergeant came up behind them and said, "That's just the way those damned Englishers say 'lieutenant,' you uneducated sonsabitches. Now get back to the trenches, all of you!"

That was all there was to it, but it was enough to plant an idea in the heads of Jace and Aaron. And that wound up changing everything.

Next time we all got together, Hank and Pike were part of the bunch too. They fit right in, natural as could be, what with being from the West and all. There were rumors floating around the camp about the Tacker Gang, of course. I figure Calvin Gechter spread most of 'em, thinking that if he couldn't get back at us one way, he'd get back at us another. Some of the stories said that we'd gunned down a hundred innocent victims during our holdups, which was a bald-faced lie, of course. Truth of the matter was, we'd never killed anybody and only wounded a few people. Roy always said that careful planning did away with the need for shooting folks. So it was likely Hank and Pike had heard some tales about us, but if that was so, they didn't say anything about it.

We went over to Lake Como on that Sunday afternoon and watched the fellas rowing around in little boats. The lucky ones had gals with them, but some of those rowboats were filled up with doughboys looking for any sort of diversion to pass the time, and the way they carried on, it was a wonder none of the boats tipped over and dumped the whole bunch in the lake. We had heard about how Jace and Aaron had jumped in to rescue those British pilots, but none of us were likely to get soaked and risk our necks over some half-drunk soldier boys.

Me, I was watching the girls and thinking about how long it'd been since I'd had a whore. Just the sight of frilly dresses and soft white skin and wide-brimmed straw hats over a mess of fluffy curls was enough to start a real ache inside me. There were plenty of places in downtown Fort Worth, just a streetcar ride away, where I could have eased that ache, but the more I thought about it, the more I realized that wasn't really what I needed. When I thought about Becky, back there at Harrigan's place in Nevada, I didn't think about what it was like to be all naked and bouncy with her. Instead I thought about how soft her hair was when I touched it, and how she'd smile at me sometimes when she thought I wasn't looking, and how sometimes up in her room we'd get to talking about everything under the sun and forget all about what we'd thought we were there to do. Now, I'm not saying Becky was in love with me or me with her or anything like that, but we liked each other, sure enough.

And that was what I missed as much as anything, I finally figured out.

Pike had talked to Sergeant Cribbage, who was in overall charge of several squads including ours, about getting assigned to the cavalry when we finished our basic training. The sergeant hadn't said yes, but he hadn't said no either. He hadn't said much of anything, in fact, according to Pike, and we decided that we'd look on that as a hopeful sign.

"What do you think of that?" Roy asked Jace.

"Think of what?" Jace asked. He hadn't been paying attention. Neither had Aaron.

"We were talkin' about all of us goin' into the cavalry," Big Boy said. "I don't know about you fellas, but I'd surely love to get on a horse again."

"You reckon the army's got any horses strong enough to carry you around, Big Boy?" I asked with a grin.

Aaron got into the spirit of the thing a little by saying, "They haul cannons around on those caissons. They ought to be able to tote Big Boy."

That was true—about the cannons, I mean. The 61st Artillery Brigade was headquartered at Camp Bowie, and we heard those big guns going off about as much as we heard airplanes flying over. Got to where we paid just about as much attention to them too.

Jace never answered Roy's question about trying to get into the cavalry. Instead he stood up, brushed off his pants, and said, "Aaron, what say we go see that Leftenant Rattigan? He told us to come on out there whenever we got the chance."

Aaron thought about it for a second, then nodded and said, "Sure, we could do that." He looked around at the rest of us. "You boys want to go? I don't reckon the leftenant would mind if we brought some pards with us."

Hank and Pike decided to pass, but the rest of us thought that would be an interesting way to pass the rest of the afternoon. Only thing was, none of us had any idea how to get out to Benbrook short of hoofing it, which would have taken the rest of the day.

Roy had a bright idea, though; we could always count on him for that. He pulled a folded-up copy of the camp newspaper, *Pass in Review,* from his hip pocket and showed us an advertisement in it. A company downtown was renting cars to soldiers for the special price of five hours for fifty cents an hour. We had that much money in our pockets, plus the nickel apiece it would cost us to ride the streetcar downtown, so we set off to rent us a flivver.

TWELVE

The last time I'd been in a car was just before that attempted bank robbery back in Reno that had nearly gotten us all killed, so I had some bad memories in my head as we drove back out from downtown in a 1915 Ford. Roy was driving, of course, and Big Boy sat in front with him. Me and Jace and Aaron were crowded into the back seat, and I thought it was a good thing Hank and Pike hadn't decided to come with us. If they had, somebody would've had to ride on the running boards.

The boys were whooping it up pretty good, and Jace yelled, "Do a Barney Oldfield, Roy!" More speed was the last thing I wanted. I was already holding on so tight my hands were going numb. I got a little less nervous when we passed the entrance to Camp Bowie. There weren't as many other cars on the road after that.

Arlington Heights Boulevard ran all the way to where the highway turned south toward Benbrook. An old man had a watermelon stand set up on the side of the road, so we stopped and asked him where to find the airfield. He gave us directions and on we went, and in a little while we were there.

Benbrook Field was a lot smaller than Camp Bowie, of course. Only a fraction as many men lived and trained there. Half a dozen runways had been plowed and paved from the pastureland, and off to one side sat the headquarters building, mess hall, infirmary, and barracks for the pilots. On the other side of the runways were the hangars where the planes were kept. I didn't know then they were called hangars; to me they were just big buildings.

A guard post was set up where the road entered the field. A fella in a Canadian army uniform stopped us and asked us our business.

Jace leaned forward from the back seat and said, "We're here to see Leftenant Rattigan. He invited us."

"Leftenant Rattigan, eh?" the Canadian sentry said. "Well, you don't look like Boche spies to me, so I'll let you go on through. You'll find Leftenant Rattigan in Barracks Four. But watch yourselves, eh? Don't go wanderin' around."

"Much obliged, soldier," Roy told him, then drove forward slowly.

We found Barracks Four without any trouble and parked in front of it. The building had a long porch, and several men were sitting there in wicker chairs. One of them stood up as we piled out of the car. He was a lanky fella with blond hair and a little mustache, and he still had a small bandage stuck on his forehead. "Hello, lads!" he called to us. "I see you remembered my invitation."

He came down the steps from the porch and shook hands with Jace and Aaron. They introduced him to the rest of us, and that was how we met Leftenant Edmund Rattigan.

He was a friendly fella, just like Jace and Aaron had said he was, and it didn't seem to bother him at all that he was an officer and we were just enlisted men. He insisted that we call him Edmund and said, "Since we're not in each other's army, I don't see any need to be quite the sticklers for protocol we might be otherwise."

"Me neither," Roy said, and the way he sounded, I think he actually understood what Edmund was talking about.

For the next hour, Edmund showed us around the airfield and introduced us to some of the other pilots. Most of the men were Canadian, with only a few Britishers like Edmund mixed in. He was an instructor, he told us. Most of the Englishmen were. Once the Canadian boys were trained in flying the planes, they would head overseas.

While we were looking around the place, Edmund got a serious expression on his face and said, "Bloody bad luck about Charles, my copilot in that trainer that crashed. I kept the plane airborne as long as I could after the engine started to cut out. Nine times out of ten, landing in a lake like that would have been safer than trying to put her down on dry land. Charles just happened to hit wrong when the impact came."

"Those aeroplanes fall out of the sky like that very often?" asked Big Boy.

"All too often," Edmund replied with a solemn nod. "We've lost several men in crashes."

"Looks like gettin' ready for war is just about as dangerous as the fightin' itself," Roy commented. "We lost some men when an artillery shell got caught in a cannon and blew up there."

"Yes, it's a dangerous business," Edmund agreed. He grinned again, though, as we entered one of the hangars and he slapped the canvas side of one of the planes. "But it has its compensations. There's no feeling on earth quite like that of soaring high in the sky, utterly free."

It didn't seem to me like you'd be very free if you were cooped up in a little bitty space like the cockpit of those planes and that was the only thing holding you up in the air. I could think of a whole heap of places I'd rather be.

Jace didn't seem to feel the same way, though. He looked at that plane with wide eyes and asked Edmund, "You reckon I could fly in her?"

"You want to go up?" Edmund sounded surprised but pleased. "Well, I suppose that could be arranged."

"What about me too?" Aaron asked quickly. "I want to go too."

"All right. I'll have to take you one at a time, you understand, since these trainers are only two-seaters." Edmund looked around at the rest of us. "In fact, if any of the rest of you would like to see what it's like . . ."

For once I wasn't the last one to put in my two cents worth. "Not me," I said. "No offense, Edmund, but you couldn't pay me enough to go up in one of them contraptions."

"I don't reckon I'm interested either," Big Boy said. "I ain't sure it could get off the ground carryin' me anyway."

Roy considered for a second or two, then nodded. "I'll go," he told Edmund. "But give these two boys their turn first." He gestured at Jace and Aaron, who both looked as excited and wide-eyed as pups.

The wheels of the plane were braced with wooden blocks. Edmund moved them and then showed us where to grab on, and we rolled the plane out of the hangar and onto the closest runway. He checked to make sure it had plenty of gasoline, or petrol, as he called it, then got a jacket and helmet and a pair of goggles from a locker inside the hangar.

"Put these on," he said as he handed the gear to Jace. "I'll get my things from the barracks and be right back."

Jace didn't have any trouble getting the jacket and the helmet on, but he had to struggle to figure out how the goggles worked and pull them down over his eyes. When he had all of the outfit on, he glanced around at us and asked, "Well? How do I look?"

I don't know about the other boys, but I had to work to keep from laughing. He looked downright silly, if you ask me. But Roy said, "You look just fine, little brother. Like a real pilot."

Edmund came back from the barracks wearing a jacket, helmet, and goggles like Jace's. He put a hand on the edge of the front cockpit and said, "Climb up here. You'll ride in front, where you'll have the best view."

Jace hesitated. "Can you steer this thing from the back seat?"

"Have no fear, the controls back there work just as well as the ones up front. Come along now, climb in."

Jace looked around quickly and saw that the rest of us were watching him. I think he was a mite scared by this time. The excitement he had felt at first was starting to wear off as he realized that he was really going to fly way up there in the sky. But he didn't want to look yellow in front of his brother and his pards, so he used the foothold that Edmund showed him and swung up into that cockpit just like he was straddling a horse.

While Jace was settling down in the seat and fastening the belt that went around him, Edmund climbed up into the rear cockpit. "I'll have to get one of you lads to spin the propeller for me. Would you be so kind, Mr. Guinness?"

"Why, sure," Big Boy said. "Just tell me what to do."

"Stand there in front of the plane and take a firm grasp on the end of one of the propeller blades."

"Gotcha." Big Boy moved to the front of the plane and took hold of the propeller.

"The rest of you stand back, please," Edmund said to Roy and Aaron and me, so we moved back. I was more than happy to, as a matter of fact. Just being so close to that flying machine made me a little nervous.

"Switch on," Edmund called. "Normally you would have said that to me first, Mr. Guinness, and I would have acknowledged it. Now, I want you to spin the propeller as hard as you can, and as you do, I want you to say 'Contact!' "

"You bet," Big Boy said. He had hold of that propeller with both hands, and he gave it a spin that had the blades twirling around so fast you couldn't tell where one ended and the other began. As he spun it, he yelled, "Contact!"

"Contact!" Edmund shouted back at him as the engine coughed and sputtered and then burst into life with a steady roar that rose and rose. The propeller on the plane's nose was just a blur now, it was turning so fast. It kicked up a good breeze too, and raised a cloud of dust around the whole bunch of us. I raised an arm to shield my eyes from it.

Edmund reached down and fooled with something. Jace told us all about the controls later, so I found out that the main one was something called the stick. When you pushed it forward, the plane went faster, at least when it was on the ground. When it was up in the air, maybe the stick did something completely different, for all I know.

The plane rolled and bumped down that runway. Jace was sitting up stiff and straight in the front cockpit, and I figured about that time he was wishing he'd never had the bright idea of suggesting we come out here to Benbrook to see Edmund. The plane was going so fast that the tail of it lifted right up off the ground, and then . . .

Damned if it didn't fly.

I saw the front wheels come up off the runway. Big Boy slapped me on the back so hard I liked to fell down. "Look at that!" he said. "Would you just look at it, boys? Lord a' mercy, Jace's flyin'!"

He sure was, or at least he was riding in that airplane, and it was flying. Once those wheels left the ground, it was like somebody had untied the ropes that held the plane down. It zoomed up into the air and turned so that we could see that double set of wings tilting way over to one side. If I'd've been Jace, I would've needed a clean pair of pants right about then. I was scared just watching.

But then the plane leveled out again. It zipped one way, then zipped the other way, then turned and flew right over us. As it came over the field, the wings dipped a little one way, then the other, like the thing was waving at us. All of us waved back, shaking both hands over our heads and whooping and hollering. Some of the British and Canadian pilots had come up to see what was going on, and they got a big kick out of the way we were carrying on.

"I can't wait to get up there," Aaron said.

He didn't have to wait long, because Edmund only flew with Jace for about ten minutes. Then he brought the plane in for a landing. It looked smooth as silk to me, the way those wheels touched down on the runway, but Jace said later it was a pretty good jolt. As the plane slowed down, we ran after it. Edmund did something to the controls that made the tail swing around as he came to a stop, so that the plane was aimed back down the runway, ready to take off again. The engine sputtered to a stop, and the propeller gradually slowed down. It had stopped by the time we got there.

"Hey, Jace, you flew like a bird!" I called to him. He gave me a little wave. Those goggles were still pulled down over his face, so I couldn't see much of his face. He unstrapped himself and stood up in a crouch, then swung a leg over and carefully climbed out of the plane. When he landed on the ground, he swayed suddenly, like he was going to fall over, so Big Boy reached out and grabbed his arm to steady him.

Edmund hopped down from the other cockpit and asked Jace, "Well? What did you think, lad? Did you enjoy flying?" He looked over at the rest of us. "It was Jace who did that wing waggle over the field, you know. I told him how to perform the maneuver, and he executed it perfectly."

Right then I knew Edmund was either mighty brave or didn't have any common sense at all. I wouldn't have let Jace even touch the controls, let alone move the wings. He could have flown that plane right into the ground. I reckon Edmund knew what he was doing, though.

Jace ripped that helmet and those goggles off, and I saw that he was grinning so hard his face looked like it was about to split wide open. "I did it!" he whooped. "I did it! I flew!" He grabbed Aaron by the shoulders and shook him. "Did you see me?"

"Sure I saw you," Aaron told him. "How could I miss you, sittin' up there big as life in that aeroplane?"

Jace moved over to me, grabbed my shoulders, and shook me just like he'd shook Aaron. "Did you see me?" he asked.

"Yeah, I saw you, you tarnal idiot," I told him. "Now quit shakin' me!"

He must have gotten the shaking out of his system, because he didn't try to grab Roy or Big Boy. He just paced up and down beside the plane and said over and over again,

"I never knew there was anything like that. I never knew there was anything like that."

If you ask me, *that's* the way he should have acted back there in Nevada at Harrigan's with that pretty brown-haired whore. I couldn't see getting so worked up over sitting in a hunk of machinery.

"All right, lad," Edmund said to Aaron. "Your turn."

For a second, I thought Jace wasn't going to give the flying gear to Aaron. He wanted to hang on to it himself. But he gave in and let Aaron get dressed in the garb. Aaron looked just as outlandish as Jace had.

Before he climbed up into the cockpit, he asked Jace, "Was it scary?"

"At first," Jace said. "But once you get up there . . . man, there's nothing like it. You got to experience it for yourself."

Aaron got settled down and strapped in, and Edmund took off again. He did the same sort of zipping around as before, and as he flew over the field, the wings did that up-and-down motion again. "That's the wing waggle!" Jace said. "I did that."

When Edmund landed, Aaron was shaky but excited, just like Jace had been. "It's something, all right," he told us as he stripped off the flying jacket. "We were up so high it seemed like I could see forever. I halfway expected to see France from up there."

"We'll all see France soon enough," Roy said as he held his hand out for the gear. I reckoned he was right about that.

Roy was the last of us to go up for a spin, as Edmund called it. He had a sober look on his face when he climbed down from the cockpit, not giddy like Jace and Aaron had been. He took the goggles and helmet off and shook hands with Edmund. "Much obliged for takin' me up," he said. "That was something, all right."

"If you'd care to go up again sometime—" Edmund began.

Roy shook his head. "Nope. I reckon once was enough. But I appreciate the offer."

It was late in the afternoon by then, and we had to return that rented car to downtown Fort Worth and then ride the streetcar back out to the camp. So we said our good-byes to Edmund, and he told us to come back any time. Jace and Aaron said that they would, but the rest of us just told him so long.

Jace and Aaron had their heads together all the way back into town, and they were still talking on the streetcar as we rode to the camp. We got back in time for evening chow, and that was when they sprung the surprise they had cooked up on us.

"Roy, that was a good idea about all of us volunteerin' for the cavalry," Jace said as the five of us sat around one of the tables in the mess hall. "Aaron and me have been thinkin' about it, though, and we're not sure that's what we want to do."

"Oh?" Roy didn't sound particularly surprised. He knew his brother pretty well, so he was probably the only one who saw what was coming—besides Jace and Aaron, that is. "What is it you want to do then?"

The two of them looked at each other and grinned, and Aaron said, "We're goin' to be aviators."

"You mean you want to fly them aeroplanes for the army?" Big Boy asked.

"That's right," Jace said. "I reckon we'd be good at it."

I couldn't stop myself from saying, "That's crazy! You think you could fly planes better'n you can ride horses? Hell, you never even sat in one of those contraptions until today!"

"Maybe not," Aaron said, "but it sure felt natural to both of us, didn't it, Jace?"

"Natural as can be." Jace looked at Roy and went on. "You went up with Leftenant Rattigan, Roy. You know what it's like. You can understand how we feel."

Roy gave a slow shake of his head. "No, not really. I'm glad I had the experience, but I didn't really care for it. That don't mean you boys shouldn't like it."

"Edmund was right," Aaron said. "Bein' up there in the air makes you feel so free it's like there's not hardly anything holding you to the earth anymore."

Me, I wouldn't like feeling like that, and I said as much. I've always enjoyed having both feet on the ground. But there was no convincing those two of that. They were like kids who'd just gotten their first taste of something sweet, and they wanted more.

"You boys do what you want to," Roy told them quietly, after Big Boy and I got through telling them they'd lost their fool minds. "The Americans have an airfield not far from here, and for all I know, they're looking for more pilots. All you can do is ask."

"That's just what we're goin' to do," Jace said. "Tell 'em that here's two more American boys ready to fly!"

I might think they were crazy, but I knew Roy was right. It was their decision to make.

Besides, it wasn't long after that I had more problems of my own.

Fact is, I like to died.

THIRTEEN

A few mornings later, when Reveille blew, I rolled out of my bunk as usual, only when I stood up the room started spinning around me. It was going about as fast as the propeller on that airplane Edmund had taken Jace and Aaron flying in, and before I knew it, I felt a hard thump and found myself staring up at the top of the tent. I had fallen over backwards.

They got us up before dawn, so it was gloomy inside the tent, but I could tell that somebody was leaning over me, and a second later Roy said, "Drew? What's wrong, son? You fell over like somebody cut your hamstrings."

"I . . . I don't know, Roy," I managed to say. "The whole place is spinnin'. . . ." Then I started to cough in hard, dry spasms that shook me right to the middle of my insides.

Roy put his hand on my forehead, then took it away and said, "Damn, you're burnin' up with fever."

Now that he mentioned it, I did feel a mite hot—and cold at the same time.

Roy slid an arm under me and lifted me like I didn't weigh anything. "Let's get you to sick call," he said.

I barely remember him awkwardly pulling my clothes on me and leading me out of the tent. It was a long walk to the hospital, but there was no other way to get there. The morning was overcast, with clouds so thick it was still dark as night outside even though dawn was breaking. A wind that seemed doubly cold to me blew, thankfully, at our backs as we trudged south from the infantry tents, Roy with an arm around me to steady me.

The hospital had all wooden buildings, about seventy of them on sixty acres on the western edge of the camp, north of the trenches. Being the healthy sort, at least up until this particular morning, I hadn't spent much time there. But it sure felt good to be out of the wind when we tramped into the building where sick call was held. Even though it was early, quite a few men were already there. The room was filled with coughing and hacking and wheezing.

I leaned on Roy and said, "You better get out of here. You'll catch what the rest of us have got, sure as blazes."

He just shook his head. "Nope, I'll stay. I'm not afraid of the grippe."

That was what it seemed like most of us on sick call had. But as we found chairs and I looked around the room, I saw that some of the men were broken out in spots, and others had jaws that were swole up like they had stashed a big wad of chewing tobacco in there. I was no doctor, but I had heard that measles and mumps were going around the camp, along with the influenza. It looked like we had all three kinds of contagion brewing in there.

I had to wait a long time before a medical corpsman got to me, and before he even took a look at me, he glanced at Roy and said, "What are you doing here, soldier? You look healthy as a horse."

"It's my pard here," Roy said, indicating me. "He's the one who's sick. I just helped him down here."

The corpsman sniffed. "Well, we'll take care of him now. You've done enough goldbricking for one day. Get back to your outfit."

I saw Roy's eyes narrow, and I knew he didn't cotton to being talked to that way. He had brought me here to help me, not to get out of work himself. But he didn't say anything to the corpsman. He just stood up and patted me on the shoulder. "Take care of yourself, hoss," he told me. Then he looked at the corpsman and made one comment. "You better take care of this boy."

The corpsman didn't know what a fine line he was walking. He said, "Don't worry, we will," and shooed Roy away. Then he put his hand on my forehead, looked in my eyes, felt of my neck, and thumped me on the chest. "What seems to be the problem, soldier?" he asked when he'd done all that.

"I don't feel so good," I said, and I wondered if the fella was blind or just stupid. "Everything's spinnin' around, and I'm freezin' cold one minute and burnin' up the next, and I've got this cough—"

"It's autumn. Most people don't react well to a change in the seasons. You feel a little warm, but I think you're all right to go back to your squad. You can come back this evening if you don't start feeling any better."

I blinked in astonishment. "You're sayin' . . . there ain't nothin' wrong with me?"

"I'm saying we have too many men lying abed already who could be out there training to fight the Hun. Now move along, Private. You've already wasted enough of the army's time."

I didn't like his attitude either. He was just a corporal, but he was acting like a general. And he didn't give a damn that I was sick. I was so woozy I reckon I wasn't thinking straight, or I wouldn't have done what I did next.

I stood up and threw a punch at the son of a bitch.

I missed, of course. The shape I was in, I couldn't hit anything I aimed at. He yelled, "Hey!" as my fist flew right by his head. I stumbled forward, with not a chance in hell of keeping my balance. Next thing I knew, I'd fallen flat on my face and that corpsman was yelling for help.

He got it, but not the sort he probably wanted. If it was up to him, he'd have had me thrown back in the stockade for trying to clout him. Instead, strong hands grabbed hold of my shoulders and rolled me over, and I looked up into the worried face of a young woman in a white uniform.

Now, I've heard fellas who have seen gals in situations like that describe them as looking like angels. A few even think that they've died and gone to heaven. But I knew this woman was real right away. I could tell because of the painful way she started prodding and poking all over me.

But she was pretty as an angel, and that's God's honest truth.

I saw short blond hair under that white cap on her head, and her eyes were the dark blue of a mountain lake. Sharp eyes, showing that she was smart. And angry eyes, right that minute. She looked up at the corpsman and said, "This man has a high fever. Why isn't he in a ward?"

"He's all right," the corpsman said. "I see them like this all the time. They feel a little poorly, so they think they can get out of their work—"

"Shut up and help me with him. He needs to be in a bed."

"Hey, you can't talk to me that way! You're just a nurse!"

She stood up and said, "I'm a nurse who can have you thrown out of the medical corps and back into the trenches if you don't start doing your job, mister. Now give me a hand unless you want to try to find out if I'm right." I could tell from the way she talked that she was a Texas girl.

Hell, yes, I fell in love with her right then and there. Wouldn't you?

I sort of faded out again, and when my senses came back to me, I found myself lying in a bed in a big, high-ceilinged room with a lot of other beds in it. Most of them were full. I was in my underwear, lying on clean sheets with a couple of blankets pulled over me. It felt mighty good. So did the heat coming from an iron stove a few beds away from me.

I didn't feel like doing much of anything except lying there, so that's what I did. After a while, a heavyset gent with glasses and a white coat came around and saw that I was awake. "How do you feel, Private?" he asked me.

"Not too good, but maybe a little better than earlier, sir," I said, figuring that he was an officer as well as a doctor.

He nodded. "That's fine. You'll be all right with a few days of rest. I hope." He sighed. "Unfortunately, we can't do much with you influenza cases except let the sickness run its course."

"Is . . . is that what I've got?"

"That's right, son. But you'll be fine as long as it doesn't turn into pneumonia."

I'd heard about men dying of pneumonia in the hospital. I felt scared when he said that. Pneumonia was something I couldn't fight back against. A fist or a knife or a six-gun couldn't touch it. The whole thing was out of my hands, and knowing that made me more scared than ever.

"Get some rest," the doctor told me. I managed to nod, and he moved on to check on the fella in the next bed.

I wondered where that blond-headed girl was.

Didn't have to wait long to find out. She showed up a little later. I saw her come into the ward, and watched as she made her way through the long room, stopping at nearly every bed. Sometimes she adjusted the covers or fluffed up the pillow; other times she poured a drink for the patient from pitchers on little stands between the beds. When I saw that, I felt mighty thirsty. Sometimes she just spoke to the patients and smiled at them. I realized I wanted one of those smiles more than I wanted a drink of water.

It seemed to take her forever to get to my bed, but finally she was there, leaning over me and asking, "How do you feel now, Private Matthews?"

She knew my name. That made something jump inside me. I tried to talk, to tell her I was fine, but I couldn't make the words come out. Nothing but a croak came from my mouth as I opened and closed it, and I was seized by a fit of mortification as I realized I probably looked like some sort of fish.

"Just a minute," she said, and didn't seem bothered at all by my stupidity. She poured some water in a glass and then put her other hand behind my head, holding it up so that I could drink. The water was warm and sort of flat, but coming from her it tasted as good to me as a drink from a cold, clear mountain stream.

She lowered my head back onto the pillow and said, "There. Now, let's try again. How are you?" She smiled at me.

That was all it took. I said, "I'm fine, ma'am, just fine."

"No, you're not. You have the influenza. I'm just a nurse, but I can tell that much. That corpsman didn't have the brains God gave a horned toad."

She had that right, sure enough. I would've laughed if I'd had the energy. Instead I grinned and said, "Nope, he didn't."

"Well, you're in good hands now. Just rest and let us take care of you."

"Yes, ma'am."

"My name is Nurse Palmer."

"Yes, ma'am, Nurse Palmer," I said.

"But you can call me Janine."

"Yes'm." I licked my lips and said her name. "Janine." As far as I was concerned, there never was a prettier name, nor a prettier girl.

I could tell she was about to move on, but before she did a new fear struck me, and she paused when she saw the worried frown on my face. "What is it?" she asked.

"You're in here . . . with all of us sick folks. What's goin' to keep you from . . . gettin' sick too?"

"Don't worry about me. I've had the influenza, and measles and mumps too, when I was younger. I'll be fine."

"You don't . . . look sickly."

Janine laughed. "It was a long time ago. I'm perfectly all right now."

I sure couldn't argue with that.

I was in the hospital for two weeks while I recovered from the influenza. Half a dozen men from my ward died during that time, but that was pretty good, considering. The death toll in some of the other wards was worse. I give a lot of credit for that to Janine and the other Red Cross nurses.

They worked like dogs, day and night, to keep that place clean and to make the patients as comfortable as possible. There wasn't much in the way of medicine they could use to fight an epidemic like this, so they had to make do with good, careful care and trust to the Good Lord. That was why most of us came through it all right.

Some of the other fellas accused me of being Janine's pet, and while I denied it, I knew they were right. And I enjoyed every minute of it too. She came to see me several times a day, and even sat on the foot of my bed while she talked to me. She started out asking me questions about my life, and I told her about being born and raised in Peaster. After that I had to do some pretty fancy dodging and dancing to avoid telling her about all the unsavory activities that had dominated my life since then. I sure didn't want to tell somebody so nice about rustling cattle and running from the law and robbing banks and associating with outlaws and gamblers and whores. So whenever I could, I got her to talk about herself instead.

She was a hometown girl, born and raised in Fort Worth. Her father owned a hardware store downtown. She was nineteen years old, she told me, and she wanted to do something important with her life, only she wasn't sure just yet what it was going to be. So in the meantime, she was serving as a Red Cross nurse here at the base hospital.

Seemed to me like that was pretty important, and I told her so. That made her blush, and she was even prettier that way.

She talked too about visiting on her grandfather's ranch when she was a kid. He had a spread out on the Brazos, in Palo Pinto County, and Janine said, "We'd go swimming in the river when it was high enough. Sometimes, I'd even sneak down there by myself and swim without any clothes on."

That was a mighty bold thing for a girl to say to a fella in those days, and as she said it, she blushed again. My throat got dry as I couldn't help but think about what she might have looked like, diving into the Brazos all naked, and I had to swallow hard. She must have known what I was thinking about, because her blush got deeper and deeper. I felt like I had to say something, so I said, "I went swimming in the Brazos once."

"You did?"

"Yep. Nearly got stuck in some quicksand too."

"Well . . . I'm glad you didn't."

"Me too."

I reckon the whole thing sounds sort of foolish, but trust me, it didn't to the two of us. We didn't care what we were talking about, as long as we got to spend that time together.

Then the fever and the cough got worse, and the doctor looked more concerned every time he checked on me. I just knew that I was developing pneumonia, until I woke up one morning covered with sweat. The fever had broken. I still had the cough, but it was better. After that I started improving by leaps and bounds.

Finally, the day came when Sergeant Cribbage showed up. I was surprised to see him. "I'm told you're going to be discharged from the hospital today, Matthews," he said to me. "The question is, now what do I do with you?"

"Well, Sarge, I reckoned I'd go back to my squad."

"They've been training for the last two weeks while you've been lying here in this hospital bed. You're behind, Matthews."

It seemed odd that the sergeant was talking to me so quietlike, instead of in his usual bellow. That was enough by itself to throw me for a loop, and what Sergeant Cribbage was saying confused me even more. "You mean I can't go back?" I asked him.

"I ought to move you to another squad that's not as far along as your old one. That's what I ought to do." The sergeant rubbed his jaw and frowned at me. "But I'm not going to. Those friends of yours are being transferred to the cavalry, and I'm going to send you with them."

I felt that funny leap inside myself again. "I'm goin' with Roy and the boys?"

"That's right." The sergeant looked around, and I don't think he wanted what he said next to be overheard. "The army's famous for taking men with natural talents and utterly squandering them. I'm not going to let that happen here. You see, Matthews, I know all about the Tacker Gang.''

''You do?''

''I made it my business to find out about you and your friends after that incident with Private Gechter. Sooner or later, there's going to be trouble with you five.''

I shook my head. ''No, sir. We're tryin' our best to be good soldiers.''

''Don't call me sir. And don't tell me that you weren't trying to kill Gechter that day.''

''He wanted to shoot me.''

''So you struck back the only way you know how. You don't back down, and you fight to the finish if you have to. That's the kind of man I want in the front lines.''

I didn't know whether to feel proud or nervous that he felt that way. I still didn't know much about war, but it seemed reasonable to me to think that the fellas up front were usually the ones who died first.

''I'm forming a new squad and sending you to the cavalry,'' the sergeant went on. ''It'll be you, Guinness, Tacker, Ball, Carson, and three other men.''

''Wait a minute, Sarge. You forgot Private Gault, and you only mentioned one of the Tackers.''

''That's because Gault and Private Jason Tacker are being transferred to the Air Corps at Barron Field.''

I closed my eyes and sighed. Those two had gone ahead and done it. I'd hoped they would have gotten some sense in their heads by now, even if Roy and Big Boy had to pound it into them. It looked like Jace and Aaron were going ahead with their plan to become aviators.

But at least I'd be together again with Roy and Big Boy and new pards like Hank and Pike. I opened my eyes and nodded and said, ''Thanks, Sarge. Thanks for puttin' me in the cavalry.''

Sergeant Cribbage just looked at me for a minute and then said, ''Save your thanks, son. You may not be so grateful when you find yourself in France.''

•   •   •

Finding out that I was going to be in the cavalry with at least some of my pards helped soften the blow of leaving the hospital. It wasn't that I liked lazing around all day; I was starting to get a mite antsy, ready to be up and doing something again. But leaving meant that I wouldn't see Janine anymore, and I wasn't sure I could stand that.

I was buttoning up my uniform tunic when she came into the ward and walked over to me. "Well, it's about time we were getting rid of you," she said sternly. "We need this bed for a soldier who's really sick, instead of one who just wants to lollygag around."

I looked over at her sort of sharp-like, wondering why she would talk to me that way when up until then I'd thought she liked me just fine . . . maybe more than fine. That was when I saw the twinkle in her eyes and the way her mouth tugged up just a little at the corners. She was having some sport with me, so I decided to give her the same back.

"I'm just glad I survived," I told her. "I swear, if the diseases don't kill you, the way they take care of you in this hospital will."

We both laughed then, and she put a hand on my arm. "I'll miss you, Drew," she said. "Please take care of your-self."

"I will," I promised. "And Janine . . . I'd like to see you again sometime. Not here in the hospital, I mean."

She hesitated, then said, "I . . . I suppose that would be all right. Do you know where I live?"

"No, ma'am, I'm afraid not."

"My father's house is on Summit Avenue. You can take the streetcar downtown and walk over there some Sunday afternoon."

I nodded. "I'll sure do that."

Major Connery came by then. He was the field director of the Red Cross, and Janine stepped back to let him shake my hand and bid me farewell and best wishes. "Take care of yourself, son," the major told me. "We don't want all our hard work getting you through the influenza to go to waste."

"No, sir, it won't," I said.

He moved on to say good-bye to some of the other patients who were being discharged. That left Janine and me to have one last moment together, and I resolved to make the most of it. Before she could stop me, I reached out and took hold of her hand. She looked a little surprised, but she didn't jerk back.

"Janine," I said, "I think you're just about the swellest gal I've ever known."

"Why . . . thank you, Drew."

"And you may slap my face for this," I hurried on, "but I just can't help it."

I leaned forward and kissed her.

It wasn't much more than a peck on the lips, but it packed just as much punch as anything I'd ever done with Becky or any other whore. In fact, it felt like somebody had slugged me in the belly.

I know, these days a fella and a gal have to do a whole lot more than that to get their hearts beating faster. But that was a different time, and when I straightened up from that kiss, Janine and I were both feeling it mighty strong. I could tell by looking into her eyes how much it had affected her. I felt the same way.

"Good-bye, Drew," she whispered.

"Don't worry," I said. "I'll see you again."

But that was a promise I came all too close to not being able to keep.

FOURTEEN

"I'm Sergeant Randall, and for the next three weeks I will be attempting to turn you ignorant, worthless sonsabitches into cavalrymen! Do I make myself clear?"

Naturally, we hollered as loud as we could, *"Yes, sir!"*

"You've had it easy so far, but now playtime is *over*! Do I make myself clear?"

"Yes, sir!"

"Your horse is now the most important thing in the world to you! More important than your children, more important than your wife or your sweetheart, more important than your dear, saintly, gray-headed old mother! From now on, your horse is more important to you than your *balls*! Do I make myself clear?"

Well, we still hollered "Yes, sir!" but I reckon we were a mite less enthusiastic this time.

We were lined up for our first formation after being transferred to the cavalry. The remount depot was at the eastern end of the camp, several miles away from the trenches where we had trained earlier. In fact, the stables were on the very edge of the camp, not far from the Trinity River and Rock Springs Park.

We had genuine wooden barracks to sleep in, instead of tents, so we all figured we'd come up a step in the world. Sergeant Randall didn't see it that way, though. He spent a good hour telling us how he'd been a Rough Rider with Teddy Roosevelt during the Spanish-American War and how worthless we were compared to the men he'd served with down there in Cuba and how mad he was that the army had sent him such a no-account bunch to turn into cavalrymen. "I'll bet none of you miserable excuses for soldiers even know which end of a horse eats and which end the shit comes out of!" he shouted at us.

I might have spoken up and told him that a few of us did know the difference, but I had already learned one of the army's main lessons: Never volunteer. So I kept my mouth shut, and so did everybody else.

The sergeant motioned to one of his corporals, and the fella led out a horse. It was a good-looking animal, a chestnut mare wearing an army saddle, which was considerably different than the saddles the boys and I were used to. For one thing, it didn't have a saddlehorn, and the pommel and the cantle were lower. But I supposed since we wouldn't be roping any cattle over there in France, it didn't really matter if there was a horn to throw a dally around.

Sergeant Randall swung up onto the horse. He mounted smooth, like he had been doing it all his life. Then he started cantering back and forth in front of us, riding a little stiffer and straighter than what I was accustomed to. After a minute he spurred the horse into a gallop, rode out a ways from us, hauled it around in a tight turn, and galloped back.

He dismounted and yelled, "By the time I'm through with you, you'll be able to do what I just did! Not as well, of course, but at least you won't be an embarrassment to your country, or even worse, an embarrassment to *me*!" He lowered his voice a little and squinted at us and went on. "Because I promise you, if anybody ever asks you what incompetent sergeant taught you how to ride, you won't have to worry about answering. I'll be there before you can even open your mouth . . . and I'll kill you."

He sounded like he meant it too.

For a minute, he just kept glaring at us. Then he raised his voice again and asked, "Does anybody here *think* he knows how to ride?"

That was a direct question, so I figured I ought to answer it. I lifted my hand, and beside me Roy and Big Boy did the same. I had my eyes front, so I didn't know if anybody else in the formation volunteered or not. But Sergeant Randall spotted the three of us, and he stalked right over to us.

He sneered at Roy first. "Hell, you're as old as Methuselah." Then he looked at Big Boy. "I'm supposed to put an ape like you on a horse?" Then it was my turn, and I reckon the sergeant must have seen something he liked— or disliked—about me, because he pointed at the horse and yelled in my face, "Mount up, soldier!"

I did like he told me to, only I sort of went about it in my own way. As I came up to the mare, I held out my hand and let her get a good sniff of me. I talked low and friendly to her at the same time, and then I gathered up the reins. She didn't shy away, so I slipped my foot in the stirrup and swung up. I was pleased with myself when I looked over at the sergeant.

He was staring at me with his mouth open, like he'd never seen the like before. After a minute, he lifted his arm and flapped his hand at me. "Ride! Ride!"

So I turned the mare around and rode one way across the training field, then the other. I wasn't wearing spurs, but I never saw the horse that I couldn't handle better with the heels of my boots than with rowels. It felt so good to be in a saddle again, even that funny army saddle, that I kept going, turning the mare again and urging her into a gallop. I leaned forward, one hand holding the reins, the other tangled in her mane, and called softly to her, getting all the speed I could out of her.

Damn, it felt good.

So I was even more pleased with myself when I brought the horse to a stop in front of Sergeant Randall and stepped down, still holding the reins. He was red-faced and wide-eyed, and his breath was coming fast between his teeth. I should have known better, but I gave him a cocky grin anyway and asked, "How was that, Sarge?"

He punched me in the mouth.

I saw it coming, but I was so surprised I didn't even try to get out of the way. His fist caught me flush in the mouth, and I was lucky I didn't lose some teeth. I went flying backward and came down hard on the seat of my pants. Sergeant Randall stood over me, so mad he was trembling, and pointed a shaking finger at me. "Don't you ever try to show me up again!" he hissed at me. "I hate you fucking cowboys!"

Right about then, the feeling was mutual. I looked over at the other fellas, and I could tell that Roy and Big Boy were about to break ranks and come after Sergeant Randall.

I rubbed the blood off my lips with the back of my left hand, and used my right to motion to Roy and Big Boy to stay where they were. Most of the recruits were gaping, as if they couldn't believe that Randall had hit me, but the corporals didn't look a bit surprised. I reckon that was a run-of-the-mill occurrence for them.

I got to my feet and said painfully, "Sorry, Sarge. Just thought you wanted to see what I can do."

"I don't want to see anything from you except your ass as you're getting back in formation! Now move it!"

I got back in line next to Roy and Big Boy, and Randall sneered at the whole lot of us and asked, "Anybody else want to ride the horsey?"

There were no takers.

That was how our cavalry training started, and I sure as hell hoped things were going better for Jace and Aaron with the Air Corps.

Barron Field, at Everman, southeast of Fort Worth, was a busy place in those days. The American fliers of what was sometimes called the Army Air Corps, and sometimes the Army Air Service, trained there, and so did a few of the Canadian pilots from the Royal Flying Corps. Altogether, they made up quite a bunch, according to Jace and Aaron. Nearly every week, they threw big shindigs at the West-

brook Hotel in downtown Fort Worth, a fancy place with
a big gold-plated statue of a nearly naked woman holding
court in the lobby. The aviators called her the Golden Goddess, and claimed that she would bring them luck when it
came time to face the German fighters in the air over
France.

In the meantime, they had to survive the training at Barron Field, and that wasn't so easy. The boys flew planes
called Morse Scouts, and to hear Jace and Aaron tell it,
they weren't much good.

Their instructor was a captain by the name of Harvey
Gallagher, and on the first day of training, Captain Gallagher told the assembled pilots, "All the *good* planes are
already over in France, being used to shoot down the Boche. So you boys are going to have to learn on these trainers. We figure if you can live through this, you won't have
any trouble overseas once you get into the cockpits of some
real planes."

Those Scouts and a few Curtiss Jenneys were all the air
corps had at Barron Field, and Jace and Aaron learned
mighty quick to be extra careful on their takeoffs and land-
ings, because that was when the engines of the trainers had
a tendency to just stop running for no good reason. It was
possible you could still bring the plane down safely if the
engine cut out while you were coming in for a landing; if
it happened while you were taking off, the plane would
usually just nosedive back into the ground and sometimes
explode.

Man, you couldn't have gotten me in one of those things
to save my life.

Jace and Aaron seemed to like it, though. The day they
each soloed for the first time, they came over to Camp
Bowie in a taxi to take us to the Westbrook with them. I'd
never seen either of them more excited.

"I don't know that we ought to be goin' to a party for
aviators," Roy said. "We sort of like to keep our feet on
the ground."

"There won't be any flyin' tonight," Jace told him.

"But I reckon some of the fellas will be pretty high," Aaron put in with a grin.

Roy saw it wasn't going to do any good to argue. "All right, we'll go with you. If nothin' else, maybe we can keep you young bucks out of trouble."

Getting a pass to leave camp wasn't any trouble most of the time. Unless somebody in the squad had really fouled up, or unless we had guard duty, Major Hallichek, the CO of our cavalry brigade, didn't mind signing passes. I think he figured that soon enough we'd be overseas and he ought to let us enjoy ourselves while we had the chance.

Sergeant Randall didn't feel the same way, of course. He didn't want anybody enjoying themselves while he was around. Making folks miserable seemed to be his life's work. But there was nothing he could do about it as long as we had signed passes and got back to the camp before lights out.

We dressed in our fanciest uniforms and piled into the taxi. Jace and Aaron were sporting patches on their sleeves for being members of the Air Corps, and the rest of us proudly wore our cavalry insignia. That made us feel better than the regular doughboys who were riding the streetcar as we drove past it heading for downtown. We weren't officers, but we weren't lowly recruits anymore either.

The Westbrook was where all the newly rich oil millionaires gathered, Jace told us, as well as being the headquarters for the aviators' festivities. The lobby of the hotel was well and truly packed when we got there, and we had to push our way into the jolly crowd. I stared up at the statue of the Golden Goddess looming over the lobby, and as I studied the statue's curves, I thought again about Janine and how much I missed her. Then I felt a flash of guilt for being reminded of her by a statue of a naked woman, when I hadn't done any more than give her a quick kiss. I didn't have any right to be thinking of her like that.

But try as I might, I couldn't help it. I told myself right then and there that I was going to go see her the next weekend.

We wound up getting a table in the Rathskeller Grill, just off the hotel lobby. That was sort of out of the way of the main party, but still pretty crowded and noisy. A waiter in striped pants and a white jacket brought us a bottle of champagne. That was Jace and Aaron's idea, and they paid for it, a mighty high price too. There were seven of us around the table, since Hank and Pike had come along too, and when we each had our glass filled with the bubbly stuff, we clinked them together over the center of the table.

"To wild times," Jace said, and I thought that was a good toast.

Aaron added some to it by saying, "To the wild times we've had . . . and the wild times we're gonna have."

"Damn well bet ya," Big Boy chimed in.

The rest of us didn't put in our two cents worth; we just drank up. Then, while Aaron started refilling all the glasses, Jace told us about how they had each flown one of the trainers by themselves that day.

I couldn't help but ask, "Weren't you scared?"

"Well, maybe a little," Jace admitted. "But once I got up there, I didn't really think about anything except what the instructors had taught me to do. And about how pretty it was, with all that land stretchin' out so far in the distance. Remember what it's like up in the high country of a mornin', when the air's so clear and it looks like you can see forever? That's the way it is when you're flyin'. It's just like bein' a bird."

Being a bird was something I never aspired to, but if it made Jace and Aaron happy to risk their lives in a few scraps of wood and canvas put together with baling wire, then so be it.

We polished off that bottle of champagne, and then Hank sprang for another one. We took it out into the lobby and passed it around. There was all sorts of singing and carrying on, and I found myself standing arm in arm with a Canadian colonel in full-dress uniform and a fella wearing scuffed-up cowboy boots and a tuxedo. I found out later that the Texan was a rancher from West Texas who'd leased his land to an oil company and made three million dollars on the deal. All in all, it was a pretty raucous evening.

And by the time we got back to the camp, it was late . . . a little *too* late.

The main entrance to Camp Bowie was where Crestline Road crossed Arlington Heights Boulevard. We dropped off the streetcar several blocks before we reached that stop. There were only five of us now, since Jace and Aaron had headed straight back out to Barron Field from the Westbrook Hotel in the taxi. Getting off the streetcar early was Roy's idea. He had drunk less champagne than the rest of us, so I reckon he was thinking clearer. He pulled his watch out of his pocket and checked the time by the faint light coming from a nearby business that was closed for the night.

"It's after lights out," he told us in a low voice. "That means if we try to get back in the camp the usual way, the guards'll arrest us for bein' AWOL."

"Hell, they already know we ain't there," I said. "They found that out when they did bed check."

"The sarge may know we ain't in our bunks, but he can't prove we're not on the post somewhere," Roy pointed out. "If we can get in and get back to our barracks with nobody seein' us, Randall won't be able to do a thing."

What Roy was saying made sense to me, so I nodded. That made my head spin almost as bad as it had when I came down with the influenza. I wasn't sure why I was so light-headed when all I'd had was some of that fizzy champagne. I never got that drunk on Harrigan's rotgut whiskey, and it was a hell of a lot more potent. I guess I just wasn't used to champagne.

Sergeant Randall had told us that he'd rip the balls off anybody caught sneaking late into camp—his words, not mine. So we were mighty careful as we made our way along Lancaster Avenue to University Drive, where we turned south. University led right past the stables and the remount depot, and that seemed to be the best spot for our needs. The camp didn't have any fences around it, but guards walked the perimeter night and day, and the shadows of the stables would give us places to hide while we tried to slip by the sentries.

Roy led the way. We followed him through the alleys that ran between the stables, stopping every time he hissed at us. We stood still and quiet, not making a sound as a guard paced by, then moved on once the fella was gone. That happened several times before we reached the front of the stables. From there, we could see our barracks about a hundred yards away on the other side of the training field. All the buildings were dark. The night air was cold, and thick with the smell coming from the stables. We were all used to that smell, so it didn't bother us. What worried us was the three-quarter moon, which was flirting with some clouds. It was dark, then silvery light, dark, then light, as the clouds moved across the moon. If anybody was looking out across that training field while we crossed it, and the moon came out from behind a cloud, we'd be spotted for sure. Still, there was no other way to get to the barracks. We had to cross that open ground somewhere, and straight across would be the quickest way.

Roy waited until the edge of a good-sized cloud touched the silver disk of the moon, and then said, "Let's go."

I found out later that charging across that training field in a running crouch was a lot like going on a night raid on the battlefield. But right then, all I knew was that I wanted to reach the safety of the barracks before the moon came out from behind that cloud. Our lives weren't riding on the outcome, but our freedom sure was, because if we were caught sneaking in like this, we'd wind up in the stockade for sure.

We made it, but just barely. As we jumped up on the porch of the barracks, the moon emerged and light washed all over the training field again. Our boots made quite a bit of racket as they thumped into the boards of the porch, and as we turned toward the door, it was yanked open and a man came out of the barracks, shooting out like a wolverine leaving its burrow to attack something.

"I knew it!" Sergeant Randall said, and I swear, there was genuine jubilation in his voice. "I knew I'd catch you cowboy bastards sooner or later! You're going to spend the rest of the war in the stockade for being AWOL!"

"What are you talkin' about, Sarge?" Roy said, sounding just as innocent as can be. "We've been right here all along. Haven't we, boys?"

"That's right, Roy," I said.

"Been back from town for hours," Hank put in.

Randall was wearing his uniform pants and an undershirt. The night was pretty cold, but he didn't seem to mind the chill. I could see in the moonlight that his hands were clenched into fists, and he was bouncing up and down on the balls of his feet, like a kid who's so excited about what's going to happen that he can't hardly stand it.

"You're liars, all of you," he said. "You weren't in your bunks at lights out, and nobody could find you. You were off the post!"

"You got no proof of that, Sarge," Roy said mildly. "We were over in the stables playin' cards after we got back from town. Just lost track of time, that's all. And we're mighty sorry about it too."

Randall's breath rasped in his throat. He wasn't the brightest fella in the world, but he could see that unless he had proof we were off the post past lights out, he couldn't punish us like he wanted to. He could give us some extra KP for being out of our bunks, but that was about all.

"Some of the sentries must have seen you sneaking back in," he said. "I'll find someone to swear to it."

That didn't seem very likely to me. For one thing, none of the guards *had* seen us as we made our way through the stables. And nobody was going to lie and say they did, because then they'd be in trouble themselves for not challenging us. As far as I could see, Randall could maybe make our lives miserable—which he was already doing most of the time anyway—but he couldn't have us thrown in the stockade. He couldn't make us miss out on the war.

Well, the way things turned out, maybe the stockade would have been better after all.

But I know that's not true. None of us wanted to be locked up. That was why we'd joined the army in the first place, to keep from being sent to prison for that attempted bank robbery in Reno.

"You think you're so damn smart," Randall said to us. He was breathing so hard from being mad that he sounded like a bellows in a blacksmith shop. "You'll find out. Just wait'll you get over there to France. You'll find out what stupid bastards you really are."

"Whatever you say, Sarge," Roy told him. "Right now, though, we're mighty tired, so I reckon we'll turn in."

"Go ahead." The sergeant's voice got low and hard. "Dream about being dead, cowboy. Because that's the way you're all going to wind up." He crossed his arms over his chest and gave an ugly laugh. "I'm not even going to give you extra KP for this little escapade. Do you know why? No point in it. You're all walking dead men already."

We went inside and left him out there on the porch muttering and cussing. I caught a few of the words.

"... don't know what it's like ... going to die ... every damned one ..."

None of us really believed him. Not then. But I'll give him credit. Sergeant Randall was a genuine, tin-plated son of a bitch.

But sometimes he knew what he was talking about.

FIFTEEN

A lot of the big houses on Summit Avenue are still there, perched on the edge of a bluff just west of downtown Fort Worth overlooking the Trinity River. The neighborhood was only a couple of miles from the cavalry barracks, so since the day wasn't too chilly, I walked over there the next Sunday to see Janine.

The folks who lived there in those days were pretty well-to-do. I could tell that from the size of the houses, the well-kept lawns, and the big trees that shaded them. The view was the sort that people with plenty of money liked too. I remembered Janine saying that her father owned a hardware store, and obviously it was a successful one. I started to get a little nervous about meeting her parents, despite the fact that I was wearing my best uniform and had the flat cap that went with it perched at a jaunty angle on my head.

I found the Palmer house without any trouble. It was three stories tall and painted a robin's-egg blue, with a lot of dormer windows trimmed in white. A wrought-iron fence ran along the front of the yard, with a hedge just on the other side of it. Large flower beds were laid out in front of the porch, and I imagined that in summer they were mighty pretty and colorful. Now, in late winter, they were bare, without even any shoots poking up through the earth.

For a few minutes, I stood on the sidewalk in front of the house and just sort of looked at it, working up my courage. I even thought about turning around and walking back to Camp Bowie before anybody inside could notice me. But then I took a deep breath and blew it out and thought about how the boys would rib me if I showed up back at the camp too soon, and I reached out to lift the latch on the gate in the iron fence.

As I went up the walk toward the porch, I thought I saw a curtain move a little at one of the windows. Somebody had seen me coming. Was it Janine?

I didn't know, but it sure wasn't her who opened the door after I rapped on it a few times with the brass lion's-head knocker set in the center of it. The fella who stood there just inside the door was tall and had gray hair and a mustache. His eyes were deep-set, and they looked at me with what I had to say was suspicion.

"Yes?" the fella said.

I snatched my cap off my head and said, "Good afternoon, sir. Would you be Mr. Palmer?"

"I am. Who are you, and what do you want, soldier?"

"I'm Private Drew Matthews, and I'm here to see Miss Janine Palmer, sir."

That admission took a lot of guts. It's funny, but I never thought about needing courage whenever the boys and I walked into a bank that we planned on robbing, even though it was always possible that we'd be killed. But telling Janine's daddy that I'd come to pay a call on her . . . well, that wasn't near as easy. I can still remember, all these years later, how it made me weak in the knees and how my heart was thumping so hard in my chest.

"You must be the young man from Camp Bowie she nursed through the influenza," Mr. Palmer said. He stuck his hand out at me. "I'm Warren Palmer. Come in, son, come in."

It took me a second to realize that despite his stern appearance, he was giving me a friendly welcome. I shook his hand and walked into the house. The foyer had a high ceiling and expensive wallpaper on the walls and a comfortable rug on the floor. An arched doorway on the right led into a parlor, while a door to the left opened into a more formal sitting room. A hallway from the foyer ran toward the back of the house and a staircase. Everywhere I looked I saw thick rugs and fine furniture. The Palmers lived mighty comfortable-like.

"I'm sorry to bust in on you like this, Mr. Palmer," I said as he closed the front door behind us, "but your daughter invited me to visit, and since I'm off duty this afternoon . . ."

"Yes, I understand." He had a folded copy of the *Fort Worth Star-Telegram* in his left hand, and he used it to usher me into the parlor. "Have a seat, and I'll let Janine know that you're here. I expect she'll be down in a few minutes."

"Yes, sir. Thank you. Sir."

He smiled a little. "You're not in that army camp now, son, and I'm not an officer. Mr. Palmer will do just fine."

"Yes, sir, Mr. Palmer," I said.

He chuckled and vanished down the hall, leaving me alone in the parlor. I wondered where Janine's mother was, and I remembered her saying that her mother wasn't very well most of the time. Mrs. Palmer was probably resting upstairs.

While I waited for Janine I looked around the parlor. There was a fireplace on one wall with a small fire burning in it, and on the mantel were several framed photographs. In one of them was a young man I recognized as Mr. Palmer, even though the picture had been taken probably thirty years earlier. He was standing behind a woman in a fancy gown and had his hand on her shoulder. The woman reminded me of Janine, and I figured I was looking at her mother. The picture had likely been taken on their wedding day.

Next to that photo was one of a baby with fluffy fair hair. Janine. I recognized her eyes, even at that early age. The other pictures lined up across the mantel were like a history of her life, starting when she was a toddler. In each photograph, she was a few years older than in the one before. Walking from one end of the fireplace to the other was like watching her grow up right before my eyes. At the far end was a family portrait, with Janine and her mother sitting in chairs and her father standing behind them. From the way Janine looked, the picture hadn't been taken too long ago. Her mother had certainly changed from that first photo, though, and I could tell by her pale, drawn face that she wasn't healthy.

"Studying the family history?"

I turned around, surprised. I hadn't heard her come in, which just goes to prove that while going through army basic training may strengthen the body some, it doesn't sharpen the senses like living a life on the dodge from the law does.

"Hello, Janine," I said, ducking my head. "It's mighty nice to see you again."

"You can't see me if you're looking down at the floor, silly." She came across the room to join me in front of the fireplace, and stood so that I didn't have any choice but to look at her. "Father told me you were here. I'm glad you came to call on me, Drew."

"Well, I . . . uh . . . I appreciate the invitation." Finding something to say was a struggle, just as it had been when I first met her. Since then, I had gotten used to talking to her, but that was only at the camp. Standing here in her parlor and trying to make conversation was a lot different from doing it in the hospital ward. Maybe it would have been easier if she'd been wearing a white dress and had a dark cap on her hair, like she did when she was volunteering as a nurse, instead of a soft-looking pale blue dress with white lace around the collar and the cuffs. She was so pretty I wanted to take her in my arms and hold her, and then I thought about that naked statue in the lobby of the Westbrook Hotel, and the two images sort of got mixed up inside my head. I felt my face starting to get hot, and I just had to clear my throat.

"You don't have to be nervous," Janine told me. "My father hasn't killed one of my suitors in a long time."

"You've had a lot of beaus, I'd expect."

She shrugged, and like everything else, did it prettily. "Not so many. Boys seem to like prettier girls."

"There ain't any such thing," I told her without stopping to think about it. "You're the prettiest girl I've ever seen."

Now she was blushing. We could have lit up the room, between the two of us, with the red glow we were giving off. It was her turn to look down at the floor, and after a second she turned and said, "Let's sit on the divan."

We settled down at opposite ends of a divan with cushions that were too soft to really be comfortable. There was a respectable distance between us, and I was determined to keep it that way. Janine was no whore. I wanted her to know that I respected her.

"Well, tell me all about your cavalry training," she said. "I haven't seen you since you were released from the hospital, you know."

"I know, and I'm sorry I haven't made it out here to see you until now. The boys and me have been pretty busy."

"I'm sure you have. Tell me about it."

So I told her, only I left out some things, like the way Sergeant Randall cussed us out all the time, and how we'd gone to the Westbrook and gotten drunk on champagne, and how we'd snuck back into the camp after lights out. I suppose without all that stuff, it wasn't much of a story, because after a few minutes she started to look a mite bored. I didn't mention the other things, though, because for all I knew her daddy was right outside the parlor listening, and I didn't want him thinking some sort of hooligan had come calling on his daughter.

"Jace and Aaron are in the Air Corps now, you know," I went on, and that perked her up a little.

"They are?"

"Yep, they've gone down to Barron Field to learn how to fly aeroplanes. They're goin' to France to shoot down German planes and become aces." That was what they called fellas who shot down a goodly number of enemy planes, I had learned from talking to Jace and Aaron.

"That sounds terribly exciting," Janine said, and I felt
a flash of jealousy because she was more impressed with
what Jace and Aaron were doing than she was with me.
"But terribly dangerous too," she added.

"I reckon the whole thing is dangerous, no matter where
you are or what you're doin'. That's why it's war."

She nodded, real serious-like. "You're right. I wish you
didn't have to go, Drew."

I shrugged. "It was my own choice." I didn't tell her
that the other choice was prison.

"Yes, but I'm going to be so worried about you while
you're overseas. . . ."

Without me noticing, she had scooted over some on the
divan, so that she wasn't all the way at the other end anymore. Fact is, I could have reached right out and touched
her. That wasn't what happened, though.

What happened was that *she* reached out and touched
me.

All she did was lay her left hand on my right arm, but
I could feel the warmth of her fingers through the sleeve
of my tunic, and it sure enough did things to me. My insides started flopping around, and before I knew it, I'd
taken my left hand and put it on top of her right hand. She
smiled at me and turned her hand over, so that our fingers
laced together, and I sort of pulled her toward me—not
hard, mind you, and she wouldn't have had to come unless
she wanted to. But we wound up with hardly any space
between us on that divan, which wasn't easy to do considering how we sunk down into those soft cushions. Her face
was only a few inches from mine. Her eyes were so bright,
and her breath was warm against my cheek, and I forgot
all about her father, didn't even think about where he might
be as I slipped my right arm around her shoulders and
kissed her.

This was a real kiss, not like that quick peck at the
hospital the day I was released. That kiss had packed a hell
of a wallop, but this one was even more powerful. I'd never

tasted anything as hot and sweet and wonderful as Janine Palmer's mouth. . . .

Well, sure enough, we got interrupted. But it wasn't her father coming into the room or anything like that that made us both yelp a little and jump apart. It was somebody pounding on the front door of her house like they were trying to knock the blasted thing down.

Janine was red-faced and breathing hard, and I suspect I was too. She jumped up and smoothed her dress down real quick-like, even though it wasn't wrinkled. "I'll get it, Father," she called as she started toward the foyer. I stood up and trailed behind her, and as I did, I heard footsteps coming down the stairs at the rear of the house. Mr. Palmer hadn't even been downstairs; he'd been upstairs, likely keeping Mrs. Palmer company, and that meant I could have kissed Janine to my heart's content for a while if some son of a buck hadn't come along and started pounding on the door. Even though I didn't know who it was, I was already mad at the fella.

Then Janine swung the door open and I saw Roy and Big Boy standing there on the porch of the Palmer house.

I sure hadn't expected to see the two of them. I'd told them where I was going before I left the camp, and I supposed they had walked over here too and asked around the neighborhood to find out where the Palmers lived. They looked a little frazzled, like they had been hurrying, and I knew something had to be wrong.

"Glad we found you, Drew," Roy started to say, but I interrupted him.

"What do you want?" I asked, and I reckon I didn't sound too happy about it either.

"We came to fetch you," Big Boy said.

"To fetch me? What in Hades—"

I stopped short, realizing that Janine was standing right there and hearing her father coming up the hallway behind me. I didn't want them to hear me cussing.

Mr. Palmer stepped up beside me and nodded to Roy and Big Boy. "Hello, gentlemen," he said, then looked at me. "Are these men friends of yours, Private Matthews?"

"Yes, sir. This is Private Tacker and Private Guinness."

Mr. Palmer was a good host. A couple of doughboys might show up unannounced on his doorstep, but he was hospitable anyway. "Won't you come in, gentlemen?" he asked Roy and Big Boy.

"Thank you, sir," Roy said, "but I'm afraid we don't have time. We just came to tell Private Matthews here that he has to get back to Camp Bowie right away. We all do."

"But I've got a pass," I said to Roy, trying not to grit my teeth too hard when I did. "I don't have to be back until tonight."

"Yes, you do," Roy said. "We all do. The word's gone out. Our cavalry unit has to report to the depot downtown tonight."

My eyes got wide, and my stomach felt empty and half sick all of a sudden. "But that means—"

"We're headin' overseas," Big Boy finished for me. "We're on our way to France at last, fellas."

SIXTEEN

Janine and I just looked at each other, and I could tell she was thinking the same thing I was: This was just about the most unfair thing that had ever happened. Here we were, just getting to know each other pretty good, and the danged old war had to go and get in the way. No, sir, it wasn't fair at all.

I wasn't going to give up without a fight. I said, "I thought the 36th Division wasn't scheduled to go overseas until this summer."

"We ain't in the 36th no more," Big Boy said. "All the cavalry units've been transferred again."

Roy said, "We're in the 4th Army Corps, 90th Division, Headquarters Troop. We'll take the train to New York and ship out from there."

All I could do was shake my head in stunned amazement. The troops training at Camp Bowie would be there for several more months, and I had planned to take advantage of that time to court Janine. I hadn't thought much beyond that, hadn't even given a whole lot of consideration to the idea of whether or not I'd ask her to marry me when I got back from France. I sure as hell couldn't propose to her now, with her father standing right there in the foyer and Roy and Big Boy waiting on the porch. Besides, I'd only kissed her twice. We weren't hardly at the marrying stage yet.

So all I could do was turn to her and swallow hard and say, "I . . . I reckon I'd better say so long, Janine."

Her blue eyes were wide and wet. "I don't want you to go, Drew," she said in a half whisper.

"I don't have any say-so about it," I told her, and my voice was just as husky as hers was. "But I'll be back. I'll come and see you as soon as we get back from France," I promised.

Mr. Palmer clapped his left hand on my shoulder and stuck out his right. I shook with him again, and he said, "Good luck, son." To Roy and Big Boy, he added, "Good luck to you boys too."

Roy nodded and said, "I reckon we'll need it, sir."

Mr. Palmer cleared his throat and said, "Janine, I'll be going back upstairs now to sit with your mother. Come up when Private Matthews has left, won't you?"

"Of . . . of course, Father," she said, and he squeezed my shoulder and then went upstairs.

Roy knew what was going on. He said to me, "Don't dawdle, Drew. There's not much time."

"I'll catch up to you boys in a minute," I told him.

He nodded and said, "Come on, Big Boy."

Big Boy tipped his cap to Janine before he and Roy left. "Nice seein' you again, ma'am," he said. "I reckon you're as pretty as ever."

Roy took hold of his arm. "Come on, Big Boy," he said again. "Let's give these youngsters a little privacy."

Big Boy grinned, but he went with Roy. They went back to the sidewalk and stood waiting for me just outside the gate, their backs turned.

If I was going to do or say anything else, now was the time for it. I turned to face Janine and put my hands on her shoulders. I was tongue-tied as all get out, but I managed to say, "I think you're mighty fine, Janine. I don't reckon I've ever met a girl like you. I . . . I hope you'll think about me while I'm over there in France."

"Of course I'll think about you," she said, sort of ragged-like, "and I'll write to you every day."

"I don't know if I can promise that or not. I never was much of a hand for writin'. But whenever I get the chance, I'll send you a letter. You got my word on it."

"Oh, Drew . . ."

She sounded like she was about to start crying, and I didn't want that, so I kissed her again. I pulled her tight against me and held on for dear life, and she put her arms around my neck and held on to me just as hard. We had to pack all the kissing we might have done over the next few months into that one moment, and I think we did a pretty good job of it.

When she finally took her mouth away from mine, she rested her head on my shoulder for a minute and whispered, "You come back to me. Swear it."

"I'll come back. I swear it."

During those days of '17 and '18, I reckon there must have been hundreds of thousands of American boys who made that same promise, maybe millions. Maybe not every man who swore the vow really meant it, and some gents probably said it to more than one gal. But I meant it, more than I'd ever meant anything in my life.

"Good-bye, Drew."

"Good-bye . . ."

Neither of us said anything about love. We didn't have to. It was already there, and we knew it.

Down by the gate, Roy started to whistle. "Good-bye, Old Paint," that was the song. I can hear it now clear as day, just like I heard it then.

"I got to go," I said, and I gave her one more quick hug and then let go of her and stepped back and put my cap on. I turned and hurried down the walk and didn't look back. I told myself I wasn't going to.

But I just had to when I heard her sweet voice floating down the street after us as she called, "Good-bye, Drew!" A glance over my shoulder told me that she was still standing there on her porch, waving one hand above her head.

"That's enough, Drew," Roy said as he walked along beside me, and I knew he was right. It was hard, but I didn't look back again.

"You bastards are nowhere near ready to go overseas, but I suppose there's not really any choice." Sergeant Randall sounded genuinely sad as he saw us off, and I knew he was going to miss having us around. But he'd get a new bunch of recruits in a day or so, and he could make their lives a living hell, so I didn't waste any time feeling sorry for him.

Besides, I was too busy feeling sorry for myself as we boarded the train that would take us to New York.

"No need to go mopin' around, Drew," Big Boy told me. "You're just like a lovesick calf. That girl'll be waitin' for you when we get back. I'd bet money on it."

"How do you know we'll ever get back?" I asked him as we moved along the crowded aisle of the train car. As usual, there were more soldiers in there than there were places to sit, and they were all carrying duffel bags too.

"Ain't no doubt in my mind we will," Big Boy said. "Think about all the times we could've got killed. Think about all the lead we already dodged from folks who're a lot better shots than them Germans."

Maybe he had a point. I had never put much stock in superstition, but considering all the jobs we'd pulled without getting shot up, maybe we did have some sort of charmed life. Something had protected us, that was for sure.

But I wasn't going to count on it, whatever it was, keeping us safe from hundreds of thousands of Boche who wanted us dead.

We'd gotten on the train too late to get seats, so we had to stand up, bracing ourselves against the rocking motion as the locomotive pulled out of the Fort Worth depot. It was nine o'clock at night, a hell of a time to be leaving, and I could see lights from all the buildings spread out across what had once been rolling prairie less than seventy-five years earlier. Civilization . . . that was what we were on our way to protect. This war was going to make the

world safe for democracy, or so President Wilson said. I
hoped he was right.

I hated to think that I might be giving up a life with
Janine for anything less.

"Sure wish we'd been able to tell Jace and Aaron where
we're goin'," Roy said with a sigh as he leaned against the
wall next to me.

Big Boy said, "They'll find out, next time they come to
see us. You reckon we'll run into 'em over yonder in
France?"

"I hope so." Roy turned his head and looked out into
the night through a window. I could tell he was thinking
about his brother. He'd taken care of Jace for a long time,
but now Jace was on his own.

When it comes right down to it, I reckon we all are.

That's what I was thinking as the train rolled on into the
night, heading east.

Everything we saw once we left Fort Worth was new to
me. I'd seen some of the western part of the country, but
none of the East. The train curved up to St. Louis, where
we got our first good look at the Mississippi River. To
somebody who had grown up in Texas, where a river could
be a few feet wide and a foot and a half deep, the Mississippi was really something. It seemed more like a lake to
me than a river. I couldn't imagine that much water rolling
steadily down to the Gulf.

Chicago was the next major stop, and I did some staring
out the windows at the buildings, so many of them and so
tall. I had thought Fort Worth was a big town.

From Chicago, the route turned east again. There was a
lot of pretty country in Illinois and Ohio and Pennsylvania.
Some of it we passed through at night, when we couldn't
see anything except an occasional light from a farmhouse
or a cluster of lights that marked the location of a small
town. As interesting as it all was, I was starting to feel a
sense of loss. Some of that probably had to do with Janine,
but she wasn't the only reason I was blue. With every clack
of the train's wheels over the rails, I was leaving the West

farther and farther behind. I might never get back there, and even if I did, it might not be the same place. All of us—Roy, Jace, Aaron, Big Boy, and me—had been holding on to something that was fading away, a time that had never really been ours to start with, but one that we had claimed anyway and tried to make real. Now it had slipped through our fingers like smoke, and I figured we would never be able to capture it again, even if we made it back from the war safe and sound.

Something besides Murph Skinner and the Gunderson boys had died in that Reno bank that bloody day, and I couldn't help but mourn it and them, even that no-good double-crossing bastard Murph, because he had been part of the thing that was gone too.

I was pretty damned moody by the time we got to New York.

Of course, the army didn't care one way or the other how I felt. They just bundled us all off the train and into trucks that took us down to the harbor. I caught a glimpse of buildings that were even taller than the ones in Chicago, but that was all. When we got to the docks, the officers rousted us out of the trucks and up long gangplanks onto big iron ships. I'd seen pictures of such oceangoing vessels before, but I never thought I'd actually be on one of them. It was late morning when we boarded, and by early afternoon, a whole convoy of troop ships was steaming down the East River and out of New York Harbor, the propellers churning the dirty water as they were turned by powerful turbines. We passed the Statue of Liberty and got a good look at her, and the officers took advantage of the opportunity to remind us that that was what we would be fighting for once we got to France. Some of the troops got a little choked up listening to the speeches, and I have to admit I was one of 'em. I might have been an outlaw and a bank robber, but I was as patriotic as the next fella.

The trip from Fort Worth had been hectic, so much so that we hadn't even had a chance to think much about what we were doing. Now, faced with a sea voyage of a couple of weeks, there was nothing for us to do *but* think.

And be sick. Can't forget about that.

I'd never been on any boat before, let alone a huge ship like that troop carrier. And the Atlantic wasn't just a little pond either. I'd never imagined that waves could be so tall or could pound a ship so roughly. Even before that first day was over, I was at the rail with hundreds of other fellas, all of us heaving until it seemed like all of our insides had come up. Roy was the same way. For some reason, though, Big Boy never got sick. Maybe he was just too big for the motion to affect him much. Whatever the reason, Roy and I were sure jealous of him for a while, until we got our sea legs.

We were quartered several decks below the top one, in long, narrow rooms lined with bunks stacked three high. Big Boy took one of the bottom bunks, of course, and Roy claimed the one just above him. That left me, as the youngest and limberest, according to Roy, to climb into the top bunk every night. Hank Ball and Pike Carson were in a couple of bunks across the aisle from us, and the rest of our squad was nearby. The walls were painted an ugly shade of green, and the place was bare of any decoration. Utilitarian, that's what you'd call it, although I didn't know that word then. The bunks were hard, and the little bit of heat that came in through a vent in the wall didn't do much to warm up the cold, damp air.

Major General Henry T. Allen was the commanding officer of the 90th Division. As part of the Headquarters Troop, we fell under the more immediate command of Major Wyatt Selkirk. I supposed they were good officers; I didn't know for sure because I didn't have that much army experience, only a few months. It was Major Selkirk who came up to me and Roy and Big Boy as we stood on deck one night. The worst of the seasickness Roy and I had suffered through was over by this time. We had been at sea for almost a week.

I knew there were more ships out there, close by somewhere, but I couldn't see them. Fourteen ships had left New York in the convoy, and the rest of them were running without lights, like the one we were on. I had noticed that, but hadn't really thought about it. I sure wasn't thinking about it as I rolled a quirly and then lit it with a kitchen match I flicked to life on my thumbnail. The night was a little warmer and the sea wasn't as rough, and the simple fact that I wasn't puking my guts up made me feel pretty good. I tipped my head back and blew smoke up at the stars I could see winking through gaps in the clouds overhead.

That was when Major Selkirk came up to me and swatted that cigarette right out of my hand. "What do you think you're doing, soldier?" he asked me, and I could tell I was in trouble.

"Just havin' a smoke, sir," I said.

"Well, do it belowdecks, you damned fool. Don't you know there are subs out there? The Boche could have been watching through a periscope when you lit that match!"

I suddenly felt cold all over, despite the fact that the weather had turned almost pleasant. "Subs?" I said. "You mean submarines, sir?"

"Of course that's what he means," Big Boy said. "Ain't it, Major?"

"That's right, Guinness," Major Selkirk said. "The Germans call them U-boats. I call them damned sharks."

We'd heard about how German submarines prowled the shipping lanes of the Atlantic, venturing nearly all the way to New York sometimes. They figured the ocean was their private pond, and so far the Allies hadn't been able to do much to disabuse 'em of that notion. The sailors who made up the crew of the troop ship loved to torment their doughboy passengers by spinning yarns about all the ships they'd seen torpedoed and sunk in these cold, choppy waters. They told us about how sometimes when a ship was sinking, its spilled fuel floated on top of the water and caught fire, so that it looked like the sea itself was burning. Men forced to abandon ship who got caught in something like that couldn't do anything except scream and burn and die. But if the fire didn't get you, the sailors said, the real sharks might, and they explained to us how those devil fish could bite a man clear in two and how they went into a frenzy of shredding and killing whenever they smelled blood in the water. Then there was the danger of drowning, of being caught on board a sinking ship and taken to the bottom with it. Sometimes, they said, little pockets of air got caught in the ships that went down, and a fella might live down there for a while before the water finally got in and filled his lungs and crushed him. Seemed like the more gruesome the story, the more those sailor boys liked telling it to us doughboys.

Me, I just tried not to think too much about what might happen if German submarines attacked us.

But the major was right: Lighting that quirly had been a damned stupid thing to do. It was bad enough that the overcast was breaking up. If the moon came out, we'd be in plenty of danger of being spotted just from that, without some fool like me waving a match around like a beacon.

"Sorry, Major," I told him. "It won't happen again."

"See that it doesn't," he said. "Maybe you'd better get belowdecks."

"Yes, sir," Roy said with a nod. All three of us started to turn away from the rail, and that was when we saw a bright flash from the corners of our eyes and heard a loud *whump*!

We all jerked around and saw flames suddenly shooting into the sky from one of the other ships in the convoy. It was steaming along about five hundred yards in front of us and two hundred yards to port, which was how those navy boys said left. As we watched in horror, there was another explosion, then a third, the biggest one yet. That ship pretty much blew right in two. It was too far away, of course, but I imagined I could hear the screams and curses of the men who were dying over there.

Major Selkirk's hands gripped the railing real tight as he watched the destruction. I felt sick again, but it wasn't from the motion of the waves now. "Did . . . did I cause that, sir?" I forced myself to ask.

Without looking away from the fiery, sinking ship, he said, "No, Private, you didn't. Those torpedoes caught them on the far side. The Boche sub couldn't have seen that match from where they launched their torpedoes. It was just pure bad luck.''

Or good luck for us, I suppose. I know it sounds bad, but along with the anger and the sorrow I felt at the thought of hundreds of American boys dying, I was mighty glad I wasn't one of them. Some won't admit it, but I reckon most fellas who have sailed or ridden in harm's way have felt the same way at one time or another.

We had all forgotten that the major had ordered us to go belowdecks, and it seemed to have slipped Major Selkirk's mind too. Maybe it just didn't matter anymore. Word spread fast that the Germans were attacking the convoy, and men poured up from their quarters to line the railing all around the ship and watch. There wasn't a damned thing we could do, of course. The navy had their big guns going and were shelling the area where they thought the submarine was, even though it was entirely possible the sub had already slipped away.

I guess the boys just didn't want to sit there in those cramped, windowless quarters belowdecks and wait for death to come to them. They wanted to be up in the open air, where they could at least maybe see death gliding toward them through the black waters. All I know is you couldn't have paid me enough to go back down there, and a lot of the other fellas surely felt the same way.

That was a mighty long night, but when the sun came up in the morning, we were still alive and the ship was in one piece, still steaming toward Europe.

SEVENTEEN

The convoy lost three ships to German raiders during the voyage to France, but not the one that Roy and Big Boy and I were on, as I reckon you've figured out by now. I was pretty edgy for the rest of the trip after the night of that first attack, when I'd seen for myself how quickly and unexpectedly the German subs could strike. Everybody on board was nervous, in fact, even the sailors who had made the Atlantic crossing several times.

We landed at a place called Boulogne, in the north of France. Just like on the night of the first submarine attack, all the troops turned out and stood along the deck rails to watch as we came in sight of land. When we got closer to shore, I could see this big stone pier sticking way out into the harbor. Those French folks had come out onto the pier and were waving their arms over their heads and yelling greetings to us. We whistled and whooped and waved back at them as the ship steamed past. They knew we were there to help them run the Germans out of France, and it felt good to know they appreciated us.

It was a long way to the front from where we landed, but all of France was considered a war zone, so when we went down the gangplanks we were wearing our helmets instead of caps or hats. I never got used to my helmet; it was heavy, and it reminded me of an upside-down iron soup bowl. But it came in handy a few times, I've got to admit.

"Feels good to have dry land under our feet again, don't it?" Roy said when we'd disembarked from the troop ship.

"I don't know," said Big Boy. "I sort of got used to bein' on that boat."

"It didn't make *you* sick," I told him. "I don't care if I never ride on another boat again, except for the one that takes us home when this fracas is all over."

Major Selkirk and the other officers got the headquarters company lined up, and we marched through the streets of Boulogne to the railroad depot. Folks turned out all along the way to watch us go past. This was the first time I'd ever been in a foreign country, except for a trip across the Rio Grande to Juarez, where I hadn't seen much of anything but the inside of a whorehouse. The French people were as friendly as could be, which makes sense when you remember that we were there to save their bacon. But I think they would have been friendly anyway, especially the gals who smiled and waved and looked mighty pretty in their long skirts and low-necked blouses that left their shoulders bare. Considering the way I'd left things with Janine, I felt a little guilty about grinning back at them and looking down those blouses . . . but I grinned and looked anyway.

Boulogne was an old town. You could tell that just by looking at it. The whole country was old. If not for telegraph wires and paved roads, some of the villages we visited might as well have been unchanged for the past two or three hundred years. Some places reminded me, oddly enough, of Spanish missions I'd seen scattered across the American Southwest. They didn't look anything alike, but they had the same air of age about them.

We got on a train in Boulogne and headed for Paris. That was where the headquarters of the American Expeditionary Force, commanded by General Black Jack Pershing himself, were located. Having still been in Texas a few years earlier, I'd heard a lot about old Black Jack and how he'd chased Pancho Villa across Mexico. He was supposed to be a pretty salty son of a gun, and I wondered if I'd ever get to meet him. Didn't seem very likely, seeing as how he was a general and I was just a lowly private.

This part of France was pretty nice and didn't show any physical signs of war, not like a lot of the places we saw later that had been bombed so much they might as well have been on the moon. The German advance had never gotten this far—never reached Paris, in fact, although the Boche had gotten within thirty miles of the City of Lights, as the French called it. I'm getting a little ahead of myself, though.

The French railroad cars were smaller than the ones we'd ridden in in America. They were boxcars, with no bunks, and were called "Forty and Eights," since they could carry either forty men or eight horses. The horses might have been cramped. I know for damn sure the men were. Still, riding in them was better than having to march all the way to Paris.

We didn't see much of the most famous French city. The train rolled right on through, and what we could see of Paris from our boxcars was all we saw of it. Big Boy said, "Reckon we ought to come back here for a visit if we ever get liberty, boys."

Roy nodded and said, "I wouldn't mind." He knew, like the rest of us, that this war was the only chance a bunch of country boys like us would ever get to see such sights.

Our destination was a nice little village called Vosges, a nine-hour ride by train east of Paris. This was the center of the training ground that had been set up the year before for American troops entering the war. Once they got there, they spent some time learning the ropes of this sort of fighting from the French and British troops who had been at it a lot longer, before being sent to the front. By now, in the early spring of '18, American units were involved in the war all up and down the line, and replacements, like us, didn't have to wait as long before getting their feet wet.

Still, according to our officers, we would be there for a while before moving up.

That was all right with me. Vosges was a beautiful place. It had suffered some artillery damage from being shelled by the German guns, but most of the buildings were intact. They were built of stone and wood and looked like something out of a picture book. We pitched our tents in a field next to a church, and it was mighty pretty of a morning, with mist rising from the long sweep of plowed ground between our encampment and a line of trees that marked the course of a creek. Turning and looking the other way, we could see the steeple of the church shining in the sun and the little cemetery behind it that was surrounded by a black iron fence and full of well-tended graves decorated with bunches of flowers. If it hadn't been for the constant booming of artillery in the distance, it would have been one of the most peaceful scenes on earth.

After we'd settled in, the officers came around and got us in formation. Major Selkirk inspected the Headquarters Troop along with a couple of other officers, one from France and one from England. Our cavalry unit would be carrying messages among the various HQs of the three armies, since it was hard to keep telegraph and telephone lines strung up and working under the German barrage. Information had to get through one way or the other, so it was usually sent by wire and by courier both. That didn't sound so bad; it reminded me, in fact, of yarns I'd heard about the Pony Express. But I wondered when we'd get to do some actual fighting against the Germans.

Major Selkirk talked to the French and British officers for a while, then said to the assembled troops, "Men, do you hear those guns? You'd better get used to them, because the Germans keep them going night and day. We'll probably have little advance warning when a barrage is targeted toward us, so be alert at all times. There are bunkers where you can take shelter if shelling begins. Wear your helmets at all times. Now, Major Chapman and Major LeCarde want to say a few words to you."

The Frenchman went first. "I am Major Jacques Le-Carde," he told us in a heavily accented voice, "and on behalf of France, I want to welcome you and express to you our deepest gratitude. As Lafayette went to your aid when your country sought to throw off the yoke of your oppressors, so you have come to our aid in our hour of great need, and we shall be eternally thankful."

That comment about America throwing off the yoke of its oppressors made the Britisher, Major Chapman, look a little sideways at Major LeCarde, since the Frenchie was talking about the Redcoats, of course. But he just cleared his throat and said, "I want to echo the sentiments of my illustrious French comrade in arms. Your President Wilson has said that this war will make the world safe for democracy, and so it shall. God save the Queen, gentlemen, and God bless the United States of America."

With that, we were welcomed to the war. And it was the last speechifying we heard for a while. From there on out, it was mostly just hard, dirty work.

"Like *this,* you bloody git!" The British sergeant stabbed the bayonet on the end of the rifle at my belly.

Instinct took over, and I said, "Whoa!" as I twisted out of the way. I don't reckon he would have really rammed that sharpened length of steel into my stomach, but seeing it coming at me that way, I wasn't able to keep still. Of course, when I jumped out of the way, that threw the Britisher off, and he stumbled and fell facedown in a puddle of mud.

We'd had some bayonet training back at Camp Bowie, but our officers here in France seemed to think that wasn't enough. So we'd been assembled on a makeshift drill field and a group of British noncoms had come over to give us some pointers. The one who'd been working with my group was a big fella named Gordon Carruthers, and it was clear from the way he acted that he didn't have much use for Americans. He liked us even less now, I figured, because his pards were getting a good laugh out of it as he pushed himself up off the ground and wiped sticky black mud from his face.

"Sorry, Sarge," I said. "Thought for a second there you were really goin' to stick me with that thing."

"You sodding barstid!" he yelled at me—or something like that. I never did really understand all that British cussing. "I'll teach you to make a fool of me in front of me mates!"

I was glad he'd dropped the rifle with the bayonet attached to it on the ground and hadn't picked it up yet. If he'd had it in his hands, I reckon he would have tried to run me through. As it was, he just swung one of those big fists nearly the size of a ham at my head.

Sergeant Randall had been able to punch me because he'd taken me by surprise. I saw this one coming and ducked out of the way. That threw Carruthers off balance again, but even though he stumbled, he didn't fall down this time. I backed off fast and said, "Hold on, Sarge. No need for us to fight."

"Shut your bleedin' Yank mouth!" he roared at me as he lunged toward me again.

Yank? Was he calling me a damn *Yankee*? I wasn't going to stand for that. I might get in trouble for it, but I stepped up anyway, meeting his charge and slamming a fist right in the middle of his face.

It didn't slow him down a lick.

He had a good fifty pounds on me, and when he crashed into me, we both went down. It seemed to take forever for me to fall, and as I did, I was vaguely aware of the yelling that came from American and British troops alike as they gathered around us. Nothing like a fight to draw plenty of attention, and Carruthers and I were giving them one. At the rate it was going, though, it wasn't going to last long. I hit the ground hard on my back, with the Englishman's weight crushing down on me from above, and for a few seconds I couldn't breathe or move or even think.

Then the weight was gone all of a sudden. I rolled over and got my arms under me, then pushed myself up onto hands and knees and started trying to drag air back into my body. More yelling made me look up, and I saw that Big Boy had taken a hand in the fight.

"Pick on somebody your own size!" he was saying as he drove Carruthers backward with a left and a right and another left. The punches came so hard and fast I could barely follow them, but I saw how the Britisher's head jerked back and forth each time Big Boy hit him. Big Boy moved in closer and buried his right fist in the sergeant's stomach, doubling Carruthers over. That put him in perfect position for the left uppercut that Big Boy threw next, and it hit with a sound like an ax biting deep into the trunk of a tree. Carruthers straightened up and flew backward, landing right in the middle of the group of English sergeants who had been cheering him on. Several of them spilled off their feet, and they were mad too as they scrambled back up.

"Get that bloody Yank!" one of them yelled, and they all charged at Big Boy.

Well, it was Katie-bar-the-door after that. Roy and me and the rest of the boys from the Headquarters Troop weren't going to let those English noncoms gang up on Big Boy, so we jumped into the fracas too. I grabbed one of those Britishers who was a lot closer to my size than Carruthers had been and jerked him around so that I could punch him in the face. He went down, but before I had a chance to feel good about that, somebody jumped on my back from behind and started whaling away at my head. I twisted, trying to throw him off, and we both wound up falling.

It was a pretty good brawl while it lasted. The Englishmen were outnumbered, but they were all tough hombres, I'll give them that much. I rolled around on the ground, wrestling with the one who'd jumped on me, until I got shed of him and landed a couple of punches on his head. I got back up just in time for somebody else to clout me on the jaw. That was the way it was all over that drill field, men everywhere slugging and gouging and kicking and not really caring who they were fighting. It went on for several minutes until the military police arrived with whistles and billy clubs. Eventually they broke up all the fights, although it took them a while.

I was on my hands and knees again, my uniform covered with mud. My helmet wasn't on my head, so I started looking around frantically for it, knowing I'd be in even more trouble than I already was if I lost that soup bowl. I saw a rounded shape in the mud a few feet away and scrambled over to it. I pulled it out of the sticky goop and wiped off enough of the mud to see my name written inside the lining. It was my helmet, all right.

That was when I became aware that the drill field had gotten awfully quiet in the past few seconds.

I looked up, still on my knees, and saw that everybody else had fallen into a ragged formation. A country lane ran alongside the drill field, and a command car was stopped on that little road. Several officers had gotten out of it, including a medium-sized fella in high-topped boots and a cap with a short bill. He was carrying a walking stick and had two stars on the shoulder epaulets of his uniform tunic. His expression was stern, but it looked to me like the mouth under the thick mustache was trying hard not to smile.

He was General John J. "Black Jack" Pershing, commander of the AEF and the fella who was pretty much in charge of all the Allied forces in Europe by this time. Had to be. I jumped to my feet as fast as I could, holding the helmet down at my side.

"What's this?" the general snapped. "Some sort of skirmish?"

The major who headed up the military police detail that had stopped the brawl saluted smartly and said, "The situation is under control, sir. We were just about to arrest these men for fighting."

Pershing strolled out onto the drill field, not paying any attention to the mud he got on his boots. Everybody had formed up into ranks as quickly as possible, not caring who they lined up beside, so there were Americans and Englishmen standing next to each other. Pershing looked them up and down and then said, "You're supposed to be fighting the Central Powers, gentlemen, not each other."

Big Boy, bless his heart, never cared whether or not somebody was a general. He spoke right up, saying, "Beggin' your pardon, sir, but this here English lunkhead was tryin' to kill a pard o' mine." He pointed with his thumb at Sergeant Carruthers, who was standing at attention several yards away.

"Lunkhead, is it?" Carruthers yelped. "Why, you damned colonist—"

General Pershing lifted his walking stick, and Carruthers shut up. "That'll be enough," the general said. "Where's this 'pard' of yours, Private?"

Big Boy nodded toward me. "Right over there, sir."

I swallowed hard. I had wondered if I would ever meet old Black Jack, and now I was going to. I wasn't sure I wanted to, under these circumstances.

Pershing ambled over and looked at me. After a couple of seconds, he said, "You need to put that helmet on, soldier. It won't do you any good if it's not on your head."

"Yes, sir," I said as smartly as I could. I clapped that soup bowl on my head and tried not to wince as it banged against my skull. The mud that was still inside it slid down the sides of my face. I figured that right then I was just about the most foolish-looking sight anybody had ever seen.

"So you're the cause of this affair," Pershing said. "What happened?"

I tasted mud in my mouth, and I wanted to spit real bad. But I couldn't with the general standing right there, so I swallowed instead and said, "Bayonet trainin' got out of hand, sir."

Pershing nodded. "I see. You're so eager to get involved in the war that you're willing to fight even your instructors, is that it?"

"Well . . . not really, sir. I just thought Sergeant Carruthers was goin' to stab me in the belly, and I reckon I reacted a mite too strong."

"Westerner, aren't you?"

"Yes, sir. From Texas originally, and lately from Nevada."

"I saw a lot of you cowboys when I was involved in the Villa affair," Pershing said. "You are an arrogant, reckless, violent bunch."

All I could do was nod and say, "Yes, sir, I reckon you're right."

The general turned and looked at the military police major who had followed him out onto the drill field. "I don't think there's any need to arrest these men. We need replacements on the front, and they'll be moving up soon enough as it is."

"Yes, sir," the major said. He looked a little disappointed that he wasn't going to get to throw all of us in the stockade. He couldn't very well argue with General Pershing, though.

Pershing looked at me again and said, "I hope you'll fight the Boche with as much enthusiasm as you brought to this battle, Private."

I nodded. "Yes, sir, I intend to."

"Well, then, carry on." Pershing stopped himself and looked back as he started to turn away. "Not with the brawl, mind you."

He got back in the car with the other officers, and it disappeared down that country lane. The military police herded the rest of us into groups and sent the British noncoms back to their units. Our bayonet training was over.

I supposed that when it came to using those bayonets, we'd just have to finish learning on the job.

EIGHTEEN

We didn't know it at the time, but Jace and Aaron weren't in Texas much longer than the rest of us were. Just a few weeks after we got to Vosges, the two of them, along with the other fellas in their squadron, arrived at the place that would be their home for the next few months: the Allied aerodrome at Belleville, northeast of Paris.

Jace was the first one to jump down from the back of the truck that had brought the American aviators out there. He propped his duffel bag against his leg and looked around at the air base. The terrain was flat, of course. Had to be so that the runways would be level. The planes were kept in hangars like the ones back at Benbrook Field and Barron Field in Texas, but instead of barracks buildings, the fliers stayed in thatched-roof cottages that had once been farmhouses . . . before war had come to France. Even regimental headquarters was housed in one of the picturesque little buildings. Like a lot of places, war had forged a mixture of old and new there at Belleville.

Aaron let out a whistle of admiration as he hopped down beside Jace. "Take a look at that," he said, nodding toward a plane that was being wheeled out from one of the hangars.

It was a sleek-looking single-seater biplane, and painted on the sides of the fuselage just back of the cockpit was an insignia of concentric red, white, and blue circles called a roundel. That marked it as belonging to one of the American aero squadrons, even though the plane itself had been manufactured in France. It was a Spad 13, and although Jace and Aaron had heard plenty about these plucky little fighters, this was the first one they'd actually seen.

"Lordy, I can't wait to go up and take a spin in one of those," Aaron said.

"You'll get your chance soon enough, Gault," said the commander of the squadron, a colonel named Peyton, who had gotten out of the cab of the truck to join his fliers. "We'll practice a few days to get used to these Spads; then we'll start taking our turns in the regular rotation."

The other aviators had piled out of the truck. Hefting their duffel bats, they walked over to the cottages where the squadron was housed. As Jace and Aaron reached one of the little buildings, a couple of men in flying jackets came out of it carrying their helmets and goggles. Both of them had lean, tanned faces and the grim look of men who had seen plenty of combat. One of them, who had a hawk nose and deep-set eyes, pointed over his shoulder with the thumb of his free hand and said, "There are a couple of empty bunks in there, men, if you're looking for a place to sleep."

"Yes, sir, we are," Jace said. "Much obliged for the offer."

"Hope you don't mind a couple of greenhorns movin' in with you," Aaron added.

"You won't be greenhorns for long," the second man said. He had the same sort of piercing gaze as his companion. "You'll either be old hands like us—or dead." Then he smiled, making him look not quite as grim, and stuck out a hand. "I'm Wentworth, and this is Allard. Welcome to Hell, boys."

It wasn't quite that bad, Jace told us later, at least not for the first few days. He and Aaron spent that time practicing

in the French-built Spads. Comparing the Spads to the
Morse Scouts and the Curtiss Jenneys they had flown back
in Texas was like comparing a top-notch quarter horse to
a swaybacked burro. The Spads were more powerful, more
agile, and a joy to fly, according to Jace. Sometimes it
seemed like the planes were part of them, responding instantly to the merest touch of the controls as they looped
and soared through the sky.

I reckon they were good planes, all right. But I think
most of it was the fact that Jace and Aaron were good
pilots. It was like those boys were born to fly.

So neither one of them seemed to be particularly nervous
when it came time for them to make their first flight over
No Man's Land, the strip of contested territory between the
front lines of the Allies and the Central Powers. The two
pilots called Allard and Wentworth had moved on, assigned
to some special mission, but there were still half a dozen
wily old veterans in the squadron, to go along with the
replacements who had come from the States. A dozen
planes took off from Belleville that morning to fly a scout-
ing mission over the German lines.

They had hardly leveled off at about two thousand feet
after climbing from the runway when more planes appeared
in the sky in front of them, heading southwest toward Paris.
Jace knew right away they were German, because along
with the training flights in the Spads, he and Aaron had
also spent quite a bit of time learning how to identify enemy planes. The group flying toward them had half a dozen
Gotha bombers in it, carrying explosives they likely
planned to drop on Paris. The rest of the bunch were Fokkers flying escort, painted a bright red and blue and decorated with black crosses.

Jace looked over to his right, where Aaron was flying,
and saw that Aaron was grinning broadly under his helmet
and goggles. Aaron pointed at the approaching German
planes, then gave Jace a thumbs-up sign. Jace returned the
thumbs-up and the grin.

It was time to put everything they'd learned over the
past couple of months into practice.

A twin set of Lewis .303 machine guns were mounted just in front of the Spad's cockpit, their firing rate synchronized with the propeller. Each of the guns had a circular drum of ammunition mounted on top of it. Jace settled his feet on the controls and wrapped a hand around the firing grip of each gun. It was almost like having a pair of .45s in his hands again, he told us.

Colonel Peyton and one of the veteran aviators were flying point, and they waved the others on as they swung toward the Germans. Several of the Fokkers peeled away from the Gothas and came to meet the American threat. Jace saw them coming and knew he should have been scared, but somehow he wasn't. Up there so high above the ground, with the wind in his face and the roar of his plane's engine in his ears, he seemed isolated. It felt almost like the other planes weren't even real, he said. They were like the figures on a chalkboard his instructors had drawn back at Barron Field, when he was learning what to do in a dogfight.

Then, suddenly, flame geysered from the barrels of the twin Spandaus on a Fokker that was speeding right at him, and everything was all too real.

Jace kicked the Spad to the right and into a climb, zooming above Aaron's plane. He glanced down as he flew by and saw that Aaron was firing too, flame licking out of the muzzles of his Lewis guns. Jace banked back to the left and came around in a tight turn. The Fokker that had fired at him was now below and in front of him, in perfect position for the kill. Jace nosed the Spad down, and his fingers closed over the triggers of the machine guns.

The roar of the guns was even louder than that of the engine, and the smell of exploded powder mixed with the hot, oily stink that came from under the cowling of the plane. Jace squeezed off several bursts as he dove toward the German, and through his goggles he saw the bullets stitch across the left wing of the Fokker and then strike the cockpit. The German pilot jerked and shuddered and slumped forward against the stick, and the Fokker bounded ahead for an instant before diving toward the ground.

Jace looked around, warned by instincts honed by a life on the outlaw trail. There was no time to think about the fact that he had just killed a man. One of the German fighters had climbed to the same level he was on, and now the Fokker was closing in fast from behind.

Before Jace could even start to dodge out of the way of the Fokker's guns, Aaron flashed in from the side, raking the engine cowling of the German plane with slugs. Black smoke started to pour out of the engine, blinding the pilot. Flames shot up amidst the smoke. The Fokker went into an out-of-control spiral toward the ground.

Aaron swung his Spad around and flew even with Jace for a minute. They traded grins again, and Jace nodded his thanks. Aaron had likely saved his life.

Another of the Fokkers had been downed in the fighting, and the rest of the bunch broke off and returned to their positions around the Gotha bombers, guarding the big, high-powered planes. Colonel Peyton motioned his men toward the Germans. So far the Americans hadn't lost a man, and they were going to stop those bombers from reaching Paris if they could. The Germans in the Fokkers would do their best to see that the Gothas got through.

For the next twenty minutes, the American fighters swooped and soared around the German bombers, but the Fokkers kept them from getting through. One of the American planes went down in flames. Jace didn't know at that point who the pilot was, but he saw the explosion far below when the Spad hit the ground, and knew that the unlucky fella couldn't have lived through the crash. He had a bad few seconds as he looked around for Aaron and couldn't spot him, but then he saw Aaron's plane on the far side of the Germans, still searching for an opening so that he could get in and destroy one or more of the bombers.

Colonel Peyton veered away from the Gothas, and the other members of the squadron followed his lead. They headed back toward Belleville. Jace looked over his shoulder to see if the Fokkers were pursuing them, but the German fighters were still grouped around the bombers.

They had lost three of their group, but they had done their job. The bombers would get through.

It was a pretty grim bunch that landed at Belleville a little later.

Jace and Aaron were the first ones out of their planes. They stalked over to where Colonel Peyton was climbing down from his Spad. Jace saw the look on Aaron's face and knew Aaron was about to grab the colonel's arm, so he put a warning hand on Aaron's shoulder.

That didn't stop Aaron from saying, "Damn it, we let 'em get away! Why'd you call us off, Colonel?"

Peyton turned toward the two of them. The rest of the squadron walked up behind Jace and Aaron to hear the colonel's answer. To give himself a minute, Peyton stripped off his helmet and goggles before he said, "There were too many of them. We couldn't have stopped all the bombers, even if every one of us had given his life trying. We're here to win a war, gentlemen, not to commit suicide."

That answer didn't sit very well, especially with Jace and Aaron. "We lost a man for nothin' then," Jace said bitterly.

"The Germans lost three Fokkers," the colonel pointed out. "We inflicted more damage than we suffered."

"What about the damage in Paris when them Gothas drop their bombs there?" Aaron asked.

Peyton shook his head. "There are antiaircraft gun emplacements in Paris. It'll be up to them to stop the bombers, or to at least make them pay a high price for any damage they inflict."

Aaron's eyes narrowed, and he said, "Seems to me you're a more *cautious* fella than I thought you were, Colonel."

The colonel's jaw tightened. Aaron had called him the next thing to a coward, and for a second Jace thought Peyton was liable to bust Aaron right out of the squadron. But then an older flier who had been stationed there at the Belleville aerodrome for a while sauntered up and said, "Colonel Peyton's right. We might have downed one or two of those bombers if we'd continued the attack, but it would have cost every man—and every plane—in the squad." He reached up and patted the fuselage of the colonel's plane. "We can replace pilots easier than we can replace these aircraft, boys. We hurt the Boche a little today. Tomorrow we'll hurt him a little more, and the day after that, and the day after that." He started to walk away, then paused and looked over his shoulder at Jace and Aaron and the other pilots. "*That's* how you win a war."

Jace and Aaron thought about it, looked at each other, and shrugged. The fella might have a point, but that didn't mean it was easy to swallow.

"You'll all get another crack at the Boche," Colonel Peyton said. "Before this is over, you'll get all the fighting you could ever want."

Turned out he was right, of course.

For the next couple of months, Jace and Aaron flew out of Belleville three, sometimes four times a week. It was a while before either of them downed another German plane. They learned that actually hitting anything when you were shooting from a plane that was whipping around and diving and shaking was a lot harder than it looked, which was why sometimes tens of thousands of bullets would be fired during a dogfight without anybody getting shot down. The fact that each of them had downed a German plane during their first battle was a stroke of blind luck.

Their records inched up, though, until Aaron had shot down four of the enemy and Jace three. Naturally enough, they had a sort of rivalry going to see who would become an ace first. That took five kills. Plenty of joshing back and forth went on between them about the whole thing.

That was during the day, and also at night, when the pilots would get together in one of the cottages and play cards, pass around jugs of French wine, and sing bawdy songs. Later on, when he was in his bunk trying to sleep, that was when things would start to get to Jace, and the beads of cold sweat would pop out on his forehead as he thought about the men he had killed . . . and how close he had come to joining them on several occasions.

They met another Westerner who passed through Belleville briefly, an Arizonan named Frank Luke. He played poker with them one night and asked if they'd ever thought about attacking one of the big German observation balloons that floated over the front, tethered to the ground by long, thick ropes.

Aaron shook his head and said, "Those balloons've got too many antiaircraft guns standin' guard over 'em. It'd be danged hard to get through to 'em."

"Yeah, but if you did, think about what big targets those sausages are," Luke said. "And with them bein' filled with gas, I reckon you could set one on fire pretty easy by strafin' it."

"If you want to try, you go right on ahead," Jace told him.

"I intend to."

And of course, that's what he did, Jace explained to me later. Frank Luke shot down so many of those German sausages that he got to be called the Balloon Buster. Jace told me Luke never seemed to really care whether he lived or died, as long as he got to kill a heap of the enemy along the way. Seems to me a fella like that should have gone down in flames—died with his boots on, that was the way we would have put it—but instead he was killed the next fall when he had to land his damaged plane behind German lines. Naturally enough, he wasn't going to surrender, so he blazed away with his .45 at the Boche who surrounded him until they shot him to pieces.

But there I go, getting ahead of myself again. There was still a whole summer to get through, and it was a humdinger for all of us.

NINETEEN

"I swear, Big Boy," Roy called, "them kids follow you around like you was the Pied Piper in that old story."

That was true enough. We had moved from Vosges to a village closer to the front called Saint Baptiste, and even though it had been heavily damaged by the German shelling, there were still a lot of youngsters there. And all of them seemed to have decided that Big Boy Guinness was just about the dandiest thing they had seen in all their borned days. He couldn't walk down one of those streets that was pockmarked with shell holes without having a danged parade following him within a couple of blocks.

Big Boy grinned at Roy and me, who were sitting on some rubble in front of headquarters and watching him as he came back from the quartermaster's depot down the street. "I know," he said. "Ain't it somethin'?"

He turned around and picked up one of those French kids, a little boy about five years old, and put him on his shoulder. The kid let out a squeal of laughter and grabbed on to Big Boy's neck, then yelled something in French to his pard. I'd picked up a little of the lingo since we'd been there, and I thought the kid was saying something about how he had climbed a mountain. That description fit Big

Boy, sure enough. He almost made two of even the full-grown French fellas.

Big Boy used his right hand to keep the kid balanced as he came on down the street. In his left he had a canvas sack, and when he got to me and Roy, he thrust it into my hands and said, "Hold that, will ya, Drew?" Then he lowered the kid to the ground careful-like and reached back to take the sack from me.

Roy knew what he was up to. "Those apples were supposed to be for us, Big Boy," he said.

"Aw, I know it," Big Boy said as he reached into the sack and pulled out a shiny red apple. "But I reckon these sprouts need 'em more'n we do."

He handed the apple to the kid he had given a ride on his shoulder. The little boy snatched the apple and took off. Some of the bigger kids might have chased him and tried to take it away from him, but Big Boy stopped them by rumbling, "Hold on there." He pulled more apples from the sack and started tossing them to the other kids in the crowd.

It didn't take long to empty the sack, and when the apples were all gone, so were the kids. They'd all run off to hunker down somewhere and enjoy their treats. Roy looked at the empty street and sort of sighed.

Big Boy grinned sheepishly and said, "Don't tell me you wouldn't've done the same thing, both of you."

"I don't know," I said. "Been a week since I've had a fresh apple. Would've tasted mighty good."

"Big Boy's right," Roy said. "Those kids are hungrier'n we are."

I couldn't argue with that. At least, as American troops, we had our rations. The French folks living in Saint Baptiste didn't have anything to eat except what they could grow in their gardens, and it's damned hard to plow and cultivate a plot of ground with German artillery barrages exploding all around you. The best farmer in the world can't grow anything in a shell hole.

I reckon there had been some milk cows in the village at one time, but they'd long since been slaughtered and eaten. Every so often a truck loaded with black market food made it through from Paris, but the prices were so high most folks couldn't afford to buy enough to keep them fed. Some families couldn't afford to buy *any* food. The grown-ups went hungry a lot of the time, and the kids scrounged for whatever they could get from the British and American soldiers. I felt sorry for them. The only way to really fix things, it seemed to me, was to win the blasted war and drive the Germans back to Germany.

An officer came out of the headquarters building behind us and said, "Private Matthews." We all turned around and saluted him, and he held out a flat leather pouch toward me. "Take these dispatches to Colonel Greer of the British Fifth Army at Soissons."

That was a good-sized town about twenty miles east of Saint Baptiste. I'd never been there, but I had studied maps of the front until I knew it backwards and forwards. I took the pouch, saluted again, and said, "Yes, sir."

Roy spoke up. "Sir, could we accompany Private Matthews? We don't have any other assignments right now."

The officer hesitated. "I suppose it would be all right. Return as soon as those dispatches are delivered, though."

"Yes, sir," Roy and Big Boy said together.

I knew why they had asked permission to go with me: They were hoping to see some action. Ever since we'd gotten to Saint Baptiste, the Germans had seemed content to lay back in the weeds and not try anything other than their shelling. Earlier in the year, before we'd gotten overseas, the Boche had made two strong pushes to the west, and everybody seemed to think it was only a matter of time before they tried a third one. Soissons was a lot closer to the front, and Roy and Big Boy thought they might actually see some German troops if they went along.

It didn't matter to me why they were coming. I was just glad for the company.

We went to the stable and saddled up our horses. As I slung the pouch over my shoulder and then swung up into the saddle, I was reminded again of the Pony Express. In a way, I was carrying the mail, just like those Pony Riders.

Orphans preferred—that was what the advertisements had said when Russell, Majors, & Waddell started looking for fellas to ride those Pony Express routes. I reckoned that fit us too. None of us had anybody in the world, except for each other.

Then I thought about Janine, and knew that wasn't true.

For the first part of the trip, I wondered what she was doing and how she was getting along back there in Fort Worth.

Then I found myself wondering if she'd met some *other* doughboy she liked as much as me, maybe even better. Maybe right now, halfway around the world, she was kissing some other soldier, or maybe even . . . even . . .

It was probably a good thing that a German artillery shell whizzed overhead right then and blew the hell out of the road about a hundred yards behind us. That got my mind right off the ugly things I'd been thinking.

The explosion was so powerful it threw us forward in our saddles. I grabbed on to my horse's mane to steady myself, and clamped down on its flanks with my knees in case it bolted. All three of the horses broke into a run, but we had them under control. Roy looked over at me and called, "You hit?"

I shook my head. Big Boy was all right too, I saw when I glanced over at him. We pounded on down the road, which right along there was lined with trees. Behind us, another shell fell, only this time it was a little off to the side instead of directly on the road. I looked back and saw whole trees flying up into the air from the force of the blast.

Getting caught in the middle of a bombardment like that meant you had to rely on the luck of the draw. There was no way of knowing where the next shell would fall and no way of protecting yourself from it. But it would probably be a little safer off the road, we knew, since the Germans had observation balloons directing their batteries' fire and they tended to concentrate on roads. So we veered away from the path, cut through the trees, and took off across country. That might make finding Soissons a little harder, but we couldn't get there if we got blown to pieces along the way, now could we?

Anyway, as it turned out, locating Soissons wasn't that difficult, because that was where the Germans were aiming most of their barrage. Half the town seemed to be on fire when we arrived. We hadn't had any more close calls on the way, but as soon as we reached Soissons, that's all we had. Shells crashed to our right, our left, behind us, and ahead of us. Debris falling back to earth pelted our helmets and stung our horses, making them jump. A hellish confusion had the town in its grip. What few civilians were left there were trying to get out as fast as they could, carrying their meager belongings on hand-pulled carts or in wheelbarrows or just in their arms. Military trucks roared up and down the streets, competing for space with horse-drawn caissons carrying cannon. Everything and everybody was headed west, out of town and away from the Germans. It wasn't a retreat. It was a rout.

But I still had that pouch full of dispatches to get to Colonel Greer, so I pulled my horse to a stop next to some British troops struggling with a balky team of horses attached to a caisson and yelled at them, ''Where's British Fifth Army HQ?''

A couple of them looked at us like we were crazy, and the rest ignored us. One of the men shouted over the crash of artillery shells, ''Get out of here, you bloody Yanks! We're abandoning this position!''

I'd learned by now that the British called all of us Yanks. They didn't mean they'd mistaken us for damn Yankees, so I didn't take offense this time. I just hollered back at this fella, ''I have to find Colonel Greer!''

He waved an arm at the next street over and then turned away, his expression making it clear he wasn't going to waste any more time with us. I looked at Roy and Big Boy, and then we all turned our horses in the direction the Britisher had indicated.

The next street was as crowded and full of chaos as the one we'd just left, but after a minute I spotted what looked like it might be a command car with a Union Jack fluttering from its roof. I sent my horse in front of it, forcing the driver to jam on his brakes. The car rocked to a stop, and a red-faced officer popped out the back door. He was a colonel, and I hoped he was the right one.

He started cussing me out, but I stopped him by saying, "Colonel Greer?"

"I'm Greer," he admitted. "What do you want?"

I thrust the pouch at him. "Dispatches from Saint Baptiste, sir."

The colonel's eyes widened, and he said, "My God. You rode into this hell to deliver *dispatches*?"

"That's what I was told to do, sir," I said.

He shook his head, hurried over to the horse, and reached up to take the pouch from me. "Very good, soldier, you've carried out your orders. Now, I'd suggest you and your friends get the bloody hell out of here as fast as—"

He stopped short and frowned for a second, then said, "Do you know where Chateau-Thierry is?"

I had to stop and think a minute, and while I was doing that, Roy said, "It's south of here, ain't it, sir, on the Marne River?"

"That's right," Colonel Greer said. "Do you men think you could reach there on horseback?"

Big Boy said, "We can get most anywhere on horseback, Colonel, happen we don't get shot out o' the saddle or blowed up along the way."

"Excellent! If you'll wait just a moment . . ."

I wanted to get out of there, as the colonel had been about to advise us to do before he had gotten whatever bright idea had hold of him now. He ran back to the open door of his command car, reached inside, and dug around for a minute. Then he came back clutching another of those leather dispatch pouches.

"Take this to Chateau-Thierry," he said as he stuck the pouch up at me.

I didn't know whether to take it or not. "Our CO said for us to come right back to Saint Baptiste," I said doubtfully.

"Damn it, man, if we don't stop this German advance, they'll be *in* Saint Baptiste in a few days! Do you think your commanding officer will like *that*?"

I had to admit he wouldn't much care for it. But I still didn't take the pouch. I pointed at it instead and asked, "Who would I deliver that to?"

"Whoever is in charge of the Allied forces you'll find there. There are vital intelligence reports in here concerning the German push."

Seemed to me like what the Germans were doing was pretty obvious. They had finally gotten around to moving again. They were pounding the hell out of the Allied front, and then attacking behind those barrages in an attempt to drive us back toward Paris. I couldn't see what use some intelligence reports saying the same thing would be to anybody.

But we were supposed to cooperate with the British and French forces whenever we could, and besides, when our officers back at Saint Baptiste found out the Boche had taken Soissons, they'd likely think we were dead anyway. We might get in trouble for reporting back a few days late, but it would be worth it if we could help stop the German advance.

I looked at Roy and Big Boy, and Roy said, "It's up to you, Drew."

"Yeah, we're just along for the ride," Big Boy added.

"Well, hell," I said, and I reached down and took the pouch from that British colonel. "I reckon we might as well ride on down to Chateau-Thierry."

"Good man." He shook my hand. "Godspeed, lad. Good luck to all of you."

We were sure likely to need it. Instead of riding west, away from the front, we were going to be heading south right alongside where the Germans were pushing forward.

Looked like it was going to be a race to see who got to Chateau-Thierry first, us or the Boche.

As we rode, I thought about the maps I had studied and tried to figure out the best route to our destination. Chateau-

Thierry was a little west of due south from Soissons. One
thing about France, there were plenty of the narrow country
lanes heading just about any direction you wanted to go.
Roy and I talked about it for a while and decided that every
time the lane we were on forked, we would bear to the
right. That would take us in the general direction of Chateau-Thierry.

That worked for a while, until we topped a small rise
and saw a broad valley stretched out in front of us across
our path. And following that valley, heading west, were a
bunch of Germans.

We reined in quick-like and then edged our horses back
into the cover of some trees beside the lane. "Damn, would
you look at that?" Roy said, but he wasn't really asking a
question. None of us could tear our eyes away from the
German column.

We saw trucks and tanks and a whole heap of infantry
in gray uniforms and iron helmets even uglier than the ones
we wore. The whole bunch stretched almost from one side
of the valley to the other. There must've been thousands of
them.

"Well, we can't ride through that," Roy said.

"Nope, I reckon they'd spot us," Big Boy said.

"We'll have to go around," I said. "We can get in front
of them." I pointed to the leading edge of the German
army. It hadn't reached the far end of the valley yet.

"It'll take some hard ridin'," Roy said.

"We've rode hard before."

Big Boy grinned and said, "Yeah. We can pretend we're
tryin' to get out in front of a sheriff's posse that's chasin'
us."

Roy heeled his horse into motion. "Let's go then. We're
wastin' time."

We cut across country again, following the little ridge
that formed the northern side of the valley. It was only a
matter of time before the Germans saw us. Big Boy was
the first one to notice their reaction. He pointed and called
to us, "Look there, boys! Motor-sickles!"

Roy and I looked down into the valley, and sure enough, a couple of motorcycles with sidecars attached to them had left the convoy and were bouncing up the slope toward us. We leaned forward in our saddles, urging the horses on to greater speed, but I doubted if they could outrun the motorcycles. We could turn back and take to the woods to the northwest of us, but that would mean the Germans would have us cut off from Chateau-Thierry. We wouldn't have any choice but to abandon the mission. I wasn't ready to do that, and neither were Roy and Big Boy.

"Wish I had my old Winchester," I heard Roy mutter. "I'd pick off those damn Huns."

I wished for a rifle too. We never carried our Springfields on assignments like this, since they weighed too much and were too awkward to handle on horseback. We were each armed with a 1911A Army .45, and had some extra ammo clips in our pockets. We had practiced with the semiautomatic pistols enough to know they were good guns, but they didn't have the range we needed now. If the Germans got close enough for us to use them, that meant we'd be in range of their guns too.

That was the way it worked out. Those motorcycles roared up onto the top of the ridge about twenty yards behind us, going so fast that they actually left the ground for a second before coming back down. The path along the ridge was fairly flat there, and they started closing the gap between them and us pretty quick-like. I undid the flap of my holster and pulled the .45, then twisted in the saddle and squeezed off a couple of shots at them. While I was doing that, I saw the passengers in the sidecars shooting at us.

Thing of it is, neither the back of a running horse nor the sidecar of a bouncing motorcycle makes for a very good place to aim. All any of us could do was sort of throw lead in the general direction of the enemy.

I knew that we weren't going to reach the head of the valley so that we could cut across in front of the Germans before the motorcycles caught up to us. If I had figured that out, then so had Roy and Big Boy, who had been in tough spots a lot more often than me. So I wasn't particularly surprised when Roy yelled over the pounding of our horses' hooves, "Keep ridin', Drew, no matter what happens! Get to Chateau-Thierry!"

"Wait a minute!" I called back to him. "What do you think you're—"

He didn't let me finish. He shouted, "Let's take 'em, Big Boy!" and hauled back on the reins. Big Boy did likewise, and as I looked back over my shoulder, I saw them hauling their mounts in a tight turn so that they could charge right back into the face of those Germans.

I started to stop and go after them, but I remembered what Roy had told me. He and Big Boy were counting on me to get through and deliver the pouch to whoever was in charge of the Allied forces at Chateau-Thierry. They were going to slow down the Germans and give me that chance.

I never will forget how shocked those Boche soldiers were to see a couple of crazy Americans riding right at them, whooping and shooting. As it turned out, that was the best thing Roy and Big Boy could have done. Roy drilled the driver of one of the motorcycles, and the fella went head-over-heels backward off the contraption. The German in the sidecar grabbed for the handlebars, trying to steer, but he was too late. Motorcycle and sidecar both dipped down off the ridge and turned over, flipping several times and crushing the passenger before the gas tank of the 'cycle blew up.

The other motorcycle went into a skid as the driver tried to avoid running into Big Boy's horse. That dumped both driver and passenger. Big Boy's mount trampled one of them, and Big Boy shot the other one.

I saw most of that in a series of glances over my shoulder, and when I realized that Roy and Big Boy had disposed of all the Germans who had been chasing us, I started to slow down a little. Maybe they'd still have time to catch up to me and we could head on to Chateau-Thierry together. The two of them turned their horses and galloped after me.

That was when one of the German cannons in the column below finally got loaded and aimed in the right direction, and it flung a high-explosive shell up there at the top of the ridge. Roy and Big Boy disappeared in a huge blast that threw dirt and rocks high into the air.

TWENTY

Let me tell you, I rode with tears in my eyes for a long time after that. I made it safely around the German column and headed on south toward Chateau-Thierry, because I knew that's what Roy and Big Boy would have wanted me to do, but I don't mind admitting that I was still crying by the time I made camp that night in some thick woods. Two of the best pards I'd ever had were dead.

I call it making camp, but it wasn't really. I would have kept riding after night fell, only I was worried that I might lose my way and blunder into the German front like had almost happened before, and my horse was worn out too. If I rode that poor nag into the ground, I'd never get where I was going in time. So I found a place in the woods and slid to the ground, then unsaddled the horse and hobbled it so that it could graze but wouldn't wander off. There was a little trickle of water that meandered through the trees, too small to even call a creek, but the horse and I were able to drink our fill from it. Then I sat down with my back against a tree trunk, ate some rations from my pack without even tasting them, and tried not to think about Roy and Big Boy. I didn't figure there was any way in Hades I would fall asleep.

But I did.

When I woke up, it was dawn. My muscles were so stiff they practically yelped out loud when I forced myself to get up and look for my horse. For a bad couple of minutes, I couldn't find it, but then I heard a rustling in the brush and a long brown nose thrust itself through the bushes.

I got the saddle on the horse and hauled myself up on his back. As I left the woods, I rode mighty cautious-like. I didn't hear any of the clanking and rumbling that would accompany the movement of an armored column like the one we'd seen the day before, but that didn't mean there weren't any Germans around. I sure didn't want to stumble into a nest of Boche.

I hadn't dreamed any the night before, leastways not that I remember, but now that I was awake again, I couldn't help but think about how Roy and Big Boy had died. I wasn't choked up about it this morning. I was mad. I wanted to kill every German I could get my hands on, even though I knew that wouldn't bring my friends back.

But I didn't see any during that day, and I suppose it was a good thing I didn't. As out of my head with rage as I was, I probably would've attacked them and gotten myself killed. As it was, I was able to make my way through the dense forest that surrounded the town of Villers-Cotterets and then swing southwest toward Chateau-Thierry. The route I was following from Soissons was turning into a giant oxbow.

One more night on the road, or rather in the woods near the road, and then I was closing in on Chateau-Thierry. For all I knew, the Germans already held the town, but I would at least try to complete my mission. By afternoon, the lane I was following intersected a larger road that led right into Chateau-Thierry, according to the signs I saw.

Signs weren't all I saw. Coming down the road toward me from the west were several trucks flying the American flag.

I kneed my horse out in front of them and held up a hand, palm out. The trucks came to a stop, and a young lieutenant hopped out of the first one. "Identify yourself, Private," he said to me.

"Private Drew Matthews, Headquarters Troop, 90th Division, Fourth Army Corps," I told him. "Carrying dispatches from Colonel Greer of the British Fifth Army to the commander of the Allied forces at Chateau-Thierry."

The lieutenant smiled a little at that. "You've come all the way from Soissons on horseback with the Germans sweeping over that ground like no power on earth can stop them?"

"That's what I was told to do, sir."

He held out his hand. "I'm Lieutenant John Bissell of the Seventh Machine Gun Battalion. I suppose I'm the commander of the Allied forces in Chateau-Thierry, since that's where we're bound and no one else is there right now."

"Then I reckon this is yours, sir," I said as I gave him the pouch.

He looked through the documents inside and nodded, as much to himself as to me. "Just as I thought," he said. "If the Germans are going to be stopped, it has to be here. Otherwise they're liable to be in Paris by mid-summer." He was talking to himself too, but then he looked up at me and asked a question that took me by surprise. "Do you know anything about handling a machine gun?"

I frowned and said, "No, sir, I don't reckon I do."

"You can carry a box of ammunition, though. I had to leave one of my men behind with a broken leg when the orders came to move up, so I'm shorthanded. What about it, Private? Care to join us?"

"Is that an order, sir?"

"No, just a request."

"What is it you plan to do, if you don't mind me askin', sir?"

He was a good-looking young fella, but right then he was as grim as any old-timer. "We're going to dig in at Chateau-Thierry and not allow the Boche to cross the Marne, no matter how many of them we have to kill."

That sounded pretty good to me. I was thinking about Roy and Big Boy again as I nodded and said, "Well, then, you can count me in, Lieutenant."

Chateau-Thierry might have been a pretty place under other circumstances. It was a typical French town full of narrow streets and steep-roofed houses. The Marne cut it in two, with most of the town on the north side of the river. The Marne itself wasn't very wide, and it ran through a channel that was bordered by stone walls, with a street on each side of it. I could see all that from where I crouched along with Lieutenant Bissell and the other fellas of his squad from the Seventh Machine Gun Battalion.

We were at the corner of a building about a block from the river. Once we had gotten to Chateau-Thierry, we had discovered that some French troops, *poilus* as they were called, were dug in on the south bank to the east of our position. More American machine gunners were coming up behind us, but we were the first ones there at what the lieutenant said would be the most strategic spot to defend. An iron bridge crossed the Marne there.

Bissell pointed across the bridge. "That's where we're going," he said. "Right over there."

One of the men in his squad said, "You sure about that, Lieutenant?"

"The Boche won't expect to find any of us on the north bank of the river. We'll take them by surprise when they start their advance tonight."

He seemed mighty certain that the Germans wouldn't try to cross the Marne until after dark, and I figured he was probably right. There were some small hills just north of Chateau-Thierry, and the Germans already had those under their control. Their big guns were set up there, and they were pouring fire into the town on the south bank. As a shell exploded about two blocks behind us, making us all crouch a little lower, I said, "Reckon it could be a mite safer over there at that."

The lieutenant grinned. "You've come far enough with us, Matthews. Thanks for helping to lug our ammo, but we can take care of things from here. You can head back to wherever your outfit is."

My outfit was a long way from there. Roy and Big Boy were dead, and for all I knew, Jace and Aaron were too, either that or off flying high in the sky somewhere. So I said, "I'll stick, Lieutenant. You can always use an extra hand."

"True enough," he said, and clapped me on the shoulder. "As soon as it starts to get dark, we'll go."

When twilight began to settle down over the town, about a dozen of us dashed across that bridge, our boot heels ringing on the iron surface. We had two machine guns with us and several boxes of ammunition. Bissell led us across the street that bordered the north bank of the river and along another street that ran perpendicular to it. Nobody seemed to be paying us any mind. The French citizens of Chateau-Thierry had long since lit a shuck out of there, and the Germans hadn't come into town yet. We had the place to ourselves.

When we'd gone about a hundred yards from the river, Bissell split the squad into two groups, each taking a machine gun and setting up behind some rubble that would give us a little cover. A hundred yards ahead of us, two main roads came together to form the avenue we were on. I was in the lieutenant's bunch, and he nodded down the road and said, "That's where they'll come from."

"And we'll be waitin' for them," I said.

"That's right, Matthews."

Seemed like a pretty fair plan to me, other than the fact that the twelve of us would be over there by our lonesome, and if the Germans got between us and the river, we'd be in pretty bad shape. I took a deep breath as I thought about that, and told myself that fighting Germans was what I'd come overseas to do. That was the reason we had joined the army in the first place. If we hadn't wanted to be in this war, we could have taken our chances in a Nevada prison. Besides, there were other considerations.

"I'll even the score for you, boys," I whispered to myself, thinking about Roy and Big Boy.

Nothing happened for a while, except for the Boche continuing to shell the hell out of the Allied positions on the south bank. As darkness settled down, the sky took on a reddish glow that told me a lot of fires were burning. Artillery shells screamed overhead and blew up on the far side of the river. It never quieted down, and it never seemed to get completely dark. We sat at our guns and waited, and during a rare lull in the barrage, I heard voices shouting in the distance ahead of us.

They were talking German.

But the attack we expected at any moment didn't come, and the night stretched out longer and longer. That played hob with our nerves, let me tell you. We couldn't move, couldn't talk, couldn't smoke. All we could do was sit there and wait for the killing to start.

Finally the sun came up, and the Boche came with it.

They streamed down both those roads, just as Lieutenant Bissell had predicted, and came together to form a gray-coated wave that rolled down the avenue toward us. We held our fire as they came closer and closer, and from the way they were acting, I could tell they didn't know we were there. Then Bissell yelled, "Fire!" and both machine guns opened up.

The roar they made was mighty loud, but not loud enough to completely drown out the screams of those German soldiers in the first ranks as the bullets ripped through them. I've heard it said that an accurate volley is like a scythe mowing down wheat, and I reckon that's right. Those Boche soldiers fell, their blood spraying into the air so that drops of it came pattering down around their bodies like red rain.

My job was handing ammo belts from the boxes to the fella who fed them into the machine gun. That gun went through bullets so fast there wasn't hardly time to think about anything else except getting another belt from the box and thrusting it into the waiting hands of the loader. My head was down most of the time, so I didn't see all the havoc we wreaked on that German charge. All I knew was that we turned it back.

All along the Marne as it ran through Chateau-Thierry, the Boche were trying to cross the river. American and French machine guns on the south bank turned them back. The squad I was with was the only one on the north side of the river, however, and it's not bragging when I say we probably did more damage than any of the other bunches. We were closer to the Germans to start with. Hell, they were practically on top of us for a while, before they cut and ran.

During one of the breaks in the fighting, I stuck my head up above the pile of rubble and took a look along the avenue. It was a foolish thing to do, and I was lucky a German rifleman didn't put a bullet through my noggin. But nobody shot at me, and I got a good look at the piles of bodies clogging the street. There were so many shot-up Germans lying there that the soldiers in the next charge would be running toward us on a carpet of their dead comrades.

Seeing all that carnage should have made me feel better, I thought. I'd helped even the score for Roy and Big Boy. But even though I was damn glad we'd killed so many of the enemy and held them off from the river, it didn't do a thing to bring back my pards. Somehow that didn't seem fair.

Almost before I knew it, the sun had set and night was falling again. We had fought all day, and we were starting to run low on ammunition. Lieutenant Bissell said, "It's time we got out of here," and I couldn't have agreed more. Now that the Germans knew where we were dug in, they could skirt around us in the darkness and catch us in a cross fire, and there wouldn't be a thing in the world we could do about it. While we had a chance, we disassembled those guns and headed for the Marne. I didn't bother to take the box I had carried over there. It was empty now.

We were just about back to the bridge when the blasted thing blew up.

The explosion sent us staggering against the walls of the buildings. I threw my arm over my face to protect my eyes from debris. "Damn it!" somebody in the squad screamed.

"That wasn't an artillery shell," Bissell said grimly. "The bridge was mined. Our boys blew it up so that the Boche couldn't use it."

"But we're still over here!" I yelped.

The lieutenant grinned at me, but he didn't look too pleased. "Someone obviously forgot about that."

"What do we do now?" asked one of the other fellas.

A rifle bullet whined off the wall over our heads. The Germans were coming down the avenue again. It wouldn't take them long to figure out that we weren't waiting for them this time.

"There's another bridge a few blocks away," Bissell said. "Come on!"

We loped through the darkness toward the other bridge, and as we did our gunners on the south bank started raking the far side of the river. Bullets being fired by our own men bounced and sang around us. We used what cover we could find, but speed was more important than stealth now. If we didn't reach that other bridge before the Germans did, we'd never get across it.

That was one hellish run, and when we'd covered the several blocks to the other bridge, we discovered that we were too late. The Germans hadn't quite gotten there, but they were close enough that they were firing across the bridge, and the Americans on the south bank were returning that fire. If we tried to make a run for it across the bridge, we would have been chopped to pieces in a matter of seconds.

Along this stretch of the Marne, there was a narrow space between the low stone wall that bordered the street and the river itself. Lieutenant Bissell hopped over that wall and called to us, "Set up the guns here!" I suppose he was thinking that if we couldn't retreat, we might as well get back into the fight.

That's what we did. Those gunners were good at their job, and in a matter of minutes, they had the machine guns set up again and started blazing away at the Germans closing in on the bridge. The Germans weren't expecting that, and once again, we mowed them down. That made them

fall back, and would have given us a breather and maybe
a chance to get across the bridge, but our boys on the south
bank were still firing.

Still, we couldn't stay there for very long, pinned down
like we were, so Bissell said, "Let's give it a try! Bring
the guns and the wounded and come on, men!"

We had three fellas who had taken bullets and had to
be helped along, but we sure as blazes weren't going to
leave them behind even if they did slow us down. We ran
onto the bridge, and then the thing that we had all feared
came true. The American gunners on the south bank heard
our boots thudding on the bridge and took us for Germans,
so they concentrated their fire on us. We ducked back,
somehow avoiding getting anybody else wounded, and
flung ourselves off the bridge and down behind that wall
again.

"Blast it!" Lieutenant Bissell said between gritted teeth.
"We have to let them know we're Yanks."

Well, that gave me an idea. I wouldn't ever lay claim
to being a damn Yankee, but I could sure do a passable
Rebel yell. So I tipped my head back and let one rip at the
top of my lungs, and that *"Yeeee-hawwww!"* was so loud
that some of the gunners on the south bank heard it and
held their fire out of pure shock. No German ever made a
sound like that.

As the shooting died down, Bissell lunged out onto the
bridge again and yelled, "Lieutenant Cobey! Lieutenant
Cobey!" I sure hoped that Cobey fella, who had to be one
of Bissell's fellow officers, hadn't caught a bullet during
the fighting.

Then I heard somebody else yell, and it was one of the
sweetest sounds I'd ever heard. He was hollering, "Cease
fire! Cease fire!"

Bissell turned, waved at the rest of us, and shouted,
"Come on!"

He didn't have to tell us twice.

We ran across that bridge like Satan himself was after
us, and after spending a day and a couple of nights in Hell,

I reckon that's what we thought. Because that's what Chateau-Thierry was for a while: Hades itself.

But we made it back safe, and not a single German soldier set foot on the south bank of the Marne. I'd have a hell of a story to tell to the fellas when I got back to Saint Baptiste.

Only Roy and Big Boy wouldn't be there.

TWENTY-ONE

But they were, and if that wasn't enough of a shock, Jace and Aaron were with them.

I was so surprised to see them standing in front of the headquarters building when I rode up that I didn't even get down from my horse. I just sat there in the saddle, staring at them with my mouth open.

"Gonna catch some flies there if you ain't careful, Drew," Big Boy said.

"Wouldn't be the first time," Aaron said. "That boy hangs his jaw open more'n anybody I ever saw."

Big Boy had a bandage around his head, and Roy limped on his left leg as he came toward me with his hand outstretched. I leaned down and took it without thinking. "Good to see you again, Drew," he said. "We were afraid you hadn't made it, but then we heard that you'd been in the battle at Chateau-Thierry. A lieutenant name of Bissell sent word to Major Selkirk and said that you came in mighty handy."

I finally figured out that I ought to dismount. I swung down from the saddle and said, "When that shell exploded, it didn't kill you, did it?"

Jace nudged Aaron and said, "Observant, ain't he? He can tell Roy and Big Boy ain't dead."

"The blast knocked us and our hosses down," Big Boy said. He touched the bandage on his head. "Some o' the debris gave me a good clout on the noggin, but you know it'd take more'n that to hurt this ol' skull."

"I got a good-sized gash on my leg too," Roy added, "but we were both able to get back on our horses and light a shuck out of there. The Boche followed us, just like we hoped they would. Could be they didn't even know you were still alive."

"But how'd you get back here?" I asked.

Roy gave a modest shrug. "Rode like sons o' bitches."

I looked at Jace and Aaron. They were mighty fancy in their Air Service uniforms. "What about you two?" I asked them. "What are you doing here?"

"Liberty," Jace said.

Aaron added, "We've done so good at shootin' down them Boche planes, the boss figured we deserved some time off."

"We're gettin' a break too," Big Boy said. "Reckon they felt sorry for me with this busted head, so I'm gettin' liberty to rest it up."

"Yeah, well, time we get back from where we're goin', you'll be more addled than ever, Big Boy," Roy said dryly. He turned back to me. "Best pack a bag, Drew. Major Selkirk's got your pass waitin' for you on his desk, so you're goin' with us."

"Wait just a damned minute," I said. This was all moving too fast for me. Here I'd spent nearly a week mourning Roy and Big Boy, when they'd been alive all the time. Not only alive, but evidently planning to go on some sort of lark once I got back. I asked, "Just where do you think we're all goin'?"

"The City of Lights," Jace said, and Aaron let out a whoop.

"That's right," Roy said. "We're goin' to Paris."

•   •   •

Once I thought about it, I felt a little guilty for believing that Roy and Big Boy were dead just because I'd seen that cannon shell go off between me and them. Of course, the explosion had been a lot closer to them, but still . . .

Anyway, once I got over the first shock of seeing them, I was mighty pleased to find out they were alive. And it was great that the five of us were together again and on our way to Paris together for some time away from the war. After everything that had happened, I felt like we needed it.

Not everybody was that lucky, though. Our new pards, Hank Ball and Pike Carson, were still assigned to the Headquarters Troop and wouldn't be going to Paris with us. If they had gotten to go along, everything would have been perfect, I remember thinking.

But as it happened so often, things didn't quite work out the way we thought.

The five of us hitched a ride on an empty supply truck on its way back to Paris. For the first couple of hours, we still had German artillery shells falling not too far from us, but gradually we drew out of range of the bombardment. We could still hear it, though. We could hear the distant rumble of the big guns on both sides of the front line even when we got to Paris. It was night when we got there, and the cannons sounded so much like thunder I glanced at the dark sky, halfway expecting to see the flicker of far-off lightning.

The sky wasn't really very dark. Paris was so lit up, befitting its name, that the glow spread all the way up to the heavens. I wondered why the French didn't turn out some of those lights, so that the German bombers that cruised over the city from time to time would have a harder time finding their target. Reckon it was more a matter of attitude than strategy. The French didn't want to admit how close Germany had come to overrunning them and taking over the whole country. Keeping Paris so brightly lit up was just one way of the French thumbing their noses at the Boche. More power to 'em, I figured.

It was a toss-up what the fellas wanted to find first once we got there: some of that fancy French champagne, or some of those fancy French whores. Or in Big Boy's case, a surrounding of food that didn't come from a ration tin. We walked around the streets for a while, wide-eyed and taking in all the gaiety, until we settled on a place that looked like it might be able to provide everything we wanted. Like a lot of the other buildings, it looked like the owners had tried to cover up every square inch of the outside with flags. Most of them were the French Tricolor and the American Stars and Stripes, but I saw the Union Jack from England and Canada, too. Plenty of folks were going in and out of the place: French soldiers, French civilians, Tommies from the British army, and dozens of Yanks. A little garden dotted with tables sat to one side of the entrance, and it was full too, with waiters scurrying back and forth tending to the customers at the tables. Bright lights above the main doors spelled out the words *CASINO AMERICAIN*.

"Looks like our kind of place," Big Boy said to Roy. "What say we take a *pasear* in yonder and find out?"

Roy looked around at the rest of us and got eager nods from everybody. "All right," he said. "But keep your eyes open. No telling what we might run into in there."

At first glance, all we were going to run into were folks who seemed mighty glad to see us. A fat, white-haired fella in a fancy suit with a red sash across his big belly met us at the door and practically fell all over himself ushering us into the place. Right behind him was a tall, skinny gink who took charge of us and led us across the crowded room, hollering in French and shouldering folks out of the way with a lot more strength than it looked like he should have had. Everybody in the place was laughing and shouting to be heard over the raucous music that came from an orchestra playing on a bandstand on the far side of the room. Everywhere you looked, it was mighty jolly.

The skinny fella brought us to a booth with a bench running around the table in a half circle. He bowed and waved his arms toward it like he'd known we were coming and had saved this spot special for us. Roy nodded our thanks and pressed a couple of francs into his hand. The fella lifted his other hand and started snapping his fingers. I don't know how he expected anybody to hear him over the general uproar in the place, but evidently somebody did, because a slick-haired, red-jacketed waiter popped up out of the crowd.

"*Vive les Americains*!" he greeted us. "What can I bring you?"

"Champagne!" Aaron and Jace said together.

"Whatta ya got in the way o' grub?" asked Big Boy.

"Ah, *la cuisine*!" The waiter looked so excited I half-way expected him to lean over and kiss Big Boy on the cheeks, like I'd seen some of those other French fellas doing from time to time. If he did, I thought, he'd likely wind up getting tossed clear across the room.

Instead, he just spouted a lot of fast talk in French until Big Boy held up a hand to stop him. "Just cut off five o' the biggest steaks you can find, wave 'em in front of a candle, and bring 'em on out here. Fry up a mess o' taters and bring them too. You understand?"

The waiter's head bobbed up and down. "*Oui, oui*. Steak and tay-tairs." He turned and disappeared into the crowd.

"You reckon we'll ever get any food?" Jace asked.

Aaron said, "Even more important, you reckon he'll remember to bring the champagne?"

He brought it, all right, or rather, a couple of other fellas did while our original waiter was carrying out a huge platter of food. The other two had this big bucket on wheels, and it was full of ice. Resting inside it at an angle was the biggest damn bottle of booze I ever did see. They dragged it out of the ice, popped the cork out of its neck so that the champagne inside spilled out the top, then poured the stuff into big crystal glasses for us. By that time, the first waiter had our food on the table, and we were ready to dig in. He had brought a lot more than steak and potatoes. There were several different kinds of vegetables on the plate too, and everything was covered in some sort of sauce that tasted better than it looked. We washed the food down with champagne, and things got pretty damn merry in a hurry.

When we were through eating, Aaron waved our waiter over and said, "Now, Pierre, I know you got to have *mademoiselles* in here somewhere. Bring 'em on!"

The fact of the matter is, there were plenty of women in the room already, and had been ever since we got there. It was just that they were all with other men. I know there are bound to be some ugly French women, but there sure weren't any in the Casino Americain that night. Every one I saw was just as pretty as a picture.

On the way into Paris, I had mulled over the question of how I was going to celebrate this liberty. I'd gotten a good start with all the food and drink, but now I had to decide if I was going to take the next step. Was I going to find me a whore and take her upstairs or not? It wasn't like I had never bedded a soiled dove before.

But I hadn't been with one, or with any woman, since I'd met Janine. We hadn't made each other any promises; there hadn't been time for that. She had no call to expect me not to mess around with any other woman when I'd never done anything more than kiss her a couple of times.

But whether Janine would expect it of me or not, I knew as I sat there in the Casino Americain that it just wouldn't seem right to go romping with a whore.

Some desperado I was, I told myself. I was getting downright respectable.

Once Aaron had called for the *mademoiselles,* it wasn't five minutes before we had a whole covey of quail around us. They crowded around the table with us, and Jace and Aaron and Big Boy didn't waste any time staking their claims and heading up a staircase our friendly waiter pointed out. The gals that were left for Roy and me slid up against us and cooed in our ears and let their hands get downright brazen. Roy kissed the *mademoiselle* next to him, and I was left with my gal looking at me expectantly. When I didn't do anything, she started to pout and said, "You not want to kiss Colette, Americain? Colette is not pretty enough?"

Now, I didn't believe for a second that her name was really Colette. It was probably Bertha or Agnes or something like that. And she knew she was pretty; a look in any mirror would have told her that. She just didn't like the idea that I was acting like I wasn't going to take her upstairs.

I reached down and took her hand and put some coins in it. That cheered her up, and she worked even harder for a few minutes, trying to get me interested. I wanted her, right enough. She was pretty, with lots of curly dark hair, a dress that came way down on her bosom, and hands that really made a fella sit up and pay attention, if you know what I mean.

But every time I started to seriously consider going with her, the image of Janine's face filled my mind, and I remembered what it had been like between us . . . and what it could have been if we'd had the time.

I reckon every man's had a few moments when he sure wishes he wasn't already in love with some woman. That was one of 'em for me.

So I was mighty glad when Roy gave his gal some money, patted her on the bottom, and said to her, "I'll see you later, honey. That's a promise. Right now I've got a hankerin' to play some cards."

"I'll come with you," I said quickly.

The two gals probably hadn't understood everything he said, but they got the idea they were being shooed off. They didn't much like it either. But both of them had been paid, even if it wasn't the going rate, and they hadn't had to do much to earn the coins. They looked at each other and shrugged, and then Roy's gal said to him, "You come and find us when you are ready, no?"

Roy nodded and said, "Damn right."

The whores moved off into the crowd, and Roy and I stood up and stretched. Our waiter hurried up, a worried look on his face. He probably thought the gals had done something wrong and made us mad.

Roy put his mind at ease in a hurry. "You got any games of chance in this place?"

The waiter's eyes widened. "This is a casino, *monsieur.*"

"I know, I'm just joshin' you. Point us toward the poker tables."

"Certainment, monsieur."

The gambling rooms were upstairs too, on the second floor of the place. It was almost as crowded there as it was downstairs. I saw roulette layouts, faro tables, and fancy-dressed gents dealing blackjack and a game I'd picked up from the French troops called baccarat. That wooden box the cards were dealt from didn't look much like a shoe to me, but like I heard a fella say once, it seems like those French folks have a different word for everything. The poker tables were tucked away in an alcove almost like an afterthought. Games were going on at all of them, but I saw a couple of empty chairs at one of the tables. Roy and I started toward it.

Another fella in a fancy suit got between us and the table. *"Excusez moi, monsieurs,"* he said, "but that is a, how you say, private game."

"We've got money," Roy said. "Unless they're playin' for awful high stakes, I reckon we can pay the ante."

The fella still didn't want to let us by. "The game, as you say, is high stakes. High stakes indeed. The owner of the Casino Americain himself is playing."

That sounded like pretty lofty company to me, and if it had been up to me, I would have just let it go and settled for another game. I sort of wanted to try my hand at that baccarat.

But then we heard a burst of laughter, accompanied by some heartfelt cussing, coming from the table where Roy and I had been headed until the casino worker got in our way. Roy leaned to the left to look around him and see what was going on, and I leaned to the right.

What we saw made us both straighten up in a hurry and look at each other.

"You say the owner's playin'," Roy said to the fella in the fancy suit. "Would he happen to be that blond gent

with the little mustache? The one who just raked in that
big pot?''

The fella didn't have to turn around and look. He just
nodded and said, *''Oui.''*

''Now, ain't that interestin','' Roy murmured.

I was thinking the same thing. Because we had seen that
gent before, the man at the poker table who was laughing
and sipping from a glass of champagne with the light from
the chandelier overhead glinting brightly on the diamond
ring he wore. The last time we'd laid eyes on him, the only
time we'd ever seen him until now, had been long months
earlier and half a world away in the foothills on the eastern
slopes of the Sierra Nevada, in a little roadhouse we just
called Harrigan's place.

The owner of the Casino Americain was the crooked
gambler called Ford, the bastard who'd cheated us out of
our loot from the Flat Rock bank job.

TWENTY-TWO

"Much obliged for the advice," Roy said to the Frenchie who had stopped us. "We'll try our luck somewhere else."

The fella waved smoothly to the games in the rest of the room. "Please do. *Bon chance*, gentlemen."

We headed toward one of the roulette wheels. I leaned close to Roy and hissed, "You know who that was?"

"Damn right I do," he said. "I didn't figure we'd ever run into him again. We better find the rest of the boys and let them know."

"They won't take kindly to bein' interrupted right about now."

"I don't care. Luck's dropped that son of a bitch in our laps, and I intend to even the score with him."

I took a deep breath. I couldn't blame Roy for feeling the way he did. The fiasco at Harrigan's place had set the stage for something even worse, the attempted bank robbery in Reno that cost Murph Skinner and the Gunderson boys their lives and the rest of us our freedom. If not for what Ford had done to us, we likely wouldn't even be here in Paris now.

Some folks don't believe in coincidence. They can even be downright nasty about it. As for me, I'm not sure about coincidence.

But I sure as hell believe in Fate, and that's what was staring us in the face.

At the same time, even though I understood how Roy felt, I wasn't sure I wanted to get mixed up in some sort of ruckus. We had come to Paris to enjoy ourselves, not to get in more trouble. I wasn't sure how in the world Ford had wound up in Paris as the owner of a casino, but it didn't matter. There were plenty of other places to gamble and drink and whore around.

"Better not go bustin' in on the boys right now," I told Roy again. It was a delaying tactic, that was all, but at least it would give him some more time to think. "For one thing, that'll likely draw attention to us, and we don't want that."

He stopped and rubbed his jaw in thought for a second. "You're right," he finally said, "and I should have seen it myself. We've got to play this careful-like, so that Ford won't have any warning of what's about to hit him."

I looked at Roy and knew we were in for it. Now that Ford had been delivered up to us, Roy wasn't about to let him off the hook.

We played a little roulette and actually won a few francs. Roy still wanted to play poker, so he waited until a chair opened up at one of the other tables so that he could sit with his back toward Ford. It was pretty likely Ford wouldn't recognize any of us in our uniforms, but Roy didn't want to take a chance and neither did I. I kept my face turned away from Ford as I drifted over to the faro table, feeling the urge to buck the tiger.

I've always been pretty good at faro, and I was quite a few francs richer by the time Jace, Aaron, and Big Boy ambled down the stairs and stopped in the gambling room. They all wore the lazy look of contentment that followed a good bout of slap-and-tickle with a pretty woman. Seeing them looking around, I glanced over at Roy and caught his eye. He had noticed the boys too, and as soon as the hand was over, he cashed in his chips. I did the same, and together we went over to meet the three of them.

"Don't stop gamblin' on our account," Big Boy greeted us. "I might do a little cardplayin' myself."

"Not tonight you won't," Roy told him. "Come on. We're all going back downstairs."

His tone of voice told them that something was up. Without any arguments, they followed Roy and me down the stairs to the first floor. The booth where we had sat before was occupied, but we were able to find places at the long horseshoe-shaped bar that ran around three sides of the room.

"What's up?" Jace asked after the bartender had brought beers for all of us. "Something got you spooked, Roy?"

"Not spooked, just mad," Roy said. "There's a fella here we know."

Big Boy said, "The place is full o' soldiers. Ain't no surprise that we're acquainted with some of 'em."

Roy shook his head. Keeping his voice pitched low enough so the bartender couldn't overhear, he said, "This ain't a soldier I'm talkin' about. It's the fella who owns this place. His name is Ford."

That drew blank looks from the boys. Back at Harrigan's place, they hadn't seen Ford as close as Roy and I had, and they didn't remember him by name. Big Boy put into words the thought they were all thinking. "Who?"

"That crooked gambler from Harrigan's place," Roy said. "The one who stole all our money."

Big Boy frowned. "I recollect him now. But that's crazy, Roy. What would a fella from out West be doin' all the way over here in France?"

"We're here, aren't we?"

"That's different," Aaron said. "We're soldiers. We signed up to come over here."

"Maybe Ford did too. Maybe once he got over here, he decided he didn't like it and deserted. Sounds about like something he'd do."

Roy didn't know it at the time, but he'd hit on something that was pretty close to the truth. We found out later that Ford had had to get out of Nevada in a hurry when some other gents he'd fleeced at the poker table had started making things too hot for him. Joining the army and becoming

one of the troops who were being shipped overseas by the
hundreds of thousands had seemed to him like a pretty good
way of dropping out of sight. But once he'd arrived in
France, he hadn't wasted much time in taking off for the
tall and uncut. With the loot he'd stashed in his gear, he'd
been able to buy into this place, and within a month, his
partner in the casino had died, run over in the street by a
truck that was never found, leaving Ford the sole owner.
Didn't surprise me a bit when I found out about that. Ford
was just up to his old tricks.

For the moment, though, all we knew was that Ford was
here, and we owed him. It was a score Roy intended to
settle, and naturally, there was only one way to do it.

Roy finished off his beer and said, "Let's get out of
here."

During the early days of the American presence in the
war, our troops had stayed in the old Pipincerie Barracks
when they were in Paris, but by this time, there were too
many of us for the barracks to hold. Several hotels had been
taken over by the AEF, so we headed for one of them that
was several blocks away from the casino.

The hour was late, but the streets were still thronged. I
supposed they stayed that way twenty-four hours a day. The
air in Paris was that of a celebration. You couldn't tell from
the way these folks acted that only a few months earlier,
the Boche had been an hour away from the city. Even now,
if the resistance of the Allies was to collapse, the Germans
could have been in Paris in less than a day and a half.

But our lines weren't going to collapse, and to judge
from the way the citizens of Paris were acting, the war was
as good as over. I knew that wasn't true either. There was
still a long, hard, bloody way to go.

Tonight the war was just about the last thing on our
minds. Roy was wrapped up in his plans for settling the
score with Ford. "There's got to be a hell of a lot of money
in a place like that," he muttered as we walked along the
avenue.

I knew where that line of thinking was taking him, and
so did the others. "That loot might as well be ours," Aaron
said.

"Seems fittin'," Big Boy rumbled. "Ford stole our money, so I reckon we can steal his."

"Sounds like a good idea to me," Jace said.

What they were all overlooking was the fact that we'd stolen that money in the first place from the bank in Flat Rock. It wasn't really ours. There was a time when I'd have felt like we'd earned it by virtue of the fact that we'd risked our lives to take it, but my thinking had turned around some over the past months.

Still, I couldn't argue with the fact that Ford had done us dirty. He needed to be taken down a notch or two, and we were just the boys to do it.

We sat up most of the night in one of the hotel rooms, planning how we were going to make Ford rue the day he'd ever crossed the trail of the Tacker Gang. And you know what?

It felt good.

One thing I'd already discovered about the army was the fact that if you didn't mind laying out a little cash, there was always a fella who could get you whatever you wanted, whether it was legal or not. All we had to do was ask around the next morning, and we found the gent we were looking for.

Or rather, he found us, since the meeting had been arranged so that we would get to the rendezvous first. We went to a fancy museum called the Louvre and looked at the paintings for a while before a burly sergeant with a cigar in his mouth sidled up to Roy and asked, "You Tacker?"

"That's right," Roy said.

"Pomerantz," the fella said around the cigar. He didn't offer to shake hands. "I hear you men are in the market for some merchandise."

"We need civilian clothes and some guns that aren't army issue."

"I don't wanna know why, do I?" Pomerantz asked.

"Nope. You sure don't."

Pomerantz took the cigar out of his mouth. "By nature, I ain't the curious type. When do you need the stuff?"

"As soon as possible." We were due back at Saint Baptiste by six o'clock the next day, so we had to hit the casino tonight or not at all. It didn't even strike us as odd that we were planning to hold up the place at gunpoint, but none of us wanted to be AWOL. That seemed like a worse crime to us now.

"I'll see what I can do." Pomerantz gave Roy an address and said, "Be there at five o'clock this afternoon. Got to warn you, though. This is gonna cost you."

"It'll be worth it," Roy said.

That was a long day of waiting. We did some sightseeing, and I knew I was looking at the sorts of things that I'd never see again—the cathedral of Notre Dame, the Eiffel Tower, the Arc de Triomphe. We ate lunch in the prettiest little sidewalk cafe you'd ever want to visit. But all I could think about was what we were about to do. I couldn't decide if I was excited, or worried, or both. Once you'd ridden the outlaw trail, a part of you was always still a desperado, I suppose, and my heart was pounding with the anticipation of pulling another job. At the same time, we'd sworn an oath when we joined the army, and turning outlaw again seemed to go against it.

But it was just this one time, I told myself, and it was for a damned good cause—revenge.

We were at the place where Pomerantz told us to meet him at five o'clock. It was a dingy little bar on a back street, and he was waiting for us. He took us upstairs and gave us the clothes and the guns he had scrounged up someplace. The pistols were short-barreled Colts, .32-caliber, not as powerful as I'd have liked, but they would have to do. The clothes were dark suits and felt hats. Pomerantz named a price for the whole thing, and it took all of us pooling most of our francs to pay him. He folded the bills and pocketed them along with the coins we handed him, then said, "Let me tell you a few things about the Casino Americain."

"Where?" Roy said.

Pomerantz shook his head. "Don't even try to bullshit me, buddy. I know that's where you went last night. I figure you're planning on robbing the joint. That's your business, not mine. But seeing as you're fellow Americans, I thought I could fill you in on a few things that might come in handy."

"I ain't admittin' nothin' . . . but I'm listenin'."

"Good," said Pomerantz, "because I'd like to see that bastard Ford get the wind knocked out of his sails. I had a good business arrangement with the Frenchie who owned that place before Ford came along. I still think there was something fishy about the way Ford got his hands on the whole place." Pomerantz told us then about how Ford had deserted and gotten into the casino business, then waved his cigar and said, "What you're going to have to do is get into Ford's office. That's where the safe is. Better do it on the q.t., though, because he's got at least a dozen Apaches working for him."

"Apaches?" Jace asked in surprise. "What're redskins doin' here in Paris?"

Pomerantz snorted and shook his head. "Not that kind of Apaches, Young Wild West. French thugs. Handy with a knife, and they'd as soon gut you as look at you. Anyway, if I was going to rob that joint, I'd try to get my hands on Ford himself and make him open the safe. Then he'd be my ticket out of there."

"If you don't like Ford, why don't you just turn him in to the army?" Roy asked. "He's a deserter."

"Nah, a firing squad's too good for him." An ugly grin spread across Pomerantz's face. "I'd rather see him really hurt. You guys looting that safe will be a lot more painful to him than if he was shot."

I could believe that. Some fellas, and Ford struck me as one of them, loved money more than they loved life itself. Was a time, and I'm ashamed to admit it, when I was almost the same way myself. But I'd learned my lesson.

And before the night was over, Ford was going to learn his.

TWENTY-THREE

The casino was just as busy that night as it had been the night before. We sauntered in wearing our civilian clothes, with those felt hats pulled down jaunty-like in front of our faces. The same fat man who'd greeted us so eagerly was there again, and he ushered us in with the same enthusiastic arm-waving and acted like he'd never seen us before. This time, we bypassed the first floor and headed straight for the gambling layout on the second floor. No one tried to stop us, and we weren't searched for weapons.

We had left our uniforms bundled up in an old jalopy parked down the street. Roy had rented the car for the evening with what was left of our cash except for five francs. If he and I hadn't won some money the night before, we wouldn't have had enough to make our preparations for this job.

Now that Pomerantz had tipped us off, I recognized the guards stationed around the place. Probably some of the fellas in fancy suits who were so obvious could handle themselves all right, but the real muscle belonged to the men who leaned casually against the walls here and there. They had dark, scowling faces and wore tight, short-sleeved shirts and those dinky little caps the French called berets.

Rather than Indians, they reminded me of Mexes I'd seen in some of the border towns along the Rio Grande, fellas who were always ready for trouble, whose dark eyes didn't miss anything that was going on. Getting to Ford with them around was going to be tricky.

Roy wasn't just about to back out, though, not after coming this far. He had one coin left, so he played it on the roulette wheel. His number came up, and the fella running the wheel pushed a pile of chips over to him. Roy said to let it ride and the fella arched an eyebrow at him, then spun the wheel again. The same number came up. A murmur came from the folks standing around watching.

Roy would have really drawn some attention if he'd let his winnings ride again, but that wasn't what we wanted right then. Instead he gathered up the chips and split them between us, so that we could all gamble. Pretty soon the little ripple his daring play had caused was forgotten.

All of us were looking for Ford. We scattered out through the big room and kept our eyes peeled for him. It occurred to me that he might not even be here tonight, in which case all our plans were likely for nothing. According to Pomerantz, Ford was the only one we could count on being able to open the safe. Some of his lieutenants probably knew the combination too, but we wouldn't have any way of knowing which ones.

I worried for nothing. We had been there about an hour when Ford showed up. I happened to be looking toward a narrow door when it opened and he strolled through into the main room of the casino. During the moment the door was open, I saw a hallway beyond it. That had to be where the office was located.

There was a bar on the far side of the room from that door, keeping the gamblers well supplied with liquor. Ford sauntered toward it. I looked around for Roy, and when I spotted him, he was already looking at Ford. I didn't have to tip him off, nor any of the other boys either. All of us had already noticed Ford, Jace and Aaron and Big Boy recognizing him from Harrigan's place now that they knew to look for him. I wondered how we were going to get close enough to him to grab him without his men noticing.

That was when Fate took a hand again, which I suppose is fitting enough, since that was what had brought us and Ford to the same place to start with. Big Boy was glancing over his shoulder at Ford while he played blackjack, and without thinking about what he was doing, he tapped his finger on his cards. The dealer hit him again, and a pleased noise from the other folks around the table made Big Boy pay attention to what had happened. He'd just hit twenty-one, and the dealer went bust trying to match him. The stakes were sizable, so Big Boy raked in a pile of chips.

That was the start of a streak, and before you knew it, Big Boy had a lot of winnings in front of him. Folks were drifting over to the blackjack table from all around the room, so it didn't arouse any suspicions when Roy and Jace and Aaron and I joined the crowd. Everybody was rooting for Big Boy, of course. No gambler likes to see the house win.

"Looks like I'm a lucky fella tonight," Big Boy said proudly as the pile of chips mounted. And luck was all it was too, blind luck. We certainly hadn't planned things this way.

Roy was standing beside me. I felt him stiffen suddenly, and when I looked past him, I saw what had made him react that way. Ford had come up to the table, and lo and behold if he didn't reach up and clap a hand on Big Boy's shoulder. "Well, my friend, it looks as if the goddess of fortune is favoring you tonight," he said heartily.

Give Big Boy credit. I might have been thrown for a loop, but not him. He just grinned at Ford and said, "Yeah, it appears you're right."

That was true in more ways than Ford knew, because I was watching him pretty close, and I could tell he didn't have a clue who we were. I reckon that hurt almost as much as anything else. What he'd done to us back in Nevada was so unimportant to him that he'd forgotten all about us.

We'd remind him soon enough, I told myself.

"Why don't you come have a drink with me?" Ford asked. "I always like to visit with the big winners."

"Well . . . sure. I suppose I could do that," Big Boy said
as he gathered up his winnings. "But I've got some friends
with me. . . ."

Ford slapped him on the back again. "Bring them along.
The more the merrier, as they say."

I glanced at Roy. A fella would have to be a fool to
pass up such an opportunity, and none of us were fools.
He gave a tiny nod, and we fell in behind Big Boy as Ford
led him toward that narrow door.

Big Boy looked back at the bar on the other side of the
room. "I thought we were goin' to get a drink," he said.

"We are," Ford told him, "but not the swill my men
serve at the bar. No, I've got a bottle of fine cognac back
in my office that has our names written on it. By the way,
what is your name, friend?"

Big Boy thought fast. I knew he hadn't expected to have
to come up with a phony name tonight, but he didn't want
to give Ford his real one. With a lack of hesitation that I
couldn't do anything but admire, he said, "Parker. George
Leroy Parker."

Well, of course, that was Butch Cassidy's real name, but
Ford didn't seem to know that. He said, "Pleased to meet
you, George. I'm Chuck. This is my casino."

Big Boy looked around. "Mighty nice place. You must
be proud of it."

"Oh, I am, I am." We reached the door, and Ford
opened it for Big Boy and stepped back. "After you, gentlemen," he said to the rest of us.

I was a little leery of having Ford at our backs, but he
didn't seem to be up to any tricks. I had figured out what
he was doing: The dealer at the blackjack table must have
passed him some sort of signal that Big Boy was winning
too much. By steering Big Boy away from the table with
the offer of a drink, Ford had interrupted that winning
streak. I figured that was the only reason he was being so
hospitable.

Turned out I was wrong. Ford had more on his mind
than that.

No sooner had he shut the door into the gambling room behind him than the door at the other end of the hall opened. A couple of those Apaches and two brawny fellas in suits stepped out of the office. The Apaches had knives in their hands. Behind me, I heard Ford move quickly, and he said, "That's far enough. I'll have that money back now, Parker."

He still didn't know who Big Boy really was. He would have pulled this trick on anybody who was lucky enough to win a big chunk of money. Then the fella would wind up in an alley with a lump on his head, if he was really lucky. If he wasn't, one of those Apaches would slip a shiv between his ribs.

But tonight, Ford had caught more than he bargained for in his trap.

I was the closest to him, so I twisted and threw myself toward him. I saw the gun in his hand, and grabbed his wrist before he could do anything with it. As I shoved his gun hand up with my left, I buried my right in his belly.

That hallway was too narrow for much fighting. Ford and I bumped hard against the wall as we wrestled over the gun. While we were doing that, Big Boy charged those Apaches. They weren't expecting that. He got his hands on them before they could bring their blades into play and cracked their heads together. They dropped the knives and slumped to the floor. The two fellas in suits tried to reach under their coats for their guns, but Jace and Aaron were faster. They had their pistols out and leveled at those two boys in the blink of an eye.

Meanwhile, Roy had come to help me. He reached over my shoulder and rapped the short barrel of his gun against the side of Ford's head. Ford grunted and sagged, and his grip on his gun loosened enough for me to jerk it away from him. Roy got his free hand around Ford's neck and shoved him up against the wall, bouncing his head painfully against the wood. He pushed the muzzle of the .32 against Ford's nose.

"You damn tinhorn," Roy said in a low voice. "Still up to your tricks, ain't you?"

Ford couldn't do anything but gag with Roy's hand so tight around his throat. He was starting to turn purple.

"You were going to turn your bully boys loose on us, weren't you?" Roy went on. "You can't even let a man win fair and square. When he does, you murder him and steal the money back."

Ford made some more strangled noises.

"Well, you're not goin' to get away with it this time. You didn't know who you were tryin' to lead like lambs to the slaughter. You didn't figure on the Tacker Gang."

I thought I saw a little recognition mixed in with the growing desperation in Ford's eyes then. He recalled the name, if nothing else about us.

"That's right," Roy said. "We're here for our money, you son of a bitch. The money you stole from us back in Nevada."

I grimaced. I'd just as soon Roy hadn't told Ford who we really were. The idea was to loot the safe as civilians, then go back to Saint Baptiste as soldiers. But Roy was so carried away with settling the score with Ford that he wanted the gambler to know who was getting the best of him. I hoped the satisfaction would be worth it. I hoped we wouldn't wind up in prison—or in front of a firing squad—because of it.

Jace and Aaron had gotten the other two men to take their guns out careful-like, put them on the floor, and kick them away. They pushed those two gents back into the office at gunpoint, and Roy hauled Ford away from the wall and shoved him after them. Ford stumbled over the unconscious Apaches. Big Boy had gathered up their fallen knives.

We all crowded into the office, and Big Boy shut the door after he'd dragged the Apaches inside. Tucked into one corner of the room was a big iron safe like the ones we'd seen in countless banks back in the States. Roy pointed at the safe and said to Ford, "Open it."

Ford was rubbing his throat where Roy had had such a tight grip on it. He rasped, "Go fuck yourself."

Roy slashed that .32 across his face.

I never did hold with pistol-whipping people. That seemed like too much of a brutal, ugly thing to do. But right then Roy was in an ugly mood. "Open it," he said again.

Ford had staggered against the desk when Roy hit him. He straightened and wiped the back of his right hand across his cheek where the gunsight had opened up a gash. Blood welled from it and smeared his face and hand.

"No," he said.

Roy eared back the hammer of the pistol and pointed it at the bridge of Ford's nose. "I'll kill you. Don't think for a second I won't."

Ford was crooked as a dog's hind leg, but he had sand. He just sneered and said, "Go ahead, cowboy. Pull the trigger. Then you'll never get into that safe. Thirty seconds after that gun goes off, the rest of my men will be back here, and they'll carve your balls off and make you eat them."

Well, we'd gotten ourselves into a nice tight little corner. Ford was right—we needed him to open the safe. We couldn't just dynamite it like we'd been forced to do on some of our other jobs.

Roy wasn't going to give up, though. He said to me, "Cover him," and as I lined my pistol on Ford, Roy turned to Big Boy and said, "Give me one of those knives."

Big Boy handed over one of the blades and asked, "What are you goin' to do?"

Roy looked at Ford's two men, who were backed up against the wall under the guns of Jace and Aaron. The two Apaches were still out cold in a heap on the floor.

Roy said, "Let's just say Ford gave me an idea with that crack about carvin' off somebody's balls." He started toward Ford's henchmen.

They didn't have as much nerve as their boss. I saw both of them go pale. Ford said quickly, "They don't know the combination to the safe. You might as well kill them."

There was only one reason Ford would say such a thing. At least one of them *did* know the combination. Roy grinned at them, but his eyes were as cold as a blue norther.

Suddenly, Ford lunged away from the desk, throwing up his left hand. Light from the ceiling fixture reflected on something in his fingers. It was a letter opener, I saw, and I knew he must have snatched it up and hidden it in his hand when he stumbled against the desk. He aimed it straight at Roy's back.

I clouted him over the head with the pistol as hard as I could.

Ford went down. The other two gents made to jump away from the wall in the confusion. Big Boy grabbed one of them by the wrist and slammed it up against the wall. With his other hand he drove the knife he still held all the way through the gent's forearm and into the wood, pinning it there. The guy would have let out a screech of pain, only Big Boy clapped a hand over his mouth before the sound could come out. The fella went limp, held upright by Big Boy's hand and the knife through his arm.

The other man threw his hands up again, backed hard against the wall, and said mighty quick-like, "I'll open the safe for you! God, you people are crazy!"

Roy put the tip of the other knife against the man's throat. "Mister, you don't know the half of it."

After that, everything went smooth for a few minutes. The fella opened the safe, just like he'd promised to do, and we cleaned it out. I couldn't keep track of how much money was in there, but it was a sizable amount. We shoveled it into a couple of canvas bags Jace found in Ford's desk. Ford looked to me like he was still out cold. Thin lines of blood trickled from his ears and his nose.

"Is there a back way out of here?" Roy asked the one fella who was still conscious. The other gent had passed out from the pain of having his arm stuck to the wall with a knife. Roy added, "Don't even think about lyin' to me, mister."

"I won't," the man said fervently. "There's another door there in the hall . . . you can't see it, it's hidden, but I can open it for you. The passageway on the other side of it leads right out into the alley."

Roy cocked his head and looked at the fella. "You're an American, aren't you?"

"Yeah, me and Phil both are." The man nodded toward his pard hanging on the wall. "We met Ford on the troop ship coming over here, and he talked us into deserting with him."

"Bad mistake," Roy said. He shoved the fella toward the door. "Let's go."

We went out into the hall. Like the man had said, there was a hidden door that looked like more of the same paneling as the rest of the wall. He pressed some sort of latch and swung the door open, and that was when Ford stumbled out of the office, his face all bloody, and yelled, "Help! Help! Kill the bastards!" He jerked up the gun in his hand and started firing.

The first bullet caught Ford's own henchman in the throat and spun him around. Blood fountained from the wound and sprayed across the fancy paneling. The fella tumbled toward me, and I grabbed him and threw him out of the way.

Roy's gun cracked, and Ford staggered back. He must have gotten the gun from his desk, but it hadn't done him much good. All he'd managed to do was kill his own man and catch a slug in the chest in return. He dropped the gun, pawed at the air, and fell again. This time, I knew, he wouldn't be getting up.

But the shots and the yelling had alerted the guards in the gambling room, and the door to it burst open. Apaches and fancy-suited gunmen poured through the opening as we ducked through the hidden door and ran down a dark corridor. I sure as hell hoped the door at the far end wasn't locked.

It wasn't. We spilled out into an alley as guns started to bang behind us. I wished I had one of Lieutenant Bissell's machine guns right about then. One of those babies would have mowed down Ford's men without any trouble. As it was, we had to run like the dickens and throw a few wild shots behind us in an effort to keep the Apaches from pursuing us too closely.

Roy was leading the way, and I hoped he knew where he was going. Finding your way around the mountain trails of the high country was one thing; running in pitch blackness through unfamiliar Parisian alleys was another. But after a minute we came to a lighted street, and Roy called, "This way!"

As usual, we went where he followed, and as usual, he was right.

We turned onto a side street, and there was the rented jalopy, just waiting for us. I never saw a prettier automobile in my life. The rest of us piled in while Roy hit the starter and Big Boy turned the crank. The motor grumbled and complained, and I had time to ask myself what would happen if it didn't start. Then it caught with a roar, and Big Boy swung up onto the running board while Roy stomped the foot feed.

Ford's boys slung a few more shots at us, but none of them came close. Roy whipped that French flivver around a corner, and we were gone into the night, richer in both money and the knowledge that Ford had finally gotten what was coming to him.

The supply truck came up behind us as we walked along a country lane the next morning, heading back toward the front lines. We were dressed in our uniforms again and had our duffel bags slung over our shoulders. Down in the bottom of those bags were stacks and stacks of francs. I would have preferred good old American greenbacks, but you take what you can get, I reckon.

We had pushed the jalopy off into an abandoned quarry before dawn and had been hoofing it ever since. The civilian clothes and the guns had gone into the brackish water at the bottom of the quarry along with the car. Now there was nothing but the stolen money to connect us with the robbery of the Casino Americain and all the shooting that had gone along with it.

Roy stepped out into the middle of the lane and waved his arm, flagging down the supply truck. A couple of doughboys looked out curiously from the cab. The driver asked, "What in blazes are you fellas doing out here?"

"We've been on liberty in Paris," Roy told them. "Missed our ride back to the front. Reckon we could hitch a lift from you boys?"

The driver grinned. "If you don't mind riding on some lumpy bags of potatoes. That's what we're carrying."

Big Boy said, "After last night, them bags o' taters are goin' to feel like feather beds, fellas."

That got a laugh from both of the doughboys. They figured we'd gone on a toot in Paris and were hung over. It was fine with us that they thought that way. We threw our duffel bags in the back of the truck and climbed up after them.

By late afternoon, we were almost back to Saint Baptiste. I had dozed quite a bit along the way, even though those potatoes weren't nearly as comfortable as feather beds. I was sitting up and rubbing my eyes when Big Boy said, "Fellas, I been thinkin'."

"That's a bad sign," Aaron said with a grin.

"No, I mean it," Big Boy said, and we could all tell he was serious.

"Somethin' botherin' you, fella?" Roy asked.

Big Boy scratched his head. "I been thinkin' about all that money." His voice was pitched low enough so that the doughboys up in the cab couldn't hear us over the rumble of the engine. "What're we goin' to spend it on out here in the middle of a war?"

It was a good question, and none of us had an answer. We hadn't thought that far ahead. We'd just wanted to get back at Ford for what he'd done to us in Nevada.

"And it ain't even American money," Big Boy went on. "Somehow, stealin' French money just ain't the same."

"What're you sayin'?" Aaron asked. "You think we ought to take it back to the casino?" His laughter showed how ridiculous he thought that idea was, and the rest of us agreed with him.

"Not hardly." Big Boy looked around at us. "I think we ought to give it to them kids in Saint Baptiste."

"Kids!" Aaron yelped. "You want to give a fortune away to some ragtag kids?"

"Well, to their folks, really, but they could use the money to help feed those littl'uns. You know how much everything costs now. Hell, we don't have to worry about goin' hungry, 'cause the army's goin' to feed us. But they do. That money could keep some of 'em from starvin' to death.''

Jace and Aaron were fixing to argue with him, and I was pretty much thrown for a loop myself. But Roy thought about it for a minute and then said, "That's a good idea, Big Boy. It'd put that money to good use. The folks in Saint Baptiste would have to agree never to say where they got it, though.''

"They'd go along with that," Big Boy declared. "I've gotten to know some of 'em, what with bein' friends with the kids and all. They'd agree to whatever we asked of 'em, Roy.''

"It's settled then," Roy said, and the look he gave me and Jace and Aaron told us that he meant it. He had gotten what he wanted out of the deal. When you come right down to it, I guess we had too. I had already started to wonder about what I'd do with my share. Using it to help feed a bunch of hungry kids seemed to be as good a thing as any.

Aaron grumbled about it a little, but he went along with the idea too, and by the time we made it to Saint Baptiste, all of us were pretty happy about the whole thing. We'd all spent a lot of our lives not caring much about other folks. It would feel good to do something just because it was right.

We wound up not getting to enjoy the feeling for very long, though. As soon as that truck came to a stop in front of the makeshift kitchen and we swung down from the back, we saw Hank Ball coming out of the headquarters building across the street. We started toward him, all grins and laughter, then stopped and fell silent as he looked up at us. His eyes were as hollow and dark as a pair of abandoned wells.

"Good Lord, Hank," Roy said. "What happened?"

Hank just looked at us and said in a flat voice, "The Boche got Pike last night."

TWENTY-FOUR

We couldn't hardly believe that Pike Carson was dead, but we knew Hank wouldn't josh about something like that. Pike was his best friend in the world. And he had proved it with his last act on this earth.

"We were just walkin' along the street," Hank told us as we sat solemnly around a table in the mess hall. "The Boche artillery opened up on the town, like they do about half the time, and we headed for the nearest bunker. But before we could get there, a shell hit the building we were goin' past, and the whole front wall started to come down on us. Pike grabbed hold of my arm and slung me out ahead of him, so that the worst of the debris fell clear of me. It got him, though." Hank took a deep, shaky breath. "Crushed him to death. He never had a chance."

Roy shook his head. "That's mighty tough, Hank. Mighty tough."

Hank swallowed hard and looked around at us and said, "And the worst of it is, I know Pike would have wanted to go in the saddle. He loved to ride more'n anybody I ever saw. Always said that a job you can't do from horseback is a job that ain't worth doin'."

I thought for a minute Hank was going to cry, and none of us wanted that. We wouldn't have known what to do if he had. But he tightened his jaw and repeated what Roy had just said to him. "Yeah, it's mighty tough."

"Come on back to the barracks with us," Big Boy said. "I think I know where I can lay my paws on a bottle of that cognac stuff." He glanced around at the rest of us and saw that we were all in agreement. We could use a little of our loot to buy the cognac. That would still leave plenty of francs for the children of Saint Baptiste.

"French booze is awful expensive," Hank said.

"Don't you worry about that," Big Boy told him, but didn't say any more. We didn't want Hank to know what had gone on in Paris.

We got the cognac, and we all got drunk. Hank told us more stories about how he and Pike had worked together in Hollywood in the moving pictures, and some of the yarns got pretty wild and racy before the night was over. According to Hank, some of those actresses were mighty fond of cowboys, even if they were only riding extras and stuntmen. By the time he was through, Hank was laughing again as he recalled those times, and it was good to hear. We all hoped that maybe remembering the good things would help him get over Pike's death.

But after that, Hank Ball was never the same. Never.

We were on the move that summer of '18. Jace and Aaron went back to their air service squadron, of course, and kept shooting down those German planes. As for me and Roy and Big Boy, our unit pulled out of Saint Baptiste and headed east . . . but not before we were able to slip those stolen francs to several of the families in the village, who passed on some of the money to other families. The mayor himself came to thank us, and we had to shoo him away so that nobody would get suspicious of us. I think he understood.

The Boche were retreating. Their big push had ended at the Marne in Chateau-Thierry, where they had been unable to break the back of the combined French, British, and

American resistance. They had taken their best shot, and it had failed. Now they were falling back, and we were pushing ahead.

With the Germans on the run, their artillery wasn't nearly as effective, and somebody higher up in the chain of the Allied command decided that we didn't need to send messages by horseback anymore. Our telephone and telegraph lines were more secure than they had been since the war started. So that sort of put me and Roy and Big Boy out of a job, and since the army couldn't stand for that, they took us out of the cavalry and put us where they could use us.

The trenches.

I'd heard about trench warfare ever since before we'd shipped out from the States, and that summer I got to know it first-hand. It's about the most miserable way of fighting I ever saw. Anybody who talks about the glory of war never spent any time huddled in a muddy ditch with bullets whizzing by about four inches over his head while trying to breathe air thick with the stench of dead bodies and mustard gas. We'd stay in the trenches for three or four days at a time, the Germans in their own positions a couple of hundred yards east. Then we'd charge over the barbed-wire-littered hell of No Man's Land, and the Germans who weren't killed in the attack would pull back a few hundred more yards, and we'd settle down in the trenches we'd just captured, and then a few days later we'd do the whole damned thing over again.

Sometimes, when I was crouched there in the stinking mud with rats running over my boots, I'd hear the engines of planes and look up and see them fly over, and I envied those pilots like Jace and Aaron. Sure, they were up there without much protection in those crates, but at least they could breathe clean air for a little while.

Like I said, it's a miserable way to fight a war.

By the middle of September, we were closing in on the town of Apremont. For the moment, the front lines had stopped shifting around, but within a day or two, the orders for another advance would come, and it would be up and

over the top for us again. In the meantime, Roy and Big
Boy and I found the driest spot in the trench that we could.
Some drizzle had blown through earlier in the morning, but
now the sky was just overcast. We sat down on some empty
ammunition boxes to enjoy our lunch. We each had a bis-
cuit and a hunk of cheese and a piece of some sort of meat.
None of us were over-curious where the meat had come
from.

"Look there," Big Boy said suddenly. "Ain't that
Hank?"

Sure enough, Hank Ball was coming toward us along
the bottom of the trench. There were boards to walk on,
but they sunk down in the mud so that they didn't help
much. Hank's boots made a sucking sound with every step
he took.

Over the summer Hank had grown thinner and thinner,
until he was just a shadow of the fella he had once been.
I never saw him smile anymore—not that there was a whole
lot for any of us doughboys to smile about—and the last
time I'd heard him laugh was that night when we all got
drunk and he reminisced about Pike. All Hank wanted to
do was kill Germans, and he begrudged the time taken by
anything else, like eating and sleeping.

"Howdy, Hank," Big Boy greeted him. "How you
doin'?"

Well, anybody with two eyes could see that Hank wasn't
doing worth a damn, but none of us had given up on him.
We hoped he would pull out of the sinkhole that had hold
of him. But it was starting to look like that wasn't going
to happen.

"I heard we're not movin' up again for a while," Hank
said. "The big push is goin' to be up the line at Saint
Mihiel."

Big Boy grinned. "Well, that's sure enough fine with
me. The way we've been goin', I thought we was goin' to
have to chase them Boche all the way back to Berlin. Let
some other fellas do the chasin' for a change."

Hank shook his head and said, "No, that's not right. If
we just dig in and wait, we won't get to kill any more of
those bastards."

"Maybe not right now," Roy said, "but our turn'll come again soon enough, you can count on that. Me, I won't mind goin' a day or two without being shot at—or havin' to shoot at somebody else."

"That's just not right," Hank said again. "We're here to kill the Boche, like they killed Pike."

Roy and Big Boy and I looked at each other. Hank's voice was flat and soft, and we could hardly make out some of his words. His jaw was slack, and his eyes were wide. I've seen fellas look like that when they were hopped up on something, but I knew that wasn't what was wrong with Hank. The problem with him was that he just had too much hate for the Germans inside him. It wasn't a war anymore to him. It was a personal fight.

I could understand that. It had been that way between the five of us and Ford, and we had risked our lives to put things right. That had been a small grudge, though. We hated one man. Hank Ball hated a whole country and everybody in it.

Roy held out the hunk of cheese from his ration tin toward Hank. "Sit down and have some lunch," he said. "Might as well enjoy the fact that it ain't rainin'."

Hank shook his head. "No, I've got something to do."

"Well, come back by here when you're through," Big Boy told him. "We're always glad to see you, Hank."

Again, he shook his head, and said, "I won't be back."

I didn't like the sound of that, and neither did Roy or Big Boy. We put our rations down and started to stand up as Hank turned toward the wall of the trench. "Hank, hold on a minute," Roy said.

But Hank wasn't paying any attention. He slung his rifle on his back and started to clamber up out of that trench.

Roy jumped toward him and reached out to grab his arm. "Hold on there, Hank! Where do you think you're goin'? Our orders are to stay put."

Hank didn't say anything, didn't even turn around to face Roy. He just drove his elbow back into Roy's chest, breaking the hold on his arm and knocking Roy into Big Boy.

"Hank, wait!" I yelled as he started to scramble up, using the footholds and handholds carved into the side of the trench. I grabbed at him too, but missed. He threw himself over the top, and his boots were the last we saw of him as he leaped out of the trench.

"Damn it!" Roy said. "We'd better get him back down here!" He started to climb up after Hank.

I had expected the German machine guns on the other side of No Man's Land to open up on Hank as soon as his helmet popped into sight. The Boche guns were quiet, though, and I hoped the gunners were asleep on the job. Maybe there would be time for us to catch up to Hank and drag him back down in the trench. Big Boy and I started up after Roy.

I don't reckon it ever even occurred to us to let Roy go by himself.

I was holding my breath as we came out of the trench. This wasn't the first time I'd gone charging across No Man's Land, but every time before, the Germans had been softened up first by an artillery barrage. Now there was nothing to keep them from shooting us to doll rags, except maybe the sheer surprise they must have felt when they saw us coming.

Hank was out in front, about twenty yards ahead of us. He was weaving through the rolls of barbed wire and the craters where shells had exploded, and the obstacles he couldn't avoid he jumped over. I kept expecting him to get hung up in the razor-sharp stuff and fall, but somehow he managed to stay on his feet. As he ran, he unslung his Springfield and pointed it toward the German lines. With a yell, he started shooting.

That got the attention of the Boche defenders, right enough. A machine gun opened up, and I saw dirt kicked high in the air by the bullets slamming into the ground near Hank's feet. He kept going, not seeming to notice.

Being the youngest and the fastest, naturally I pulled out ahead of Roy and Big Boy. Hank had slowed down when he started firing his rifle at the Germans. I thought maybe I could catch up to him, tackle him from behind, and knock him down. Then we'd have to crawl back to our trench and hope the Germans didn't find the range before we got there.

It didn't work out that way. I was about halfway between Hank in front of me and Roy and Big Boy behind me when something slapped at my left side. It wasn't much of an impact, but it was enough to throw me off stride. I let out a yell as I lost my balance and tumbled down, barely avoiding a tangle of barbed wire.

Hank looked back when he heard me cry out, and he must've thought I was wounded worse than I was. He screamed in rage and took off toward the German lines again, maddened that he had lost another friend. I looked up from where I had fallen in time to see him stop short as a burst of machine-gun fire punched into his body. He fell over backward, his uniform already dark with blood.

"Drew!" Roy yelled behind me. He and Big Boy were coming on.

I raised up enough to wave my arm at them. "Get back!" I shouted. "Get back in the trench! I'm all right!" Then I ducked back down with my face in the dirt, because bullets were starting to sing past my ears.

I found out later that Roy had started to come on after me anyway, but Big Boy grabbed his arm and slung him back toward the trench. He had seen what I had already figured out. The place I had fallen was a little depression in the ground, and as long as I kept my head down, the German machine guns probably wouldn't be able to draw a bead on me. Those guns could only be lowered a certain amount on their emplacements. If the overcast stayed in place when night fell, it would be dark enough so that I could crawl back to our lines without the Boche seeing me.

So Big Boy did the smart thing: He dragged Roy out of the line of fire and both of them went diving back into the trench, leaving me and Hank sprawled there among the shell holes and barbed wire of No Man's Land.

That was fine with me. I didn't want anything happening to Roy and Big Boy. It was bad enough we'd already lost Hank.

I was breathing hard and my heart was going a mile a minute in my chest. I figured the first thing I ought to do was find out how bad I was hurt. I was lying facedown, and I couldn't get my hand over to my side where I'd been hit. I waited until there was a lull in the machine-gun fire coming from the Germans, then rolled over as quick as I could, being careful to still stay in the little depression in the ground. The movement brought more fire, which I'd expected. It seemed like I could see the bullets themselves, flying through the air about six inches above my face, but I reckon that was just my imagination.

Now I could reach my left side by carefully sliding my right arm over my belly. My fingers found the bullet-torn, blood-wet spot on my uniform and probed underneath it. The wound hadn't hurt much at first, but now it was starting to sting pretty good. I found a shallow gash a few inches long where a slug had plowed a furrow in my side, but that was all. I breathed easier after that. I could live without such a small chunk of meat, and it wasn't likely I'd bleed to death from a wound like that. I still had to worry about blood poisoning, but I'd deal with that after I got out of No Man's Land. I was more sure than ever now that if I could hold out until nightfall, I'd be able to get back to the Allied lines.

"Drew!" That was Roy's voice, coming from the trench. "You all right out there, Drew!"

"Yeah!" I called back over the continuing chatter of machine-gun fire. "I'm aces, Roy! Just stay there, and I'll see you later!"

Big Boy shouted, "What about Hank?"

"He was hit bad! I think he must be a goner!"

Only he wasn't, as I discovered when the guns fell silent again a little while later. After all the hellish noise they'd been making, the silence seemed to ring and echo, and then suddenly in the middle of it I heard a sound I'll never forget.

It was a faint, bubbly rasping, and I knew it was the sound of Hank trying to draw breath into his bullet-torn lungs.

"Roy!" I called. "Hank's still alive!"

"Stay there, Drew!" Roy told me without hesitation. "You can't get to him!"

"I got to try!" I shifted a little as I said that, and as I did a bullet whined through the wire right next to me. I let myself down flat on my back again and started to cuss. If I moved, the Germans would not only nominate me but more than likely elect me. I couldn't get to Hank. I couldn't do anything but lay there and listen to those machine-gun bullets searching for me.

Even if I'd been able to reach Hank, there probably wouldn't have been a thing in the world I'd be able to do for him. I knew he'd been hit five or six times, and it was a miracle he was still alive.

Only, miracle might not be the right word. Usually a miracle is a good thing, and Hank would have been better off if that burst of fire had killed him right off the bat. He let out a gut-wrenching moan from time to time, and I hoped like blazes he was unconscious.

Roy and Big Boy probably heard his cries too, and I reckon the sound ate at them just like it did me. But none of us could do a damned thing but wait.

Then things got worse. Along toward the middle of the afternoon, the clouds started to break, and the sun began peeking through the grayness. Shafts of light slanted down bright and hot on the shattered land where I lay.

I squinted my eyes against the glare, and beads of sweat popped out on my forehead. When they rolled into my eyes, all I could do was blink. I couldn't raise my head or lift my arm to wipe them away.

I could stand being uncomfortable. The bad thing about the sun coming out was that once night fell, the moon and the stars would be out too. There would be enough light for the Boche gunners to aim at me if I tried to make a run for the trench or even if I tried to crawl. That meant I was still stuck right where I was.

The sun dropped slowly toward my feet, and finally got down low enough so that I couldn't see it anymore. That was a little relief. It didn't last long, because Roy called,

"As soon as it's dark, Drew, we're comin' to get you."

"No!" I yelled back. "It won't be dark enough, Roy, you know that! Stay where you are, damn it!"

"Hold on there! Who's the leader of this gang anyway? I give the orders around here, old son!"

"Blast it, Roy! I don't want you gettin' killed for no reason. I'm all right out here, I swear it!"

I hoped that Big Boy would talk some sense into him. Roy would be throwing away his life to come up out of the trench now. The Germans knew Hank and I were lying out there, don't think for a minute they didn't. Every time they stopped shooting, I figured they were trying to lure Roy and Big Boy out of the trench in hopes of retrieving us.

The sun set and the shadows gathered, and I watched the stars wink into being high in the heavens. Back home, I'd spent many a night hour lying in my bedroll, looking up at the stars, and they were as pretty here in France as they were in Texas or Nevada. Somehow, though, they were different, and I found that I missed those Western stars. I wondered if I would ever see them again.

My side hurt like the dickens, but I forgot about that when the German guns stopped again and I realized I couldn't hear Hank breathing or groaning anymore. I closed my eyes for a minute and hoped he'd finally found peace.

"All right, Drew!" Roy called. "I'm comin' to get you before the moon comes up!"

"No! There's too many stars—"

And then I heard a *whump!* and a smaller pop, and a new star blossomed into life above me. It was a flare fired from the German lines, and it cast a harsh, garish white light all over that section of No Man's Land as it drifted back down to earth. More guns than ever before opened up, and I couldn't help but raise my head to see what was happening. I saw Roy and Big Boy go diving back into the trench, and a wind stirred the hair on my head. I knew that breeze had been a bullet, so I dropped my head back down.

The Germans had been too quick on the trigger. If they'd waited another thirty seconds to fire that flare, Roy and Big

Boy would have been too far away from the trench to reach it when the shooting started.

The Germans kept that up for a while, shooting flares into the air like fireworks on the Fourth of July. They didn't stop until the moon rose. It was nearly full, and it lit up that battleground almost as well as the flares.

Well, I'd stick a while longer, looked like, I told myself. My mouth was bone dry and my head hurt, but the pain in my side had dulled down to an ache that wasn't too bad. Under the circumstances, it was best that I find something positive to think about.

I reckon I went a little out of my head for a while. I watched the moon as it climbed through the sky, and instead of seeing the face of a man in it, I saw Janine. Not only that, but it seemed like she leaned down right over me, and I could feel the cool touch of her fingers on my brow as she murmured, "Poor baby. Poor, poor baby."

I never told that to anybody else. But I swear, it was like she was right there with me. That helped me get through it all for a while.

Then the singing started.

At first I thought I really had gone crazy. But I wasn't the only one who heard the weak, ragged voice singing, "O, bury me not . . . on the lone prairie . . . where the . . . the coyotes howl . . . and the wind . . . blows free . . ."

It was Hank Ball singing as he lay there about twenty yards from me. I had thought he was dead an hour or two earlier, but I reckon he had just passed out. Somehow, even shot to pieces like he was, he had hung on, and now, for some reason I couldn't even come close to understanding, he was lifting his voice in song.

I did the only thing I could. I joined in.

And I wasn't the only one. The German guns had stopped firing again, and I heard more voices coming from the trenches. Big Boy's deep, booming bass, and Roy's wobbly baritone, and the voices of other men I didn't know, and we were all singing with Hank, for Hank, so that he would know he wasn't alone. Again he sang, "O, bury me not . . . on the lone prairie . . ." And then I heard a long sigh from him and no more words. I stopped singing, and a minute later somebody else stopped, then another and another, until everything was quiet again in No Man's Land. This time, there was no doubt in my mind. For Hank, the fighting was over.

For the rest of us, it went on.

I lay there under the moon and stars and waited to see what would happen when the sun came up.

What happened was that our artillery boys shelled the hell out of the German lines, dropping such a barrage on them that all they could do was hide and pray. They didn't care anymore about some wounded Yank doughboy stuck in No Man's Land. Roy and Big Boy came charging up out of that trench, and Roy grabbed hold of me while Big Boy slung Hank's body over his shoulder. We hurried back to the trench and half climbed, half fell into its muddy sanctuary. A medical corpsman was waiting to clean and bandage the wound in my side.

There was nothing anybody could do for Hank. He was dead, just as I'd thought. I hoped he had heard the rest of us singing with him during the night, so he'd known that he wasn't alone. But in the long run, I don't suppose it mattered whether he had been aware of it or not.

Where he had gone, everybody winds up going alone.

TWENTY-FIVE

The Allied push at Saint Mihiel was every bit as successful as Black Jack Pershing and Marshal Foch and the other generals must have hoped it would be. Once we got moving, we went a long way in a matter of days, and by late September we had pushed the front line back beyond Pont-a-Mousson.

I went along too. That bullet crease on my side wasn't enough to keep me out of the action. When the orders came for us to move up, one of the medical corpsmen who had been tending to me said something about sending me back to Paris to recuperate. I just picked up my rifle, said, "Not hardly," and got out of that field hospital. We had the Boche on the run, and I was damned if I was going to miss out on the end of things.

North of us, a fella named Patton was giving the Germans hell with his tank corps around some thick woods called the Argonne Forest. The Boche fought every step of the way, but their steps were all backward now. What little news we got from the rest of the world wasn't about who was going to win the war, but rather about how the politicians were haggling over what to do after the Central Powers surrendered.

First there was a little matter of making sure they did surrender, and we went about that chore as best we could.

The Germans had been mighty proud of what they called the Siegfried Line, which was a defensive position they said couldn't be broken. Well, we took care of that, and during a rainy October, they fell back to the Hindenburg Line. None of us had any doubt that they wouldn't be able to hold it either.

Of course, it wasn't all fighting. We had a few minutes here and there to grab a bite to eat and wash out our socks and play a hand or two of cards. Roy and Big Boy and I even had some visitors one day, and we were mighty glad to see them.

Jace and Aaron came wobbling up on bicycles, of all things, to the dugout that was our temporary home. We saw them coming, and Big Boy let out a whoop. "Where'd you find them mustangs, boys?" he called out to them. "Better be careful, or they're liable to throw you!"

They came to a stop, and Jace grinned and said, "At least we haven't been set afoot, like you fellas."

Aaron added, "Hell, Big Boy, it's been so long since you've been on a horse, I'd swear your knees ain't bowed no more!"

Big Boy took a playful swipe at both of them, and then there was a lot of hand-shaking and back-pounding. When that was over, Roy said, "What are you boys doin' here? They throw you out of the Air Corps?"

"Not likely," Jace said. "We're aces! Aaron's shot down eight planes, and I've got six."

Aaron jerked a thumb back down the road behind him. "We've moved to an aerodrome about two miles that way. We'll be flying patrols over this section of the front. Shoot, it's like the whole gang's together again!"

I pointed up at the sky. "Except we'll be down here and you and Jace will be up there in the wild blue yonder."

"Yeah, but what's a few thousand feet?" Aaron asked with a grin.

"A hell of a lot, when it's straight up!" Big Boy said.

"Well, you watch for us when we go flyin' over to-morrow," Jace told us. "We'll waggle our wings at you."

"We'll be watchin'," Roy said. I could tell he was mighty glad to see his brother again and to know that Jace and Aaron were all right. We all expected that the war would be over in another month or so, since it didn't seem likely the Boche could hold out any longer than that. With any luck, we'd all make it through to the end.

And then we'd have to decide what to do with the rest of our lives as free men. I knew a couple of things already: I wasn't going back to being an outlaw—and I was going to see Janine just as soon as I could.

Nothing makes a fella fight harder than having his back against the wall. I reckon those German troops felt like they had gone as far as they were going. They stiffened, and when the next Allied push came, they held, at least for the time being. During the long retreat, artillery hadn't played much of a part, but now, with the front lines relatively stationary again, the barrages started up. The German long guns pounded us hard. Their fire was deadly accurate, and we knew it was because of the observation balloons we saw floating over the front. The fellas up in those gasbags could signal down to the gunners on the ground and tell them how to drop those shells right in our laps.

It wasn't any surprise that our planes started going after those balloons hot and heavy.

By this time, we knew Jace's and Aaron's Spads by sight. They swooped over our lines at least once a day, dipping their wings one way, then the other, as they set out to attack the observation balloons or escort Allied bombers on raids into German-held territory. It always made me feel a little better knowing they were up there, sort of like angels looking out for us, although Jace and Aaron would have made about the most unlikely angels anybody ever heard of.

We had moved up into the forward trenches again, right on the edge of yet another No Man's Land. I couldn't look

out across that shattered ground without thinking about
Hank Ball and the day and the night I had spent lying under
the German machine-gun fire. I wished the damned war was
over.

The steadily growing roar of airplane engines behind us
made me glance up. A flight of Spads zoomed overhead,
and sure enough, the two on the right end of the formation
dipped their wings. Jace and Aaron were at it again. The
planes arrowed toward a cluster of German balloons that
had drifted toward the front lines.

But I reckon those balloons were bait, in a way, because
as our boys went for them, more German planes than I had
ever seen before in one place came zooming out of a cloud
bank to the south, their guns blazing.

"Son of a bitch!" I yelped as I pointed at what was
happening in the sky. "The Boche were waitin' for 'em!"

Roy and Big Boy and I all scrambled up to the top of
the trench where we could have a better view, not caring
that the Germans on the other side of the line might be able
to draw a bead on us. We watched as a whole horde of
those Fokker triplanes roared around the Spads, practically
swallowing the Allied planes. I tried to keep my eye on the
planes being flown by Jace and Aaron, but it was next to
impossible, the way those crates were dodging and darting
around. We had witnessed dogfights over the lines before,
but never anything as spectacular as this. Planes burst into
flame and went spiraling toward the ground, and it wasn't
only our boys who were being shot down either. We gave
as good as we got, and several of the Fokkers were destroyed in the first few minutes of the battle.

"That's it," Roy muttered each time one of the German
planes was hit. "That's it." His face was drawn in haggard
lines, with his brother and his friend up there in deadly
danger. We all knew it, and we were all holding our breath
to see what was going to happen.

Looking back on it now, I don't suppose there was ever
much doubt. The Germans had planned their ambush too
well, and there were too many of them. In less than ten
minutes, there were only a couple of the Spads left in the

air. I knew it was too much to hope for, but I wanted those two to be Jace and Aaron. I wanted them to cut and run, to get out of there while they still had a chance.

That was what they tried to do, and as they turned and headed toward the Allied lines, I got a better look at the planes. My heart practically jumped out of my throat. I recognized the markings on both of the Spads. My pards were still alive.

But then some of the Fokkers moved to cut them off, and Jace and Aaron were forced to bank away from the front lines. It was like those triplanes were herding them back toward the German side. A minute later, it became obvious what the plan was. The Fokkers were driving the two Spads in range of the antiaircraft batteries that protected the observation balloons. The German pilots were going to let the gunners on the ground take care of the last two American planes.

Roy pounded his fist against the ground. "No, damn it!" he said. "Break away, Jace. Get away from 'em! Come on, boy . . ."

But there was nothing Jace or Aaron could do. They flew right into a curtain of antiaircraft fire, and even from this distance, I saw how the explosions jolted the Spads and set them on fire. I knew that in the cockpits of those planes, Jace and Aaron would be fighting hard to keep control of them, but it was hopeless. They each managed to prevent the planes from going into a spin, but keeping them in the air was impossible. They slid steadily toward the ground, vanishing out of sight beyond a low hill. A minute later, an explosion sounded in the distance.

"No!" Roy yelled. He was holding his Springfield so tightly that not a bit of blood remained in his hands.

Several of the Fokkers flew over the spot where Jace and Aaron had gone down. Then they turned and roared toward the front lines again. I knew what they were doing: The bastards were going to fly over No Man's Land and taunt us. Rub it in our faces how they had destroyed a whole flight of Allied planes and killed the pilots.

Not today, I thought. There wasn't going to be any bragging today.

I was numb from the knowledge of Jace's and Aaron's death, but there was a spot of anger deep inside burning as bright and hot as the sun. I came boiling up out of that trench as the German planes reached No Man's Land, and Roy and Big Boy were right beside me. Big Boy was holding a grenade, and he heaved it up in the air as hard as he could at the Fokkers.

Of course, bringing down a plane by throwing a hand grenade at it is pretty far-fetched, and when that grenade went off, it wasn't anywhere close to the German planes. But just the sheer audacity of it must have gotten to the Boche pilots, because they turned sharply and some of them headed back toward the German lines. A couple of others flew on toward us.

That was fine with me and Roy. We were already firing our rifles toward them as fast as we could.

By all rights, the German machine gunners should have gotten us, but the other fellas in our trench saw what was happening and took a hand in the game. They opened fire on the German gun emplacements and made those Boche soldiers hunt for cover while Roy and Big Boy and I were out in the open. That gave us a chance to empty our Springfields at the low-flying Fokkers.

As a kid, I'd brought down many a bird on the wing with an old single-shot rifle, and Roy was an even better shot than I was. I reckon it surprised the hell out of those German pilots when our bullets started ripping through the canvas of their planes and thudding into the engines. To my satisfaction, I saw smoke start to come from both planes.

One of them went out of control, spun, and crashed at the edge of No Man's Land, the impact throwing dirt and debris high in the air as the plane smashed up. In an instant, the wreckage was sheeted in fire. The pilot managed to clamber out of the cockpit, but he was ablaze too, and screaming. For a second, I thought somebody ought to put a bullet through his head and put him out of his misery.

Then I thought, why waste perfectly good lead?

The second plane's engine was sputtering and choking as it flew over us, so close to the ground that it seemed like I could reach up and touch the landing gear. In fact, I instinctively ducked a little, worried that one of the wheels might knock my helmet off. Of course, the plane was higher than that—but not much. It slammed into the ground behind our lines, but the pilot had kept its nose up so that the blow was a glancing one. We turned to watch as the Fokker slid and skidded a hundred yards or so, plowing up the ground as it did so.

"Come on!" Roy said. "That son of a bitch is mine!"

We knew he was talking about the pilot. Roy wanted to settle the score for Jace and Aaron up close, so that the Boche could look in his eyes and know what he was dying for. We scrambled down into the trench and then back out the other side of it, and took off at a dead run toward the wrecked plane.

We weren't the only ones with that idea. More of our troops were closing in on the Fokker, and they were closer than we were. Shots began to crackle, and I figured the pilot was taking potshots at our boys with his side arm.

"Don't kill him!" Roy shouted. "He's mine!"

It looked like we weren't going to get there in time, so Roy did the only thing he could. He stopped in his tracks and dropped to one knee, then brought his reloaded Springfield to his shoulder. He sighted just for a moment at the pilot, who had slid out of the cockpit and was crouched next to one of the crumpled wings. Roy fired, and the pilot staggered and dropped the pistol he had been firing at our troops as they closed in on him.

Roy hadn't shot to kill, though. He had drilled that Boche pilot's forearm neat as you please, and under other circumstances, I would have let out a whistle of admiration for his aim. I was still caught up in the excitement of the fight, though, and shaken by what had happened to two of my best friends in the world. I just ran on toward the downed Fokker with Roy and Big Boy.

When we got there, the wounded pilot was struggling in the grip of a couple of doughboys. Blood covered one side of his face, and more blood dripped from his arm where Roy had ventilated him. He was cussing up a storm in German. Roy shut him up by pressing the point of his bayonet into the Boche's neck just under the chin.

"Shut your filthy mouth," Roy said. "I ought to cut your throat right now, Fritz. My brother was flying one of those last two planes, and the other pilot was a pard of mine."

I didn't expect the fella to speak English, but he did. He glared at Roy through the one eye that wasn't swollen shut, then abruptly laughed. "You fool!" he said, his voice strained from the bayonet point pressing into his flesh. "American fool! Those fliers are not dead."

Roy's eyes widened in surprise, and I reckon mine and Big Boy's did too. "What did you say?" Roy grated.

"The last two Spads did not crash. They landed safely."

Big Boy said, "But we heard somethin' blow up."

"The gas tank of one of the planes exploded, but not until the pilot had gotten out of it." The German's lips were pulled back from his teeth in an expression that was half a grimace of pain, half a cruel grin. "By now they have been taken captive, and they will soon wish their planes had crashed!"

Roy's shoulders tensed, and I knew he was about to drive that bayonet right through the German's neck. That would get him in no end of trouble, so I reached out and grabbed hold of his arm and pulled him back. "Wait a minute, Roy," I said. "Think about what this fella just said."

"I know what he said!"

"Jace and Aaron are still alive!" I knew I had to get through the anger in Roy's mind. "They're still alive, Roy, you hear me?"

"Of course I hear you. What—"

If he hadn't been so upset, he would have seen it right away. As it was, it was up to me to do the sort of thinking that he usually did.

"If Jace and Aaron are still alive," I said, "that means we can go get them."

TWENTY-SIX

"Absolutely not," the colonel said. "It's out of the question. I'm not going to risk any men on a rescue mission this late in the game."

"But Colonel . . ." Major Selkirk said.

The colonel shook his head. "Forget it, Major. I know these men want to retrieve their friends, but those two American pilots—*if* they survived the downing of their planes—will just have to endure being prisoners of war for a time. As soon as an armistice is signed, I'm certain the exchange of prisoners will begin too."

Major Selkirk turned to look at Roy and Big Boy and me, as if to say, *Well, boys, I tried.*

But that wasn't good enough. Not hardly.

We were in the 90th Division headquarters bunker, a couple of miles behind the front lines. The captured German pilot had been brought there for medical treatment and interrogation, and he had repeated his story about seeing Jace and Aaron land relatively safely and then be captured by Boche troops. "Perhaps you could work out an exchange," he had suggested with a sneer. "Since one German pilot is worth at least two American fliers, my commander might be willing to turn them over if I am released.''

That idea hadn't gone over too well. The colonel wanted to wait for the armistice that everybody knew was coming.

But when was it going to come? That was what nobody knew.

And what would happen to Jace and Aaron in the meantime?

Roy managed not to show it while we were in HQ, but he was fit to be tied. As we started back toward the trenches, he let it all out, cussing a blue streak for several minutes and then saying, ''If that stuck-up officer thinks I'm goin' to sit on my butt while my brother and my pard are right over yonder in German hands, then he don't know Roy Tacker.''

''What can we do?'' I asked. ''I thought goin' after Jace and Aaron was a good idea too, but you heard what the colonel said.''

''Ain't none of the Tacker Gang ever been overfond of rules,'' Big Boy said.

''I need to do some thinkin' on this,'' Roy said, stalking on toward the front, his rifle held tightly in his hand. ''When I figure it out, I'll let you know. I reckon I can count on you two to back my play.''

''Damn right,'' Big Boy said. ''You didn't even have to ask.''

Roy glanced over at me. ''What about you, Drew? You didn't say nothin'.''

I took a deep breath and told him, ''You're the boss, Roy. Always have been.''

But I remembered Reno, and how close we had come to disaster several times when we hit Ford's casino in Paris, and I wondered if there was ever going to come a time when all this helling around would stop.

Then I thought about Jace and Aaron, and knew that if I needed to walk through Hell a little more, I could manage it for them.

● ● ●

The major knew us pretty good by then, and I wasn't surprised when he showed up late that afternoon and said, "You three are relieved. Fall back and let someone else worry about the front tonight."

"We ain't been on duty that long," Roy said. "I reckon we're good for a while yet. But we're much obliged for the offer anyway, Major."

"It wasn't an offer, Private. It was an order."

For a second, I thought Roy was going to tell Major Selkirk what he could do with his order. But then Roy just shrugged and said, "All right." He turned to me and Big Boy. "Come on, fellas."

We followed him a couple of hundred yards down to a connecting trench that ran away from the front. The three of us turned and went out of sight of the major, and Roy stopped.

"This don't change anything none," he said. "We're still goin' after Jace and Aaron."

"The major'll be on the lookout for some sort of trick," I told him.

Roy nodded. "Yep. But he won't be expectin' what I got in mind."

I didn't much like the sound of that, but Big Boy and I just looked at each other and shrugged. Roy was calling the shots.

We took advantage of the opportunity to get some supper. Any other time, we would have followed that meal with some sleep in one of the bunkers. Instead, Roy headed for one of the artillery emplacements.

I didn't have any idea what he wanted with those big guns and the fellas who fired them. It was twilight right along about then, and the cannons were silent for the moment. The bombardment would start again once full darkness fell. I was glad nobody was shooting. Those big guns were hell on the ears when you were close to them.

Most of the artillerymen had trained at Camp Bowie, and we knew a few of them slightly. Roy found a couple of fellas we were acquainted with, and before you could say Jack Robinson, we were all sitting around that gun em-

placement smoking cigarettes and swapping yarns about
Fort Worth and basic training. It was a pleasant enough
way to spend an evening, considering, and I was sorry to
see it end when the orders came over a field telephone for
the bombardment to commence again. We said our so-
longs.

Only we didn't start back to the bunkers where our unit
was assigned. Instead, Roy led us to a fenced-in corral behind the cannons. The moon was coming up, and in its
silvery light I saw Roy grin as he turned to Big Boy and
me and asked, "Do you boys still remember how to ride
bareback?"

I saw then what he was planning to do, of course. We
were going to turn horse thieves and take some mounts
from this corral. The horses would get us across the front
lines. Nobody, not even the major, would be expecting a
dash like that.

"I reckon I can manage," Big Boy said.

"Me too," I put in without hesitation, but I added, "Are
you sure about this, Roy? If they stop us, they're liable to
shoot us for tryin' to desert."

"We ain't desertin'. We'll come right back as soon as
we get Jace and Aaron loose from the Boche."

"The brass won't know that."

"I'm goin'," he said flatly. "You boys best make up
your own minds what you're goin' to do."

"Nothin' to decide," Big Boy said. "Let's go get our
pards."

Roy looked at me. *God help me,* I thought, and then I
said, "Let's go."

With all the cannons going off, nobody heard the horses
whinny as we slipped into the corral and cut out three
likely-looking mounts. Of course, none of them was really
what you'd call a saddle horse. They were draft horses,
plain and simple, and their job was to pull the caissons on
which the cannons were mounted. But they would do in a
pinch, and after we'd rigged some rough halters with pieces
of cord we cut from our gear, they weren't too balky. Back

home as a boy, I'd ridden mules plenty of times, and these animals were a lot better than that.

We couldn't ride the horses across No Man's Land, not with the way it was covered with barbed wire and shell holes. But a road ran east from Verdun, on our side of the front, to a village called Etain, behind the German lines. The artillery barrages from both sides had done quite a bit of damage to it, we'd heard, but at least it didn't have any barbed wire on it. Etain was likely where the German forces in this area had their headquarters, and that was where Jace and Aaron would have been taken after they were captured. So that road was what we were bound for, and once we were on it, there would be no turning back.

I figured someone would challenge us as we rode north-west toward Verdun, but no one did. Maybe the sentries took us for French refugees when they heard the slow, steady clip-clop of those draft horses' hooves. And nearly everyone's attention was turned northeast, toward the front. Nobody was looking for trouble behind the lines.

I hoped the Boche were the same way once we got over in their territory. A little carelessness on their part would go a long way toward getting us back out of there with our hides in one piece.

We left the lane we were following and cut across country before we got to Verdun. This was like carrying messages again, as we had done a few months earlier when we first got into the war. It was harder to find our way by the stars over there in France than it would have been if we were home, but we managed. Roy had always had a nose for the right trail, and he didn't let us down. We snaked around Verdun, and sure enough, we hit a broad, hard-packed road that wasn't too shot up. It had to be the one we were looking for.

"All right, boys," Roy said to us in a low voice as we reined in at the edge of the road. "Ready to gallop?"

"Ready as we'll ever be," Big Boy said. "You reckon these nags got much speed in 'em?"

"We're about to find out," Roy said. He tightened his hold on his horse's makeshift halter and drove his heels into its flanks. "Hyyyahhh!"

That horse broke into a run, and Big Boy and I were right behind Roy on our mounts. Their hooves drummed on the road and the wind blew in my face, and it was almost like being back in the West again, on the run from a sheriff's posse. The road ran through some woods, and I knew there were American Marines and doughboys out there in the darkness, getting ready to push on when the order came. I heard a few startled shouts, and somebody took a shot at us. The bullet didn't come close enough for us to hear it, though.

We must have looked a sight, dressed in our muddy uniforms with those soup-bowl helmets tightly strapped to our heads and Springfield rifles slung on our backs. I would have given a lot right then for a Stetson, a duster, a Winchester, and a Colt .45. Hell, if we'd had all that, we'd have been ready to take on the whole damned German army.

The miles fell behind us, and those horses kept running. They may not have been Thoroughbreds, but they ran like champions that night. It wasn't long before we figured we were in German-held territory. Roy reined in and held up a hand, signaling for Big Boy and me to stop. He unbuckled his helmet and sailed it off into the woods to the side of the road.

"We're not doughboys anymore, fellas," he said. "I reckon we're outlaws again."

That sounded good to me. I never did like that damned helmet. I pitched it into the woods after Roy's, and so did Big Boy.

Then we unslung our rifles and held them in front of us as we rode off the path and started across country again. We tried to keep the road in sight, though, so it could lead us to Etain. The sky in the east was turning pink, and we knew dawn wasn't far off. By now, Major Selkirk likely knew that we were gone. There would be nothing but trouble waiting for us when we got back.

But it would be worth it if we could bring Jace and Aaron with us.

The sun still wasn't quite up when we reached Etain. Like most French villages, it would have been a mighty pretty place if it hadn't suffered the ravages of war for the past four years. Some of the buildings were bombed-out ruins, and others were heavily damaged, though still intact enough to be used. We watched the town wake up from a wooded hill just to the west. The place was full of German troops, tanks, cannons, and equipment, as we had expected. I heard the whistle of a locomotive floating on the early morning air as a train pulled into or out of the station on the far side of the village. But there was one surprise. A steady stream of cars moved to and from a large house on another hill north of the village, crossing a stone bridge over a creek with deep banks as they did so. It was more than a house, really—more like a mansion. I pointed it out to Roy, and he said, "More than likely some rich French fella lived there, and the Boche took it over to use as their headquarters. It'd be just like 'em to commandeer an estate like that."

I nodded, because what he said made sense. Big Boy rumbled, "If that's their HQ, ain't that where we'd likely find Jace and Aaron?"

"That's what I'm figurin'," Roy agreed. "Come on. Let's circle around, see if we can get into the place from the back."

The whole town was like a beehive that's been bumped good and hard. I wondered if there were any French folks left in the village, or if Etain was populated solely by German soldiers now. We stuck to the woods as much as possible in hopes that we wouldn't be spotted by any of them as we looped around to the north.

It was a good plan, and it could have worked out. It wasn't Roy's fault that it didn't, just pure bad luck. We found a narrow lane that ran up the back of the hill where the mansion was located, and we started up it. We were about halfway there when we heard some clanking and grinding, and a tank rolled over the little ridge at the top of the slope and started down the lane toward us.

The turret on top of the tank was open, and a German soldier was riding with the upper half of his body sticking through it, jouncing along like he wasn't expecting any trouble. But then he saw us and yelled something to the other Boche in the tank with him, and the ugly thing lurched to a stop.

"Oh, hell," Big Boy said. "We best light a shuck, boys."

We tried, but the cannon on the front of that tank belched fire and smoke, and a shell blasted on the right-hand side of the lane as we jerked the horses in that direction. Even those normally placid caisson horses, as accustomed as they were to loud noises, didn't like explosions going off that close to them. They reared and pawed the air, and it was all we could do to keep them from bolting.

"Head back down the hill!" Roy shouted. We tried to haul the horses around so we could do that. Another shell whined over our heads and slammed into the lane below us. The horses went crazy again.

"They got the range on us, Roy!" Big Boy yelled. "I'll smoke 'em out o' that tin can!" He turned his horse again and kicked it into a run that carried him straight toward the tank. With a rebel yell, he waved his rifle over his head, then brought it down and started shooting.

"That crazy bastard," Roy said, and I could tell he thought Big Boy was really something. So did I. We went after him.

It was the old-style cavalry versus the new-style cavalry, I guess you could say, and it's not really any surprise who won. Big Boy's shots ricocheted off the outside of the tank. He didn't have a human target to aim at, because the fella who had been riding in the turret had ducked back down and yanked the hatch closed behind him. The cannon belched Hell again, and the shot landed close enough to Big Boy so that the blast sent him spinning off the back of his horse. "Big Boy!" I yelled as I fired my Springfield toward the tank. Maybe I'd get lucky and one of my bullets would find the viewport and bore a hole through the driver's brain, I hoped.

Luck wasn't with us on this day, unless you count the fact that none of us got blown to pieces. Roy jumped off his horse and knelt beside Big Boy, who was shaking his head groggily and trying to sit up. I rode past them and dropped off my horse, letting it run on into the woods. I caught my balance and planted my feet wide, standing in front of Roy and Big Boy as the tank rumbled up to us. My rifle was pointed right at the thing, but the muzzle of its cannon was lined up with the three of us, and it looked about a mile wide from where we were. Still I stood there bold as brass, because, by that time, what the hell else was there to do?

The hatch on the turret popped open again, and a German voice called harshly, "Surrender, *Amerikaners,* or we will kill you."

"Go to Hell," I said, squinting over the barrel of my rifle.

"Drew." That was Roy, talking quiet behind me. "Put the rifle down, Drew. They got us, fair and square."

That surprised me. "You mean we're goin' to give up?" I asked without turning around.

"Think about why we're here, boy. We came to get Jace and Aaron. Maybe now they'll take us right to 'em."

I glanced back then, and saw the devil lurking in Roy's eyes.

"We'll all be together then," he said, "and sooner or later, the Tacker Gang will ride again."

I hoped he was right. I lowered my rifle, dropped it to the ground, and put my hands above my head.

TWENTY-SEVEN

Big Boy wasn't hurt bad, mostly just shaken up and scratched here and there by flying debris from that explosion. The tank crew marched us up the hill toward the mansion, covering us with their handguns. The house was even more impressive when we got close to it and got a good look at the manicured lawn and the freshly painted walls. War hadn't touched this place physically.

But the owners, whoever they had been, were gone, and the house was full of Boche. That made it uglier to me than any tumbledown shack I'd ever seen back in the States.

Guards carrying rifles took over from the tank crew and prodded us at bayonet point into the mansion. We were taken straight to a fancy parlor where an officer sat behind a huge desk. He looked up at us in surprise and started jabbering in German. I figured he was asking where in the Sam hill we'd come from, and the guards told him, I suppose. He stood up and came around the desk to look at us. His hands were clasped together behind his back. He was about fifty, I reckon, with short blond hair and brown eyes set deep in a tanned face. He wasn't a bad-looking fella, and I could tell he was fairly smart. He said something to us in German.

Roy shook his head. "We don't none of us savvy that Dutch lingo. You'll have to speak English, fella."

" 'Savvy'?" the German said. "This is English?"

"It is where we come from."

"Very well. I shall speak your . . . lingo, as you call it." He walked back behind the desk and faced us again. "I am General Reinhold von Junzt, the commandant here in Etain. And you are . . . ?"

We'd been told if we were ever captured that we didn't have to tell the Germans anything but our names. That was all General von Junzt got from us. Roy did the introductions.

"You are American soldiers?" von Junzt asked.

We had thrown our helmets away, but we were still wearing the rest of our uniforms. Roy looked down at his and said, "That's pretty obvious, ain't it?"

"You are not spies, or you would be in disguise. What are you doing here?"

I guess Roy didn't want to tell him we were looking for Jace and Aaron, for fear that von Junzt might deliberately keep us away from them. So he just said, "We got tired of waitin' for our orders to come. Figured we'd just go ahead and advance on our own."

"You are not deserters?"

"Hell, no," Big Boy said. "We ain't the sort of hombres who run out on our pards."

There was more truth to that than General von Junzt knew. He grunted and said, "Very well." He started to sit down, then added, "I thought perhaps you had come here to rescue the two American aviators who were captured yesterday."

That was a low-down shot, but a good one. I reckon Big Boy and I weren't able to keep the looks of surprise off our faces, because I saw the sudden spark of satisfaction in von Junzt's eyes. Roy was the only one in the room who was still poker-faced. The general settled down in his chair and smiled confidently.

"I was told that the two fliers also spoke as if they were characters in a novel by Karl May," he said. He looked at

Roy. "You and Old Shatterhand are brothers under the skin, *nicht wahr?*"

I didn't know what the hell he was talking about then. I looked into it later, and found out that this Karl May fella was like a German dime novelist who wrote a bunch of stories about a frontier scout named Old Shatterhand and his Indian pard Winnetou. General von Junzt must have been one of May's readers. It struck me as odd that Germans would read stories about the American West. We sure as hell didn't read stories about *them*.

But anyway, Roy just shook his head and said, "We don't know any pilots. We're infantry."

"That is a shame," von Junzt said with a head shake of his own. His expression became a mite grim. "I was hoping you could tell me where we could find them."

I wasn't sure right then if he was lying or not. But when he said something to the guards and then flicked his hand at us like he didn't care one way or the other anymore, I figured he was telling the truth. The guards marched us out of the parlor and took us into the basement of the house, where they locked us in what had probably been a storage room. A little light came into the makeshift jail through a high, narrow window just above the level of the ground, so that we could see each other as we looked around. Roy put into words what I was already thinking.

"They don't have any more idea where Jace and Aaron are than we do," he said, and I nodded. Yet General von Junzt had known that the two of them talked like Westerners, which meant they had been in German hands for at least a little while.

"They got away," I said. "The Boche must have been bringing them here, and somehow they got away."

"Son of a gun!" Big Boy exclaimed. "You really think so?"

"It's the only thing that makes any sense, considerin' what's happened since they grabbed us," Roy told him.

Big Boy nodded. "Well, I sure hope they took off for our lines."

I hoped the same thing. Of course, if Jace and Aaron made it back on their own, that would mean that we had made this raid into German-held territory for nothing.

And maybe gotten ourselves killed for nothing too.

Still, I would have felt like it had been worth it if I could have known right then that Jace and Aaron were safe.

And I probably would have cussed them up one way and down the other if I had known what they were really up to.

The Germans let us sweat for a while in that basement cell. Then guards showed up again and took us back upstairs to the parlor. General von Junzt was standing next to a large table with several other officers. They had a map spread out on the table, and they were talking loud as they stabbed their fingers at various places on it. More than just a conversation, this was almost an argument. I wondered what they were wrangling about.

Von Junzt let it go on for a little while. Then, when he glanced over and saw us standing just inside the door with a cluster of guards around us, he cut off the talking with a curt word or two. He made an offhand gesture, and one of the other officers rolled the map up. They all clicked their heels and saluted the general, then filed out of the room through another door. Von Junzt went to his desk and motioned for the guards to bring us forward.

"You have perhaps decided that you know something about those American aviators after all?" he asked us.

"I told you," Roy said, "we don't know any damned pilots. They don't have anything to do with doughboys who go sloggin' around in the mud all day."

"Very well. You will be taken into the village and held there until such time as you can be sent to a prisoner-of-war camp in Germany."

Roy gave him a thin smile. "Sort of bothers you that you may have a couple of Americans runnin' around loose behind the lines, don't it?"

Von Junzt shrugged. "It is nothing to me. Sheer curiosity, that is all." He gave the guards an impatient look and ordered them to take us away. That must've been the gist of it anyway, because we were prodded out of the parlor again.

This time, instead of the basement, they took us out the front door of the mansion and loaded us into the back seat of a car. It had a jump seat so that a couple of the guards could ride facing us, covering us with pistols as they did so. Two more soldiers climbed into the front, one of them sliding behind the wheel, which was on the right-hand side instead of the left. I hadn't had much experience with automobiles, but that looked wrong even to me.

We started along the winding road that ran down the hill, toward the stone bridge over the little creek between the mansion and the rest of the village.

"You got a face like the rear end of a donkey, you know that?" Roy said to one of the guards facing us from the jump seat. The fella just stared blankly at us over the barrel of his pistol. None of the other three seemed to understand what Roy had said either.

Roy leaned back against the seat and said, "They don't speak English. Didn't figure they did."

"What good does that do us?" I asked. I was pretty down in the dumps. It looked like we were going to wind up in the hoosegow after all—a Boche prisoner-of-war camp.

"At least we can talk about what was goin' on back there in the general's office, and why he's so worried about Jace and Aaron maybe bein' loose around here."

"You mean that fuss he was havin' with those other fellas?" I frowned. "I didn't understand any of that."

"Well, I did," Roy said, surprising me and Big Boy both.

"I thought you said you didn't savvy his lingo," Big Boy said.

"Figured it wouldn't hurt for him to think that." Roy grinned. "My granddaddy on my mama's side was Black Dutch. He taught me how to speak it some when I was a kid so's he could tell me dirty jokes without my mama knowin' what he was doin'. I recollect enough of it to know what the general and the others were talkin' about.''

The car slowed to take a curve in the road.

"From what I could gather, they're about to launch one last offensive,'' Roy said. "A counterattack that they hope will break the back of our push. And they're going to do it down here, away from the Hindenburg Line, where they think we won't be expectin' it. They've been stockpiling guns and ammunition and supplies down here for several weeks, gettin' ready. The last trainload is supposed to be comin' in today, and when it gets here, they'll be able to launch their strike tomorrow.''

The road went around another bend, looping back and forth as it wound down the hill toward the creek.

"Those must've been some complicated jokes your granddaddy told you!'' Big Boy said. Roy just shrugged.

"Damn,'' I said in a hushed voice. "You reckon they've got a chance of gettin' away with that, Roy?''

He nodded slowly. "Maybe. It was the general's idea. Some of the other fellas thought those supplies ought to go to the troops further north, where our big push is. But if the general's right, and they can break through the lines here and then loop up to the north and get behind our boys and the French and the Tommies . . .'' He took a deep breath. "Things could get a mite interestin'.''

That was putting it mildly. We had the Boche on the run, but if they slipped around us . . . well, the war might not be over in a month after all.

"The general don't want us, or Jace and Aaron, or anybody else who might know anything about this to get back to the Allied lines,'' I said. "That's why he was pretendin' not to care when you could tell he was really as nervous as a long-tailed cat on a porch full of rockin' chairs.''

Roy said, "Yep. That's the way I figure it.''

I had to bite back a groan as the car reached the bottom of the slope and started toward the bridge. "Lord, I wish there was some way we could get away from these old boys.''

That was when that stone bridge blew up right in front of us.

TWENTY-EIGHT

The car slewed hard to the right and bumped off the edge of the road as the driver tried to avoid the explosion. Roy and I lunged forward at the same time and grabbed the wrists of the guards sitting across from us so that we could shove the barrels of their guns away from us. Big Boy's hands shot out and wrapped around the necks of the Boche soldiers. He cracked their heads together as hard as he could, and even though they were protected by their helmets, the impact was enough to stun them. They didn't resist as Roy and I wrenched the guns away from them.

We had acted instinctively by jumping the guards, and in the meantime the driver was following his instincts by struggling to bring the car under control as it jolted across the gravel shoulder of the road. He couldn't keep it from going in the bar ditch. We were all thrown forward as it crashed to a stop about twenty feet from the bridge. I heard a lot of thudding against the roof of the car as rocks and debris from the explosion pelted down on it.

The driver and the other guard in the front seat were even more addled by what had happened than we were. The one in the passenger seat was trying to twist around so that he could bring his rifle into play when Roy shot him in the side of the head. He jerked against the window of the car, so hard that his helmet cracked the glass.

I chopped at the driver's head with the gun I'd jerked away from one of the fellas in the jump seat. The butt of it caught him just in front of the ear, and he slumped against the door on his side. For a second I thought about shooting him.

Then a couple of figures ran out of the woods that bordered the road, and I forgot about everything else. They weren't wearing their uniforms anymore, but I recognized them anyway, despite the civilian clothes.

General von Junzt had been all hot and bothered to find Jace and Aaron, and here they were less than half a mile from German headquarters.

They ran up to the car and jerked the doors open, and Roy and Big Boy and I jumped out. We did some whooping and hugging and back-pounding, but only for a couple of seconds. Then Aaron said, "Come on. We'd better get out of here."

"Yeah," Jace added. "That dynamite's liable to draw some attention."

It already had. I could hear the screeching of tires and brakes and the roaring of engines as several cars tore down the twisting road from the mansion. I knew they would be full of Boche soldiers on their way to find out what in blazes had happened down here at the creek.

The five of us ran into the woods. Jace and Aaron took the lead, since they seemed to know where they were going. We came to the creek again, slid down its steep banks, splashed across the water, and climbed out into more thick woods on the other side. I could tell we were headed for Etain, and I wasn't sure how smart that was, since the village was full of German troops.

Jace and Aaron slowed down before we got there, though, and we found ourselves crouching in a brush-choked gully that had probably been carved out by rain-water. We all looked at each other and grinned, and Big Boy asked the question that Roy and I were thinking.

"How in hell did the two o' you wind up here just in time to spring us?"

"We've been waitin' all day for them to bring you out of that place," Jace said. "We figured they'd bring you to town sooner or later, and since that road's the only one between German headquarters and the village, we planted our dynamite under it and kept an eye on the place." He took a short telescope that folded up on itself out of his pocket and held it up proudly.

"Wait just a damned minute," Roy said. "The two of you look like farmers, and you've got dynamite and a telescope. What the hell have you been doin' since yesterday?"

"Gettin' ready for the three of you to come after us, of course," Aaron said.

Jace shook his head. "That ain't strictly true. We thought you might be addlepated enough to come over here behind the lines on your own, but we weren't countin' on it. As for the clothes and the dynamite and the telescope, well, we got hold of all that stuff the way any good outlaw would."

"We stole all of it," Aaron said.

Roy still wasn't satisfied. "Why? How come you didn't just try to get back to the Allied lines?"

"We figured we'd just get shot if we did," Aaron said.

"Besides," Jace said, "we were already back here nearly to Boche HQ, so we thought we might as well make nuisances of ourselves."

"Better back up," Roy said with a shake of his head. "Start at the beginnin'."

"Well, it's simple enough," Jace said, and it was. He told us quickly how the two of them had gotten out of their wrecked planes and been grabbed by German troops, just like that Fokker pilot had told us. They had been tossed in a truck and taken to Etain, and the officers there had been ordered to bring them straight to HQ. That would have been so that von Junzt could question them, I thought. While the truck was on the road between the village and the creek, though, it had blown a tire and gone off the road, much like the car with us in it had done when Jace and Aaron blew up the bridge. They had managed to jump their guards and kill them, then escaped into the woods.

"They beat the bushes for us all day and half the night," Aaron said with a grin. "What they didn't know was that we were sleepin' snug and warm in a farmer's hayloft less'n a mile away. The farmer didn't have any need for it anymore."

"House was burned down," Jace said. "But the barn was still standin'. That's where we found the dynamite. It was old and sweaty. I reckon the farmer must've used it to blow up stumps, or something like that."

"You're lucky you didn't blow yourselves up, totin' around touchy stuff like that," Roy said.

Jace and Aaron both shrugged. "We thought it might come in handy," Aaron said. "Like Jace told you, we'd already decided to raise some hell around here and make things hard on the Boche if we could, instead of headin' back to the front."

"We got these duds off a clothesline at another farm early this mornin'," Jace said. "Found the telescope in another house that was abandoned. There's not very many folks around here anymore except the Germans."

Roy nodded. "The French are all refugees, just trying to get away from the Boche."

"We were workin' our way around behind that fancy mansion the Germans took over when we spotted some soldiers takin' you boys into the place," Aaron went on. "Can't say I was surprised to see you."

"But you were a sight for sore eyes anyway," Jace added.

"That's when we decided to mine the bridge and then wait to see what happened. Sure enough, after so long a time, here you came. We were hidin' underneath the bridge, so we lit the fuse on that bundle of dynamite and hightailed it out of there along the creek." Aaron grinned. "You know what happened after that."

It was a pretty wild story, but if there's one thing my life has taught me, it's that sometimes the wildest stories are the way things really were. No book writer could ever come up with anything quite as odd as what really goes on in the world.

"So, the Tacker Gang is all together again," Jace said. "Now what do we do?"

Roy's face settled down into sort of a grim expression as he said, "I've got a pretty good idea."

Roy had come up with some wild plans in the past—the bank job in Reno, the raid on Ford's Casino Americain in Paris—and some of them had worked out while some of them hadn't.

This was just about the wildest one yet.

But I had to admit it made sense. We were the only ones who knew what the Germans were up to with their counterattack, and if anybody was going to stop them, it would have to be us. Sure, they had thousands of men and more guns than you could shake a stick at, while there were five of us armed only with a couple of sweaty sticks of old dynamite that Jace and Aaron had saved back when they blew up the bridge.

That didn't make any difference. We had the chore to do, and once Roy had told us what he had in mind, even I had to admit that we had a chance of pulling it off. The main challenge starting out would be to avoid the German patrols searching for us, and Roy had always had sort of a sixth sense about how to avoid a posse.

"We need some German uniforms and some guns," Roy said. He looked at Jace and Aaron. "You boys know the lay of the land a little better than the rest of us. Any ideas where we could lay our hands on those things?"

"There are couriers goin' up and down the road between Etain and Metz all the time," Aaron said. "Most of 'em ride those motorcycles with the little sidecars hooked to 'em. Think that might do?"

Roy grinned. "Sounds like just the ticket."

The town of Metz was southeast of Etain, so we circled to the east, avoiding the village. Several times we had to lie low in the bushes while German patrols passed within earshot. General von Junzt had quite a few of his men searching for us. He probably wouldn't have gone to that much trouble for a handful of escaped prisoners, but with the Germans' last-ditch push coming up, he couldn't take a chance that we would get back to the front lines and warn the Allies.

The general didn't know it, but that wasn't what we had in mind at all. We were going to do a little hell-raising instead, Old West style.

Moving slow and careful-like, we took a couple of hours to reach the Etain-Metz road. Once we had, we crouched in the brush at the edge of the lane and waited until we heard the roar of an engine coming toward us. The motorcycle came into view. It had a sidecar attached to it, just like those that had chased Roy and Big Boy and me when we were trying to get to Chateau-Thierry. An officer sat in the sidecar, clutching a leather dispatch case, while the driver was hunched over the handlebars, watching the road suspiciously through the goggles over his eyes.

Roy was the best shot among us, so he was the one who aimed at the driver. He planned to try a head shot first, in hopes that he wouldn't mess up the uniform.

The pistol in Roy's hand cracked wickedly, and the driver jerked. His hands came off the handlebars. He tumbled to the side off the motorcycle, which went into a crazy skid. The officer riding in the sidecar let out a scream. The whole shebang rolled over, throwing the officer clear.

Big Boy was on the German almost before he hit the ground. He got an arm looped around the officer's neck and jerked his head back, sharp and quick. I heard the crack of bone, and the officer went limp. Big Boy dragged the body off the road and into the bushes while Aaron grabbed the driver's body. Jace and I wrestled the motorcycle back onto its wheels and rolled it and the sidecar to the side of the road.

Roy's bullet had caught the driver just below the right eye. It had made a considerable mess of the man's face, but only a few spatters of blood had gotten on the uniform. I thought the stains were small enough so that they

wouldn't be noticed easily. Roy and Big Boy went to work
stripping the bodies, while Jace and Aaron and I looked at
the motorcycle.

"Either of you know how to drive one of these things?"
I asked them.

"We flew planes," Jace said. "We ought to be able to
manage a damned motorcycle."

Aaron said, "I'll drive. I'm the closest to the same size
as that Boche."

He was right. The driver's uniform fit him like it had
been made for him, and I claimed his cast-off farmer's
clothes so that I could get rid of my army duds. Roy
climbed into the officer's uniform. Once they were ready,
Aaron turned the motorcycle around and played with it a
little, getting the feel of it. He grinned at us. "Just like
ridin' a horse," he said.

I doubted that, but he did seem to have the hang of
running the thing. He and Roy started back toward Etain,
while Jace and Big Boy and I took to the woods again. We
would meet up with them later, at the place Roy had picked
for our first strike at the Germans. He had pointed it out to
us as we circled the village the first time.

The railroad line entered Etain from the northeast. We
were able to cut across country, while Roy and Aaron had
to take a more crooked route. So we got to the rendezvous
about the same time. It was a spot where the rails crossed
a narrow country lane. Aaron parked the motorcycle smack
dab on the rails, and we waited.

That last train full of munitions and supplies hadn't
reached Etain yet; Roy knew that from what he had overheard back at von Junzt's headquarters. It was due any time
now, but it was going to make an unscheduled stop before
it reached the village.

We had been waiting a little over half an hour when we
heard a growling rumble in the distance. It grew louder,
and we knew the train was coming. Roy and Aaron stood
at the side of the tracks, while Jace and Big Boy and I
crouched at the bottom of the embankment a few yards
away, out of sight behind some fallen logs.

Roy began waving his hands above his head as soon as the locomotive came into view. The engineer must have seen him, because I heard the squeal of the train's brakes and a moment later the hiss of steam as the engineer let off some of the pressure from the boiler. I risked a glance over the deadfall, and saw that the train was indeed slowing. It came to a stop just before it reached the crossing, and Roy and Aaron jogged along the side of the locomotive to the cab. The engineer leaned down and angrily yelled something at them in German. Roy lifted the dispatch case and shook it meaningfully. Clearly, he had an important message for the engineer.

What he really had was one of those pistols we had taken away from our guards. He slowed as he reached the cab, reached into the case, took out the gun, and shot the engineer. The fella was rocked back by the bullet and fell out of sight in the cab. Roy dropped the case and jumped up into the cab, with Aaron following right behind him. Their guns cracked again.

By that time, Jace and Aaron and I were out of hiding and scrambling up the embankment toward the locomotive. We hustled up to the cab and climbed in as Roy and Aaron were shoving the bodies of the engineer and the two firemen out the other side. Roy sprang to the throttle and eased it open, and the train lurched into motion again. It knocked the motorcycle off the tracks as it started to build up speed.

I had to grin as I stood in the cab with Roy and Jace and Aaron and Big Boy. Frank and Jesse James had held up trains, but the Tacker Gang had gone them one better. We had stolen the whole damn thing, locomotive and all.

TWENTY-NINE

There were new, large warehouses along both sides of the railroad tracks in Etain. Jace and Aaron had noticed that much during their brief stay in the village. It made sense that those buildings were where the Germans were storing the munitions they had gathered for their counterattack.

"It'll be like a powderkeg," Roy had told us earlier while we were going over his plan. "If we blow up all the ammunition on this train while it's right there beside those warehouses, the whole thing will go up, and that'll be the end of the Boche's last push."

Now, as the train rocked along toward Etain, there were just a few more little matters to take care of before we could carry out Roy's plan.

Like the German officer who came scrambling over the coal tender behind us, yelling and waving a gun.

He must have been trying to signal the engineer to find out why the train had stopped for a few moments, and when he didn't get an answer, he came forward to investigate on his own. I figured that out later. Right then, I didn't care who he was or why he was there. All I knew was that the son of a bitch started shooting at us, probably as soon as he spotted Big Boy's American uniform.

I was holding a pistol that had been taken off the body of the engineer. As a bullet whipped past my ear and whined off the side of the cab, I twisted around and saw the German officer on top of the coal tender. Instinctively, I snapped off a shot, and the German went sailing off the train like he'd been jerked by a rope.

"There are bound to be some guards back there," Roy said over the rumble of the engine. "We'd better take care of them while we've got the chance."

"I'll go," Aaron volunteered without hesitating.

"I will too," Jace said, and I nodded.

"Big Boy, you stay here with me," Roy said. "I may need you to shovel some of that coal so that we can build up a good head of steam."

Big Boy nodded his agreement, but he didn't look happy about it. He wanted to go with us and kill some more Boche.

Jace and Aaron and I tucked our guns in our belts and climbed over to the tender to the first car. I looked at the way it was swaying back and forth as the train clicked over the rails, and I felt a little queasy just watching it. But that was the quickest and easiest way to reach the back of the train, where the guards were likely posted, so we clambered up the narrow ladder, pulled ourselves onto the roof, and started toward the caboose, crawling on our hands and knees.

After a few yards, we felt confident enough to stand up. I held my arms out away from my sides to balance myself. Jace and Aaron, having been pilots, were more used to taking chances, I guess, because by the time they reached the end of the first boxcar, they jumped to the next one. I gritted my teeth and followed, but I sure felt sick and dizzy during that long second when I was between cars and could glance down and see the roadbed flashing past beneath the train.

I landed with a thump, staggered a little, caught my balance again, and followed Jace and Aaron.

The train was a short one, only ten boxcars and a caboose behind the engine and the coal tender. We were nearly to the caboose when an iron-helmeted head poked itself above the roof of the last boxcar. Jace and Aaron and I spotted the German at the same time and stopped to draw our guns. The soldier didn't see us until he had climbed halfway onto the roof of the car, and by that time it was too late to drop back down out of sight. So he threw himself forward instead as we opened fire on him.

He sprawled out flat on the roof. He had his rifle in one hand, but he didn't have a chance to use it. All he could do was duck his head and pray as our bullets gouged splinters from the roof of the boxcar around him.

The pinned-down Boche got a break as one of his pards stuck the barrel of a rifle over the edge of the roof and started throwing lead at us. That made us dive for cover, only there wasn't any. We had to hug the roof of the car we were on.

The first German was able to open fire on us and give the second one a chance to climb on top of the car with him. Then they both shot at us while a third man clambered up. This wasn't looking too good. They kept swarming on top of the last boxcar. We had hoped to take them by surprise, but now they had the advantage on us.

Still, Jace managed to get a shot off that knocked one of the Germans off the train as the man stood up to try to charge toward us. That knocked some of the wind out of their sails, and it made us bold enough to try a charge of our own. The Germans came up on their knees to return our fire, and our slugs caught a couple of them.

But then Aaron stumbled and went to his knees, barely catching himself so that he didn't roll off the train. At first I thought he had just tripped, but then I saw how he had his left arm pressed across his midsection while he shakily tried to aim his pistol at the Germans with his right hand. He'd been hit, and the uniform tunic he wore was already dark with blood.

"Aaron!" Jace yelled. He had seen the same thing I had.

Aaron took his left hand away from the wound and reached up to grab hold of Jace's belt. He hauled Jace down onto the roof, even as he emptied his pistol toward the

Germans. "Keep your head down, you . . . damn fool,"
Aaron panted as I came up in a crouch behind them.
"Goin' to get it . . . shot off."

I knew he was hurt bad. So did Jace. Aaron's hand
slipped off Jace's belt, and he pitched forward on his face.
He didn't move again.

Jace let out a scream of rage. He jumped up and ran
toward the Germans, firing his pistol as he came on, leaping
over the gap between cars without ever slowing down.
There was nothing I could do but follow him.

It must have shocked the hell out of those Boche soldiers
to have that crazy American run right into them that way.
I know they stopped shooting for some reason, and that
makes as much sense as any. And it gave Jace a chance to
get among them. He slashed his now-empty pistol across
the face of a man who rose to meet him, then kicked another one off the train. I was right behind him, still with a
few bullets in my gun, and I fired them at close range into
the stunned faces of a couple of the Germans. Two more
of the Boche guard detail were scrambling off the back of
the car, no doubt trying to reach the shelter of the caboose.
Jace snatched up a fallen rifle with a bayonet attached to it
and went after them.

He rammed the bayonet through the throat of the man
who was wasting time trying to climb down the ladder at
the end of the boxcar. The German gurgled out a shriek
and fell, and he landed on the one below him. That knocked
both of them off the narrow platform at the front of the
caboose, and I reached the end of the boxcar in time to see
them slip through the gap and fall to the roadbed. The one
who was still alive when he fell screamed as the wheels
cut him to pieces.

That left just Jace and me on our feet, standing at the
back of the last boxcar. Jace was panting and making a
funny noise, and when I looked over at him, I saw tears
streaming down his face.

I took hold of his arm, then handed him another German
rifle I had slid from under one of the fallen bodies. "Better

go down there and make sure there aren't any more guards in the caboose," I told him.

I was pretty sure there wouldn't be any more Germans. All the shooting would have brought them out. But I wanted a minute to check on Aaron.

Jace nodded numbly and slung the rifle on his back, then climbed down to the platform. I waited until he had the rifle in his hands again and had kicked the door of the caboose open. Then I turned and hurried back to Aaron.

He had fallen in the center of the car's roof, otherwise he might have slid off by now. His head was twisted and I could see his face, and I knew he was dead before I even pressed my fingers to his throat in a hopeless search for a pulse. There was a big pool of blood underneath him, spreading out from his midsection.

I blinked back some tears of my own. Before everything that had happened over the past couple of days, we had thought . . . we had honestly believed . . . that all five of us were going to make it through this war.

Now Aaron was dead, his life snatched away from him just like that, and I knew it had been a mistake for any of us to hope.

I heard steps thudding on the roof, and looked up to see Jace approaching. His face was cold and hard now, and he had several rifles slung on his back, as well a pouch of some sort hung over his shoulder. "Aaron's dead, isn't he?" he asked, but he already knew the answer.

I nodded. "Yeah."

"Did he say anything?"

"He was gone when I got here."

Jace closed his eyes for a second. "All right. Let's put him down on the platform."

That made sense to me. We didn't want him to fall off the top of the train before we reached Etain. He would still be on board when the munitions blew and took the rest of us with them.

We were all going to die. I was convinced of it now. We would stay on board this train and run it right into the station, where we would blow it up and set off all the explosives in those warehouses too. It would be one hell of a blast, and what slim hopes the Germans might have left would be shattered along with everything else.

My lips curved in a little smile. Shoot, being an outlaw, I'd never expected to live to a ripe old age anyway.

We laid Aaron's body out on the platform at the front of the caboose. The door was open, banging back and forth from the motion of the train. I could see that the caboose was empty. Just as I had thought, all the guards had come out to challenge us.

"What's that?" I asked, pointing to the sack Jace was carrying.

He hefted it. "Grenades. Found 'em back here and thought they might come in handy."

I nodded and said, "They sure might. Come on, we'd better get back to the engine."

We went up the ladder. Jace didn't look back at Aaron's body, and neither did I. Aaron had crossed the great divide, and there wasn't any turning back.

For any of us.

When Jace and I jumped down from the coal tender into the cab of the engine, Roy looked back at us, and his face turned grim. "Where's Aaron?" he asked.

"He didn't make it," Jace said curtly.

"And neither did any of the Germans," I added.

"Aw, hell," said Big Boy, his face twisting a little with grief. "Damn it all to hell. Poor Aaron."

"They'll pay," Roy said, his jaw tight. "Damned if they won't."

Etain was only a mile or so away now. We'd be there in a couple of minutes. I said to Roy, "How are we goin' to set off those explosives?" Without waiting for him to answer, I went right on with a suggestion of my own. "Jace has a sackful of grenades he found in the caboose. If we could pull the pins on a few of those, it'd set off the others. That might be enough to start the ball rollin'."

Roy nodded and pointed toward one of the gauges near the throttle. The needle on the gauge was already into the red. "It ought to be, especially when the boiler blows too. I closed the relief valve."

That was good thinking on his part. Roy was always smart, smarter than the rest of us.

But the next thing he said made me think he'd lost his mind.

"You and Jace and Big Boy get ready to jump," he said to me.

"What?" That exclamation came from Jace. "I'm not goin' anywhere, Roy. I'm stayin' with you."

"The hell you are," Roy said harshly. "One of us has to stay to keep the throttle wide open and pull the pins on those grenades. That's my job. The rest of you clear out and head for the Allied lines."

"No!" Jace cried. "I'm not leavin' you, Roy!"

Big Boy leaned out to the side of the cab, looked past the engine, and then pointed down the tracks. "Looks like there's nowhere for us to go anyway," he said.

We all looked. The train was nearing a road on the outskirts of Etain, and gathered on it were some German troops. A truck was parked on the tracks where they crossed the road.

"Son of a bitch!" Roy said. "They found out some way that we took over the train."

Jace shook his head. "How?"

"I don't know, but they're sure as hell out to stop us!"

That was true. The troops had opened fire, and we had to crouch down low in the cab as bullets started to bounce around. Roy reached up to nudge the throttle as far forward as it would go. The train shook and rattled as it lunged toward the German army truck blocking the tracks.

That truck didn't stand a chance. The front of the locomotive struck it and slammed it out of the way with only a hard bump for us. The gas tank on the truck burst, and a spark from the train's wheels must have set it off. Flames roared up on that side of the tracks as the gasoline exploded with a huge *whump!*

Then we were past the blockade, and Etain was in front of us. There were more troops along the tracks, and they raked the cab with rifle and machine-gun fire as we rolled past them. I was crouched on the floor of the cab next to Roy, and I heard him grunt suddenly. He fell against me, and I had to grab onto the side of the cab to keep us both from falling.

"Roy!" I yelled in horror and surprise.

I don't know why, since we were all planning to die in a few moments anyway, but the fact that he had been shot bothered me. He put his right hand on the floor of the cab to hold himself up and pressed his left hand to his chest. A thin trickle of blood came from the corner of his mouth.

"Lordy, that hurts!" he gasped. "I don't know why these plans never go like they're supposed to anymore."

Jace and Big Boy hurriedly crawled up beside him too. "Roy!" Jace cried. "No, Roy, no!"

Roy looked around at us. His face was drained of blood now, except for what was leaking from his mouth. "You boys . . . are the best pards . . . a fella could ever have," he said. "Now . . . gimme those grenades . . . and get the hell off this train!"

"I'm not leavin', Roy—" Jace began.

Roy stopped him by reaching out to Big Boy. "Promise me . . . get 'em off of here . . . Big Boy . . ."

Big Boy took Roy's hand. "Don't know if it'll do any good, Roy, but I'll try," he said.

"The hell with that—" Jace started again. Then Big Boy shut him up with a backhand that knocked him silly. I grabbed on to Jace's shirt to steady him and keep him down out of the line of fire.

Roy looked at me and nodded. "Thanks . . . Drew. I knew I could . . . count on you . . ."

Big Boy helped Roy hitch himself up into a sitting position, propped against the side of the cab. "Here's the grenades," he said as he put the sack in Roy's lap.

Roy reached into the sack with a hand stained red by the blood welling from the wound in his chest. "Here . . . take a couple . . . there'll still be . . . plenty . . ."

I took the grenades. "Big Boy, you hang on to Jace," I told him. "I don't know where we're goin', though, with all those Germans around."

Big Boy ventured a glance out of the cab. When he looked back, he was grinning. "Them Boche must've figured out what we're up to. They're runnin' like blazes away from the center of town."

I took a look for myself. The Germans weren't even trying to stop us anymore. I hadn't noticed that the shooting had stopped, what with the roar of the engine. It had a high, shaky sound to it, and I knew the boiler was about to blow.

It was time for us to go. We might kill ourselves jumping from the train, but Big Boy and I had promised Roy, with our words and actions, that we would at least try to save his brother Jace.

Big Boy shook hands with Roy again, and so did I. The train station, which was surrounded by those warehouses full of munitions, was only about a hundred yards away. "So long, boys," Roy whispered. I couldn't hear what he said, but I knew what he meant.

Big Boy grabbed hold of Jace, who was shaking his head groggily and trying to come around. Big Boy lurched to his feet and took Jace with him, and the two of them went sailing out away from the cab. I took one last look at Roy. He had a grenade in his bloodstained left hand. He used his right to pull the pin, then dropped the grenade back in the sack and reached in to pull out another one. As he did, he looked up at me and grinned.

I jumped. There was nothing left for me to do.

Roy was alone for that last hundred yards or so, but I've often thought that maybe Aaron's spirit was there with him, helping him along, giving him a little strength as he pulled the pins on those grenades. Even without being there, I know one thing, and I'm as sure of it as the day is long.

Roy was still grinning when those grenades exploded and the locomotive's boiler blew and the munitions in the boxcars went along with them, sending out sheets of fire along both sides of the tracks that set off all the other explosives stored in those warehouses.

It was the biggest blast I'd ever heard, like the whole world was ending. Took out four or five square blocks. And Jace and Big Boy and I didn't even get the full benefit of watching it, since we were pretty shaken up by our leap from the train. Jace came through it the best, because he was still only half-conscious and let himself go limp. Big Boy broke his left arm, and I twisted both ankles so bad it was like glass grinding in the joints when I tried to walk. Big Boy used his right arm to help hold me up, though, and Jace got on my other side when he came around, and we hobbled away through empty streets as more blasts went up behind us. The Germans had abandoned Etain, at least this part of it. Nobody wanted to be anywhere near those warehouses when what was inside them blew. No matter how well-disciplined those soldiers might have been, only a damn fool wouldn't run in a situation like that.

Smoke and flame climbed into the sky behind us as we kept moving, slow but sure. None of us knew whether or not we would make it, but we were heading home.

EPILOGUE

1965

"But you did make it," the reporter said, his voice echoing a little in the grocery store.

The old man nodded. "Yep. We had a few more skirmishes with the Boche along the way, but nothin' to speak of. Anyway, it didn't much matter. They'd lost heart, especially ol' Kaiser Bill and his advisors. The Armistice was signed less'n a week later, and the war was over." The old man sighed. "The war to end wars, we called it. Sure wish it had turned out that way."

The reporter leaned back in his chair and shook his head as he closed the notebook he had filled with his scribbled notes. "That's quite a story, Mr. Matthews. Yes, sir, quite a story."

The old man frowned and said, "You don't think I was makin' any of it up, do you?"

The reporter looked straight at him and asked, "Were you?"

A smile spread slowly across the old man's weathered face. "History's whatever a bunch of damned college professors say it is, ain't it? And the meanderin's of an old geezer who happened to be there don't really mean much. Make o' that what you will.''

The reporter stood up and stretched, easing back muscles made weary by long sitting. He glanced at the front window of the store. It was dark outside. The grocery's last customer had come and gone long before.

"One last question," the reporter said. "How did the Germans find out what you were planning to do with that train?"

"Well, we found out later that one of those guards in the caboose hung out a flag that they used as a distress signal before he went out with the others to swap lead with Aaron and Jace and me. Somebody spotted it and got word to General von Junzt, and he figured out what we were goin' to do. That's why he threw everything he had at us, tryin' to stop us. Leastways, that's the way he explained it to me a few years later.''

The reporter's eyes widened slightly in surprise. "You met von Junzt again?"

"Sure did."

"Where? How?"

Instead of answering, the old man looked toward the front of the store. Headlights shone through the glass as a car pulled up at the curb. "That'd be the missus, more'n likely," the old man said as he stood up from his stool. A car door opened and shut outside. "She gets worried about me if I ain't home for supper, and I'm runnin' late today. Sometimes when I get to talkin', though, it's hard to stop.''

One of the screen doors in the entrance opened, and a white-haired woman in a print dress came in. The reporter could see what must have once been a great beauty in her face.

"Are you ever coming home, Drew Matthews?" she asked. She looked over at the reporter and stopped as she approached the counter in the center of the store. "You're one of those newspaper men, aren't you?"

He took his hat off. "Yes, ma'am. I'm sorry if I've kept your husband here past closing time.''

The old man waved a hand and said, "It don't really matter. You know what I'm like, don't you, Janine?"

The woman snorted sharply. "After all these years, I most certainly do. I know once you start spinning those yarns of yours, there's hardly any stopping you." Then she smiled at her husband, an expression full of affection. When she turned back to the reporter, she went on. "I'm sorry if this old goat's been boring you."

"No, ma'am, Mrs. Matthews," the reporter assured her. "It's been fascinating. But I guess I'd better be on my way." He extended a hand over the counter. "Thank you for talking to me, Mr. Matthews."

The old man shook with him. "You goin' to write about what I told you?"

"Yes, I am. The world needs to remember its heroes."

The old man's face grew solemn. "I don't know that we were heroes. Just a bunch of fellas tryin' to stay alive and finally do what was right for a change."

The woman came around the counter and gently took his arm. "Come along, Drew," she said. "I'll help you lock up."

The reporter lingered on the sidewalk in front of the store while the old couple turned the lights off and locked up. The main street of the little town was illuminated at each end of the block by a streetlight, but other than that, it was dark and empty. The kids who had sat on the sidewalk earlier reading their comic books had gone home, and were probably sitting in front of the family television set by now, or maybe they were reading again, or just sitting on the front porch in the warm summer night hoping for a cool breeze.

Peace, the reporter thought wryly. It was wonderful.

But there were always other things lurking out there at the edge of the darkness, things that in their ugliness and violence had to be turned back by men such as Drew Matthews and Roy and Jace Tacker and Big Boy Guinness and Aaron Gault, men who might have been outlaws once but who had become so much more. . . .

"Ah, hell," the reporter said aloud to himself. "Keep getting that hokey and you might as well give up journalism and start writing fiction."

"What'd you say?" The woman and the old man had come out of the store behind him, and the old man was locking the door.

The reporter shook his head. "Nothing. Thanks again, Mr. Matthews."

The old man opened the car door for his wife, then shut it after she had gotten in behind the wheel. He turned, stepped closer to the reporter standing on the sidewalk, and said in a low voice, "You come back some time, hear? I like to talk, and I got plenty of time these days."

The reporter nodded. "I'll do that." He hesitated, then gave in to a final burst of curiosity and said, "Mr. Matthews . . . surely men like you and your friends, after all you'd gone through, you didn't just come back to the States and settle down?"

"We damn sure did. Of course, there was that one time back in the twenties when Jace decided he wanted to go into the rum-running business, and since me and Big Boy were his pards, we naturally had to help out some." The old man started around the car toward the passenger side and lifted a hand in farewell. "But that's another story. Good night, and you drive safe now on your way back to the big city."